Mary

Clark rose, tuc **kissed her fore** **never let anyth** **He kissed her forehead again. "You can always depend on me."**

Teagan smiled. Her eyelids finally lowered. She snuggled into her pillow.

Warmth filled Althea's soul. Using a story, he had just told his daughter he'd always be there for her. A pretty smart move for a guy who obviously didn't know how to say the words himself.

Clark motioned to the door. Althea turned and walked out into the hall, with him on her heels and the glow in her warming every part of her body. This was definitely a family worth saving.

But how?

Lindsay tucked Teagan into bed, kissed her forehead and said, "I'll never let anything happen to you." He kissed her forehead again. "You can always depend on me."

SINGLE DAD'S CHRISTMAS MIRACLE

BY
SUSAN MEIER

MILLS & BOON

First published in Great Britain 2013
by Mills & Boon, an imprint of Harlequin (UK) Limited,
Eton House, 18-24 Paradise Road, Richmond, Surrey TW9 1SR

© Linda Susan Meier 2013

ISBN: 978 0 263 90148 1
ebook ISBN: 978 1 472 00537 3

23-1013

Harlequin (UK) policy is to use papers that are natural, renewable and recyclable products and made from wood grown in sustainable forests. The logging and manufacturing processes conform to the legal environmental regulations of the country of origin.

Printed and bound in Spain
by Blackprint CPI, Barcelona

Susan Meier spent most of her twenties thinking she was a job-hopper—until she began to write and realised everything that had come before was only research! One of eleven children, with twenty-four nieces and nephews and three kids of her own, Susan has had plenty of real-life experience watching romance blossom in unexpected ways. She lives in western Pennsylvania with her wonderful husband, Mike, three children, and two over-fed, well-cuddled cats, Sophie and Fluffy. You can visit Susan's website at: www.susanmeier.com.

For Jack and Helaina
(the inspiration for Jack and Teagan)

CHAPTER ONE

"TURN RIGHT."

The soothing voice of the GPS rolled into Althea Johnson's car, and she maneuvered her vehicle as directed, onto the snow-covered Main Street of Worthington, Pennsylvania. The week after Thanksgiving, the little town sparkled with the spirit of Christmas. Tinsel connected to telephone poles looped above the street. Huge evergreen wreaths decorated with shiny multicolored ornaments covered the top half of shop doors. Silver bells glistened in the sun that managed to peek through the falling snow.

But as quickly as she entered the tiny town, she exited. The GPS stayed silent so she continued up the winding road and climbed a tree-covered mountain.

Up and up she went for a good ten minutes, causing her palms to sweat as her car just barely chugged through the wet snow. Positive she'd missed an exit, she was about to look for a place to turn around when the GPS sang out, "In thirty feet, turn left."

With a sigh of relief, she braked slowly, carefully. She'd learned to drive in Maryland winters, but she'd spent the past twelve years in sunny Southern California. Her car didn't have snow tires and her driving skills were a bit rusty.

"Turn left."

Braking again, she guided her little red car down a short

lane lined with snow-coated pine trees. A huge Victorian house came into view. A pewter-colored SUV had been parked haphazardly in the driveway. A man reached in and pulled grocery bags out of the open hatch. Snow fell on him like cotton balls from heaven, covering his shoulders and back, and icing the evergreens that ringed his property. A big black dog bounced around him. A little girl clung to the hem of his jacket.

Frazzled.

That's the word that came to Althea's mind. She stopped her car, pushed open the door and slid out. The big dog bounded over with a "Woof." In one quick movement, he jumped on his hind legs, his paws landed on her shoulders and she fell backward into the snow.

Cold seeped through the back of her lightweight jeans and Southern-California hoodie. Huge white flakes billowed down on her.

Trapped by the dog—who had his paws on her chest as if he were holding her down until the police could get there— she only saw boots rapidly approaching.

"Crazy!"

The man gave the dog a nudge. The beast bounced off with another "Woof!"

He extended his hand. "Let me help you up."

She gaped at him. His face was perfect with a straight nose, angled cheekbones and the tint of five o'clock shadow, even though it was only noon. "Did you just call me crazy?"

"The dog's name is Crazy. Her given name is Crazy Dog. If she had a birth certificate that's what would be on it."

She laughed.

She came up so fast that she stopped inches away from his nose. This close, she could see his whiskey-brown eyes that perfectly matched his light brown hair.

"You named your dog Crazy Dog?"

He stepped back, putting some space between them. "After the way she knocked you down, I would think you wouldn't be surprised."

She laughed again. Cold air filled her lungs. She slapped her hands together to remove the snow.

"Let me get your back."

The words were barely out of his mouth before he turned her around and brushed the snow off her back and then did a quick sweep over her bottom.

"If this stuff melts on your clothes you'll be wet all afternoon."

Her nerve endings tingled. Her breath stuttered in and out. The intimacy of it should have made her indignant. Instead, it felt surprisingly...normal. This was a man who saw a problem and fixed it. For him, his brushing her butt was nothing more serious than that. For her...well, she hadn't had a man touch her in years. So even that simple brush zinged through her and sent the wrong kind of warmth careening through her bloodstream.

She pivoted to face him. "I'm fine. You don't have to brush anymore."

"That big, stupid dog should know her place." His eyes narrowed as he looked at her hoodie and jeans. "I'm hoping you have a coat in the car."

"I'm from Southern California." Funny how easy that came out of her mouth when really she was "from" right down the road. Newland, Maryland, was only fifty or so miles away from the green hills of Pennsylvania, where Clark Beaumont lived.

"California?" He stepped back. "Are you Althea Johnson?"

"In the snow-covered flesh." She extended her hand to shake his. "I take it you're Clark Beaumont."

He caught her hand, gave one quick pump and pulled back. "I thought you weren't coming until Friday?"

"Once I told Emily," she said, referring to the mutual friend who had told her about the job and referred her to Clark, "that I would interview with you, I drove straight through."

"You haven't slept?"

"Or really eaten for that matter."

"Wow. This is not your lucky day. Things sort of went to hell in a handbasket around here this morning when the snow started to fall."

She glanced around at the winter wonderland, understanding why he chose to live in this peaceful, beautiful slice of heaven. Even if living this far out of town probably came with complications.

"Don't sweat it. I haven't really had a lucky year." Or a lucky life for that matter, but a few months ago she'd decided not to wallow in self-pity anymore and it had worked. She laughed more. She forgot all about designer labels and getting married. She took one day at a time, did the task in front of her and didn't worry about tomorrow. And her life, even though it came with trouble, had become happier.

"Which is why you were driving back to your hometown?"

"No. I'm driving back to my hometown to see my sister. I'm interviewing for the temp job with you because of the bad year. My teaching position was cut. Rather than wait until I ran out of money and lost my apartment, I decided to go home. My sister owns a company and can give me a job the second I get to Newland, but I don't want to work in a bakery. I want to find a teaching job. And the few thousand dollars I'll make tutoring your son will give me a couple more weeks before I'll have to become a baker out of desperation." Especially since room and board came with the job.

He sniffed a confirming laugh that said he knew all about bad years, temp employment and desperation. But looking at his house, with multiple angles and levels of roofs, green shutters that accented the creamy yellow siding and ginger-bread trim along the wraparound porch, she had to wonder if the guy really knew trouble. The house only needed gum-drops and candy canes to be ready for a storybook. People who lived in storybook houses didn't know trouble.

In her head, she snorted in derision. That's what every-one had believed about her family. But behind the walls of their perfect Cape Cod *home,* their father had ruled with an iron fist. Literally.

She shivered.

Clark's eyes widened. "I'm sorry. You're freezing. Let's go inside." He glanced back at her car. "Do you want me to grab your luggage?"

She smiled politely. "Let's see how the interview goes first."

He winced. "Right. Sorry." He pointed to the house and motioned for her to go before him. "Emily was so sure you'd be a good choice as Jack's homeschool facilitator that I took the liberty of checking the references on the résumé you emailed me. So we really are just down to the interview."

"That's good." She walked to the white porch steps and began climbing. The town she'd driven through at the bot-tom of the mountain had been decked out for Christmas. But this beautiful Victorian house, perfect for a dreamy holiday, didn't have as much as a string of lights along the porch roof.

"With my housekeeper sick for the past week, every-thing's been a little off-kilter. If I hadn't gone to the gro-cery store, I wouldn't even be able to offer you coffee." He stopped. "Shoot. I forgot the groceries. You go ahead in-side. I'll get them."

She turned around with him. "I'll help."

"You're cold."

"And carrying groceries will warm me up."

She followed Clark to his SUV. He pulled out two plastic bags with handles and she took them from him.

"Just go in the front door and follow it back down the hall to the kitchen."

She nodded, but by the time she got to the door in her slippery tennis shoes, Clark was right behind her.

"If you decide to take this job, you'll have to get yourself a pair of boots."

"I guess."

"And a coat. Winters can be brutal here."

The little girl who had been hanging on Clark's coat when she arrived stood in the front foyer. Wearing a pink hooded jacket and little white mittens, she looked both adorable and warm.

"This is Teagan."

The little girl's gaze dipped to the marble floor, so Althea stooped in front of her. "Hey, Teagan."

"Teagan, this is Ms. Johnson. She's the lady interviewing to be Jack's teacher."

Teagan continued to look at the floor.

"It was nice to meet you, Teagan." She rose. Sometimes it was best to give a child her space. Eventually, she'd warm up to her. Kids always did. With a quick smile at Teagan, she continued on to the kitchen.

Clark plopped his bags of groceries on the center island. Dark wood cabinets should have given the room a gloomy feel, but the cheerful white marble countertops and warm oak hardwood floors took care of that. So did the huge windows by the wooden table that provided a spectacular view of the mountains behind the house.

"Wow."

"Thank my wife for that view. She found this land, created the design for this house."

"She's got a real eye for things." She turned from the windows just as a boy of about twelve walked into the kitchen, the big black dog on his heels.

"Dad, did you get that ham I asked for?" When he saw Althea, he stopped dead in his tracks.

"Yes, I got the ham." He faced Althea. "Althea, that's my son, Jack." He turned to Jack. "Jack, this is Althea Johnson. As soon as I get these groceries put away I'm going to interview her to see if she can become your new teacher."

Taking a bag of cans to the pantry, Clark continued putting away the groceries. Big black dog by his side, Jack stood where he'd stopped, sizing her up.

Usually she wasn't afraid of a twelve-year-old boy, especially not one so handsome. Shaggy brown hair and big brown eyes like his dad's gave him an angelic choir-boy appearance. But he also had an odd expression on his face. Almost as if he were strategizing how to get her fired—and she hadn't even taken the job.

Clark came out of the pantry. "Okay, I'll make sandwiches. Jack, you finish with the groceries and then I can interview—" He stopped, faced Althea again. "I'm sorry. You'd said you hadn't eaten yet."

"I haven't."

"Okay, here's what we'll do. I'll make cocoa for the kids and then coffee for us before I make the sandwiches. Jack and Teagan can eat out here. We'll take our lunches into the den and we'll talk while we eat."

She wasn't the kind of person who got cozy so quickly with strangers. But when she'd turned over the new leaf about her life a few months back, she'd promised herself she'd stop being so cautious. Plus she was extremely hungry. The thought of a cup of coffee and a sandwich made her taste buds dance for joy.

Clark walked to the counter, opened a rollaway door and pulled out a coffeemaker. Feeling odd with nothing to do, she said, "I could put on the pot of coffee if you show me how."

On his way to the counter to get the groceries, Jack snorted a laugh. Clark faced her with a smile. "This is a single-serve coffeemaker. I can make two cups of cocoa for the kids and an individual cup of coffee for each of us."

"Oh." And didn't she feel stupid?

While the first cup of cocoa brewed, Clark whipped around the kitchen, gathering bread and ham and retrieving milk for the coffee from the fridge, along with condiments for their sandwiches. Teagan crawled up on one of the stools beside the center island where Clark opened the deli meat and a loaf of bread. The dog clip-clopped over to her, soundlessly parking herself beside Teagan's tall chair. Outside, the snow continued to fall. Big, beautiful white flakes on a huge, silent mountain.

Silent.

She glanced around. That's what bothered her. It was as quiet in here as it was outside. Jack had put away the few things his father had directed him to, but he said nothing. Teagan sat on one of the tall chairs by the center island, just watching as Clark raced around, going between the coffeemaker and the refrigerator, gathering things for the sandwiches.

"Can I help with anything?"

"No. No. I'm fine. I'm accustomed to doing this."

Doing what? Getting lunch? Having quiet kids? Being a one-person whirlwind of activity? Because it was Tuesday, Althea suspected his wife was at work. So maybe when she was around everything was noisier?

With the ham, bread and condiments on the center island,

Clark motioned for her to come over. "Fix yourself a sandwich while I make Teagan's cocoa."

She walked over, put bread on a paper plate and noticed Teagan watching her, her dark brown eyes cautious, curious. "I can make your sandwich first."

The little girl buried her face in the dirty pink bear she held. Though they'd been in the house ten minutes, she still wore her jacket with the hood on her head and her mittens on her hands.

Clark hustled over. She tugged on his shirtsleeve and he leaned down.

She whispered something in his ear.

He said, "Okay," and went back to the coffee/cocoa maker. "We don't have that flavor."

Her lips turned down in an adorable pout, as she slid her hood off. Her hair was as dark as her eyes. The pale pink coat she wore accented both. As pretty as a princess, she blinked at Althea.

"I can help you with your coat, if you want."

Teagan's gaze whipped to her dad. He walked over with a cup of cocoa. "I'll get her coat. You just finish making your sandwich."

Teagan tugged on his shirtsleeve again. He leaned down. She whispered in his ear.

Baffled, Althea stopped slathering mayonnaise on her bread. Not only did the little girl think it normal to talk only to her dad and only in a whisper, but also Clark was so accustomed to it, he automatically leaned down to listen.

"Sure. We have marshmallows."

She almost asked Clark about it. But she knew kids hated it when adults talked about them as if they weren't in the room. Any minute now she and Clark would go into the den for her interview. She could ask him then. Delicately of course.

"Jack, do you want to make your sandwich now, too, so that I can put all this stuff back in the fridge before we go into the den?"

Jack walked over, grabbed some bread and ham and fixed his sandwich without a word.

Althea's eyebrows rose. She'd taught middle school for six years. She knew twelve-year-olds. They were sassy, moody, and the boys were always hungry. They didn't wait for an invitation to make a sandwich.

What was going on here?

Clark handed Teagan her sandwich then he brought over her cocoa, complete with marshmallows, and started the first cup of coffee. He made his sandwich and the second cup of coffee then he put away the bread, ham and condiments before he faced the kids.

"Althea and I will be in the den. If you need me, just come back and get me."

Teagan blinked. Jack nodded.

She followed Clark down a long hall off the front foyer to the den. He motioned for her to take the empty chair in front of the desk then sat on the tall-back chair behind it.

"I think we should just get right to the point."

She nodded, knowing what was coming. With a housekeeper in the hospital with pneumonia and a wife who obviously worked, this job had morphed into babysitter/teacher. She might even have to cook. Or clean up. It was not going to be the piece-of-cake, easy-money job she'd expected. Not that she was above helping out. Plus, truth be told, taking this position was about more than money. Spending four weeks close to her sister, but not really in Maryland was a stall tactic. She longed to see her sister. But she was afraid to see her dad. So finding employment close enough that Missy could drive up and visit her here in Pennsylvania might have been too good to be true.

That was usually how her life worked. Everything she thought was "perfect" ended up being a scam.

She smiled slightly. "Sure. Let's just get right to the point."

"My wife was killed in an automobile accident three years ago."

Her mouth dropped a bit. That wasn't at all what she'd been expecting. From the casual way he'd mentioned her when she complimented the view, she never would have guessed his wife had died. She'd even suspected the poor woman was at work.

"Jack did okay until this fall. Now suddenly he's failing all his classes. He's done so poorly that his former teacher quit. I need you to pack four months of learning into one month."

"That's quite a job."

"He's been over the material once already. Technically only the December material will be new." He leaned back in his chair. "He's not a stupid kid. In fact, he's very bright. I'm sure he's retained some of what he heard. This is more about getting him focused again and making him see that if he decides to slack off, there are consequences."

"Are you sure this isn't about him grieving for his mom?"

Clark sighed. "She died three years ago. He had two therapy sessions. One right after. One about a year ago. He has the techniques and tools to cope."

"But he's in a new life phase. And I'm not a therapist—"

"If you think he needs to begin seeing his therapist again, back he'll go. But I think this is more about him getting soft than anything to do with his mom. Twelve is a normal rebellion stage." He winced. "I know that because I went through one myself."

When she pictured rebellion, she didn't picture silence.

She envisioned anger. Pouting, sure. But not the control and quiet she'd seen in that kitchen.

Still, he'd said if she believed his son needed to talk to someone he would get him help. She couldn't argue that.

"So, what makes you want a temporary job?"

"As I said, I lost my job and I'm on my way to live with my sister in Maryland. I want the extra cash to give me more time to look for a teaching job."

He nodded as if remembering their conversation outside.

"Plus, she has triplets and a new husband I haven't yet met."

He frowned. "You haven't met your sister's family?"

She shrugged that off easily. She could answer this without giving away any of her secrets. "California's a long way from here. I didn't have the money to just pop home and I also couldn't take the time off work."

Accepting that, he shifted on his chair, getting more comfortable, a sign that the interview was going well from his perspective.

"Since Jack's original homeschooling program failed, I found three excellent replacement options you can use to catch him up on this semester, but there are also some incredible subject-specific websites you can use to reinforce the material."

"Sounds like you've done your homework."

"Being a single parent is something like a full-time job."

She inclined her head. She understood what was going on. He could easily handle the concrete and the obvious. Parental duties and tasks, things he could see. Insubstantial, delicate things like talking weren't as easily handled as getting groceries, finding homeschool programs or making lunch. He might be ignoring warning signs because he didn't know to look for them.

He smiled. "Do you have any questions for me?"

"Yes. I'd like to know about Teagan."

"Do you mean what will Teagan do while you teach Jack?" He tossed a pencil to his desk. "I was hoping she could color in the room you and Jack use for your class work."

"Actually, I'm more concerned about the way she only talks to you and then only in a whisper."

He laughed. "She's three-and-a-half. She's just shy."

Three-and-a-half? And her mom had died three years ago? The poor thing had been only six months old when her mom died. Technically, she didn't know her own mother. And he thought she didn't talk because she was shy?

"Really? You think she's just shy?"

"Yes. She's fine."

Althea took a bite of her sandwich to stop herself from saying something she might regret. Either this guy was in complete denial about his kids or he was right.

If he was right, if Jack was in the throes of a normal twelve-year-old rebellion and Teagan was just shy, everything would work itself out. If he wasn't—

Well, if he wasn't, these kids were suffering. They might not be huddled in a closet, desperately trying to block out the sounds of their dad beating their mom the way she and her older sister Missy had been, but they were suffering. And if their dad didn't understand, there was no one to help them.

She knew she might be reading too much into this situation, but after her own miserable childhood, when every teacher, every neighbor, and even her grandmother missed the signs that she, her sister and her mom were in trouble, she couldn't just walk away.

"I'll take the job."

He sat up. "Really?"

The disbelief in his voice made her laugh. "You were

afraid that when I'd realized I may also have to become your temporary housekeeper/babysitter this week, I'd refuse."

"I wasn't going to ask you to do the housekeeping, but if you could at least tidy up after meals it would be a big help."

Drat. Her and her big mouth.

"I have some projects at work that I should be attending to. If you could start today, I could get an afternoon of research in. I'll work from here, of course, so you and the kids will have today to get accustomed to each other. But I really do need to catch up. I missed all of last week."

His hopeful voice made her shake her head. What the heck? She wasn't doing anything else. And the sooner she sat down with these kids and tried to figure everything out, the better.

"As long as I don't have to cook."

"You can't cook?"

"No reason to cook when I lived alone."

"I'll get takeout."

She glanced across the desk at him with a smile to confirm their deal, but he rose and extended his hand to shake hers. She stood up. When she took his hand, a bolt of electricity crackled up her arm. Their eyes met and from the quick glimmer in his, she knew he'd felt it as clearly as she had.

Her gaze fell from his handsome face to his sweater-covered chest to his snug blue jeans and the crackle of electricity sparked again.

She stifled the urge to yank her hand away. It was one thing to take a job as a live-in employee, knowing *she* was attracted to her employer. She'd always been able to ignore her hormones.

But knowing he was attracted to her, too—

Weren't they tempting fate?

CHAPTER TWO

CLARK WALKED AROUND the desk. "Let's get your things from your car and I'll give you the grand tour of the house."

He motioned for her to precede him out of the den. She headed for the door and he followed, his gaze automatically dipping to her butt.

With a wince, he forced his eyes back up again. What was he doing? Yes, Althea was pretty with her sunny yellow hair and big blue eyes, and, yes, he'd felt that zap of electricity when they shook hands, but she was now his employee.

Even if she wasn't, he wasn't interested. He could have cited the usual reasons. Losing his wife so suddenly had been a shock. But discovering she'd been having an affair and that her lover was someone he'd considered a friend—that had about killed him.

The echo of the pain of the first few months after her accident still lingered. Memories of consoling Jack, the chaos of caring for a six-month-old baby alone, the cool, empty feeling of his bed, all rose up inside him every time he thought about moving on. But none of those were as bad as the ache. The solid ball of grief that weighed him down, sat in his belly like lead, even as it competed with the hurt and humiliation of discovering she'd been having an affair.

The woman he'd believed would love him forever, the woman who'd borne his children, had betrayed him.

That kind of humiliation left more than a mark. It changed a man's perspective. Caused him to make vows—and keep them.

He would never be vulnerable again.

Never.

That's why he wasn't worried about his attraction to Jack's new teacher. He was too smart to be tempted to even consider trusting someone again.

Plus, her résumé might say she was twenty-eight but she looked twenty-two. He'd already been made the town laughingstock. He didn't need to add chasing after a woman who looked too young for him.

When he and Althea reached the front door, he opened it for her. She looked back at him with a smile. "Thanks."

His heart tumbled in his chest. Had he thought her pretty? He'd been wrong. When she smiled she was breathtaking.

But he wasn't interested. "You're welcome."

They stepped out onto the snow-covered porch and he grimaced. "I should have gotten you a coat."

She glanced at him skeptically. "You have one that would fit?"

He wanted to drown in her big blue eyes and for a smart man that didn't make sense. He'd already set his mind not to trust again and that precluded falling in love, or even indulging an attraction. But how could he stop an attraction? The bubbly feeling that rose when she looked at him was natural, spontaneous.

And annoying. He hated being out of control.

"No, but even a too big coat would be better than an insubstantial hoodie."

She laughed.

The sound skipped along his nerve endings, filling him with pleasure. Damn it! Why was this happening?

She jogged down the steps. "Can't argue that. But since

we're out here already, let's just grab my suitcases and do the tour so you can get to work and I can spend some time with Jack."

He couldn't argue that. With his hormones going haywire, the less time they spent together, the better.

Her things turned out to be two suitcases, an overnight bag and a laptop. He carried the two suitcases. She carried the rest. He led her down the hall to the kitchen again, then to the suite of rooms behind it.

"Mrs. Alwine stays here when I travel. But while you're here, the suite is all yours."

She made a slow turn, taking in the big dresser and mirrored vanity, as well as the aqua-and-brown comforter and pillows that matched the aqua-and-brown print curtains.

She faced him with a frown. "So in other words, if you travel while I'm here, I'm in charge of the kids overnight."

Heat crawled up his neck. He hadn't even considered that might be presumptuous, then realized he'd done the same thing to Mrs. Alwine. The heat intensified. If there was one thing he prided himself on it was doing his fair share. Not leaving the kids to their own devices. But it seemed in being so careful of the kids, he'd been a little heavy handed with his employees.

"I guess that depends on when Mrs. Alwine comes back."

She laughed and slid out of her jacket. A rust-colored T-shirt outlined perfect breasts and a small waist. With a quick shake of her head, her sunny yellow hair swirled around her and fell in place on her shoulders.

His mouth watered, and he cursed inside his head. With her hoodie gone, she didn't look twenty-two anymore. She looked all twenty-eight of the years he'd seen on her résumé. But instead of that making her less desirable, it made her more desirable. She was right in his age range—not too young for him as she'd looked in the hoodie.

He pivoted to face the door. That kind of thinking wouldn't do either one of them any good. He needed her help. She needed some money. For both of them to get what they wanted—what they needed—they had to keep this relationship strictly platonic.

"I'll round up the kids and you can do what you want this afternoon. Maybe let Jack have a hand in choosing the new homeschooling program."

She nodded, but he didn't hang around. He bounded out of the room, found the kids, and got them set up in the den.

When everyone was settled around the big desk, Jack behind the computer, Althea on the chair beside him, and Teagan on the opposite side with her coloring book, he said, "Okay. Now I'm going upstairs to my office to work."

He closed the den door behind him with a giant sigh of relief. But Althea faced his two quiet children with a sigh of confusion.

Seeing the look of exasperation on Jack's face, she clicked off the computer monitor. "I just got here. You just met me." She smiled at Jack, then Teagan. "I don't think we should work this afternoon."

Jack said, "All right!" But Teagan jumped off her chair, scampered over to Jack and frantically tugged on his shirt-sleeve.

He leaned down, rolled his eyes, then caught Althea's gaze. "She still wants to color."

"Oh, sweetie! You can color, if that's fun for you. I'm just saying that neither your brother nor I was prepared to work today so I don't think we should."

Teagan didn't really pay attention to what Althea said. From the second the words, "You can color," came out of her mouth, the little girl raced back to her chair and put her attention on a fat coloring book and a box of brightly colored crayons.

The temptation was strong to ask Jack if she was always like this. Then she remembered Missy. She remembered how as older sister Missy had ended up assuming responsibilities that shouldn't have been hers, and she pulled back her question.

For all she knew, having to speak for his three-year-old sister could be part of the reason Jack was unhappy.

"So, do you want to play Yahtzee or Uno or something?"

Jack laughed. "Really?"

"Well, we can't just sit here and do nothing. Plus you can learn a lot from how somebody plays a game."

He slouched down on his seat with a huff and folded his arms across his chest. "You're going to analyze me."

"No, I'm going to get to know you. And if you're smart you'll also use the time to get to know me."

He sniffed a laugh. "Right." He sat up. "But I'd rather play video games."

She winced. "I'm not very good."

"Then I guess we'll see if you have a temper."

This time she laughed. "You're pretty smart for a twelve-year-old."

"Yeah. That's why I'm failing all my classes."

It would have been the perfect opportunity to get into a discussion about his classes and what he thought might have caused his bad semester, but he gave the video game instructions so quickly she didn't have time to ask. He handed her a controller and pointed at the spot beside him on the sofa. Thrust into a game she'd never seen before, she needed all her concentration just to work the controller.

In between rounds, she glanced at Teagan who quietly colored in her fat book. After an hour or so of the game, Jack said, "Hey, Chai Tea."

Teagan looked over.

"Isn't it about time for your nap?"

She slid off her chair just as the den door opened and Clark stepped inside. He stooped down and opened his arms. "I see somebody's ready for a nap."

He scooped up the little girl, and, as he rose, he saw the video game. "I thought you'd be working."

"Today is our first day together," Althea said, then added a, "Drat" when Jack killed two of her soldiers. "Anyway, we're using this time to get to know each other."

Without taking his eyes off the screen, Jack said, "We're bonding."

"Just don't bond too long. I want your grades up so you don't fall behind a semester."

He left the room and Jack tossed his controller to the sofa. "Let's go."

Baffled, she turned, her gaze following him as he walked to the desk. "Go?"

"To work. You heard him. He wants my grades up."

She rose from the sofa. "Yes. But he didn't seem to be angry that we were getting to know each other."

"You should have spent some time bonding with my dad instead of me. Then you'd know that was his angry voice."

"*That* was his angry voice?"

"Yep."

They went to the computer and checked out the potential programs Clark had chosen for his son. Jack participated as they scrolled through each one, but his responses were lackluster. She tried to revive some of the enthusiasm he'd shown while playing video games, and though he would smile, his heart clearly wasn't in his studies.

The den door opened again. Clark poked his head inside. "I ordered pizza. It should be here in a half hour or so. Jack, I'm sure Althea would appreciate the chance to clean up before we eat. So why don't you turn everything off so she can go?"

"What time is it?"

"Six."

"Six!" It had been noon when she'd arrived, probably after one before they finished the interview and got her set up in her room. That could have made it two when she and the kids got settled in the den. Maybe three before Teagan left for her nap. That meant she and Jack had spent three hours looking at programs. She supposed that wasn't too far-fetched.

"Where's Teagan?"

"After her nap, she stayed in the office with me."

"Oh. Okay." She smiled at Jack. "You and I certainly were immersed in our work."

He smiled. But he didn't say anything. She glanced at Clark then back at Jack.

He wasn't afraid of his father. *That* she recognized from her own life. She knew what a frightened child looked like. But he was terribly unhappy.

She followed Clark to the kitchen, ducked into her suite behind it to wash her hands, then joined Clark and Teagan at the table. While Jack found paper plates and napkins, Clark opened the big pizza box. The scent of tomato sauce and pepperoni invaded the air, making Althea's stomach growl.

"I guess this is what two days of going without food will do to you."

Clark gaped at her. "You really did go without food?"

"I wanted to get here. I'd already been on the road three days. After I talked to Emily, I just wanted to keep moving so I could get here and get started."

"I can understand that." He glanced back at Jack. "Hurry up, buddy, or the pizza will be cold."

At the easy way the term of endearment slipped from Clark's lips, Althea frowned. He clearly loved his son. And with Teagan sitting on his lap while he cut her pizza into tiny pieces, it was also obvious that he loved his daughter. He was simply too much of an organizer. Someone who wanted everything to run like a well-oiled machine. Because everything was "working" he didn't see anything wrong.

But there was plenty wrong. She could see it in Jack's eyes.

They ate their pizza with Clark carrying on a steady stream of chitchat. When he announced he would be getting Teagan ready for bed, she asked if she could follow along.

His face scrunched in confusion. "Why?"

"With the housekeeper gone, it's just good for me to know all the routines."

He shrugged. "Sure. Great."

She trailed behind him as he carried the little girl up the steps. They found her bedclothes first, then Teagan had a quick bath. She slipped into her princess nightgown and crawled under the covers.

Althea leaned against the doorjamb as Clark retrieved a well-worn storybook from the drawer in the white bedside table that matched the white frame of her canopy bed.

He read her a story about a bunny that had gotten lost in the woods. While most children's eyes would droop as the story lulled them to sleep, Teagan's eyes widened.

Althea frowned. Why read her a story that seemed to upset her?

But in the end the daddy rabbit found the lost bunny. He fed her soup, tucked her into bed and kissed her forehead, telling her he'd never let anything happen to her. She could always depend on him.

Happy ending.

Clark rose, tucked Teagan into bed, kissed her forehead and said, "I'll never let anything happen to you." He kissed her forehead again. "You can always depend on me."

Teagan smiled. Her eyelids finally lowered. She snuggled into her pillow.

Warmth filled Althea's soul. Using a story he had just told his daughter he'd always be there for her. A pretty smart move for a guy who obviously didn't know how to say the words himself.

Clark motioned to the door. Althea turned and walked out into the hall with him on her heels, and the glow in her warming every part of her body. This was definitely a family worth saving.

But how?

The next morning when Althea stumbled into the kitchen, she found the quiet Beaumonts all seated on the tall stools around the center island.

"Good morning."

Clark glanced up from his computer screen. "Good morning."

Today he wore dark trousers, white shirt and blue tie. His hair neatly combed and his brown eyes bright with enthusiasm, he was clearly happy to be getting back to his normal routine.

Her attraction sparked to life again, but, as always with anything to do with her hormones, she ignored it. As she prepared a single cup of coffee using the directions on the side of the coffeemaker, she nodded at his laptop. "Working already?"

"Reading the *Wall Street Journal* online."

Now why in the name of all that was holy had that sounded sexy? "Ah."

She ambled to the center island. Clark pointed at a plate of French toast. "Breakfast?"

"Yeah. As soon as I have at least one cup of coffee."

He rose and grabbed the black suit coat from the back of

his stool. "If everything's under control here, I'm going to go into the office right now. Even with email and fax machines, we couldn't get everything done we needed to get done last week while I was home with the kids. And we're hopelessly behind in preparing some important government bids."

He shrugged into the charcoal-gray overcoat that had been flung across the unused table by the French doors.

"You never did tell me what you do for a living."

"I own an engineering firm."

"Oh." The way he said that sounded sexy, too, confusing her. She wasn't the kind of woman to fall for the executive type. She had been a sucker for beach bums. Which was why she kept getting her heart broken and her bank account depleted and why she'd stopped dating.

He motioned for her to walk him to the front door. When they were out of earshot of the kitchen he said, "My wife was the brains of the operation. She was actually the engineer. I'm just a lowly liberal arts major who took business courses at university after we realized Carol wanted to start her own firm, and she'd need me to run it. When she died, I had to hire two people to replace her."

The casual, very calm way he talked about his deceased wife baffled her. Until she remembered that was sort of how Clark talked about everything. Casually. Calmly. With very little emotion.

"I also had to learn as much about the work as I possibly could so that I could speak intelligently to clients."

"So you've had a long, difficult three years."

Reaching for the doorknob, he frowned. "I would think that would go without saying."

Yeah. She supposed he was right.

"Anyway, I'll be back around six. All of my contact numbers are on a sheet in the kitchen. As you probably noticed yesterday, Teagan is fine coloring or playing by herself. Do whatever you would normally do with Jack's lessons, etc. And then spend the rest of the day however you want."

"You'll bring dinner?"

He chuckled. "Yes."

With a quick yank on the front door, he opened it and left.

She took her time returning to the kitchen. He wasn't a bad guy. Actually, he seemed like a really nice guy—a *gorgeous* nice guy to whom she was unexpectedly attracted. But he was an executive who'd handled his wife's death with the cool efficiency he probably spent on the company's tax return. He had to use a storybook to show his daughter she could depend on him.

It wasn't his fault that his kids were quiet, sad. Maybe even slightly lost. He handled things the way he knew how.

But his kids *were* quiet and sad, and slightly lost, and she ached for them.

In the kitchen, she glanced at Jack who wore jeans and a T-shirt then Teagan who wore little blue jeans with pink flowers embroidered on the pockets with a matching pink T-shirt. Her long dark hair had been combed, even though she didn't have a clip or band to keep it out of her face.

She ambled to the center island, filled a plate with two slices of French toast and sat on the stool beside Teagan.

"Are you ready to color today?"

The little girl yanked on Jack's sleeve. He bent down and she whispered in his ear.

Jack sighed. "She said yes."

Althea poured syrup on her toast, her heart aching for Jack again. The kid was twelve, isolated on a mountaintop—a beautiful mountaintop to be sure, but a lonely one. And a boy who should be in the ignoring-his-siblings stage had to speak for his baby sister.

He needed some fun.

And not just video games. Something unexpected.

"We're going on a field trip this morning."

Jack gaped at her. "Field trip?"

"Yeah. I need a coat and boots."

Teagan blinked at her. Jack frowned. "You don't have a coat?"

"I lived in Southern California for the past ten years. The heaviest thing I have is a hoodie."

Jack just stared at her.

"Come on. You're old enough to know the geography of this country. We have all different kinds of weather."

"I suppose. I just don't want my dad to be mad."

"He's the one who told me to get boots."

She turned him toward the door. "Go get your coat and your sister's coat. I swear we'll have fun."

CHAPTER THREE

JACK REMINDED ALTHEA that Teagan was too small to ride in a car without a safety seat, so they grabbed the extra one from the garage and installed it in her little red car.

The whole time they worked, Althea kept glancing back at Teagan, hoping for her to speak. Clearly excited at the prospect of getting out of the house, the little girl jumped from foot to foot. Her eyes glowed. Her smile could light the garage. But she never said a word.

As they rode down the hill, Jack chatted happily, filling her chest with the light airy feeling that comes from pleasing another person. She'd figured out he needed to get out of the house, she just hadn't realized how badly. It was a stroke of luck that she needed a coat and boots.

She parked in front of one of the meters, fed it enough to give them an hour for shopping and turned the kids in the direction of the town's general store.

In a shop stocked for winter in the mountains, she immediately found a coat and boots. The light blue jacket, black mittens and black boots she tried on not only fit, they were cute. But because she found them so quickly, their trip into town was ending too soon.

So, wearing her new coat and boots, she herded the kids across the street, telling them she wanted to see more of the town. About halfway down, she got her second lucky break of the morning: a Santa Shop.

There was nothing like seeing decorations, talking about gifts and sharing secret gift wishes to perk up children.

"Why don't we take a peek inside?"

Jack's face scrunched in confusion. "You want to go into a Santa Shop?"

"Yes."

"Why?"

"Why not?"

"Because we don't decorate until Christmas Eve?"

She took Teagan's hand. "Well, maybe we should change that this year and do some decorating beforehand?"

Teagan blinked up at her silently. It wasn't much, but she suspected eye contact was a big step for Teagan.

Jack shook his head. "If Dad hates us decorating early, I'm telling him it was all your idea."

"Good. Fine. Because it is my idea. And if he loves it I'll get all the credit."

When they reached the shop door, Jack held it open like a perfect gentleman. The scents of cinnamon, apples and bayberry wafted out to them. Old-fashioned wooden tables held rows of toy soldiers. Model trains chugged in circles around miniature towns. Ceramic villages took up another two rows. Evergreen wreaths hung on the back walls beside bundles of tinsel.

"I can't afford much," she told the kids, "but we're four weeks away from Christmas. The least we should get today is a wreath for the door. Then we'll come back every week and get something new."

Jack faced her. "You want *us* to pick out the wreath?"

"Sure. It's for your house. Your Christmas."

He stood in front of her, looking totally puzzled.

"I thought you said you decorated on Christmas Eve?"

"We do. But we only put up a tree. Dad says it's enough."

"Well, sure it's enough," she agreed, not wanting to undermine his dad or make him look bad. "But starting today and doing a little something every week to the house, a little something to remind us that in a few weeks we'll get presents and drink hot cocoa by the fire and eat peppermint sticks—well, that'll just make everything extra special."

Jack laughed lightly. "I think you're expecting a lot from a wreath."

Holding Teagan's hand, she headed for the wreaths. "You'll see. Maybe not this week but next week it will all start to sink in and then we'll have Christmas spirit all over the place."

Following a few feet behind her, Jack laughed.

Althea's spirits soared. Teagan might not be talking but she was happy. And Jack was laughing. Once they got the wreath, they could go home and start his lessons.

Around eleven o'clock, Clark began to get antsy. He'd been so focused on how much work he'd missed because of Mrs. Alwine that he hadn't thought through leaving the kids that morning.

Technically, Althea wasn't a total stranger. She was a friend of a friend. That was how she'd gotten wind of the job and why he'd agreed to interview her. Yes, he'd checked her references. But he didn't *know* her. And he'd left his kids with her.

He fished his cell phone out of his jacket pocket and hit the speed dial number for his home phone. It rang the usual four times before it went to voice mail.

He sucked in a breath. She could be in the bathroom. Or she might have turned off the ringer of the phone in the den for Jack's studying.

Or she could have kidnapped his kids.

He groaned internally, telling himself not to think like that, and rummaged around on his desk for the sheet of paper with her cell phone number on it.

When he finally found it, he punched in the digits and waited through five rings before it, too, went to voice mail.

He tossed his cell phone to the desk, telling himself not to be paranoid. But his situation was unusual. There was a reason he lived on a secluded mountaintop. A reason he hid his kids. Even discounting the possibility that someone might kidnap them because he was a wealthy man who could pay a ransom, lots of people were curious about Teagan.

He cursed, shot off his chair and grabbed his top coat. Walking through his assistant's office, he said, "I'm going home," and strode out to his SUV.

Even wanting to get to his house as quickly as possible, he made a loop around town and headed up the mountain. As his SUV rolled to a stop in front of the garage, his chest tightened. Althea's car was gone.

Frantic, he flew up the porch steps and into the foyer, calling the kids' names. No answer. Nothing but the eerie echo of his own words came back to him. Crazy clip-clopped into the foyer, nudging her nose against Clark's hand for a pat on the top of her head.

Clark stooped to pet the nuzzling dog, but his mind jumped back to the day he'd gotten the call about his wife. He'd come home from a business trip to a cold, empty house and had no idea where his kids were, let alone his wife. Then the phone had rung and he'd gotten the news that his wife was dead and his kids were with her parents.

He broke out in a cold sweat.

Cold, empty houses were never good news.

And with a guy in town who might suspect he was Teagan's father, a guy crazy enough to throw himself over Clark's wife's casket and wail—not worried about gossip or consequences—Clark couldn't take any chances Brice Matthews would see Teagan.

Even if the kids were safe with Althea, that didn't mean they were safe from Brice.

He pulled out his cell phone and dialed 9-1-1.

Though they purchased a wreath and secured it in her trunk, Althea took the kids around town to visit a few more shops and scope out potential decorations they'd buy in the following weeks. Now that she'd talked Jack into decorating the house for Christmas, she wanted to see her options.

They had just walked out of the last shop, laughing as they ate ice cream, even though it was freezing out, when two policemen rushed them.

One policeman grabbed Jack and Teagan. The other backed her into the shop wall.

"Are you Althea Johnson?"

"Yes?"

Teagan began to cry. Jack tried to squirm out of the officer's hold. "Let go of me."

"And these children are Jack and Teagan Beaumont?"

"Yes."

"We have a report that you took these kids from their home."

"I'm their babysitter. We came to town to look for a coat and boots for me." She motioned to her brand-new blue jacket and still shiny black boots. "Call their dad. He'll tell you I'm their babysitter."

"He's the one who filed the report."

Clark's SUV slid to a stop in front of the sidewalk. He bounded out and raced over, grabbing Teagan from the officer and then pulling Jack under his arm protectively. "Are you guys okay?"

Jack looked at him as if he were crazy. "We were fine until you called the police on us."

Teagan buried her face in her father's neck. Clark's expression hardened. "Teagan is not fine."

"She was," Jack insisted. "She was laughing."

Standing on tiptoes to see over the policeman's shoulder, Althea shouted, "She was. We were having fun."

"You were supposed to be home!"

"We were on our way home to start Jack's lessons. We had plenty of time. We just shifted our schedule." She pointed at her jacket. "I needed a coat. And boots." She held up her foot, displaying one of her new boots. "Remember?"

The policeman holding her back faced Clark. "So what's going on here?"

"We were just shopping!" Jack spat. "But I get it! He doesn't ever want us doing anything that might even remotely be fun." He shrugged out from beneath his dad's hold and headed for the SUV. "Take us home. Put us back in jail."

Saddened for Jack, Althea swallowed, glanced at Clark, then pressed her lips together.

A mixture of horror and confusion played across Clark's face. As if finally putting it all together in his head, he stepped back. "Oh, my God."

He looked from Jack who stood beside his SUV to Teagan in his arms to Althea still backed up against the shop wall, and scrubbed his hand across his mouth. "Oh, my God. I'm so sorry."

The policeman released Althea. "So everything's good?"

Althea forced a smile. She didn't know whether to be angry with herself for not letting Clark know she was taking the kids shopping, annoyed with him for being so damned paranoid, or to feel sorry for him.

In the end, she decided to feel sorry for him. He'd lost his wife. He didn't want to lose his kids, too. She got it. "Everything's fine. Really. Let me get them home."

The policeman looked to Clark for confirmation. He nodded. "I'm sorry. I panicked." He nearly said, "Ever since my wife's death I've been panicky," but he knew that would only make him look like an idiot. God knew it made him *feel* like an idiot. So he said nothing.

The two policemen walked back to their car. Althea ambled over, looking warm and snuggly in her new blue coat and black mittens. "Are you sure you're okay?"

He put his head back, closed his eyes. He'd just had her nabbed by the cops and she was asking him if he was okay? "I should be asking you that. I'm so sorry." He opened his eyes and forced himself to look at her. "You have the right to use whatever schedule you want." He sucked in a breath. "But I don't like the kids going into town without me. I wish you had called me before you left the house."

"You're right. I should have called you." She pressed her hand to her chest. "That's my mistake. I never thought to call. But I should have."

She put her hand on his arm consolingly. "Let's go home."

He couldn't believe she wanted to go with him. Were he in her shoes, he'd probably quit. But when he pulled his SUV off Main Street and onto the mountain road, she was right behind him. When he drove onto his lane, her little red car was in his rearview mirror. When he got out, she got out.

They walked into the echoing foyer with Teagan asleep on his arm. A dull sound rang in his ears, making his head pound. He'd never been so mortified.

Or so confused. Jack thought they lived in a jail? Teagan had laughed with an outsider?

Althea said, "Why don't you put her on her bed and I'll make us all some cocoa."

Jack sniffed with disdain. "I don't want any cocoa."

All the control he thought he had slipped through his fingers like melted snow. "Good. You can go into the den and take a look at today's lesson."

"Whatever."

He watched Jack stalk away and knew he'd handled that badly, but his head hurt and his thoughts swam like fish in a bowl. How had he gotten to this place?

He slid his gaze to Althea. "I don't need any cocoa."

"Bourbon then?"

A surprised laugh escaped. "Actually, bourbon sounds really good right now. But I'll be fine. You go work with Jack."

She shook her head. "Jack needs a minute. Forcing him to set things up on the computer by himself will be a good way to occupy him and give him some space."

He took Teagan to her room and lingered over removing her coat and boots. There wasn't any part of him that wanted to confide in anyone, let alone Jack's teacher—a woman he was actually attracted to. But, more than that, he was mortified that he'd panicked. And not just panicked. He'd panicked publicly. He'd called the police when his kids were happily strolling down Main Street.

Of course, he hadn't known that.

Still, a sensible man would have at least looked in the obvious places—

But a man who'd been blindsided by his wife's death and double blindsided by her infidelity jumped to all kinds of conclusions.

When he couldn't delay any longer, he walked downstairs. Hoping Althea had gone to the den to be with Jack, he turned right, into the living room, and there she stood in front of the discreet bar housed in a black built-in beside a huge window. She held a short glass with two fingers of bourbon.

She handed it to him. "Is neat good?"

He smiled. "I don't sully whiskey with frozen water."

She laughed. "Have a seat."

He lowered himself to the gray sofa. "You're going to quit, aren't you?"

She sat on one of the two white club chairs across from him. A glass-and-chrome coffee table sat on the gray, white and black printed rug that connected the small conversation group in the big living room.

"I'm not going to quit."

"I sent the police after you."

"You were afraid."

He downed his drink, savoring the soothing warmth as it ran down his throat. He rose to get another. "Right."

"I saw the look on your face. You were terrified."

He grabbed the bourbon bottle and poured.

"You'd thought I'd taken your kids. There has to be a reason you were so suspicious."

"I was angry with myself for leaving the kids with someone I really didn't know."

"Maybe. But something pushed you to the point that you panicked rather than check things out."

He sighed. This time he sipped the whiskey. There was no way in hell he'd recount his private failures to a stranger. A stranger he'd wronged no less.

"All right. You don't want to talk. I get it. But I also see your kids are in trouble emotionally and so are you."

He snorted in disgust. "Are you saying we all need therapy?"

"I'm saying you need to give yourself a break and need to give your kids a break. You're overorganized. Your kids seem to feel they need to be super quiet to please you."

Heat of shame filled him. The day before, he'd noticed that he'd been taking advantage of Mrs. Alwine. Was it such a big stretch to consider that he'd forced his kids to overbehave?

He ambled back to his seat. She rose from hers. "I can understand that you don't want the help of a stranger. I'm also not a therapist. But I have spent six years with kids Jack's age. I know they sass. I know they experiment with cursing. I know they sulk and whine and roll their eyes and in general make the lives of adults miserable. And Jack does a few of those things, but not often. He's too concerned with pleasing you." She sucked in a breath. "You have an opportunity here. It's four weeks before Christmas. Four weeks when you can decorate together, tell him stories about Christmases past with his mom. Watch old Christmas movies. Make snowmen. Sled ride."

He raised his gaze to meet hers.

"The choice is yours. Use Christmas to turn your family into a family again. Or let this go on. Pretend Teagan's not talking is shyness. Pretend Jack's simmering silence is part of being a twelve-year-old. And six years from now when Jack leaves home without a word of why, and with no intention of ever coming back, you'll have no one to blame but yourself."

Jack's angry comment about living in prison rumbled through his brain. He was failing as a father and though he was loathe to talk about any of this, he'd be a fool if he didn't realize he was drowning.

He blew his breath out, rubbed his hand across his mouth and finally decided he had no choice. He didn't want his kids to hate him or to be unhappy. But he also didn't want them going into town, and if the way to keep them home was to tell their current babysitter the whole story then maybe that's what he had to do.

"The day my wife died, I came home from work to find the house empty and cold."

"So when you came here today and found we'd gone, the empty house scared you?"

"Not as much as having the kids go to town." He scrubbed his hands across his mouth again. He hated this. Hated his misery. His humiliation. But he did not want his kids in town. "My wife had been having an affair. Apparently for at least a year. Brice Matthews, one of our employees, showed up at the funeral overcome with grief and sobbed over her coffin. He called me every name in the book for not letting her go—not giving her a divorce—when she'd never asked for a divorce."

"Oh, my God." Clearly shocked, she sat again. "I'm so sorry."

"That's why I don't want the kids in town."

"Because of gossip?" She shook her head. "It's been three years. Trust me. You can stop worrying. People aren't that interested in anybody's life."

"Everybody's interested in Teagan's."

Her eyes narrowed. "Teagan's? Jack's the one old enough to understand—" Then her mouth dropped open. "Oh, God. Teagan was only a few months old when your wife died and your wife had been having an affair."

"For a year before she died."

"You think people wonder if she's yours?"

"I don't think. I *know* lots wonder whether or not she's really mine."

"They've told you this?"

"No. But a few days after Carol's death, people started looking at Teagan oddly. If I'd go to the grocery store with her in a carrier, everybody peeked in to see her. Some people were more obvious than others. It took me a while, but I realized everybody thought she was Brice's child and they were looking at her to see if there was a resemblance."

"That's awful." She shook her head again, as if marveling at the stupidity of some people. "I'm sorry."

"That's the second time you've said that." He sniffed a laugh. "And I appreciate the sentiment. But you certainly weren't at fault."

"I know. But on behalf of crappy, unfair things that happen everywhere, I feel somebody has to say they're sorry."

He laughed again. His chest loosened. The knot in his stomach unwound.

Their gazes met and he smiled. "Thanks."

"On behalf of crappy things everywhere, you're welcome."

"No. I meant thanks for listening." He rubbed his hand along the back of his neck. "You're the first person I've told this story to." And he didn't feel god-awful. He felt calm, almost normal. "Anyway, that's why I don't want the kids to go into town. I don't want Teagan subjected to scrutiny or Jack to hear things about his mom he's too young to understand."

"Got it." She rose, smiled briefly. "Jack's probably got the computer up and running by now."

With that she left the room, and he flopped back on the sleek gray sofa, looking at the gorgeously appointed living room in the house so well designed "perfect" was too small of a term to use to describe it. In the end, the "perfect" house had meant nothing. Absolutely nothing.

His wife had cheated. Her affair had started before Teagan was conceived. And if Brice Matthews ever figured that out, he might lose Teagan long before he lost Jack.

He sipped his bourbon and closed his eyes. His life was a mess and though he appreciated Althea's suggestion about decorating, he didn't think decorating for Christmas was going to change that.

But at least he knew Althea would keep the kids home now.

CHAPTER FOUR

"I think I have a problem."

Even though she'd closed the den door, Althea walked down the hall, away from the room, so the kids couldn't hear her as she talked with her sister, Missy.

After her discussion with Clark, she'd tried to imagine what it would be like to lose a spouse, a wife he'd obviously believed loved him, discover she'd been unfaithful, and have poor, innocent Teagan's parentage called into question by the town gossips. The humiliation would be off the charts. But couple that with grief? She couldn't fathom the pain of that.

Her heart ached for him, but there was nothing she could do about any of that. She could, however, help him with Jack. And that's why she'd called her sister. A woman raising triplets who'd stood up to their dad and made a real life for herself out of nothing, Missy would know what to do.

"Did your car break?"

Althea winced. "Not that lucky. I got to Clark Beaumont's house early and he hired me immediately because his housekeeper has pneumonia."

"You're a housekeeper?"

"I'm just sort of helping out."

"Oh, Althea!"

"I'm fine. It's all fine."

Missy sighed. "No, it's not fine. You called me because you have a problem."

She grimaced. "Okay. Let me put it this way. It's fine that I got here early. I don't mind straightening up after breakfast and making sandwiches and opening a can of soup for lunch."

"But?"

"But the kids' mom was killed in an automobile accident three years ago. Teagan is only about three. Which means her mom died when she was an infant."

"Oh, that's awful."

She wanted to tell Missy that that was only half the Teagan story, but though Clark hadn't sworn her to secrecy she didn't feel right revealing intimate details of his life. So she stuck with the relevant facts.

"And Teagan doesn't speak. Well, she does. But she doesn't talk out loud. She tugs on her dad's or her brother's sleeve and whispers in their ears. They have to convey the message."

"Oh. Poor sweet thing."

"Clark thinks she's just shy."

"At that age, she could be."

"Yeah. I'm kind of waiting that out. The real problem is Jack. I'm here because Jack failed last semester."

"I know. Emily told me."

"Well, I don't think he failed because he's dumb or lazy or even because of mourning his mom, but because Clark is overprotective. He doesn't like the kids going into town because of gossip. He's got lots of money and a dead wife and two kids and he thinks everybody's curious about them." She grimaced at the sketchy explanation, but it was the best she could do without invading Clark's privacy.

"And you think Jack's failing is a cry for help?"

"If what he said yesterday when Clark sent the police after us is true, I think it's a cry for freedom."

"He sent the police after you?"

She winced. "It all made sense at the time. I had taken the kids shopping without telling him. When he called and couldn't get us, he panicked."

"Althea, you've got a little girl who doesn't talk, a twelve-year-old who is rebelling and a paranoid boss who sent the police after you. Are you sure you want to get involved in this?"

"I have to get involved in this. If one person had paid a little attention to us, just one teacher or doctor or neighbor, we might not have spent every damned Saturday night in a closet praying Dad wouldn't kill Mom."

"Yeah." Missy sighed with understanding. "Okay. I get it."

Althea's shoulders sagged with relief. She knew her sister would understand that she couldn't abandon these kids. "So what do I say? How can I get Clark to understand that he can't protect Jack forever? That the poor kid just wants a little freedom? Maybe some friends?"

"Well, you could try explaining that kids are pretty resilient and even if the town is curious about them, once Jack's been in school awhile he'll be old news."

"That's great! I was also thinking of telling him that I'd like to use Jack going to school in town as an incentive for him to get his grades up."

"That's an even better idea."

"Good. I'll start working on him tonight." Happy with her plan, Althea shifted subjects. "So how are the kids?"

"Eager for Christmas. But Wyatt is worse. God only knows what he bought us this year."

She laughed. "You mean you didn't like last year's RV?"

"We love the RV, but the kids are getting spoiled."

"A little spoiling never hurt anyone."

Crazy Dog bounded out of the den and up the hall. "Crazy!" She flattened herself against the wall, and the dog whipped by her, but she pivoted and raced toward her again. "Crazy! You stop running right now!"

"What in the hell are you talking about?"

"The dog. Her name is Crazy. And trust me. She deserves it."

"Have you ever thought that maybe she'd behave better if she had a better, calmer name?"

Althea laughed.

"I'm not kidding. Call her Crazy, she'll act crazy. Rename that dog." She paused then yelped, "Owen! You stop that right now!"

Althea's laughter turned to fits of giggles. "I notice Owen's name doesn't make any difference in his behavior," she said, referring to the only boy of her sister's triplets. "I can't wait to meet them."

"Can you come for supper tomorrow?"

"I don't want to miss any interaction between Clark and the kids until I fully understand what's going on." She might know the whole story, but she wasn't sure how much Jack knew, how much he understood. "Give me a few more days to observe and analyze."

"All right." Missy paused to sigh. "But tread lightly, okay? You don't want to get in over your head. Or worse, this might be nothing and you could be interfering when you're not needed."

Knowing Clark had a right to be concerned, she let that comment pass. Crazy jumped up and licked her face, her big tongue making a slopping noise.

"And, Althea. Rename that dog. Give her a calmer name and maybe she'll settle down."

Disconnecting the call, Althea laughed. She petted the

dog before shoving her off her shoulders and to the floor. "We're going to start calling you Lullaby."

The dog woofed.

She grabbed Crazy's collar and led her to the den. "All right. Maybe that one's a little too calm." She opened the door and Crazy broke loose, bounding over to the desk where Jack sat.

The force of her paws hitting the back of Jack's chair was so strong that she shoved Jack into the desk.

"Ouch!"

"Woof! Woof!"

"Crazy!" Althea patted her hands on her knees. "Get over here."

The dog bounded over and danced around her.

"My sister thinks we need to give the dog a calmer name."

Jack laughed. "A calmer name?"

"To make her behave."

"That's stupid."

"Yeah, but at this point I'll try anything." She glanced at Teagan. "Anybody have any suggestions?"

Teagan blinked. Jack sighed. "We already did this when we got her. We're not good with naming dogs."

"You have to think of something that sort of makes sense for her personality."

"Dad said Crazy Dog works."

"Yeah, but I think it just encourages her to be bad." Hearing what she'd just said, she frowned. Jack was right. It did seem stupid to change a dog's name and hope to change her behavior, but this pup was so big and gangly that Althea was desperate. "How about if we think about a name that describes how we want her to behave?"

"You mean you want to call her Angel?"

She glanced down at Crazy and she woofed.

"She'll never be an angel. She's more like the class

clown." She paused and smiled. "You know, we could give her a clown's name so she'd still be allowed to be funny, but she wouldn't have to be crazy."

Jack laughed. Teagan smiled.

Althea tapped her fingers on her chin. "The only clown name I can think of is Ronald McDonald...or Clara Bell."

As if testing the name, Jack said, "Clara Bell."

Crazy woofed and danced around again.

"I think she likes it."

Althea stooped down. Using Crazy's collar she brought her face up to hers. "Okay. From here on out, you are not Crazy. You are Clara Bell. You get to be fun but you're also a lady. Okay, Clara Bell?"

Clara Bell woofed then raced out of the den.

She and Jack exchanged a look. "I don't think it's going to work."

"My sister's pretty smart. If anybody's dumb idea could work, it's Missy's."

Jack rose and stretched. "So what are we going to do today?"

"I thought you were already working."

"I don't feel like studying right now. I want to do something fun."

She thought of dangling the chance to go to school in town as incentive to get him to work, but bit her tongue. She couldn't do that until she talked to Clark.

Then inspiration struck.

"Hey, if you spend the four hours you're supposed to spend at the computer and let me do a quick review with you, we can hang Teagan's wreath this afternoon."

Teagan bolted upright in her chair, her face glowing with excitement.

Jack sat again. "Okay."

"Okay." And now she knew a little incentive worked very well to motivate Jack.

* * *

Driving up the lane to his house that night, Clark narrowed his eyes. Something hung on his front door. He drove closer and groaned.

A big, gaudy wreath.

Anger skipped across his nerve endings, rippling to every part of his body, like waves from a stone thrown into a lake. After everything he'd told her the night before, she still left the house? Took the kids to town? Risked Brice seeing Teagan?

Grabbing his bags of fast food, he lunged out of his SUV, marched to the door and stared at the wreath. A huge circle of pine created a bed for red and gold ornaments. The ribbon of the big gold bow at the bottom cascaded along most of the lower half of the door.

It was, in a word, ugly.

He opened the door and stepped inside. After setting the fast food bags on the foyer table, he slid his scarf off his neck. Frustrated, he wondered why he'd bothered exposing his humiliation to her, if she had taken his kids to town anyway.

"I'm home."

Teagan barreled into the foyer, Crazy on her heels. She caught his arm and tugged until he leaned down.

He smiled. "What?"

She whispered in his ear.

His eyebrows rose and he winced. "*You* picked out the wreath?"

Her little head bobbed what seemed like fifty times in three seconds. Crazy woofed. Teagan caught his hand and turned him in the direction of the door. As he opened it, Althea appeared in the foyer, wearing jeans and a fuzzy pink sweater.

His prickling nerves caught fire and he froze.

Her yellow hair floated around her. Her summer-blue eyes sparkled. Everything male in him locked in on her.

Okay. Maybe the ugly wreath wasn't her fault, but this attraction was. Not that he was blaming her for his being attracted to her. But she was pretty... No, gorgeous. And obviously he was susceptible.

Teagan grabbed the door and opened it the whole way so they could see the wreath from inside the house.

Clark desperately struggled to corral a wince. "That's really some wreath."

A grin split Teagan's face, lit her eyes, wrinkled her pert little nose. The pride in her expression about tore his heart in two. Still, he'd asked Althea not to take the kids into town and she'd disobeyed him. He couldn't let that go. If she didn't obey his wishes, he couldn't keep her...no matter how good she was with the kids.

He caught her gaze. "So you took the kids to town again today?"

Arms crossed beneath her enticing breasts, Althea strolled over. "No. We bought the wreath yesterday when we were out."

"Oh." With no reason to be angry with her anymore, he was totally defenseless against her charm. She stopped in front of him, and his hormones jumped and popped. His tie suddenly felt too tight. The room grew unbearably warm.

Her blue eyes glittered with happiness as she dropped her hand to Teagan's shoulder. His daughter, who rarely spoke and most certainly didn't cotton to strangers, looked up at Althea with a wide grin.

His breath stuttered. Teagan was relating to her? Not just relating, but coming out of her shell?

The happiness that invaded his heart nearly burst its seams. Joy circled through his system like a cyclone, creating a feeling so intense it stole his breath.

Oh, no! This wasn't just about an attraction anymore. *He liked her.*

Damn it! What was he doing? He didn't want to like her. He didn't want to like anyone! He had problems. Tons and tons of problems. All caused by the first woman in his life. The last thing he needed was to get involved with another.

Lights suddenly cut across the front yard. Teagan spun to face them. Crazy barked and raced out of the house.

"Crazy!" He turned to go after her, but Teagan caught his arm and pulled him down.

"What!"

She whispered in his ear.

He gaped at her. "The dog's name's not Crazy anymore?"

Althea winced. "Sorry. We thought if we called her something calmer than Crazy she'd start behaving. So we renamed her Clara Bell."

Sliding past him, she ran out after the dog. "Clara! Clara Bell! Stop."

Shaking his head, Clark stared after her. Crazy bounded through the snow like the Easter Bunny on steroids, woofing and jumping. Althea couldn't get close enough to grab her collar but she kept trying. And she kept calling poor Crazy Clara Bell.

Teagan giggled.

Clark glanced down at her. "I see renaming the dog worked out really well."

Teagan giggled again.

Althea caught the dog before the big black SUV stopped in his driveway.

Afraid to leave her out there alone when he didn't know who was in the car, he told Teagan, "You stay here." Then he walked across the porch and down the steps as the SUV door opened and a petite blonde jumped out.

"Missy!"

Althea dropped Crazy's collar, ran to the short blonde and hugged her.

Crazy went nuts.

"Crazy!" He yelped, running over to the dog and catching her by the collar. Teagan yanked on his sleeve. He bent down automatically then groaned. "I told you to stay inside! What are you doing out here?"

She whispered in his ear.

He squeezed his eyes shut. "I know you renamed the dog, but right now Crazy fits."

"I told Missy it wouldn't work."

Clark straightened away from Teagan to see the tall dark-haired man who had spoken. He extended his hand for shaking. "Wyatt McKenzie. Husband of the woman who came up with the idea for the new dog name. And Missy," he said, pointing to the sobbing woman hugging Althea, "is Althea's sister."

Clark shook his hand once. "Clark Beaumont. It's nice to meet you." He glanced at Althea and her sister as his uncontrollable hound bounced and barked, trying to get free to join the reunion.

Althea stood hugging her sister. His heart stumbled.

She was good to his kids. She knew his secrets. And now he liked her.

This was trouble.

Althea swiped at the tears streaming down her cheeks. Clinging to Missy, she said, "I can't believe you're here."

Missy whispered, "I kept thinking about the dog and the little girl who doesn't talk and the boy who just wants friends. I had to make sure that you weren't in over your head."

Althea sniffed a laugh. "Still protecting me."

"We always protected each other."

She thought back to their days in the closet, huddled together, hiding from their dad. She remembered pooling their money so they would always have enough for lunches and football games and clothes. They were a team, but she'd been so desperate and alone after Missy moved out that she'd forgotten that.

She squeezed her eyes shut. "I have missed you so much."

"Yeah, I know. But at least it hasn't been eight years since we've seen each other," Missy said, referring to their real reunion two years ago. Once Missy had found her, she'd hopped on one of Wyatt's private planes and flown to California. She wanted to be sisters again, and though Althea had been afraid to come home because of their dad, she'd missed her sister. They'd mended their fences and become close again through video calls. "Phone calls are nice, but there's nothing like seeing someone in person."

Missy pulled out of her embrace. "You have to meet the triplets."

She opened the back door of the SUV and three kids rolled out. Two wore pink jackets and white mittens. The little boy had on a Pittsburgh Steelers' jacket. Missy sighed. "How many times do I have to tell you not to get yourselves out of your booster seats?"

"Sorry, Mom."

"Sorry, Mom."

"Sorry, Mom."

Althea hugged each one of them. Though she'd "met" them in a video call, feeling the warmth of their little bodies with each hug filled her with joy.

Then they spotted Teagan. With a yelp of happiness, they raced over to Clark and his daughter.

The first little girl, a brunette with big brown eyes, said, "Hi, I'm Lainie."

Teagan all but crawled up her father's leg. Clark bent down and scooped her up. "Sorry. She's a little shy."

Missy walked over. "Does she like chocolate cupcakes?" She lifted the lid on a basket of chocolate cupcakes with white icing decorated with red and green gumdrops.

Teagan's eyes widened. Her head snapped around and she whispered in Clark's ear.

"Yes. I think she's offering you the chance to have one." He motioned toward the porch. "But not until after you've eaten dinner."

He caught Wyatt's gaze. "I bought fast food for tonight but I can head back to town and get a few more hamburgers and fries."

"No need." Missy motioned for her husband to go to their SUV. "I have a nice supper of lasagna and homemade bread in warmers in the back of our car."

Tears filled Althea's eyes again. Her heart stumbled in her chest. She hadn't seen her sister in two years and suddenly here she was with cupcakes and lasagna. Althea's two favorite things.

As Missy and Clark and the triplets headed for the front door, Wyatt grabbed a big picnic basket and followed them.

The men and kids walked into the house without a backward glance. But at the door, Missy stopped and faced her. "Are you coming?"

Althea pressed her lips together to keep from crying. Missy walked back, slid her arm across Althea's shoulders. "Are you okay?"

She caught her gaze. "I'm so sorry I left."

"We both did what we had to do." She squeezed her shoulder. "We've talked about all this. We're okay."

She nodded. They had talked about it. Missy understood that she'd needed to leave. She'd also understood Althea's fear about contacting anyone. And now they were beyond it.

"Besides, we're going to have fun tonight."

Wyatt yelled. "Hey, get in here already. I'm sure Clark doesn't want to spend good money heating the outdoors."

Happiness bubbled through her. *Her sister was here.* She was about to eat lasagna and a cupcake. Jack would probably die of happiness having other kids to talk to, even if they were only six, half his age.

Then she looked at Clark just as he glanced over at her. Her heart warmed. Her pulse fluttered.

She might be close to her sister again, but with her other unresolved issues, was it wise to be falling for her boss? Especially when he appeared to have more troubles than she did?

CHAPTER FIVE

WYATT SET THE big basket on the center island. Missy immediately dug in, bringing out a fat loaf of Italian bread and setting it beside the basket before she opened the thermal case for the lasagna. She pulled out the casserole dish and removed the lid of the steaming tray. The sweet aroma of sauce, cheese and Italian sausage filled the air.

Althea's mouth watered.

Jack came into the kitchen, Clara Bell on his heels. His gaze roamed the room, taking in all the people. "What's up?"

Althea turned to him. "This is my sister, Missy, and her husband, Wyatt, and their triplets."

His eyes widened. "Triplets?"

The kids' heads bobbed up, their gazes honing in on Jack. Missy said, "This is Lainie, Claire and Owen."

Owen said, "Hey."

Althea said, "They came for supper." Then she laughed. "Actually, they've *brought* supper."

But before Jack could reply, Clark said, "Okay, let's get everybody's coats off. Jack, you get the dishes and silverware and set the table."

Jack headed toward the dish cabinet. Owen slid out of his coat, dropped it to a chair and followed him. "I'll help."

At first Jack looked confused and Althea held her breath.

Though he was starved for company, a six-year-old might not be Jack's idea of a playmate.

But he shrugged. "Yeah. Okay."

Missy and Wyatt helped the girls with their coats, then grabbed Owen's from the chair. "Where do you want these?"

Clark said, "I'll take them." But as he reached to take the jackets from Missy, Clara Bell leaped up, grabbed the loaf of bread from the center island, whipped around and raced between Clark and Missy who were passing the coats. Three little jackets and two adult coats, complete with mittens and scarves, flew into the air. Two scarves fell on Clara Bell's back and went with her into the hall and foyer.

Clark yelled, "Crazy!"

Jack said, "I'll get her," and ran up the hall.

Owen scrambled after him. Two seconds later Clara Bell raced back into the kitchen from the right-hand door, apparently running the circle of hallway that ringed the downstairs, scarves billowing from her back, bread clamped between her teeth.

"Clara Bell!" Althea said, reaching for a scarf and missing.

Lainie and Claire giggled and reached for the scarves, too. When they missed, they bolted after Clara Bell. Jack and Owen rounded the corner into the kitchen and raced after them.

"Kids!" Missy cried. "No running!"

Wyatt said, "I'll get them," and headed up the hall.

Clara Bell burst into the kitchen again.

Missy grabbed for her, Clark grabbed for her, Althea tried to snag her collar, but everyone missed.

Teagan calmly stepped in front of her. Clark gasped and lunged for her, but before he could get her, Clara Bell stopped dead in her tracks and laid the bread at Teagan's feet.

Teagan grinned.

Missy said, "Well, Teagan. For a little girl who doesn't talk, you certainly have a way of getting things done."

Everybody laughed but Clark. He picked up the slobbered on bread. "Luckily, when I was shopping on Tuesday, I bought a loaf of bread."

Missy started gathering the dropped coats and scarfs. "Where did you want these?"

After setting the store-bought bread on the center island, Clark took the coats.

When he returned, Missy said, "Why don't we get everything set up and eat?"

Clara Bell said, "Woof."

Clark scowled. "Oh, no. You go into the family room while we eat."

As if she'd done it a million times, Teagan walked over, took Clara Bell's collar and led her away.

Claire, the only blonde in the triplets, said, "We'll help," and she and Lainie raced after Teagan and the dog.

A few minutes later, the food was on the table and the girls returned. Lainie said, "We washed our hands."

Teagan held hers up with a grin.

"And without being told!" Clark scooped her up, walked over to the table and began organizing the seating. Because there were only six chairs, he and Jack brought in three chairs from the formal dining room. He put the triplets by their mom, with Wyatt on Missy's other side. Then he directed Jack to sit at his left and Teagan to his right with Althea in the middle of the table between both families.

Nobody spoke.

Althea exchanged a look with Missy, who smiled. "Why doesn't everybody just pass their plate up to me and I'll dish out the lasagna and we'll pass the plates back?"

Sending the plates around the table got everyone talking again. Realizing the bread Clark had bought on Tuesday hadn't been cut, Althea jumped from the table to do it. Comments on the delicious aroma of the lasagna swirled around. By the time she returned to the table with the bread, her plate of food was in front of her.

Jack took a bite of his food and groaned. "This is fantastic."

Missy grinned. "I'm glad you like it."

"My sister loves to cook. In fact, she owns a company that makes cakes."

Teagan's eyes widened.

Clark forked a bite of lasagna, but before he ate it he said, "Teagan loves cake."

Missy smiled at her. "Then I'll leave all the spare cupcakes here for you."

She grinned and nodded.

Clark frowned. "Is that good for her?"

"One cupcake a day for a few days won't hurt her."

Jack laughed. "Hear that, Chai Tea? You'll look like a cupcake when you're done."

Mouth full of lasagna, Owen giggled.

Lainie said, "Oh, gross." But Jack and Teagan laughed.

Clark shifted on his chair and addressed Missy. "Althea tells me you own your bakery."

"Yes. But I leave the management to a team. I'm so busy with the triplets that I save my work time for baking two wedding cakes a month. Because that's the part of the job I love."

He faced Wyatt. "And you do what?"

"I own a company that produces graphic novels."

Clark laughed. "No kidding."

Wyatt peeked over. "You like comic books?"

Jack perked up, too. "Only yes."

"Great. I'll have my office send up a few that won't be out until spring. You'll both be ahead of your friends."

Jack high-fived Clark and Althea's heart warmed. Two days ago, Jack wouldn't have been so open. Clark probably wouldn't have, either.

When his gaze met hers, she smiled at him.

He slowly returned her smile. Small lines crinkled around his eyes. And something happened inside her. A weird shifting. For as many problems as they had between them, she couldn't deny she liked him. A lot. Way more than a smart woman would like someone she'd known only a few days.

"Why doesn't Teagan talk?"

That question came from Lainie, Missy's little brunette with big brown eyes.

Missy said, "Hush now. She's shy."

But Teagan grinned across the table at the triplets, almost refuting Missy's words.

"She *is* shy," Clark said, "but that's because we live out in the country. She doesn't see a lot of people."

Little blonde Claire frowned. "She doesn't have friends?"

"There's really been nowhere for her to meet friends."

Owen shook his head. "That's sad."

"Owen identifies," Missy explained. "He used to sneak into Wyatt's house, looking for company."

"Too many girls in our house," Lainie said and rolled her eyes.

Wyatt laughed. "He just wanted some guy time."

Althea looked over at Jack. He looked back at her. A silent understanding passed between them. He wanted friends. No. He *needed* friends.

"Maybe you should send her to preschool," Missy suggested.

Clark didn't answer. He couldn't. The strangest things were happening. He hadn't had company in this house since his wife's death and it should have felt odd, uncomfortable.

Instead, once everyone got over Crazy stealing the bread, the mood became warm and happy.

He'd even smiled at Althea, which was a huge mistake. Every time he looked at her heat rushed through him. But now, she wasn't just a gorgeous woman, living in his home, she was a nice woman with a sister who loved her and a family. In one silly meal she'd gone from being his son's teacher to being a person.

Which would be great, except the more he got to know her the more he liked her.

And he didn't want to like her.

He'd vowed he'd never get involved again. And he was a man who kept his vows. So why was she tempting him?

The two families finished the meal talking about snow and Christmas. Clark and Wyatt supervised the triplets and Jack loading the dishwasher, as Missy and Althea spent a few more minutes at the table.

Reminding their kids they had to get up for school in the morning, the McKenzies packed up to leave. Teagan hugged the girls. Jack and Owen made plans to meet online to play some kind of video game. Missy and Althea clung to each other.

Wyatt shook Clark's hand. "We'd love to have you come to our house next week."

He winced. "I'm kind of busy, but Althea's free to visit any evening. Every evening."

Obviously disappointed, Wyatt said, "Oh. Okay. That sounds great."

Clark felt like a real heel, but he absolutely positively couldn't get any more involved with Althea than he had to be for Jack's sake. His wife had more than broken his heart. She'd humiliated him. He wouldn't risk that again.

But when Althea said good-night as he and Teagan walked to the steps for bed, her smile was so radiant that his stomach clenched. For three wistful seconds he stared at her, wishing his wife hadn't cheated, wishing he'd known she was unhappy, wishing they'd gotten a divorce like a normal couple, wishing he wasn't scarred, bruised, wounded.

But that was foolish. He was what he was. Wounded. And he did have troubles. Troubles that kept Jack at home and Teagan away from prying eyes. He'd spent three years protecting his daughter. He wouldn't drag Althea into that.

Althea got out of bed the next morning, brushed her teeth, combed her hair, and did something she hadn't done in at least ten years. She put on makeup before breakfast. Not a lot. Just a little mascara and some lip gloss.

She studied her reflection, unable to believe she was so attracted to Clark Beaumont that she'd resort to makeup.

But she was. And he was attracted to her. She'd known that from their first handshake, but after the way he'd smiled at her at dinner the night before and the look of longing he'd given her before he climbed the stairs to take Teagan to bed, everything felt different. He liked her. And for once in her life she didn't want to run. She wanted this.

She walked into the kitchen, her long chenille robe tied tightly over her boxers and tank top. Clark and the kids sat at the center island.

She breezed to the coffeemaker. "Good morning."

Out of her peripheral vision she saw Clark look up. His gaze went from the top of her combed hair, down her puritanical robe to her bare feet.

She smiled. He was looking as interested as she'd thought he was the night before.

And she was very glad for the mascara.

"So what's everybody doing today?"

She turned from the coffeemaker just as Clark rose and put another pancake on his plate. His white shirt fit his firm chest very nicely. His orange-and-brown-print tie brought out the amber color of his eyes. But it was his tidy brown hair that sent a thrill through her. This was a normal, decent guy who was interested in her. Not a beach bum. Not a guy who got drunk and beat his kids. A guy who *protected* his kids. The kind of guy a woman could make a life with.

If she didn't screw it up.

If he really was interested.

If he was thinking the same way she was.

If they actually fell in love.

That was a lot of ifs.

"I have work. Two big meetings." He waited for her to bring her coffee to the open seat across from his at the center island. "I know it will be a long day for you guys, but that's the way it is when you own a company."

When she looked into his eyes her hormones went crazy, but he was back to being overly polite and cautious with her. Which, given that they'd basically just met a few days ago, was probably a very good thing.

She glanced down at her coffee to break eye contact. She had weeks to work this out. There was no sense rushing things. In fact, it was wise not to rush things.

Clark said, "How about you, Jack? What's on your agenda for today?"

Althea quickly glanced at Jack, who froze at his father's question.

"You know, neither of you has ever reported on what you're doing."

Jack's expression became defiant. "I'm working."

"I know you are," Clark said. "I'm just curious about how far you're getting."

Althea peeked at Jack's plate and saw it was clean. His breakfast eaten, he could leave. "Jack, why don't you go into the den and set everything up. I'll be in in a few minutes."

He sighed and slid off his stool. Teagan slid off her stool, too. She walked over, tugged on Clark's sleeve until he bent down, and hugged him. She didn't whisper in his ear. She just hugged him. Then she followed Jack out of the room.

For as closed off as Clark was with everyone else, he certainly had a special relationship with Teagan. "She's something."

Clark's gaze meandered over to her. "Yes. She is."

"She has a heart full of love."

He sniffed a laugh.

"And so does Jack."

"I totally agree. His problem isn't personal. His problem is his schoolwork."

Althea stirred her coffee. "I was thinking about that yesterday, considering what I've seen in the past with the kids I've taught in a regular classroom, and I think I have an idea for an incentive to get Jack working."

His gaze met hers slowly again and this time her cheeks warmed. Of all the men she'd met in her life, happier guys, why did this man with closed off emotions make her breath stutter?

"What's your idea?"

She smiled to take some of the sting out of what she was about to say. "I think Jack needs company. Competition. Maybe even friends to toss around ideas."

"And you think I can go to the friend store and pick up a few twelve-year-old boys?"

She laughed. Okay. He'd made a joke. Maybe he wasn't so closed off after all. "No. I think we could inspire Jack to work harder, get his lessons caught up, if we told him that if he passed the required tests we'd put him in school in town next semester."

Clark's face fell. "What?"

"He's lonely. He wants friends. School is the obvious solution."

"I don't want him in school and you know why."

"But if we don't give him something to look forward to he's never going to perk up. But more than that he *needs* friends."

"He doesn't need to go to town."

"He does!"

"Damn it, Althea! We talked about this!"

She shut up. All thought of having a romantic relationship with him fell out of her brain. Closed off emotionally was one thing. Anger and yelling was another. She'd had enough of that from her dad to last her a lifetime.

Clark squeezed his eyes shut.

Damn it! The last thing he wanted to do was hurt her. He liked her. He actually wanted to do a lot more than like her. But this was exactly why he couldn't. His life was a mess and he didn't want to drag her into it as a girlfriend or lover or anything beyond Jack's teacher. "I can't send Jack to school in town because of the gossip. I don't want him to hear that about his mom."

Her eyes softened with understanding. "I know that, but that was three years ago. Kids in sixth grade won't be talking about it."

"But the teachers will."

"Who cares? They'll whisper about it for a week or so and it will drift away because your wife is gone. It's over and done. There's no fresh information."

He groaned and shook his head. "And what about Teagan? If Jack goes to school, he'll hear the gossip about her."

"Clark—" Her voice was soft again. Soft and full of sanity. "He's going to have to deal with this sometime. You can't keep him here forever."

He rubbed his hand across his mouth. "I know."

"Most people will be too kind to talk about it when Jack's around."

"Hopefully."

"Plus, he's mature for his age. He's a good boy. A smart kid. Even if the gossip gets to him, you'll be able to talk him through it."

Clark drew in a long, slow breath. Jack had failed a semester, shouted that he felt he was in a prison. Was keeping him home doing more damage than letting him go to school?

"You could also ask the teacher or guidance counselor to watch out for him…to let you know if there's gossip so you'll be ready."

He looked at the floor, then back at her again, suddenly wondering if it really was Jack he was protecting…or himself. "I haven't really talked with him about his mom since she died." Sadness rattled through him. Because he hadn't known how to talk about Teagan, he hadn't talked about any of it. "Bits and pieces here and there. But nothing serious." He sucked in a breath. "Maybe if we talked about her…" He shrugged again. "You know, if I dropped a few normal things into the conversation like what she liked for breakfast, that could pave the way for the 'big' conversation we may someday need to have."

"I think that's a great idea. You're going to be talking about this sometime. So it would be good to start small. With normal stuff. Maybe even talk about Christmas things. Did she decorate?"

"Yes. But she didn't let anybody help. There are no memories."

"So that's what you tell him. You say, 'your mom loved to decorate the house so much she did it herself.' Then if he has any questions or wants to talk, you've opened the door."

He nodded. "Makes sense." He sighed heavily, scrubbed

his hand across his mouth. "Okay. You tell him that if he gets his grades up, I'll look into sending him to school in town next semester."

CHAPTER SIX

JACK ABOUT DIED of happiness when Althea told him about her talk with his father. He dove into his studies, set the table for their lunch of canned soup and bagels and met his father at the door when he returned from work that night.

He launched himself into his arms, hugging him. "Thanks."

Clark's gaze rose to meet Althea's, as he spoke to his hugging son. "This is all contingent on you getting your grades up."

Jack stepped away. "I know. I will."

Althea slid her arm around Jack's shoulder. Looking at Clark she said, "So what'd you bring for dinner?"

"I stopped at a fish place."

"I didn't see a fish place in town."

"That's because I don't work in town. I moved my office to a big, empty warehouse in between Worthington and Greenfield, the next town over."

"Oh." And she knew why. He'd kept Jack out of school to protect him from gossip, but he'd moved his offices so he didn't have to deal with it, either.

"So, Jack, get the plates. I'll open the boxes and we'll have dinner."

They ate their fish, laughing over the fact that they would soon run out of fast food places to get supper. When dinner was over, Clark tossed his paper napkin into the basketlike container that had held his food.

"At least we never have to do dishes."

"I would do the dishes tonight," Jack said, happily gathering the boxes and paper bags to toss into the trash.

Althea caught Jack's arm to prevent him from leaving the room. "I have a better idea."

Clark peeked up at her. "Oh, yeah?"

Her nervous system went haywire. Now that they'd talked, she understood why. His heart had been on his sleeve that morning. He loved Jack but he was afraid. Not for himself but for Jack. To a woman who had grown up in a home with a dad who hated his children, Clark's love for his son was amazing.

She rose from the table. "I found a stash of Christmas decorations in the attic while Teagan was napping and Jack was working. I thought we could hang the lights."

Clark's face scrunched in confusion. "It's too early to put up a Christmas tree."

She gave him a look, trying to tell him to keep up with where she was going with this. They'd talked about him decorating with the kids that morning so he could interject things about their mom as they decorated. She was helping him get that ball rolling.

"I don't want to hang lights on a tree. I want to hang them on the porch, around the railing and along the roof overhang."

Jack cheered, Teagan clapped but Clark gaped at her. "You want to use a ladder in the dark?"

God, he was thick! Of course, he had worked all day and lots of things had happened to him in between this morning's conversation and now.

Still giving him her remember-our-talk-from-this-morning-look, she said, "There are plenty of outside lights on the front porch and around the house. Once we turn them all on, it won't be dark. Plus, there's a big storm coming on Saturday. We do it tonight or we don't do it at all."

Jack said, "Please. Please. Please."

Teagan looked at her dad with a pleading expression and Althea burst out laughing. He might have forgotten their conversation, but the kids wanted to decorate. "You're outnumbered."

He pushed back his chair and rose. "I'm also the one who's going to have to climb the ladder, which will be sitting in snow."

"We can anchor it."

Clark sighed. "Yes. We can."

Jack said, "Yay!" Teagan danced around, hugging her bear. Clara Bell woofed.

Clark shooed them all toward the front foyer. "I've gotta change into jeans. You guys get coats and boots on."

Jack helped Teagan with her coat and boots while Althea raced to the attic and retrieved the boxes of lights she'd found.

By the time she slid into her coat and boots and carried the two boxes marked Outdoor Lights onto the front porch, Clark was lugging the ladder over.

"Okay, ma'am, where do you want this?"

His imitation of a handyman made her laugh, but he wore the same tight jeans and sweater he'd had on the day she'd arrived at his house and Althea remembered why she'd instantly been attracted to him. The soft denim of his wellworn jeans caressed his butt. The sweater accented muscles hidden by his white shirts and ties. He looked happy, comfortable.

Her quilted jacket suddenly became too warm. She licked her lips.

"Althea? Ladder?"

Embarrassment flooded her cheeks. She'd been staring at him—virtually salivating over him—and he'd seen.

She peeked up, saw his twinkling eyes. Oh, yeah. He'd seen.

She shook her head haughtily, causing her hair to cascade around her. He wasn't the only attractive person in this equation and she wasn't the only *attracted* person in this equation. If he wanted to play games, he could bring it. She was ready.

"Are there hooks on the roof for the lights?"

His face contorted a bit as he thought. "If memory serves, I think there are."

She sashayed over, patted his forearm. "Then why don't you just take the ladder to the left corner?" She smiled sweetly. "You climb up, I'll hand you the lights and you can connect them."

His breath hissed out from between his teeth. He looked about ready to say something, but glanced at his eager kids and walked the ladder to the far corner of the house. He anchored the bottom before he slowly let it fall to the porch roof.

She smiled. "Want me to hold it while you climb up?"

He frowned. "I don't think we have a choice." Then his eyes narrowed. Probably because he realized she'd have a perfect view of his behind while he ascended the rungs.

She laughed. "Just start climbing."

As he ascended the first few rungs, she handed Jack the big circle of lights. When Clark got about halfway, they unwound enough of the string that he could take the end with him. He found the hook and latched it.

"It looks like there's a hook about every four feet. The next time I'll set the ladder in between two hooks."

"Makes sense to me."

He climbed down. They moved the ladder. Althea and

Jack took a few steps to the right as Clark ascended again. This time he connected the lights onto two hooks.

That process continued until the front porch roof had been strung with lights.

Clark climbed down from the ladder. Teagan yanked on his sweater sleeve. She whispered in his ear and he shook his head. "We don't turn them on until we have all the lights up."

Her little lips turned down into a pout.

"That's what Mom used to say."

Clark's head jerked up and his gaze flicked to Jack.

Althea held her breath. Sympathy for Jack mixed with the ache she felt for Clark. He didn't want to talk about Jack's mom, but he had to. They'd already decided that this morning.

A second ticked by. Two. Three. Four. Five.

Then Clark quietly said, "She was a stickler for details."

The breath Althea had been holding leached out slowly, soundlessly. But she picked up some snow and tossed it at Clark. This couldn't be a sad conversation. It had to be fun. "Like you're not?"

Stunned, Clark pivoted to face her. She nudged her head in Jack's direction, hoping he'd catch her meaning. Nobody wanted to be sad. Three years had gone by. Jack needed to remember his mom in a good way. A happy way. Especially when it concerned a holiday.

"Oh, his mom was worse." Clark picked up the second string of lights and pointed so Jack would walk with him to the far side of the porch railing. "If you think I worry about details, you should have seen your mom."

Jack laughed.

Unstringing enough of the lights that he could latch them into the hook on the porch railing, he said, "She didn't like to shop in stores or malls. So she'd go online and pore over descriptions of silly things like ornaments for the tree as if they were family heirlooms."

"Someday they will be family heirlooms," Althea reminded them. "Jack, you and Teagan should find ornaments you really like, things your mom bought, and save them for when you're adults. They'll be great keepsakes for your trees."

Jack nodded.

Althea's and Clark's gazes met over Jack's head. Clark said, "You know, we don't talk about your mom much. Is there anything you'd like to know? A memory you'd like to tell us?"

He shook his head. "I don't remember much."

Althea placed her hand on Jack's back and rubbed affectionately. "Maybe you have photo albums?"

"We have some pictures on the computer," Clark said slowly. The subject was painful, but necessary. Still, even understanding that, Althea could see how difficult this was for him.

Teagan sidled up to Althea and slid her tiny white mittened hand into hers as she snuggled against her side.

Clark unstrung enough of the lights to get to the corner of the porch. Jack followed behind him, holding the neatly wound circle of lights. They worked together as if they'd done this a million times, but from what Jack had said about their Christmases they only put up a tree. Which meant these lights had been wound by his mom, Clark's wife. *That* was probably what Clark was remembering.

A reverent hush fell over the night. Surrounded by darkness, the lit porch felt like a world of its own. Clark latched the lights into the hooks. Jack followed him, the circle of colored bulbs unwinding as Clark walked it to the next hook. Teagan held Althea's hand.

She understood why Clark hadn't wanted to talk about

his wife. She understood why he'd let a tradition or two go to the wayside. But the damage left in the wake of his necessary healing process was the emptiness, the quiet, the *silence* that seemed to permeate everything they did.

And she didn't know how to fix it. Her own life had been a dark place. Silent while her dad worked. Filled with terror when he was home.

Why had she ever believed she could help these kids? This family?

She might be attracted to Clark and she might long for a real relationship, but her problems had formed her. She'd never been anything but afraid, skeptical, wary. She didn't trust. She didn't know how to be a normal woman, forget about being a mom. And if she got involved with Clark, fell in love and married him, she instantly became a mother. Her only example of marriage was a man who beat his wife until she so feared her husband she didn't eat and died before she turned fifty.

Her thoughts that morning about having a relationship with Clark had been selfish and foolish. It might have been fun to daydream about it, but he had enough problems in his life without dragging him into hers.

When the lights were strung, they made a production number out of the official porch lighting. Teagan, Jack, Clara Bell and Clark stood in the snowy front yard, while Althea shoved the plug into the electrical outlet. Multicolored globes burst with color.

Clark's nerves crackled a bit as the first good memory of his wife rolled through him. She'd always loved Christmas. Decorated everything but the kitchen sink.

He laughed softly. "Your mom loved decorating."

Jack whispered, "I remember."

Teagan stood beside Jack. She slid her mittened hand into

his. Clark saw, and his chest tightened. Teagan knew absolutely nothing about her mother.

He stooped down in front of her. "And your mom loved you."

She blinked at him.

"You were a tiny bundle of joy. She'd wanted another baby after Jack, but years went by before we got you." He swallowed, refusing to think about the fact that it might have taken another man to get his wife pregnant. "And when you arrived it was better than Christmas."

She grinned.

He scooped her up. "Now, let's go make hot chocolate."

"None of that junk you make with water in that silly coffeemaker of yours," Althea said, while they tromped through the snow to reach her. "I'm making real cocoa."

Clara Bell bounded ahead, racing to the front door and pausing to wait for Althea to open it. They walked into the house laughing. Jack's curiosity and sadness about his mom abated as he helped Althea make the chocolate syrup they would ultimately mix with milk.

Clark removed Teagan's coat and she smiled at him, as if in approval that he'd finally talked about her mom.

The tightness that always squeezed his chest loosened a bit. Althea cued up Christmas carols on her phone, put it on speaker and filled the room with magic.

Magic.

For the first time in three years, his house felt like a home.

They drank their cocoa. Jack excused himself to go to his room to watch TV. Teagan wrapped herself around his neck and he inhaled the sweet scent of outside that still clung to her, realizing he'd never taken the kids out to make a snowman or snow angels or to have a snowball battle.

But now he could. Now he would.

"You ready for bed, Chai Tea?"

She giggled, but she also yawned.

His gaze wandered over to Althea's. He wasn't stupid. He owed this—being able to take the next step—to her. But he'd also noticed, at a certain point while they were outside, that she'd shut down. She still helped with the lights, but she'd been the one to suggest she push in the plug. She'd said that the family should stand together in the yard and see the lights come on together. Almost as if she didn't want to be with them. Didn't want to feel part of things.

But she was.

"Do you want to help put Teagan to bed?"

She shook her head, smiled slightly. "Like Jack, I think I'll watch TV."

"I was actually hoping you and I could have a chat."

"A chat?"

He caught her gaze. "Like we had this morning."

"Oh. Okay."

He knew she thought he wanted to talk about Jack and he supposed he did. But he also intended to find out what had happened out there. Why she'd shut down.

He bathed Teagan, read her a story, tucked her in and came downstairs about thirty minutes later.

He found Althea in the den, flipping through the channels on the big-screen TV. She hit the power switch as he walked inside. "I think that went very well."

"Thanks to you." He glanced around nervously, not knowing where to sit. The only chairs in the room were at the desk. Everybody sat on the sofa when they watched TV.

But she was sitting there...

And he was feeling things that he probably shouldn't, a closeness that warmed his soul. He wasn't a hundred percent sure that was a good thing, considering that he was ridiculously physically attracted to her. Still, up until that morning he'd thought sending Jack to school in town would be bad. Now he knew it was necessary, a crucial step in their healing.

Plus, she'd flirted with him. She'd tossed her hair, put her hand on his forearm, all but told him she'd be looking at his behind while he walked up the ladder.

He laughed. Good grief. He'd made it through a decorating session talking with Jack about his mom, the wife who'd betrayed him. Sitting by a woman he liked might not be a logical next step but there was nowhere else to sit and he was done being an idiot.

He plopped down beside her. "So what happened out there?"

She peeked over. "You decorated with your kids and talked about their mom?"

"No. I meant with you."

"Me?"

"Everything was going fine. You were a part of everything, nudging us along, making our conversation about Carol happen and then you suddenly shut down."

"I didn't want to intrude too much. It was your family moment. Something you guys needed," she said, sounding logical and honest, but he'd been there. He'd seen her sort of back away.

"I'd buy that if you hadn't seemed so sad."

She faced him. "But it was sad. I could all but see the heaviness around Jack's heart."

"And I could all but see the heaviness around yours."

Just as he saw it now. Her usually bright eyes had dimmed. Her always smiling mouth was a thin straight line.

He reached over and touched her hair before he even realized he was thinking about doing it. "Althea," he said her name softly, intimately. "I've told you things I've never told another person. And it's helped me. It's only fair you give me a chance to return the favor."

She licked her lips and closed her eyes.

And he knew he was right. Something big troubled her. "I've never talked about this with anybody."

"Good. It'll put us on even footing."

"I don't even know where to start."

"Start with why decorating seemed to make you sad."

"Because my mom would try to decorate every year and my dad would come home drunk and tear down the decorations, as he called her names like worthless and lazy."

"Oh." That stunned him. He'd thought she was about to tell him about an ex-boyfriend who'd dumped her. Hearing her dad was a drunk shifted his perspective so far he couldn't quite comprehend it. "I'm sorry."

She sniffed a laugh, rose and walked across the room.

She had wanted to tell him the whole story, so that he'd stop looking at her with love and respect. Yes, she'd helped him with Jack, but any good teacher could have made the suggestions she had. If it came to them dating, falling in love, or her caring for the kids like a mother for any reason, she would fail miserably. So maybe it was time to disabuse him of any fairy-tale notions he was getting because she'd figured out Jack needed to go to school.

Pacing away, so she wouldn't have to look at him, she said, "He would beat her. Usually every Saturday night. Missy and I would huddle in the closet and pray he'd pass out before he killed her."

She turned then, needing to see his reaction. She needed to see the pity that would anger her and force any romantic notions *she* had out of her head, force her to move on.

But his face stayed calm, impassive. "And no one helped you?"

"We were very good at pretending nothing was wrong. Even after he started beating Missy and then me, we could pretend we were fine in public. Missy was so perky and popular at school she was voted everything from class president to prom queen."

"You led a double life?"

"*She* led a double life."

He laid his arm across the back of the couch. "And you?"

"I was the class clown."

"Ah."

She smiled slightly. "Probably the reason I identify with Clara Bell."

He laughed.

"I left home the day I graduated high school. Didn't go to my graduation ceremony."

His eyebrows rose.

"I pretended, just as we always did. I got dressed. Kissed my mom." Tears sprang up. "Joked a bit with my dad, accepted the money gift my sister gave me." She swiped away a tear that fell. "Then when we arrived at the high school, I got out of the car and headed for the entrance to the gym that the graduates were to take. But I didn't go in. I hid behind a corner and watched Missy and my parents walk to the main entrance. Once they were in the building, I ran back home, grabbed the suitcase I'd already packed and stole my dad's car."

He sat up. "What?"

She laughed a bit. "I didn't have a car and I had to get away."

"You're a felon?"

She laughed again. "Yeah. I guess. But I was also mad. I left the way I did so that they'd be in the audience, waiting for me to step up and take my diploma but I wouldn't be there. I wanted them to be publicly embarrassed that I was gone. And they were. Missy said our dad about blew a gasket. I drove to California and got a job so I could support myself through college."

"And you made it and your sister has forgiven you. I saw her face the other night. She clearly loves you."

"Yeah, but I didn't tell you the worse part."

"There's a part worse than your dad beating you?"

"My mom died the week after I graduated." The tears rose again. This time she let them fall. "I had no idea. I wanted so badly to be free that I didn't even try to get in touch with anyone to let them know I'd arrived safely. I hated them. I hated my dad for beating me and my mom for letting him and I wanted no part of them. Then two years ago, after Missy and Wyatt got married, she finally found me and told me that she loved me, that she wanted me in her life. I was thrilled because I'd grown past all the hate I had for her, but then she told me Mom had died."

The one attempt she'd made to save herself had back-fired. It brought more pain and guilt than her father's fists ever had.

"She died without me. I never got to say goodbye. I never got to say I was sorry because for all my big talk about her never trying to rescue me, I never tried to save her, either. Missy did. When she graduated from high school she went to the city and got a job as a secretary. She rented an apartment and let me stay there almost every weekend through high school so I'd be out of danger. She tried to get Mom to go, too, but—" She stopped, sobs erupted from her. She couldn't catch her breath. Didn't want to catch her breath. She wanted to be sad. She wanted to be angry. She wanted to find her dad and slap his face for being who he was. For keeping her from her mom. But in the end she was the one who had gone. Stolen a car. Broken her mother's heart.

The next thing she knew Clark's arms were around her. "I'm so sorry."

Sobs rattled out of her. "I could have called Missy at her office and let her know where I was. But I'd stolen a car.

Stolen it. I was afraid that if I called, Dad would somehow figure out where I was and he'd send the police after me."

"You were desperate."

"I was *selfish*. I wanted out. I got out. I got on with my life as if I didn't have a care in the world and never knew my mom was dead until two years ago."

His arms tightened around her. "Shhh. That was a long time ago. And you were a kid. A desperate kid. My God. Your dad beat you."

Her only answer was a shuddering sob. He hugged her tighter. For the first time in her life she felt the warmth of true protection. He held her the entire time she cried. Cried for her mom. Cried for her sister. Cried for herself. For the little girl who had just wanted one normal Christmas.

"Do you know we never had a Christmas tree survive past Christmas Eve? My dad would always come home drunk and knock it down. He'd call us selfish for wanting gifts. Sometimes he'd find the things my mother had bought us and burn them in front of us."

Clark's breath hissed out. "He was an ass."

Her tears began to subside. "He was a bully."

"Exactly."

She pushed back, out of Clark's arms, but he caught her shoulders and studied her face. "I'm not letting you go until I know you're okay."

"I'm never going to be okay."

"Don't be silly."

She shook her head, stepping away from him. "That's actually my point. I don't know what a good relationship looks like. I dated beach bums and losers because that's where I felt I belonged. My example of a mother is someone who fears her husband. The longest commitment I ever made was to the school where I taught, and even they got rid of me."

She swallowed and looked up into his solemn amber eyes. "I don't know how to be what you need."

"Stop that." He reached for her but she ducked away from him.

"You and your family are wonderful. And you deserve much, much better than me. What happened out there while we were decorating, the part where I flirted?"

He nodded.

"Forget it. Forget anything you think you might have felt. You deserve much, much better."

She slipped out of the den and Clark stared at the door long after she closed it.

It was funny. He was thinking exactly the same thing, except in the opposite.

She deserved better than him—better than a family with a little boy who'd been overprotected, a little girl so shy she didn't speak and a father who wasn't even sure he was really a father because the wife he adored had betrayed him.

So though he didn't agree with her assessment that he deserved better, he would stay away from her. She deserved to find a man who didn't come with a houseful of problems. A man who wasn't even sure he could trust again.

CHAPTER SEVEN

ALTHEA LET AN entire week go by, waiting for Clark to resume decorating with his kids. Though the house wasn't quite as quiet and the kids were perkier, she knew they needed another burst of special attention. Thursday passed, then Friday with no offer from Clark to decorate again.

She came into the kitchen on Saturday morning a bit after nine, made a cup of coffee and sauntered to the center island where Clark and the kids sat having breakfast. The French doors displayed big white flakes of snow as they fell on the mountain. Another storm had arrived.

She set her mug of coffee on the island, across from Clark. "We have some evergreen garland and some ornaments we want to hang today."

From behind the screen of his laptop, Clark said, "That's nice."

She pushed his screen closed. "You're helping."

Jack laughed. Teagan grinned.

One of his eyebrows rose. "I am."

"Christmas is about family."

"I'm still three bids behind."

"So drop out of submitting on one of the projects and spend today with your kids."

He wanted to scowl. She could see it in his eyes. But she also knew he realized she was right. What they'd done the night they'd hung the lights was a good beginning. But he'd fallen down on the job.

"Jack, I pulled all the Christmas decorations from the attic. They're in the hallway by the attic door. If you and Teagan could start carting them down that would be great."

Jack took one final bite of cereal and headed for the door. "Come on, Chai Tea."

Bear in hand, she followed him. Clara Bell trotted after her.

"Exactly how much decorating are we going to do?"

She held back a smile. "I have terrific plans."

"I don't want to put up the tree until Christmas Eve."

"I'll give you that. But that still leaves garland on the stairway and around the doors of all the downstairs rooms. You have a fireplace." She began ticking off items on her fingers. "Which will need stockings."

He sighed. "There are stockings in the boxes."

"I know. I found them. I also saw red replacement shades for the lamps." The good mood she'd had while helping them string lights returned. But this time it was tempered with intelligence. She wasn't in any way, shape or form fit to be a mom. She also wasn't whole or healthy enough to have a relationship with a great guy like Clark. But that didn't mean she couldn't enjoy Christmas. "I found red and green placemats in a thin box marked End Tables so I'm guessing they go on the end tables in your living room. Then I thought the kids and I could take whatever is left over next week and decorate the den."

He shook his head. "What is it about women and decorating?"

"I don't know about other women, but I've never had the chance to decorate a whole house before."

"Oh."

Damn it. She didn't want him feeling sorry for her. But

she had sort of led them down this path again. She lifted her chin. "Okay. So I've never had a real family Christmas. But I'm here with a family now, so I'm not going to apologize for enjoying it."

"Good. Then I won't apologize for letting you decorate." He rose from the center island. "That is, after I help hang the garland."

"Yes!" She fist-pumped once, grabbed her coffee and followed him out of the kitchen. Jack and Teagan scurried down the stairs. Teagan held a little box marked *manger* and Jack carried a bigger box marked Assorted Ornaments.

"Did you get the box marked *garland?*" Althea asked as she and Clark paused by the steps.

"It's in there." Jack finished as he walked down the stairway and angled his head in the direction of the living room. "We carried all the boxes in there."

Clark found the container with the garland. He pulled out a long strand of fake evergreen.

Althea raced over and peered at it. "It doesn't look too bad."

Clark turned it over in his hands. "How's it supposed to look?"

"Real. I'm surprised your wife didn't buy real evergreen."

He turned it over in his hands again. "Looks real enough to me." He caught Althea's gaze. "Must have looked real enough to her."

"Must have." She walked over to the box marked Nativity Scene. "You and Jack hang that. Teagan and I will set this up."

As she and Teagan removed donkeys and sheep, shepherds and wise men from the box, she heard Jack say, "Why would you think Mom would buy real evergreen?"

Clark said, "She liked nice things."

"Oh."

"Pretty things," Clark expanded.

Althea's soul swelled. He was doing what he needed to do, telling his son about his mom, and it was coming more naturally now. "You remember how everything in the house had to be perfect?"

Jack laughed. "Yeah. I remember."

"And you couldn't run inside."

"I still can't run inside."

"Well, she was more of a stickler about it than I am."

Althea made a face and Teagan grinned at her. She turned to Clark and Jack. "What was her favorite color?"

Teagan's head whipped around and she gazed at her dad with rapt curiosity. Color was something Teagan understood.

"Pink." He paused. "No. She liked to wear pink but she really loved gray because it went with everything."

Althea laughed. "That's a detailed answer."

"Don't forget," Clark said as he pulled a string of garland between his fingers, straightening it out, testing its strength, "We build for a living. I remember her nixing colors in architectural drawings and replacing them with gray."

"Interesting."

"She said it was a way for the client or buyer to see the building's potential without being encumbered by somebody else's taste in color."

Jack said, "Huh," as if pondering that. Or maybe thinking about his mom.

The conversation died as Clark left to get the stepladder and then climbed up and began attaching evergreen garland around the doorway of the living room.

They worked quietly, but companionably. Teagan arranged the figurines in the manger then took them all out and started again. Althea smiled at her, letting her work at her own pace and do her own thing.

She glanced at Jack, looking like a cross between a little

boy and a teenager. Above him on the stepladder, Clark hung garland. To see them, no one would know that there had been so much turmoil in this family only two weeks before. She might not have turned them around, but she'd helped.

Something sailed through her. Something that felt like joy. Her head tilted in confusion. Joy. She was *happy*. She glanced at Clark. He was happy, too. Talking about his wife seemed to have taken away some of the pressure of the situation.

Just as talking about her dad, about her past, about feeling like a fake, had lifted some of her burden, too.

Not all of it. She still had to go back to Newland. She'd probably see her dad. But she didn't fear it the way she had when she arrived at the Beaumont household.

They decorated for about two hours, hanging stockings, changing lampshades, finding the perfect spot for the eighteen-inch Santa Claus statue that said, "Ho! Ho! Ho!" when Teagan pressed on his belly. She gasped and snatched her hand back.

But Clark laughed and hoisted her onto his shoulder. "He's just here to see if you're naughty or nice. He won't hurt you. I think it's time for me to get some work done."

Jack deflated. "But it's Saturday. I want to do something."

"Now." Althea put her hand on his shoulder. The living room and foyer had been decorated. Clark had talked about Jack and Teagan's mom. It might only be noon, but he'd done his fair share with the kids. "Your dad helped for two hours. He still has work to do. But I have an idea."

Jack glanced up at her.

"Why don't we bake cupcakes after lunch?"

Teagan gasped.

Jack's eyes narrowed. "You said you can't cook."

"That's because I haven't cooked in a long, long time."

"Why not?"

"I lived alone. I had no reason to cook. But," she said, gathering up boxes and placing them on the stairway to take back to the attic on her next trip up the stairs, "my sister and I both did a lot of cooking and baking when we were teenagers."

Jack made a face. "Why?"

She ruffled Jack's hair, sucked in a breath and did something else she hadn't done in ten years. She talked normally about her dad. "My dad owns a diner."

Jack's eyes widened. "He does?"

"Yep, complete with old-fashioned stools and a jukebox."

"What's a jukebox?"

Clark said, "It's a thing that plays records."

"What are records?"

"Songs," Althea corrected. She gave Clark a slight push toward the stairs and his office. "Go. You're making things worse."

He kissed Teagan's cheek then handed her to Althea and jogged up the stairs.

Althea sighed with relief. "Good. Now that he's gone I can admit I'm not a hundred percent sure I can bake good cupcakes, but we'll get some kind of cake."

Teagan smiled. Jack laughed and led the way into the kitchen.

After eating a sandwich, she and Jack scoured the pantry not just looking for ingredients for the cupcakes, but also hunting for something to decorate them. Clark hadn't thought to buy gumdrops or sprinkles on his last shopping trip and apparently Mrs. Alwine didn't use them.

Still, she found everything she needed for cake batter and the recipe from her teenage years simply popped into her head as if she'd been using it every day for the past ten years.

"The memory is an odd thing," she told Jack as he helped

her measure cake flour. "I haven't made this cake in ten years, yet I can recite the recipe as if I made it yesterday."

"My mom was like that, too."

"Really?"

"She remembered everything."

"Did she cook?"

He laughed. "No."

A stirring of happiness bubbled up in her. Up to now she hadn't cooked any more than Carol had, but right now she was baking cupcakes—

She squelched the happiness. What was she doing? Trying to be as good as or better than a dead woman? So she could have Clark? So she could be these kids' mom? She already knew she couldn't. Cooking and cleaning were nothing compared to the emotional things these kids would need. Things she couldn't provide because what she knew of childhood and teen years was hiding in a closet.

Two hours later, Clark came into the kitchen. "Just getting a cup of coffee."

"But we need sprinkles."

Clark faced Jack. "Sprinkles?"

Teagan displayed a bare cupcake. It had been slathered with pretty white frosting, but compared to the cupcakes Missy had brought two weeks before it looked incomplete. No gumdrops. No color.

He rubbed his hand across his mouth. "I really should get back to work."

"It is Saturday," Althea reminded him. Though she'd sided with him when they were done decorating, it felt like time that he should be included again. "And you've worked two hours. It's time for a break."

"And you want me to spend it going to the grocery store?" He paused. "Oh, wait. I get it. You want me to go into town for dinner."

"Actually, I was thinking about making chicken for supper."

She swore she could see his mouth water.

"Making chicken?"

"My dad had this recipe for chicken that melted in your mouth. People from three counties raved about it."

"Do you have everything you need?"

She winced. "There's no chicken in the freezer."

He downed his coffee. "Okay. So I need chicken and sprinkles."

"Sprinkles will be in the baking aisle."

"Got it."

When Clark returned an hour later, he had chicken and sprinkles. He also had potatoes, frozen vegetables, milk, cereal, gumdrops, candy canes, bread and enough groceries for a week.

With Clara Bell dancing around them, he and the kids put away the groceries while Althea picked through the bags, looking for the things she needed to make dinner.

"That was a smart trip," she said, smiling at him over the top of the bag.

"Yeah, I figured that since I was in town I'd get the things we'd need for a week."

"You'd forgotten you needed to shop, didn't you?"

He winced. "Yes."

She patted his shoulder as she walked by. "Don't worry. You're actually doing very well for a guy who's accustomed to having a housekeeper."

"Yeah, Dad. You are."

At Jack's praise, his gaze met Althea's over the shopping bag he was emptying. She smiled her approval and everything inside him sprang to life. She liked him. He liked her. They worked like a team. Something he'd never done with his wife. She'd had her skills and jobs. He'd had his. Their life was more like a relay. When she had the kids, he worked. When he had the kids, she worked.

With Althea everything was homey, comfortable. What he remembered a family should be. But she thought she didn't belong.

Pulling chicken from a bag, Althea said, "So, Jack, what's your favorite memory of your mom?"

Teagan crawled up on one of the island stools, put her elbows on the marble top and her little chin on her fists.

Jack shrugged. "She liked watching movies."

Clark stopped pulling cans from the bag. "She did." Good memories came tripping back, surprising him. "She'd rent every kids' movie when it came out on DVD and on Saturday nights, we'd watch them."

He'd forgotten that. How had he forgotten the one night of the week she gave exclusively to them?

The ice around his heart melted a bit. He'd hated Carol for so long he'd forgotten how much he'd once loved her.

"Oh, that's so nice! So many days I wished my family would rent a movie."

His head snapped up, his gaze flying to Althea. Just as he was growing comfortable talking about his deceased wife, she was growing comfortable talking about her family.

"My dad usually came home from the diner late, though." She met his gaze and he knew what she was telling him. She wouldn't say he came home from work drunk because of the kids. She shrugged. "So we never did anything like that."

Anything like a family. She didn't have to say the words. He got what she was saying. But he also saw something else. The mere fact that she could speak of her family so calmly proved she was getting comfortable with them—her memories—her life.

After the groceries were on the shelves, he sneaked out of the kitchen, grabbed his coat and drove back to town. He didn't like being in town. Though no one gave him crazy looks anymore, he didn't want to risk the possibility of running into someone who would. But on his second trip to Worthington that day, his muscles relaxed. He walked into the video store and inspected the selection of movies as if coming to town was a regular occurrence. He found two he knew the kids would like, bought some popcorn at the counter when he paid for the movies and drove home. He hid the movies and the popcorn in the den and went up the back stairway to his office.

At his desk, he closed his eyes. She'd talked about her family. He'd gone to town twice in the same day. They were changing each other.

After a chicken dinner that really did melt in your mouth, Clark led them all to the den. He walked to the desk, opened the drawer and pulled out the two movies he'd rented.

Teagan clapped her hands. Jack said, "All right!" And Althea laughed. "Wow. Those are great. Thanks."

"Oh, you haven't seen the best part." He pulled out the containers of microwaveable popcorn.

"But we just ate."

"I thought we'd get Teagan in pj's and let Jack get his shower for bed then we'd watch."

She scooped Teagan off the floor. "Sounds like a plan."

They ate popcorn and watched the two animated movies about talking fish and dancing penguins. Teagan curled up in his lap and fell asleep. Jack cuddled in with Althea. With the four of them huddled together on the sofa, they looked and acted like a real family. Though part of Clark was happy he could give that experience to Althea, another part held back.

He knew what was happening. He was falling for her. And he couldn't. He shouldn't. For as much as he and the kids looked like a happy little unit now, there was trouble in their lives. Big trouble. Problems she shouldn't have to bear. Even though she thought she was the one who didn't deserve to be part of this family, he knew better. *He* didn't deserve her.

He carried Teagan to her bed, said good-night to Jack at his bedroom door and returned to the den with a heaviness in his chest.

When he opened the door, he found Althea cleaning up the popcorn bowls. "That's okay. I'll do that."

"You've done enough for one day." Her eyes actually sparkled with happiness. "The decorating was fun. And you talked about the kids' mom again, which makes Jack so happy, but also seems to thrill Teagan." She picked up the second bowl. "Going for sprinkles won Teagan's undying love, but they flipped for the movies. It was a night they'll probably never forget."

She'd gotten all the bowls, so he busied himself picking up kernels of popcorn that had fallen to the couch, not wanting to meet her gaze. He didn't know whether it was good or bad that he so desperately wanted to make her happy. But the joy that shot through him was filled with male pride and *that* was wrong. He couldn't have her, and doing things for her might only hurt her when it was time for her to leave.

"Why don't you go on to bed?"

"In a minute." She sighed. "The night was nice for me, too. Fun." She sucked in another breath. "But I didn't mean to make you feel like you had to do nice things for me when I said I wanted to enjoy being part of a family for Christmas."

"I did it for all of us."

The grateful expression on her face nearly did him in. He wanted to walk across the room, take her chin in his hand, stare into her eyes and tell her she was beautiful, that she deserved someone to treat her with respect and make her a part of things. But the "things" of his family weren't simple like dinner or popcorn or decorating. They were big, difficult problems he and his kids would face. Maybe soon, if he sent Jack to school in town.

She deserved a man who would put her on a pedestal, not drag her down with even more problems.

She walked over to him. "You're a sweet man, Clark Beaumont."

He winced. "No man wants to be called sweet."

She laughed. A light, airy wonderful laugh that filled him with the same warmth he'd had that morning while decorating.

Her hand automatically went to his forearm and he realized how much she touched him, touched Jack, held Teagan. It was as if she was reaching for contact, *begging* for contact.

"You can be sweet and still be manly."

He laughed, but she didn't take her hand off his forearm and the skin beneath it radiated with warmth.

He looked into her big blue eyes. He wanted so badly to kiss her. To really kiss her. He wanted so badly to love her. To bring her into his home, share his life.

He knew he was two steps away from falling in love with her. But he also knew she deserved better...more. Someone who could love her totally and completely. He could not. Even if he didn't have problems, Carol had scarred him. He seriously wondered if he would ever trust a woman again.

He shifted her hand away. "Don't."

"Don't?"

"You might be too innocent to know what's going on here but I see it."

She gaped at him. "Innocent?"

"You are innocent. You had a terrible childhood so you hid from life."

"Clark, I'm also twenty-eight. I've had boyfriends."

He shook his head. "I'm sure you have, but I'm equally sure you never let yourself fall in love."

She grimaced. "That transparent, huh?"

"People with problems recognize other people with problems."

"Your problems are resolving themselves."

He shook his head, paced away from her. "You would think."

"Clark, I don't think. I *know.* Jack is totally different than when I came. Teagan is coming out of her shell. Before you know it she's going to talk. Out loud."

He sniffed a laugh.

"What? Are you still worried about the gossip in town?"

"Actually, I finally see that it's time to face the gossip in town. To let Jack hear the truth, if it comes out, and process it with him. So he can heal."

"But…"

He sucked in a breath, not wanting to say what she was leading him to but knowing that if he didn't tell her, she'd never understand why he had to stay away from her.

"But the problems with Teagan aren't so simple."

"You'll handle it the same way you're handling Jack. If and when she hears a rumor, you'll explain."

He walked to the desk. Ran his fingers along the shiny top.

"Clark, that's the only way to handle it. Honestly."

He met her gaze.

"What?"

"I can't be honest."

She stared at him. He could almost see the wheels turning in her head as she tried to understand that answer. Finally, she said, "You have to be honest."

"Sure. It'll be easy to tell her she's not my daughter."

She gasped. Her eyes widened and she gaped at him.

"Why would you tell her that?" She stopped, her mouth formed an O of understanding. "Oh, my God. This isn't about gossips. This is about you. *You* don't think she's yours?"

"No. I don't."

She fell to the arm of the sofa. "Oh, Clark! You can't believe the gossip!"

He fiddled with a pen that sat on the desk. "My wife and I tried to have another child from the time Jack was two." He glanced over at her. "We couldn't."

"That means nothing! You'd already produced Jack. You weren't sterile."

"We barely slept together."

She squeezed her eyes shut.

"For the first year after Carol died, I waited for Brice to figure it out. To come to my house demanding to see Teagan or demanding a DNA test. He never did."

"So that's good!"

He shook his head. "No. He was preoccupied. He left his job working for me and had to find another—while he mourned the woman he considered the love of his life."

"You identified."

"I understood." He paced away from the desk. "About two years after Carol died, he got married. I thought he'd think of it then, but he never did." He glanced over again. "He has kids of his own now."

"You're saying you think he doesn't want her?"

"I'm saying I don't know what he's thinking, but I do know that if he ever figures it out, he'll come after her."

CHAPTER EIGHT

SYMPATHY FOR HIM created a tight band around Althea's chest. "You can't torture yourself with this."

"Of course, I can. Not just out of fear for myself, but fear for Teagan. Even if he never comes after her, she deserves to know the truth."

"But you don't really know the truth. You said you and your wife had made love a time or two."

He sighed. "A time...or two."

"So you could be Teagan's dad."

"The odds are slim."

"So get a DNA test yourself."

He strolled away, back to the desk Jack used to study and Teagan used for coloring. "Then I'll know."

"Exactly."

Anger brightened his whiskey-colored eyes. "Don't you see? I don't want to know! Once I know, I might have to face the fact that she's not mine. As long as there's doubt, she could still be my little girl."

"As long as there's doubt you'll worry."

"Better to worry than to know."

"But what if she's yours?"

"Did I tell you how small of a chance there is?"

"If she's yours, you won't ever have to worry about

whether or not you should tell Teagan. You won't have to tell her anything."

"And if I find out she's not mine? What about then?"

"You'll figure it out."

He shook his head. "As long as I don't know then I don't have to face the fact that I might be keeping Teagan from her real father. Once I know I have to make some very difficult choices."

"Look, at some point you're going to have to tell her. Why not have the truth?"

"Haven't you been listening? The truth is the one thing I'm trying to avoid."

"Oh, yeah? How about imagining how you'll feel if you discover she's yours."

"So relieved I'll dance on this desk."

"Which is exactly why you should do it. You can't run from this. You can't spend your life worried that some guy from your past will waltz in and ruin your future."

"The night I came home from Carol's wake and was bathing Teagan for bed, I about exploded from fear. So I told myself to just get through the next few days and prepare myself to lose her. But Brice never came. And I never sought him out because I love Teagan. I'd watched her birth, walked the floor with her. She'd been my little girl for six months by then. I didn't want to give her up. I don't want to give her up now."

She walked over to him. "You said he moved on, but from the way you stay out of town, I'm guessing he still lives in Worthington."

"He does."

"And you live on a mountain so removed from everybody else that if it weren't for your job, you'd be a hermit. It's not good for you. Not good for the kids. You have to face this."

He ran his hands down his face. "I don't want to."

But even he heard the waning conviction in his voice. He'd held back from doing the right thing out of fear. Yet that same fear kept him hostage. Kept his kids prisoners. They couldn't go on like this anymore. "I'll look for a lab online."

When Althea strolled into the kitchen on Sunday morning, the room was as quiet as the first day she'd arrived. Jack and Teagan stared into their cereal bowls. Unshaven, in pajamas and a robe, no computer in front of him, Clark stared straight ahead.

She set the coffeemaker in motion and faced the center island. "So, why's everybody so gloomy today?"

Jack shrugged. Hugging her bear, Teagan gave her a pleading look. Clark's gaze met hers slowly. The pain in his eyes melted her heart. Knowing he had to face the truth about Teagan was killing him and she suspected the kids were reacting to his mood.

And who could blame them? Their daddy was sad.

Holding her now finished mug of coffee with both hands, she strolled to the center island. "You know, the mall in Hagerstown is open for shopping today."

Jack's head jerked up. "You wanna go shopping?"

"I have to buy gifts for my sister and her kids. Maybe even something for Wyatt. I could use your help."

Clark rose from his stool by the island. "That's a great idea. You and the kids go shopping."

Teagan grinned, crawled down from her stool and hugged Althea's legs. Warmth filled her, along with a determination to make sure Clark didn't undo all the good he'd done the day before by being so solemn today. If it took getting the kids out of the house, away from him, that's what she'd do.

"I'll take Teagan upstairs and get her dressed."

Jack hooted and hollered. Clara Bell danced around and followed him up the stairs. In Teagan's bedroom, she found a warm sweater and jeans for the little girl and brushed her hair. The fine dark strands fell into place, but her bangs were too long to go without something to hold them out of her eyes. "You wait here one minute. I'm going to get you a clip for your hair."

She raced down the stairs, but when she reached the kitchen and saw Clark still sitting on his stool staring straight ahead, she stopped short. It wouldn't do him any good to stay home, either. Not if he spent the day moping. He needed to get out. Needed to get his mind off possibly losing Teagan.

"You should come with us."

He snorted a laugh. "Frankly, I want some time to think."

"Thinking is over. Decision is made. You're getting the test. So now you have a choice. Make everybody so miserable that you'll regret it if the results come back in your favor. Or make everybody so miserable that Jack will realize something is up and all the good you've done over the past few days will go down the tubes."

He sighed.

She walked over, put her hand on his shoulder. "You're not spoiling my first ever real family Christmas."

He sniffed a laugh.

"I'm serious. If this is your last Christmas with Teagan, you'll regret it if you don't make it wonderful."

He looked down at the center island, then back at her. "I may tell her when she's old enough to hear, but even if she's not mine I won't let her go. I'll fight for her tooth and nail. She's been with me for three years. He's never even thought to get a DNA test. And if he does, and he comes after her, I'll fight him."

She patted his back. "That's the spirit!"

He chuckled, but his stomach clenched. For the past three years, he had pretended everything was fine because he didn't know for sure that Teagan wasn't his. Once he got that test and discovered the truth, he'd be living a lie.

Still, Althea assembled the kids, got their coats, slid little boots onto Teagan's tiny feet and was waiting at the front door for him when he came downstairs. The second he stopped beside Althea, who held Teagan, Teagan pointed at the shiny red clip in her hair.

"What's that?"

She grinned.

"That's a clip I bought last year to wear in my hair for a Christmas party." She smiled at Teagan. "I think it suits the day."

He kissed Teagan's cheek. "I think it does, too." He shrugged into his coat. "So, we're going to the mall?"

Jack fist-pumped. "Yes!"

Althea laughed.

But Clark wondered if this was the first day of living a lie or the last day he could honestly pretend Teagan was his.

She crawled down, out of Althea's arms, and walked over to him. Raising her arms, she silently asked him to carry her.

He reached down, hoisted her up and she kissed his cheek. Warmth blossomed through him. Though he knew getting the DNA test was the right thing to do, he wanted this day. Every hour. Every minute. Every second.

They piled into his SUV and carefully headed down the snow-covered mountain toward town. Instead of driving along Main Street, he veered to the left, circled the little town and headed for the Interstate.

Sitting on the passenger's side seat, Althea slid a sideways glance at him.

He cleared his throat. "Interstate is faster."

She nodded.

The trip took an hour. In spite of the falling snow, the parking lot was jammed to capacity. Clark let them off at the mall entrance and found a parking space. He left his SUV so far back in the lot that by the time he reached them, standing in the center of the rows of shops for the outdoor mall, he was covered in snow.

In Althea's arms, Teagan leaned over and brushed the snow from his hair. He laughed. "Thank you."

She grinned.

He glanced around at the brightly lit stores, the garish decorations, the bustle of people. His stomach tightened. This was the place everyone from town shopped.

As if reading his fear, Althea reached over and tapped his forearm. "Where to first?"

He shrugged. "You're the one who needs to shop."

She glanced at Jack who had wandered away, toward the big front window display of an electronics store. "You need to shop, too. And this would be a great day to ferret out what a certain someone wants for Christmas."

Teagan grinned.

Althea pinched her cheek. "And you, too."

"So that's what this is all about?"

"That's part of it. While I check out things for the triplets, you can scope what makes a certain three-year-old smile." She nodded at Jack. "I can go to the electronics store pretending to want something for Wyatt and you can see what games Jack gravitates to."

He loosened his shoulders. With a mission in mind, this shopping trip didn't seem so bad after all.

"So." She directed him to a store. "Let's start with finding something for the triplets." Looking behind her she called, "Jack, are you coming?"

He scrambled over.

Christmas carols blared through the store. A chorus of "We Wish You a Merry Christmas," followed them as they trudged to the back and the children's clothes.

Teagan on her arm, she stopped at a rack of little girls' holiday dresses. She pulled out a red velvet dress trimmed in white fur that made it look like something one of Santa's elves would wear.

"This is pretty."

Teagan smiled.

"Come on, this warrants more than a smile. It's adorable. I can see Lainie in it. And maybe the blue one for Claire with her big blue eyes and yellow hair."

Teagan frowned.

"Seriously?"

She scrambled down from Althea's arms. Althea expected her to go to her dad. Instead, she bolted off.

"Teagan!"

Instantly alert, Clark ran after her. Althea ran after Clark and Jack scrambled after her.

In and out of rows Teagan bobbed and weaved, so short it was difficult for Althea to keep track of her. But she could see Teagan was backtracking, going toward the front of the store. The door opened and closed. Althea gasped and raced toward it, knowing Teagan had gone outside. On the sidewalk, she spotted Teagan headed for a toy store. The little girl was too short to reach the door handle so she slid in when a pair of grandparents walked out. Althea, Clark and Jack bolted after her. They wound through rows of toys just far enough behind Teagan that they couldn't grab her. But she suddenly stopped at a doll display.

Althea screeched to a halt when she reached her. Clark followed suit. Jack stopped behind him.

Althea stooped in front of Teagan. "Never do that again."

She grinned and pointed at a doll. A baby wrapped in a pink blanket with a pacifier in her mouth.

"She's cute."

Teagan nodded.

She smiled, as an idea occurred to her. "Is this what you think the triplets would want? Owen might not appreciate that."

Teagan shook her head furiously.

"So it's for the girls?"

She shook her head again.

Althea peered up at Clark, who crouched down in front of Teagan. "Who wants this then?"

She pointed at herself.

"Oh, so *you* want it?"

She nodded. Her face came alive with a happiness Clark had never seen before. She didn't just like the doll. She liked being out. Seeing things. Shopping. Sadness crept over him. He'd deprived her and Jack of so much because he was afraid. Though he'd realized the night before that Althea was right—he had to know the truth about Teagan—he felt it even more strongly now. His kids couldn't be hidden anymore. They had to have normal lives. Even if it meant that ultimately he'd have to fight Brice Matthews for custody of the little girl he considered his.

Lifting Teagan, he rose. "Thank you for telling me what you want, but you know I'm only Santa's ambassador."

She frowned. Her head tilted.

"You remember Santa, the guy in the red suit who brings the gifts?"

She nodded.

"Well, I'll tell him that you told me this doll is what you want."

Jack pointed to the back of the store. "Or she could tell him herself."

Clark's gaze followed the direction of Jack's point and he saw Santa. A tingly hope filled him. "Would you like to tell Santa yourself?"

Her eyes widened with fear and she buried her face in his neck.

Althea patted the little girl's back. "It's a nice idea, but it might be too much for one day."

"I was hoping…"

She smiled at him. "But today's not the day. Today's the day for looking around. Maybe getting some caramel popcorn."

Teagan's head snapped up.

Clark said, "If you're good."

She nodded furiously.

He laughed.

Althea browsed the toy section with Teagan following her around, pointing at gifts. Half she thought were good choices for the triplets. The other half she wanted for herself.

On the guise of looking for something for Wyatt, they strolled to the electronics store. Pretending not to notice Jack, they let him wander away. Though Clark stayed with Althea, the store was small enough that he could see everything that caught Jack's attention. He made mental notes of game names and gadgets. By the time Althea chose something for Wyatt and they walked out of the electronics everybody was shopped out.

Clark said, "How about we find the caramel popcorn and head home."

Carrying four huge bags, Althea agreed. "I've never this much money on Christmas before."

Clark led them to the vendor with the popcorn. "did you do for Christmas before?"

"Normally nothing."

He held back a grimace. He should have known than to ask that. He bought the popcorn and they down the long parking lot to the SUV.

They packed Althea's bags in the back of the

it warmed up and then headed home. The big box of popcorn sat beside Teagan's car seat and she reached in and grabbed a handful.

"Hey, you can't have that until after lunch!"

Jack groaned. "But we're starving."

Clark winced. He'd noticed they hadn't eaten their breakfast. He'd been in such a black mood that no one had eaten. But his mood was so good now, his attitude so positive, that he caught Jack's gaze in the rearview mirror and said, "So let's stop in town for pizza."

Jack said, "All right."

The trip back to town flew by. He parked beside the pizza shop and got out of the car. When he opened the backseat door and began to unstrap Teagan, both Althea and Jack gaped at him.

"What? I thought it would be faster if we ate the pizza here."

Jack scrambled out of his seat belt. "Sounds good to me!"

Althea followed close after him. "Sounds good to me, too."

The scent of tomato sauce and warm crust greeted them as they entered the little pizza place. They sat at a table with a red-and-white checkered tablecloth, and Clark found a booster seat for Teagan.

The waitress came over. They ordered a large pizza with everything, three colas and a glass of milk. Then Althea got and walked over to the old-fashioned jukebox.

"Here, Jack. This is a jukebox."

He walked over. "Oh. It's kinda weird. Why not just listen to your iPod?"

She laughed and fished out some change. "What do you want to hear?"

He shrugged.

"How about Christmas songs?"

They chose some music and walked back to the table. As they waited for the pizza, the little restaurant began to fill. Half the people who came through the door walked up to the high counter to get takeout orders.

Finally their pizza arrived and they dug in. Clark handed out slices to Jack and Althea, then cut a piece into tiny bites so Teagan could eat it.

With Christmas carols filling the air, and warm delicious pizza filling their tummies, everything was perfect. The joy of it filled Clark to bursting and he knew he owed Althea for this. Right at this moment, he could almost believe that when he got the results of the DNA test he would learn that Teagan was his. And the fear would be over. The niggling doubts that stopped him from enjoying his life, his kids, would be gone.

And maybe he wouldn't have to worry about dragging Althea into his troubles. He'd only have to worry about the fact that he couldn't trust.

But what better way to learn to trust than with a woman who constantly proved her worth?

After a quick supper of salads made from things they fou... in the refrigerator, Althea cleaned the kitchen, then joi... Clark and his kids in the living room for TV. Shop... pizza and making salads as a family had gotten Cla... his nerves and had turned Jack chatty.

But the day had been too much for Teagan a... asleep on Clark's lap. Gently cradling her, he r... sofa.

Althea rose, too, to help put the little gir... stopped her with a wave of his hand. "I'll... Jack relax."

He returned in ten minutes, telling A...

bathed her, simply slid her out of her clothes and into pajamas. She nodded.

He smiled at her.

And her stomach plummeted. She couldn't describe the look in his eyes, the way his smile affected her, but she knew that—in her entire life—nobody had ever looked at her quite like that.

She turned her attention back to the television, her nerves tingling.

Ten minutes later, Jack yawned and stretched. "I'm tired, too."

As he walked past Clark, Clark grabbed his hand and squeezed. "Too much time walking outside."

Jack sniffed a laugh. "It was still fun."

"Yeah. It was."

Jack grinned, happier than Althea had ever seen him. "Good night."

She and Clark said, "Good night," and Jack left the den.

Althea turned her attention back to the TV. Out of the corner of her eye, she noticed Clark shifted on the sofa, bringing his knee up to the cushion so he could see her.

That's when it hit her that they were totally alone.

"I'm sort of tired, too."

She squelched a sigh of relief. She'd probably imagined he was looking at her differently. She faced him with a smile. "Good night, then." She pointed at the TV. "I'll turn everything off."

He smiled and nodded, but didn't get up from the sofa. Instead, he leaned toward her, caught her shoulders and pulled her to him. His lips met hers softly.

Her heart knocked against her ribs and she tried to slide away, but he kept her where she was, moving his lips across again.

Warmth exploded inside her. Her breath shivered out.

She wanted to wrap her arms around his neck, pull him to her, and lose herself in him and the kiss that was so gentle and sweet.

But he drifted back. Smiled again. "Good night."

Then he left the room and she sat staring at the door.

Hadn't they decided they weren't going to pursue this?

CHAPTER NINE

ALTHEA COULDN'T BELIEVE he'd kissed her. The next morning when she got out of bed, her lips still tingled from it. She stared at herself in the mirror, equal parts of happy and confused. She knew he liked her. She liked him, too. But they were supposed to be smarter than to start something that wouldn't work.

When she walked into the kitchen, her gaze traveled over to him, and he smiled at her.

Her nerves twinkled like lights on a Christmas tree.

"So what are you guys doing today?"

Jack rambled off a list of his lessons as she made herself a cup of coffee.

When he was done, Clark turned on his stool to face her again. "So what are you going to do this afternoon?"

His beautiful, perfect smile could have lit the room. Her limbs froze, as real fear rattled through her. She didn't know how to be in a normal relationship. But she was already halfway in love with Clark. And she didn't want to run or hide. She wanted this.

"I think…" Because her voice cracked, she cleared her throat. "I think I'd like to go see my sister today."

One of his eyebrows arched.

Okay. So he'd figured out the kiss had rattled her. Wasn't ̣esty part of a real relationship? It was good that he knew.

"Do you want to take the kids?"

"I could."

He laughed. "Why don't you wait until I come home? Call Missy let her know you're coming tonight."

She nodded. A shivery feeling rippled down her legs, knocking her knees. She'd never wanted and feared something simultaneously. But looking at Clark's happy expression, seeing the kids eating their cereal and even Clara Bell jumping around, she knew she wanted this.

If it killed her she would get over this fear that she wasn't good enough.

Clark arrived home promptly at six. Handing the keys to his SUV to her, he said, "I know you have a car, but I'd feel safer if you took this."

She glanced at the keys, then back up into his eyes. God, he had gorgeous eyes. And he was generous and kind and smart…

Okay. She was smitten. That's why she was going to see Missy. To learn how to deal with this. "Thanks."

He caught her by the shoulders, bent down and kissed her lightly. "Have fun."

She nodded, smiled at him and headed out the door, her knees knocking and her stomach clenched but her heart soaring. A real, normal man liked her. And she was already as close to loving him as she could be without actually falling. She could have a life…a home. A real home. With happiness and holidays. Safety and love.

The drive to Newland took an hour. Part of her wanted to squeeze her eyes shut as she drove through town, but practicality wouldn't allow that. So she drove through, eyes open, looking at buildings that hadn't changed much. The grocery store. The hardware. The library. She slowed Clark's big SUV, taking it all in.

It was like traveling back in time. Except, she didn't experience the fear she'd expected. Even this close to the diner her nerves were steady. She passed the short wide building that housed her dad's restaurant and smiled. No fear. No weirdness. Lights still lit the diner, and customers still sat in the booths along the wall of windows.

She sucked in a breath. As long as she didn't go into the restaurant, she wouldn't see her dad. There was nothing to be afraid of.

A little farther down the street, she saw Missy's Bakery. Cupcakes decorated the big sign above the door of the little shop. Pride sizzled through her.

Missy had done it. She hadn't merely broken free of their nightmare. She'd started over. She'd married a great guy. She had her own business. She raised her kids without fear.

Awed, she pulled the SUV into the parking space in front of the bakery and got out. Shoving her hands into the deep pockets of her blue coat, she stared up at the pink-and-blue Missy's Bakery sign. She looked at the cute cupcakes, smiled at the wedding cake in the front window, thrilled with everything her sister had accomplished.

"Pretty impressive, ain't it?"

She gasped and her knees about buckled. Her short, stocky father stood right beside her. His hair had thinned out and life had worn lines in his face, but he still had the same air of superiority, the ability to instill fear.

"Our little Missy, all grown up. Becoming a big girl in this town."

She licked her suddenly dry lips and refused to look at him, while she plotted whether or not she could spin away and race back to Clark's SUV before he could catch her.

"Nice SUV you're driving."

"It's my boss's." She found her voice, if only to keep him from making incorrect assumptions about her.

"Fancy. What do you do these days?"

Everything inside her told her to run. She couldn't imagine why he was outside Missy's Bakery when the lights were still on in the diner. But that was how it went with her dad. There was never anywhere to run. No way to hide. It was as if he had radar and always knew where she was…unless she was three thousand miles away.

She mumbled, "I'm a teacher."

"Hump. Not as highfalutin' as your sister."

His attempt to goad her got lost in her fear. She told herself she didn't have to stand here and even talk to him, told herself no one would blame her for simply turning and walking away, so she did. She turned, walked to the SUV and opened the door.

"Still no time for your old man?"

Ignoring him, she climbed inside.

He shook his head and kicked snow like a little kid. As she pulled out onto the street, he waved.

Her hands shook so badly she could barely drive. She forced herself to focus and when she turned onto the street for the house where her grandmother used to live, the house where Missy and Wyatt now lived, her eyes bulged. Not only had a huge addition been attached to her grandmother's little Cape Cod, but the house next to it—the one owned by Wyatt's family—had also been remodeled.

She parked in the wide driveway, behind the huge RV, her heart in her throat. Every bad memory she had rolled through her brain. The fear. Her mother crying and begging. Missy reading to her in the closet, telling her not to be afraid, telling her someday they would get out.

Tears filled her eyes. Missy had gotten out.

And she had, too. As long as she was away from Newland, she was okay. Her tears fell off her eyelids and rolled down her cheeks. She pulled down her gearshift and silently let the SUV roll backward out of Missy's driveway.

Missy had always been the strong one. She wasn't strong. Fear still haunted her.

She didn't have to talk to Missy. She already knew she wasn't ready for what Clark wanted.

When Althea arrived home, Clark watched her take off her coat, completely confused. The red rims around her eyes told him she'd been crying. He'd expected her to come home happy, bubbly...

Ready.

For what he wasn't entirely sure himself. The kiss had knocked him for a loop. And she'd let him kiss her before she'd left that evening. He thought they were carefully moving toward something.

Maybe he was wrong?

Or maybe he was reading too much into this?

Except—he glanced at his watch—she hadn't been gone long enough to visit her sister. The length of time was only enough to drive to Newland and turn around and drive back.

Now he was really confused.

Following her down the hall toward the kitchen, he said, "Hey, you're back early."

She wouldn't look at him. "I changed my mind about visiting Missy."

"Really?"

She said, "Yeah. The drive was fun. It was nice to get out of the house but I wasn't in the mood to talk tonight."

He stopped following her. Wasn't in the mood to talk? He'd thought she needed to talk? That that had been her purpose in going. "Okay."

She turned and smiled at him. "The drive was relaxing, but I'm actually tired and I think I'm just going to my room to watch a little TV."

"You don't want to help put Teagan to bed?"

She shook her head and walked down the hall that led to her suite of rooms. A few seconds later he heard the door to her room click closed.

He ran his hand across his mouth. What had just happened?

She spent the week barely speaking to him, though it didn't seem obvious because Jack talked nonstop. From his constant chatter, Clark figured out that Althea wasn't skimping on Jack's lessons. If anything, they were pulling ahead and Jack was jazzed. His grades were up. His mood was good. He'd be going to school in town in January and Clark wasn't afraid.

But Althea was gone. Quiet. Not talking. Barely eating.

Something had happened on her trip to town and if it killed him he would get her to tell him.

Saturday morning, Althea woke later than normal. Worried about how she'd spend a whole weekend avoiding Clark, she dallied another twenty minutes in her room, waiting to hear the noise of him and the kids having breakfast, but she heard nothing. As the hands on her clock clicked toward ten, she told herself that she'd probably slept through their breakfast.

She ambled into the empty kitchen and made herself a cup of coffee. Before she could turn and go into her room, Teagan raced into the kitchen and over to her, plowing into her knees. Jack followed close behind her. Both kids wore their jackets and mittens.

"Are you going out to play?"

Clark walked into the kitchen. "No. They're going to my parents'." She noticed the pair of sixty-year-olds behind him. "Althea, these are Mona and Dave Beaumont. My parents. Mom and Dad, this is Althea. She's Jack's teacher."

His parents said, "How do you do," and smiled at her.

"It's nice to meet you."

His mother clapped her hands. "Come on, guys. We have to get going. Snow's coming again."

Jack said, "Bye," and pivoted away from her. Teagan smiled until Althea got the message and stooped down. Then she hugged Althea with all her might, spun away and raced to her grandmother.

Clark followed them out of the kitchen, but returned in what seemed like seconds.

"Already had the car packed," he said as he walked to the coffeemaker. He popped in a single serve packet and put a mug under the drip. "So they're off. I'm glad you got up in time to say goodbye."

The room fell silent as she processed everything. The kids were gone and they were alone. *Alone.* Never once had he talked about the kids leaving for weekends. So why suddenly were they spending a weekend away?

Finally she said, "Is this a regularly scheduled visit?"

He pulled his now-full mug from the coffeemaker. "I thought the kids could use a break. My mom's always wanted to have them a weekend before Christmas to help decorate, bake cookies, that kind of stuff. But my parents live in town so that never happened. Anyway, now that I'm beyond that, I called her to see if she wanted them this weekend and she was thrilled." He looked at her over the rim of his mug. "Plus, I think you and I need to talk."

Fear about suffocated her. "Talk?" She should go to Missy's. She almost said the words, but remembered running into her dad and those words froze on her tongue.

"About what happened between us."

A wonderful kiss. The generous offer of his car. The way he let her go to her sister's. The easy, familiar way he accepted her.

Longing welled up inside her. He was the kind of man

any woman would want. But she didn't fit into his life. Her father reminded her of that. A woman whose idea of love and marriage was abuse had no clue of how to be the lover of a man like Clark. A woman who'd spent her childhood hiding had no idea of how to be a mother to his children.

"I thought we'd kind of silently agreed our getting involved was a mistake."

He smiled over the rim of his cup. "I was giving you time."

She swallowed. "Time?"

"To think through whether or not you want to be involved with me."

Every fiber of her being yearned to. But she could hear the cigarette-roughened voice of her dad, talking about how successful Missy was. And the realization, standing beside him, that the only way she'd ever gotten free of him had been to run.

She would run again. Except this time she wouldn't steal a car or have only two hundred dollars in her pocket. As soon as her task with Jack was finished, she'd have a few thousand dollars. Enough to keep her while she sent teaching résumés to states like Texas or Idaho. States so far away no one would ever find her.

"I'm not who you think I am." She tried to smile at Clark, but knew her attempt had been weak at best. "I'm one of those people who does better alone."

With that she walked into her room and closed the door. The thought of being cooped up in the twelve-by-twelve space all day made her think again about going to Missy's. But she couldn't. She wouldn't. Not only did she not want to see her dad, but what if she drew her dad's attention to Missy again? What if he began harassing her?

She couldn't risk it.

She spent two hours sitting by a window in a pretty aqua

club chair, watching the snow fall, and an odd memory surfaced. When it snowed like this, big, wet flakes, she and Missy had made snowmen. Living in California for the past decade, she hadn't even seen a snowman let alone made one. She suddenly, desperately needed to be out of this room, but more than that, she needed to do something. Something that reminded her of the one good thing she could remember from her childhood.

She had a coat, boots and mittens. So it wasn't as if she was ill prepared. Plus, Clark had undoubtedly retreated to his office to work. No one had to know. No one had to see her. And the kids would love the snowman when they got home.

She peeked out her door. Kitchen was empty.

She could do this.

Clark glanced out his office window and burst out laughing. Unless he missed his guess, she was building a snowman.

Stretching, he rose from his desk and walked to the window. She looked adorable in her blue coat and black mittens, but something was wrong. Something big enough that she needed the physical diversion of rolling a huge ball of snow.

He left his office, grabbed his coat and shoved his feet into sturdy boots. He exited through the front door, so she wouldn't see him and sneaked up behind her.

"What are you doing?"

She spun to face him, her mittened hands flattened on her chest as if he'd scared the tar out of her. A reaction he found a little drastic.

"Are you going to tell me what's up?"

She swallowed. "I'm fine."

"Oh, hell, no. You're not fine."

Her chin lifted. "I am." She turned away and put her attention on the second ball she was rolling to be the middle of her snowman.

Okay. So the direct approach wasn't getting him any-where. He sucked in a breath. The air was crisp but not frigid. Big white flakes of snow billowed around them. The silence intensified the peace in his soul. Peace she'd helped him find. Whatever was wrong, he wouldn't let her go through it alone.

But if she wouldn't talk—he stooped down, grabbed two handfuls of snow and packed them into one big snowball—then he'd just have to loosen her up.

Ten feet in front of him, she labored over her snowball, her butt in the air, her arms straining as she rolled it, gathering more snow.

He gave his big snowball one final pat before throwing it at her butt.

Thwack. Direct hit.

She shot up straight and pivoted to face him.

He bent and built another snowball. Before she could say anything, he tossed it at her middle. It landed with a wet thunk.

Her eyes widened. "What the hell are you doing?"

"Loosening you up."

He bent again.

"Loosening me up? For what?"

Whack. He hit her again. This time in the thighs.

Her widened eyes narrowed. "Oh, you are so dead."

"I don't think so. I think you've been in California too long to be really good at a snowball battle."

She bent, gathered snow, threw it at him and missed.

He laughed. "See? I was right. Of course, anybody with any recent snowman experience knows that you don't roll the snowball that you have to put on top of your first snowball."

Thwack. She hit him right in the chest.

"You think I'm a lightweight?" She scooped up more snow. "I might have been in a warmer climate for years, but this isn't exactly brain surgery." She hit him again. "There's a very low learning curve on snowball throwing."

This time he was smart enough to duck away from her snowball. It whizzed past him. As he ran, he bent and scooped up more snow. He turned and tossed it at her. Direct hit.

She didn't waste a second. Chasing him, she gathered snow. He lost sight of her when he ducked around the side of the house. He stopped, flattened himself against the wall and worked to slow his breathing. When she flew around the side, he caught her arm and pulled her to him.

The stunned expression on her face had laughter bubbling from him. He breathed in the fresh air, savoring this one precious, wonderful moment that he knew he'd remember forever.

He wasn't afraid. He wasn't angry. He wasn't unhappy. He was with somebody who made him laugh.

"I think this is against the rules of the Geneva Snowball Convention or something."

He laughed again. His heart swelled with a wonderful freedom that intoxicated him. Already holding her one arm, he hooked his hand around the second so he could pull her closer. He didn't give her two seconds to realize what he was about to do. He swooped down and kissed her.

Thoroughly. The way he'd wanted to kiss her from the second she'd shaken out her pretty yellow hair. He moved his lips across hers roughly, but enticingly, feeling her yield beneath him.

The world around them became a reverent hush as he realized he was falling in love again. Differently this time. Not with a partner. Not with a friend. But with...someone he adored.

He wasn't quite there yet. He was wise enough to hold back a bit. But he was on the brink.

When her hands crept up his arms and slowly slid to his neck, he smiled against her mouth. Unless he missed his guess, she was falling, too. Their lips moved against each other, tongues mating in the silent world.

But she suddenly pulled away. Stepped away. Turned away. "Don't."

He reached out to catch her shoulder and force her to face him, but she shrugged him off.

"Okay. Fun and games are over. I like you and you like me. Why are you rejecting me?"

She said nothing.

He put his hands on his hips and looked up at the snow that fell to his face. "You know what? You were a bit shaky but agreeable until your trip to your sister's." He paused, frowned. "Who you never actually visited. What the hell happened?"

She still said nothing.

"Do you want me to get another snowball?"

She peeked back at him. "I was winning that fight."

"In your dreams. If I'd wanted to destroy you I would have." He took a step toward her. His voice softened. He ran his hand down her knit cap to the yellow hair that peeked out beneath it. "What happened that night? Tell me. Maybe I can help?"

She sniffed a laugh. "Right. That's exactly what my dad wants. He wants you to feel sorry for me. Then he can swoop in and tell you his sob story so you'll give him money. Or maybe he'll blackmail you and just demand money."

He held up his hand. "Wait! What are you talking about?"

"The night I was supposed to visit Missy, I stopped on Main Street when I saw her adorable little bakery. I couldn't believe it and had to look at it close up."

"I get that. You're proud of her."

"Yeah. It was great until suddenly my dad was standing beside me."

"Oh."

"He liked your car by the way. He guessed you must have some money just from the look of it."

"That doesn't mean I'm going to give it to him."

She snorted in derision. "Oh, you don't know my dad. He's a con man and a bully, remember? Once he finds a mark, he doesn't let go."

"And you consider me incapable of calling the police?"

She sniffed a laugh. Peeked back at him again. "You'd just call the police?"

"You are talking to the guy who wouldn't take his kids to town for three years." His chest puffed out with pride. "I take care of my own."

She laughed.

"You told me to think positively about Teagan. You told me not to let gossip or negative things get me down. Now I'm up because of you. I'm ready for whatever happens. You can't wallow in misery, when you wouldn't let me wallow in misery."

She laughed again as a funny feeling assaulted her. She gave herself a second to examine it and realized it was hope. She faced him. "This is a little more than wallowing. He's going to come after your money."

He shook his head. "Let him try."

She pressed her lips together, drew strength from his strength, confidence from his confidence. After all, her dad was fifty miles away. Why should she cower now?

"I still think I won that snowball battle."

He put his arm across her shoulder and led her back to her two big snowballs that would eventually be a snowman. "Yeah, but I won the war." He kissed her again. Happiness bubbled inside her. This was what sharing your life felt like.

She knew it. She'd never had it before, but there was no mistaking the feeling.

He broke the kiss. "Let's finish the snowman and surprise the kids."

She nodded. Pieces of her broken heart began to knit together.

He bent to pick up her second snowball. With a grunt, he lifted it and put it on the first snowball. "You think you could have lifted that alone?"

She shook her head. "No. Not alone." And maybe that's what life was all about. Realizing you couldn't do the heavy lifting alone.

"Want some hot chocolate?"

He grinned at her. "Yeah. But we've got one more layer of snowman. Then we have to find him a hat…and some eyes. Maybe some twigs for arms."

"You've done this before."

"Everybody's done this before."

Maybe everybody had, but it was the first time she'd shared something with a man, something that though not intimate was personal. She tucked the memory away. She was still scared. She was still vulnerable. She knew she could—would—make huge mistakes that might send him running, but today he was hers.

That afternoon, she shooed him out of the kitchen so she could make dinner. All the cooking lessons her father had given her came rolling back. Except this time, her fear didn't resurrect. Clark was right. If her father came here, if he tried to blackmail her, or even have her arrested for stealing his car, she would deal with it. Actually, as soon as she got the money for tutoring Jack, she would give her dad a certified check and make him sign a paper saying that was a total payoff of her debt to him.

She smiled. Now that Clark had her thinking logically, she was thinking very logically.

While her pork chops baked she raced into her bedroom and began a search for attorneys. She intended to pay her dad the money for the car, but she didn't want to be afraid anymore. She needed to get him to sign something. So he'd never have anything to hold over her head again.

Twenty minutes later she returned to the kitchen to check on her scalloped potatoes and pork chops. The entire room smelled divine. Like a home. Her home. She set the table by the French doors so they could watch the snow fall. She found candles and dimmed the lights so the snowfall would be even prettier. More romantic.

When Clark walked into the kitchen and saw the candles, he stopped. "Wow."

Nerves invaded her. "You don't like it?"

His gaze ambled to hers. "I think it's very romantic."

"That was the look I was going for."

"You're okay with this?"

She laughed. "First you push. Now you're pulling back."

"I'm not pulling back. I just want to make sure I'm not pushing too much."

"You're not."

But when they were on the couch in the den that night, watching an old movie, and his arm slid across the sofa, over to her shoulders, warmth tingled through her along with a shiver of fear. He was so special. He deserved a wonderful love in his life and she knew…she just *knew* that she'd screw this up somehow if they went too fast.

Using his arm around her shoulders, he pulled her closer, snuggled her against him. The dual reactions of fear and need spiraled through her. The temptation was strong to lay her head on his shoulder, close her eyes, just enjoy this.

Why shouldn't she? She might eventually ruin everything, but tonight he was hers.

She sucked in a quick breath, let her head lean to the right an inch, two inches, three inches...

"Dad!"

Clark bolted up. "Did you just hear Jack?"

She jerked away. "Yes!"

He popped into the room, Teagan on his heels. "Gramma says she's sorry but she forgot about some Christmas cookie thing she has tomorrow."

Clark jumped up off the sofa. Althea slid to the far end before she also rose.

"Cookie thing?"

"I think she said it's an exchange." He grinned. "But she said we can come back next weekend."

"Next weekend is Christmas."

Jack laughed. "I think she knows."

Clark tossed her an apologetic look before he put his hands on the kids' shoulders and herded them toward the door. "It's late. You guys had a busy day. Time for bed."

When they were gone, Althea fell to the sofa, grateful for the reprieve. But deep down inside, she admitted she might have been lucky tonight. She wasn't ready for what her body seemed to want with Clark.

Still, she and Clark lived together. One of these nights he'd kiss her again, hold her again...

And though she wanted this, she wasn't ready.

CHAPTER TEN

THE NEXT MORNING when Althea strolled into the kitchen and stopped at the counter to make her cup of coffee, Clark could see she was nervous. He'd felt the tension in her the night before. He'd felt her stiffen when he'd put his arm around her while they watched TV.

But she also hadn't run. She might have been nervous, unsure, but she'd laid her head on his shoulder—albeit only for ten seconds before the kids came home.

"So, Grandma said that any night this week we could come back and stay over to make up for not being able to stay over last night."

"Sounds good to me."

Teagan clapped her hands over her mouth, her big brown eyes growing even bigger.

Clark smiled. "I'm surprised you're happy to stay away from the house without me."

She grinned.

Jack said, "She ate more cookies than she painted."

Althea joined them at the center island. "Your grandma makes painted cookies?"

"Santas and Christmas trees—" Jack counted off on his fingers "—bells, sleds, churches, elves. They're sugar cookie shapes and the paint is icing."

"I've made those."

Clark's chest tightened. She'd probably made those for her dad's diner. She was talking again, opening up, albeit slowly because she wanted what he wanted. A relationship.

He watched her fuss over Teagan's breakfast. She'd said she wasn't innocent, that she'd had boyfriends. But he had a sense that none of her boyfriends had been dads...or older than she was. Having a relationship with him was probably different than anything she'd done before. And for a girl who had been abused, different was probably scary.

He didn't intend to run from this, but he also wouldn't push her. This was as new for him as it was for her. They had plenty of time.

"Well, I'm going upstairs to the office." He turned and headed to the door, but on second thought, he stopped. "I only want to work until noon, so what do you say we go to town and get pizza for lunch again?"

Teagan gasped and threw her hands across her mouth. Jack said, "All right!"

Althea perked up. "Now, there's a good reason for all of us to get out of our pajamas."

Althea and Jack played video games until it was time to get dressed to go to lunch. She took Teagan into her room and they poked through the drawers to find something cute to wear out.

"Did you keep the clip for your hair?"

She nodded and raced to her dresser. She lifted a little Cinderella figurine and produced the sparkly red clip Althea had put in her hair a few days before.

Her heart melted. Clark was doing the best job he could with these kids but from the way Teagan hid her clip, like a treasure she didn't want stolen, she could tell Teagan would love to be more girly.

"You know, while we're in town for lunch, we could pick up a whole pack of clips for you."

She nodded eagerly.

And maybe tonight she'd mention to Clark that they should take Teagan shopping for clothes, let her pick out some things. Right now she had nothing but T-shirts, sweaters and jeans in her closet. Maybe she'd like a dress?

With Teagan and Jack ready to go, Althea headed back to her room. She showered quickly and walked to her own closet. She rifled through hangers of sweaters and jeans, suddenly wishing she had something prettier, too. For the first time in her life, she wanted to dress up, look special, look feminine…not like the girlfriend of a guy who spent his life surfing. No bikini. No ripped jeans. No hoodies. She wanted to look pretty.

But since she didn't have anything but jeans, she found her neatest pair, slipped into a red sweater and hunted for the red clip that matched the one she'd given to Teagan.

When she stepped out of the hall into the kitchen, Teagan grinned.

She smiled at her. "We're sort of twins now."

Clark's face scrunched in confusion. "Why?"

She pointed at her clip. "I have one. Teagan has one."

"Oh. That's cool." He feigned excitement for Teagan's sake, and she suppressed a happy sigh. This was what she loved about him. He probably couldn't give a flying fig about matching clips, but he knew it meant something to Teagan, so he made a big deal out of it.

In a flurry of passing hats and finding mittens, they put on their outdoor clothes and headed to the garage and Clark's SUV. He strapped Teagan into her seat as Jack buckled himself into the seat beside her. Althea took her place in the passenger's seat beside Clark.

Behind the steering wheel, he smiled at her. "Ready for pizza?"

She nodded, smiling. Such wonderful, inconsequential talk. Like a real family. Like people who loved each other.

It might be too soon to be in love, but it wasn't too soon to behave like people who cared about each other. She was starved for it, intrigued by it, so enamored with the idea of being in love, being in a real family, acting like a normal person that her heart felt like it could explode.

Now if she could just get past the damned fear.

The drive to town took the usual twenty minutes. Clark got Teagan out of her seat. Althea made sure Jack was okay. They walked up the decorated street to the pizza place.

Warmth greeted them as they stepped inside. The waitress remembered them. Jack ordered the pizza, making Clark laugh and Althea relax. All this might seem special to her, but it was normal for a family. *Normal*. And if she could relax, be herself, this could all be hers one day.

They sipped their soda and chatted about Jack's schoolwork for the twenty minutes it took for the pizza to bake. It arrived with a flourish. Napkins and paper plates were passed. Clark cut Teagan's slice into tiny pieces. The waitress brought second sodas.

Other customers finished eating and left. New customers arrived and filled the seats around them. They ate their pizza. Clark paid the bill, and they walked out onto the street.

Althea didn't want it to end. She wanted to walk up Main Street again, see the decorations with Clark and the kids, enjoy the brisk air, talk about nothing some more.

"You know, Teagan's hair looks great with the red clip, but there are lots of colors she could wear. In fact, if we got some hair ties, I could put her hair in pigtails tomorrow or a ponytail."

In Clark's arms, Teagan gasped. Clark frowned. "Would you like some hair ties?"

She nodded.

He smiled. "I think most of the shops are closed today, but if Althea doesn't mind, she could bring you back tomorrow and get them then."

She froze. He would let her take the kids to town…on her own? He'd made such great strides in letting go of his fear that Althea was bolstered by his success. If he could let go of his fears and accept that the kids needed breathing room, then surely she could put her fear about a relationship aside.

"The drugstore's open."

Clark and Althea glanced down at Jack.

"It is?"

"Yeah and it's got the girly stuff in it."

Clark peeked over at her for confirmation.

"Drugstores always have makeup and clips and hair ties." She grinned. "Girly stuff. We could get her clips now." Which would extend their trip, helping her adjust to the fact that she fit here. With this man. His kids. In their life.

"Okay. Then let's go to the drugstore."

The wind whipped up as they walked to the very end of Main Street. A brand-new brick building housed the popular chain store. Althea pulled her jacket hood up over her hair as they walked across the almost empty parking lot and the wind swirled around them.

She held the door open for Clark, who still carried Teagan. Inside, they all stomped their feet on the mat in front of the door and removed their mittens.

"Is there anything else we need while we're here?"

Althea glanced around. "Well, if you need soap or shampoo or hair spray," she teased. "This is the place to get it."

They ambled up and down the aisles grabbing a few items like aspirin and foot powder.

Clark shook his head. "I only ever shop at the grocery store. I'd forgotten there's a whole world of products out here."

She laughed. "You really need to get out more."

The bell above the main door tinkled as another customer arrived. Clark picked up Q-tips and tossed them into the basket Jack had retrieved. He turned away from the shelf with a smile, but his smile suddenly froze and he stopped.

Confused, Althea followed his gaze to the tall dark-haired man who had just entered.

"Hey, Clark."

Clark stiffened. "Brice."

Brice? Althea's eyebrows rose. *The Brice?*

Her gaze flew to Clark. His face had hardened. His eyes had narrowed. His arms protectively hugged Teagan to him.

Teagan.

She hadn't worn a hat because she wanted everyone to see the red clip in her dark brown hair—hair the exact color of Brice's. She glanced at her eyes. Not whiskey-colored like Clark's but dark brown like Brice's.

She stifled a groan.

No wonder Clark worried. Teagan had Brice's coloring.

Thick, icy tension filled the space around them. Clark said nothing. Brice said nothing.

"We're just here for a few things," Althea said, putting her hands on Jack's shoulders and pulling him close to her. "So we need to get going."

Brice nodded. He nudged his head in the direction of the prescription counter. "I'm picking up something for my mom."

Not knowing what else to say, Althea said, "It was nice to see you," before she shepherded Clark and the kids away from him.

Clark didn't say a word on the drive home. Neither did

Althea. What could she say? "I see why you're worried. Teagan looks just like him"?

He might need to talk about it, but that seemed a cruel way to bring up the subject. And they certainly wouldn't talk about it in front of the kids.

When they got home, he locked himself away in his office. Althea entertained Teagan and Jack. At six, she reheated the leftovers from their dinner the night before. But when she knocked on his office door, Clark said he wasn't hungry.

He did come out two hours later to help get Teagan ready for bed.

When she was bathed and in her pink princess pajamas, he read her the story about the bunny that had gotten lost in the woods. In the end of the book, when the daddy rabbit found the lost bunny, fed her soup, tucked her into bed and kissed her forehead telling her he'd never let anything happen to her, Teagan nestled into her pillow. Comforted. Happy.

She could always depend on her daddy.

With the story complete, Teagan's pink bedroom grew quiet. Clark rose, tucked her into the covers, kissed her forehead and said, "I'll never let anything happen to you." He kissed her forehead again. "You can always depend on me."

Teagan smiled. Her eyelids lowered.

Althea's eyes filled with tears. Teagan's favorite story wasn't just a story that comforted her. It comforted Clark, too.

As he passed the mirrored dresser, he picked up Teagan's hairbrush.

He stepped out of the room and closed the door.

She caught his gaze.

He sighed. "There's enough hair in here that the lab I

found should be able to get something usable for a DNA sample."

Her breathing stilled. "I thought you'd already done that."

He shook his head. "I was a little preoccupied." He flicked his gaze to her again. "Happy."

"Oh." She swallowed. Grasping for something to say, she said the first thing that popped into her head. "So how'd you get Brice's DNA?"

"I didn't. I don't want to know if she's his. I'm going to find out if she's mine. I'm sending my DNA."

He wouldn't look at her. A wall of distance sat between them.

She licked her dry lips. "And what's going to happen if it comes back she isn't your daughter?"

He shrugged. "Haven't figured that out yet." He sucked in a breath. "But after seeing him today, happy or not, able to pretend or not, I realized I can't put this off anymore. I have to know."

Without another word, he walked down the hall toward his bedroom. His shoulders hunched over, his steps slow, he looked like a man on his way to the gallows.

Sympathy overwhelmed her. His wife had been the one to make the mistakes, but he was the one suffering.

The mood the next morning was agonizing. Familiar silence permeated the room. She saw the package on Clark's briefcase, noticed the lab name neatly printed on the front.

Their gazes met as she sat down at the island with her cup of coffee.

Breaking the unbearable quiet, she said, "So Jack's going to be taking the tests today to see if he's ready to move into the next semester."

Clark worked up a smile. "That's great. Good luck, buddy."

Confident in the way only a twelve-year-old can be, Jack shrugged. "I'm going to ace this."

Clark chuckled. "Good."

The kitchen fell silent. Teagan munched on toast, grinning at Althea when she looked her way. She watched Clark's gaze amble over to his little girl and watched pain skitter into his eyes.

Everything inside her felt for him. If she could, she would take his pain. He was such a good man that it didn't seem fair that he had to suffer. He was a good person, an honest person, something she'd longed for all her life.

She swallowed. She had longed for this her entire life. A family with a man who protected his kids. A man who knew how to love.

Whether it was convenient or not, difficult or not, she loved him and she would not let this break him.

Clark returned home from work as down as he left. Althea tried to cheer him up through dinner.

"Jack was done with his tests twenty minutes before the average time."

"That's great."

"I think he deserves a treat tonight."

Clark met her gaze over the dinner table. "A treat?"

"I was thinking we could decorate the tree."

Jack gasped. "It's too early."

"It's less than a week before Christmas Eve." She sent a hopeful look Clark's way. "Besides, it's not like there's a law against decorating trees early when everybody seems to need a boost."

Catching her meaning, Clark sucked in a breath. "I suppose we could."

"I pulled the tree decorations from the attic and left them

in the hall by the door again. Why don't you go get them, Jack?"

Jack said, "All right," grabbed Teagan's hand and flew out of the kitchen.

"It's not right for anybody to be sad this close to Christmas."

Clark sniffed a laugh. "So mine's the mood you're trying to boost."

"Not trying." She smiled. "I will boost your mood. But this is good for the kids, too."

She heard the thump, thump, thump of the big box being dragged down the stairs and Clara Bell's "Woof! Woof!"

She jumped out of her seat. "I think I better go help him."

Clark motioned her down. "You finish your dinner. I'll help."

Understanding that he might want some private time with the kids, Althea stayed behind, lingered over her dinner and put the dishes into the dishwasher.

When she couldn't delay any longer, she walked into the living room where Clark sat on the floor, artificial tree limbs sorted out in a big circle around him. Jack stood over his shoulder. Teagan stooped beside him.

"So what's up?"

He sighed. "I've always hated this tree."

Jack's eyes widened. "You have?"

"Yes. Now it isn't just artificial. It's old and artificial. I think I'd like a real tree."

Althea peeked over at him. He shrugged. "If we're going to make this our best Christmas ever, we should have a good tree."

Understanding what he was doing, she nodded. "I think that's a great idea. Is there a tree farm around here?"

Clark rose from the floor. "There are probably ten tree

farms around here. But the best one is about five miles east."
He faced the kids. "Get your coats."

Driving to the tree farm, Clark said, "This will be our new tradition. Going out a few days before Christmas and picking our own tree."

Althea's entire body tingled with happiness. She'd never helped choose a tree. But, better than that, she knew this adventure was good for the kids, as well as Clark. "I love real trees."

The closer they got to the tree farms, the happier he seemed to be. Not only did the tree shopping seem to take his mind off the DNA samples he'd sent that morning, but also this was a family who needed some new traditions.

When they arrived at the tree farm, Clark climbed out and helped Teagan out of her car seat. Carrying her, he walked to the makeshift stand in front of what looked like hundreds of rows of trees lit by huge overhead lights.

"We're here for a tree."

The old man running the stand pointed to the right where dozens of trees leaned against the side of an old building. "We have some pre-cut here or you can pick your own."

He glanced at the trees then Teagan's eager face. "I think I'd like the kids to have the experience of picking our own tree."

Her heart splintered in two for him and she suddenly understood. As he was putting together the artificial tree, he must have realized this might be his last Christmas with his little girl. And he intended to make it the best Christmas possible.

With Clark and Teagan leading the way, they started down one of the rows of trees. The music being piped around the farm shifted from "Here Comes Santa Claus" to "We Wish You a Merry Christmas." A light, powdery snow began to fall. Clark stopped in front of a tree.

"Look at this one."

She had to crane her neck to see the top. "I think it might be a bit too tall."

He nodded and started down the row again.

Teagan turned in her dad's arms and grinned at Althea who laughed. "We Wish You a Merry Christmas" floated around them. Caught in the spirit, Althea began to sing, too.

"We wish you a Merry Christmas. We wish you a Merry Christmas. We wish you a Merry Christmas and a Happy New Year."

"Glad tidings we bring to you and your kin." Jack joined in. Althea laughed and put her hand across his shoulder.

"We wish you a Merry Christmas," Clark joined in. "And a Happy New Year."

He stopped. "Hey, look at this one."

Althea and Jack stopped. The tree was tall, but not too tall. Bushy branches and a bright green color indicated a healthy tree.

"I think it's perfect."

"I think it's perfect, too." Clark looked to Jack. "What do you think?"

"I think it's great."

His voice was hushed, solemn, as if it was his first Christmas. In truth, it might actually be his first real Christmas since his mom's death.

Althea rubbed her hand across the top of his shoulders. "Wait until we get it decorated. I found so many beautiful ornaments in the boxes in the attic."

Jack nodded. "Should I go get the guy with the axe?"

Clark laughed. "I think a saw will be enough."

The caretaker sent one of his employees back with Jack to help cut the tree. He wrapped twine around the branches to make it possible to tie it to the top of the SUV. They were quiet on the way home, so Althea turned to face Teagan and Jack and began to sing, "We wish you a Merry Christmas."

Because that seemed to be the only song both she and Jack knew all the words for, they repeated it until Clark pulled in the driveway.

Shutting off the SUV engine he said, "Okay. Enough!" But he laughed. Jack laughed. Teagan giggled and Althea's spirits lifted. The dark cloud that seemed to have been hovering over Clark's head was gone. His eyes glowed with happiness as he and Jack wrestled the tree into the house.

Teagan stayed at Althea's side, her little mittened hand tucked firmly in Althea's.

And for the first time in her life she felt that she belonged. Not as a teacher or friend, but as someone more. Someone special not just to Clark, but to the kids, too.

Familiar fear tiptoed through her. Right now, making a Merry Christmas for the kids, she was good. Knowledgeable. All she had to do was figure out what *she* wanted, and do that for the kids. But what happened in January or February? What happened when they fell? Had a problem with a bully? This wasn't like school where she had a principal for backup or parents to call in for a consultation. She would be on her own and she had no idea how to handle kid troubles.

Jack and Clark installed the tree in the stand, then filled the bowl with water. Jack immediately walked over to the box of lights, but Clark stopped him. "It's late. Plus, we've had enough fun for tonight. Let's save some for tomorrow."

Jack looked about to argue but Althea said, "Tomorrow we can string popcorn and we'll have that to hang on the tree, too."

He said, "Okay."

"Great." Clark scooped up Teagan. "You guys can go find something on TV while I get Chai Tea ready for bed."

Jack headed for the den with Althea on his heels. But

she remembered she'd washed Teagan's favorite nightie that day. The fear nudged at her again. She'd forgotten laundry. Left it in the dryer like a single woman did. Not a mom. Not someone responsible for kids.

Telling herself to stop thinking of her failings, she changed directions. She pulled the clothes out of the dryer and hastily folded them. Carrying the armload of Teagan's T-shirts and pajamas, she raced up the stairs and into Teagan's bedroom.

Clark rushed in behind her.

She displayed the pajamas. "I forgot I'd washed these today."

He showed her a bottle of bath gel. "I forgot we'd run out of this last night."

Their gazes caught. Her fear eased a bit. Even seasoned father Clark forgot things a time or two. It might have been last minute that each had remembered, but they had remembered. In some ways that actually made them more compatible.

She smiled.

He smiled.

"We wish you a Merry Christmas and a Happy New Bear."

At the sound of the sweet little voice, both Clark and Althea pivoted to face the bathroom.

Clark whispered, "She's singing."

Too stunned to speak, Althea nodded.

As Teagan repeated "We Wish You a Merry Christmas and a Happy New Bear" over and over again, Clark and Althea sneaked up to the bathroom door, which was open a crack. They peeked inside.

Naked, waiting to go into the tub, Teagan sang to her dirty pink bear.

"Is she singing to the bear? Wishing the bear would have a happy Christmas?"

Althea pressed her hand to her mouth to stifle a laugh. "I think she's singing about a happy new bear because she doesn't have any frame of reference for a year, but she does know what a bear is."

"Oh." He paused. His eyes softened with love. "Look how beautiful she is."

"And how happy. She loves you Clark. She'll always be your little girl."

He blew his breath out on a long sigh. "Let's not kid ourselves, if the DNA tests come back that she's not my daughter chances are Brice will figure it out himself sooner or later."

"Maybe not."

"And what am I supposed to do if he doesn't? Keep her from her biological dad?"

She didn't know what to say, so she said nothing. Clark was in a horrible catch-22.

He opened the door and walked inside. Picking up Teagan, he tickled her tummy then put her in the tub. "We heard you singing."

She blushed and pressed her lips together.

Althea sat on the rim of the tub and ran her hand down Teagan's silky hair. "Oh, sweetie. You have such a beautiful voice. We loved hearing it."

She shook her head and looked down at the bubbly water around her.

She wasn't going to talk.

With a glance at Althea, Clark said, "Let's get you bathed and read your story."

Obviously relieved, Teagan nodded enthusiastically.

But walking down the stairs after Teagan was in bed, Clark sighed heavily. "You know that if a psychologist gets a hold of her and realizes she doesn't talk, only whispers, they'll crucify me. They'll call me unfit and I'll never keep her. I'll be lucky to even get visitation rights."

Althea caught his arm. "That's if the DNA tests come back saying she's not yours. And if Brice sues you for custody. Don't borrow trouble."

He squeezed his eyes shut.

"Hey. Come on. I saw what you were doing tonight. You were working to make this the best Christmas ever. Don't stop now. Don't panic now. Keep going."

He hugged her. "Thank you."

She laughed. "For telling you not to borrow trouble? Or for bossing you around?"

"For being here. For making me face the truth. For not letting me get negative."

His arms tightened around her, and warmth filled her. She couldn't remember a time when somebody really wanted her around. Needed her. She might not be the best candidate for mom, but if Clark loved her she would make it work.

She prayed the DNA results came back saying Clark was Teagan's father.

Until then, she would keep this family happy.

CHAPTER ELEVEN

THE NEXT MORNING, she got up before Clark and had pancakes on the griddle when he entered the kitchen.

"What's that smell?"

She laughed. "It's breakfast. I worked the opening shift at the diner my last two years of high school. I make a mean pancake." And if she was going to do the job of keeping Clark and his kids happy while he awaited the DNA results, then she wasn't going to fudge or pretend. She wouldn't shy away from things she wanted to do, no matter how painful the memories. She would pull out all the stops—do everything she could do—to make these next few days happy.

"Mmmm." He sat on one of the stools around the center island as Teagan sleepily ambled into the room, bear under her arm.

Clark pointed at the stack of pancakes Althea walked to the table. "Look at those."

Her eyes rounded and she smiled.

"Teagan loves pancakes."

"Well, you are in luck," Althea said as she set the plate of pancakes on the center island and sat on the stool across from Clark. She picked up Teagan's plate. "How many do you want? Seven?"

She giggled.

Jack strolled into the room.

"Hey, buddy."

"Hey."

He slid onto a stool.

Clark pointed at the plate of pancakes. "Look. Althea made pancakes."

He roused himself a little. "Pancakes are good."

They passed syrup. Clark cut Teagan's pancake. Althea dug into her own.

"So what are you going to do today?"

Jack glanced up at his dad. "I don't know. What do you want me to do?"

"Well, you finished your studies so I guess you can choose."

"You mean if I want to play video games all day I can?"

"It's sort of like a vacation. You finished your work. You get the reward of time off."

He leaped off his stool. "Cool! I'm going to call Owen. See if he can play Wizard World with me online today."

Clark pointed at his plate. "First you have to eat."

He slid back onto the stool.

Clark gobbled his breakfast, grabbed his briefcase and headed for the door. As always, Althea followed him, giving him a chance to give her special instructions for the day if he had any.

Instead, he set down his briefcase, pulled her to him and kissed her. "I'll see you at dinnertime. Do you want me to bring home something?"

Too stunned to speak, she shook her head. He smiled. "Later."

She nodded.

He opened the door and closed it behind him.

She stared at it. Happiness swirled through her. One step at a time she could do this.

Midmorning, when Jack was in the den playing video

games, Teagan sat coloring at the desk beside him and Althea studied a cookbook, looking for something special for dinner, the doorbell rang.

She jumped off the stool, calling, "I'll get it," as she passed the hall to the den.

Without thought, she grabbed the doorknob and yanked open the door with a festive, "Happy holidays."

"Well, happy holidays to you, too, baby girl."

Her dad.

Her chest froze as her gaze whipped around. The kids weren't behind her. She prayed they stayed in the den then pivoted to face her dad again.

"Get out."

"Hell, I'm not even in. I'm on the damned porch." He smiled at her. His gray whiskers lifting as his jowls rose. His beady eyes crinkling at the corners. "Besides, is that any way to treat your dad?"

"You were never a dad to me."

"Ah, hell, kitten. I did the best I could with what I had."

She gaped at him. "You had a successful business, a beautiful wife, two daughters who worked like slaves for you. And you rewarded us by beating us. You're a criminal."

He sniffed a laugh. "That's fancy talk from somebody who stole her daddy's car."

She shut up. Fear shivered through her. She recognized that voice. The warning voice. Hide before you get hit.

"In fact, that's pretty much why I'm here. I want blue book value on that car. Not what it's worth now. What it was worth the day you took it."

Her chin lifted. "You never paid us for working at the diner. I think of taking that car as evening the scales."

"State police don't see it that way. I ran a hypothetical past them and they say I'm entitled to restitution…or I can have you locked up."

Her heart stuttered. She automatically took a pace back. He could be lying. He always lied. But this wasn't something to test him on. Eventually, she intended to pay him, but she couldn't today. Not only was her bank account empty, but she also hadn't printed out the receipt and release form she'd found at the legal site online. Plus, if she told him she would pay him later, he'd hound her to borrow the money or give him a post-dated check—or something. And then he'd be back because she didn't yet have a release for him to sign.

"I don't have any money."

He peered into the foyer. "Seems like your boyfriend does."

"He's not my boyfriend. I'm his son's teacher."

"So what do you get for this gig? Has to be good. More than a teacher's salary."

Her heart stumbled again.

He pointed his index finger at her nose. "I'll be back after the holidays. You have money for me then."

He smiled, turned and walked away.

She closed the door behind him then leaned against it. Her knees shook so much it was everything she could do not to slide down to the floor and wrap herself in a tight ball. Hot, prickly fear enveloped her. But it wasn't fear for herself. It was fear for Teagan, Jack and even Clark.

This was why she couldn't have a relationship. Anybody she brought into her life would have to deal with her dad.

When Clark arrived in his office, he had thirty-seven emails waiting. But he saw only one that concerned him. Jack's test scores.

He blew his breath out on a sigh and prayed the results were good because Jack was counting on this. Althea was right. He needed to go to school in town, needed friends.

But if he failed and had to enter school a grade below his peers that might be worse than not going to school at all.

Slowly, deliberately, he clicked on the email and the message popped up on his screen. As he read the scores, his frown lifted into a grin. Jack had done it!

He sat back on his chair. *Althea* had done it. She'd worked real magic on his family.

He called the house to see if she'd be free to go to the school with him that afternoon but got no answer. Realizing she might have taken the kids Christmas shopping, he chuckled...then stopped himself. *He'd chuckled.* He really wasn't afraid anymore. Wasn't dead inside. She'd brought him back to life.

He called the school and set an appointment to meet with the principal that afternoon. He tried the house again, but again got no response, so he went to the redbrick school alone.

He sat in the office, in a chair meant to accommodate a middle-school kid, feeling tall and gangly. He jumped out of his seat when Mrs. Osborne stepped out of her office.

"Mr. Beaumont?"

"Yes." He extended his hand to shake hers. "I'd like to enroll my son for the next semester."

"That's wonderful." She directed him to go into her office. "I trust you have his transcripts."

The first ten minutes Clark took care of the business of transcripts and qualifications, then he sucked in a breath and did what had to be done.

"Jack's mom was killed in an automobile accident three years ago."

Mrs. Osborne laid her arms on her desk. "I remember."

"There was gossip."

She winced. "I remember that, too."

"I'm afraid it will resurrect when he returns to school."

"It might. But the interesting thing about middle school is that the kids don't really care so much what their parents do. They're quite self-absorbed."

He laughed. "For once that would work in my favor." But he quickly sobered. If the DNA test results came back that Teagan wasn't his, he had some big decisions to make and those decisions could impact Jack.

He sucked in another breath. He didn't want to tell his secrets, his shame, to a complete stranger, but he did want Jack to be protected.

"Just in case these kids aren't so self-absorbed, how about if you have Jack's teacher report anything unusual to you."

She brought her hands together and knitted her fingers. "Define unusual."

"You know…if he's bullied, teased, that kind of thing."

"We're very proud of our antibullying policies. We will protect your son. But, it's also our policy to alert parents if there's any extra trouble."

He nodded. Rose. He couldn't ask for anything more than to be apprised. But he still had a sense he was leading his son into a den of lions and it sickened him, resurrected his anger with his dead wife, made him feel powerless.

Never in his life had anyone been able to make him feel powerless…until Carol.

When Clark arrived home, Althea could see he was antsy, nervous. Their moods fit and she was glad. With him upset, it was unlikely he'd notice she was upset.

She'd intended to make something fancy and festive for supper and instead only had the mental energy to open two cans of soup and make cheese sandwiches.

Teagan loved it. Jack ate three sandwiches. Clark barely touched his food.

When the kids disappeared before having to stack the

dishes in the dishwasher, Clark sniffed a laugh. "Well, we sort of made our bed on that one."

A shiver raced through her at his unexpected choice of words. "Our bed?"

He met her gaze. "Neither one of us talked enough to slow down the kids' eating and keep them here long enough to do dishes."

She almost laughed at the silly way she'd misinterpreted him, but nerves overwhelmed her. If she wanted to have a life with Clark, she didn't just have to tell him about her dad's visit. She had to admit her dad had found her. Wanted money. Would probably want more money, even after she paid for the car.

"I visited Jack's school today."

"Oh." Good news. Thank God. She could certainly use it.

"I got his grades this morning." He shook his head. "Damn. I should have printed them out and shown him."

Althea smiled. "He knows he did well. He'll be okay waiting another day or two to actually see his scores."

"He did exceptionally well." He reached across the table and squeezed her hand. "Thanks to you."

Her spirits lifted a bit. "You're welcome."

"Anyway, I enrolled him for the next semester."

"That's great." Her spirits rose again.

"It seems great." He toyed with his silverware. "I just hope I'm not throwing him to the lions."

"Sixth-graders are bad, but they're not lions."

He met her gaze. "No, but their parents are. What the hell is going to happen if I get the DNA results back and Teagan's not mine? What if Brice picks this year to finally figure out she might be his? What if I decide Teagan has a right to know her real dad?" He squeezed his eyes shut. "Is this the right year to put him into school?"

"I don't know."

He burst from his stool. "Damn it all, anyway! What the hell was Carol thinking? How could she bring this trouble to our door? Where the hell was her head?"

She swallowed. "I don't know."

He raked his fingers through his hair. "I can't even comprehend that level of selfishness."

Althea stayed quiet. She might not have betrayed Clark the way his deceased wife had, but if she stayed, she'd bring every bit as much trouble to his house.

He shook his head as if shaking off his anger and faced her. "I'll do the dishes."

She rose. "No. I'll do the dishes. You need to get the kids and start decorating the tree we bought yesterday."

"That's right."

She smiled. "I know you want to make this a special holiday for the kids and I think having something to do every night like decorating the tree is an excellent way to do that. Don't let the past ruin the present."

He nodded. "You're right. How'd you get so smart?"

She looked away. "Oh, I am so far away from smart that you'd be amazed." She tossed a dishtowel at him. "Go or I'll make you dry."

He started out of the room, but stopped suddenly. "There's one more thing."

"Oh, yeah?"

"All this time you've been here, I've never paid you."

She tilted her head. "No. You haven't."

"So, I transferred your salary into the checking account number you gave me."

A thrill of happiness ran through her. She'd loved working here, even without pay. But that money had a purpose. It gave her choices rather than have to become a baker by default.

"I also added a bonus."

"Oh, Clark! You shouldn't have done that!"

"Hey, you washed dishes, did laundry, babysat the kids… all things that weren't in the job description when I hired you. You earned the money."

Grateful, she smiled. "Thanks."

He left the room and Althea made short order of the dishes. Her mood improved, she raced into her room and fired up her laptop. In a few quick keystrokes, she was at her banking account page and when she saw the amount Clark had deposited, her eyes bulged. Over double what they'd agreed to.

She rose, ready to go into the living room and argue, except…

It was enough money to pay off her dad.

She paced her room. The problem was no amount was ever enough money to pay off her dad. Still, if she gave him this money she needed documentation that she'd paid off the car. That their debt was settled. Before she gave him a check, she had to print out the receipt and release she'd found on the legal website, stating that her debt to him was paid in full.

But that wouldn't stop him from asking again.

And again.

And again.

Missy had told her that.

She'd told her that the only way to get rid of him was to stand up to him. And she wasn't sure she could. Oh, she would try. She would go to him with the best of intentions, but he'd baby girl her…or he'd threaten her and her knees would knock together.

She stopped pacing. She'd never been able to face him for herself, but for Clark, Teagan and Jack…

Her shoulders straightened. For Clark, Teagan and Jack, she could pay him his money, get him to sign the receipt and tell him she would call the police if he ever came near her again. That's what Missy had done. It would work for her, too.

She closed her laptop and headed into the living room. Clark and Jack had strung multicolored lights in rows on the tree. Teagan walked a shiny red ornament to one of the bottom branches and hung it.

Jack saw her first. "You missed all the cursing."

She laughed. "Lights that hard to string?"

"No. They were tangled. Right, Dad?"

"Tangled doesn't even begin to describe it."

They had two more days until Christmas Eve. The house was decorated. The tree was being decorated. They could bake cookies the next day or she and Jack could do a special project.

"I was thinking." She bit her lip. "We don't really have any more decorating to do tomorrow. We could bake cookies—"

Jack fist-pumped. "All right!"

"Or we could take the family pictures off your dad's computer and send them to a photo site. When the pictures get here next week, we could create photo albums." She paused, caught Clark's gaze. "We could make special albums for you and Teagan," she said, still talking to Jack, though she looked to Clark for approval. "Albums with memories of your mom."

Jack said, "That would be nice."

Clark smiled. "That would be really nice."

They finished decorating the tree. Clark thought of another memory or two to tell his kids. Althea's nerves calmed. She would face her dad as soon as she could sneak away. Not for herself but to protect the new family she was creating.

She was so high on happiness that she began singing "We Wish You a Merry Christmas." Jack joined in immediately. Clark soon after. Teagan grinned.

Althea stooped in front of her. "We know you know this." The little girl giggled.

Clark said, "Yeah, Teagan. We know you know this song." She giggled again.

"One of these days you're going to forget yourself and talk to us."

She laughed and hugged her bear to her face.

But that night when Althea went upstairs to put away some of Jack's laundry, she heard Teagan singing in the bathroom again and she smiled. Clark was right. One of these days his little girl would relax enough and be calm enough to forget she didn't talk out loud and she'd just speak.

She walked down the stairs feeling light and airy. Everything was working out. Once she got rid of her dad all she had to do was take life one day at a time.

She could do this.

But when she walked into the den, Clark wasn't in front of the TV. He paced back and forth behind the desk.

"What's up?"

"In all the commotion of getting Jack into school again, I forgot I was supposed to get the DNA results today."

"So soon?"

"I paid extra to have the tests expedited."

"So, check your computer now."

He faced her. "I just did. They aren't there. So much for the extra money I paid."

She plopped to the sofa. "Come on. Sit down. Watch some TV. Worrying's not going to accomplish anything."

He sat. "I just want to know."

"No matter what happens, you are her father. Even if Brice gets custody, the judge would let you have visitation. You'll never really lose her. Your role would just change."

"I wouldn't like that."

"No. But it would be better than nothing. But I don't think

you're going to lose custody. I actually think it might flip.
You'd keep custody and Brice would get visitation. You've
raised her. You're the only father she knows. No judge would
pull her away from you."

"You don't think so?"

"I think you have to focus on the positive options. Not
the negative. And that includes remembering that she could
actually be your daughter."

He sniffed a laugh. "I tell myself that a few times a day
now." He caught her gaze. "You came into my life at just the
right moment. Jack needed you. But I needed you more. I
needed someone to kick my butt and tell me it was time to
move on. I appreciate everything you've done."

She smiled, waiting for more. Telling her he appreciated
everything she'd done was a perfect opportunity for him to
tell her that he loved her. Or that he wanted her. Or even
something as simple as he liked her. But he said nothing.
He turned to the TV.

She glanced at the TV, then back at him. He wasn't the
only one who had a problem. Now that she knew how she
wanted to handle her dad, she could talk to him about it.
She needed the same support from him that she gave to him.
She wanted to share her troubles, her dreams...her life. She
wanted him to love her.

And he was watching TV.

Of course, he'd had a stressful day, made worse by the
fact that the DNA test results hadn't come as they were supposed to.

She slid close to him on the sofa. He put his arm around
her. And though she didn't nestle in, she relaxed.

Everything was fine.

But at eleven, when he excused himself to go to bed he
didn't even think to kiss her.

She watched him leave the room, reminding herself he'd

had a rough day. Hell, he'd had a rough three years that was about to culminate in either the best or worst news of his life. She couldn't fault him for being preoccupied.

The next morning she rose early again. Not only did she need to prove to herself that she could fit into this family, but also she'd promised herself she'd do whatever it took to keep them happy.

She made oatmeal—every day couldn't be a pancake celebration day—and though Jack groaned, Teagan clapped with glee. Clark also entered the kitchen looking bright and chipper.

Scooping a bowl of oatmeal for himself, he said, "Remember the email I told you I was waiting for?"

Her breath froze and she spun to face him. There was only one piece of news he had been waiting for.

"It turns out I had been worrying for nothing. The last project Carol had been working on belongs to me."

Joy burst inside her. She wanted to run to him and hug him. News like this deserved fanfare…a celebration. But he'd used code so he could tell her without letting the kids in on a secret they were too young to know. She couldn't hug him.

Of course, if they were going to have a relationship, why delay letting the kids see? Why not hug him? Wasn't that what a normal person would do?

She peered over at him. He dished oatmeal into a bowl.

She couldn't hug a man holding a bowl of oatmeal. So she smiled. "That's great."

"Yeah, Dad, I hope you get the bid."

Clark ruffled Jack's hair. "The wait is over. It's mine."

Althea chuckled at the double meaning in that and joined them at the breakfast table.

Clark said, "So today's the day you look through pictures on the computer?"

"I thought we'd do that in the morning and bake cookies in the afternoon."

Teagan gasped and clapped before she slid off her stool, ran to Clark and tugged on his shirtsleeve.

Clark shook his head and kissed the top of her head. "Nope. No more whispering. I want you to talk."

She frowned. Althea's eyebrows rose. With the worry of her paternity issues out of the way, Clark wasn't going so easy on her. She frowned and sulked her way back to her stool.

Clark ate his oatmeal reading the *Wall Street Journal,* then left for work. He didn't catch her shoulders, pull her to him and give her a quick kiss. He didn't smile at her. Actually, he was so caught up in gathering his briefcase and coat that he barely looked at her.

This time she couldn't blame it on him being preoccupied. Jack's grades were up. The DNA results were in. Now that he was free of worry and happy, he seemed to have forgotten all about her.

She shook that off. Told herself that was ridiculous. But actions spoke louder than words. He hadn't noticed her worry the day before. He'd hardly noticed her that morning.

She occupied herself helping the kids choose the pictures for the albums in the morning. But she couldn't stop the worry over his indifference that morning. To take her mind off that, she and the kids made cookies all afternoon.

When Clark returned from the office, the house was filled with the scent of sugar and cinnamon, as well as the roasted chicken, mashed potatoes and peas she'd made for dinner.

He scooped Teagan up on his way to the kitchen. When she was seated at the table, he pulled a piece of paper out of his jacket pocket and handed it to Jack.

He opened it and jumped for joy. "I knew I'd done well."

Feeling oddly left out, Althea said, "Oh, so those are your grades?"

He nodded. "Here. See for yourself. I did excellently."

Reading the report, she smiled. "I'm very proud of you."

Clark said, "I'm very proud of you, too."

They ate dinner companionably chatting about Jack's grades and his reentry into "real" school.

When they were through, Clark stole a cookie for dessert. "Jack, how about putting these dishes in the dishwasher?"

Still excited over his good grades, he happily jumped off his chair. "Sure."

Clark caught Althea's hand. "I thought you and I could have a private minute in the garage."

"The garage?" Good Lord. All day she'd worried that he didn't want anything to do with her anymore and here he was spiriting her out to the garage to kiss her. Her happiness returned in a wave of joy. She was such a worrywart!

He put his finger over his lips and made a shhh sound as he led her down the hall to the door that would take them to the garage. "I went to the mall today. And I think I got the doll Teagan wanted. I need you to look at it to be sure."

"Oh." She wasn't exactly disappointed. She wanted Teagan to have that special doll as much as he did, but for the past few days their communication had been all about the kids. About him. And then this morning he'd all but ignored her. Though he'd said he appreciated her the night before, the spark of whatever he'd felt for her seemed to be gone.

In the garage, he took the doll out of a huge bag of things he'd bought for the kids. All her odd feelings disappeared. He was getting ready for Christmas...for his kids. He might not be preoccupied with Jack's grades or Teagan's DNA, but now Christmas was on his mind. How could she fault him for that?

She smiled at him. "This is the doll."

"Damn, I'm good."

She laughed. "Yes, you are."

Suddenly, Jack appeared at the door. "Hey, Dad! Mrs. Alwine's here!"

He grabbed the doll from Althea's hands and tossed it back into his SUV before racing to the door.

Althea followed him.

A tall, thin woman stood in the kitchen, holding Teagan, who hugged her fiercely as if she'd never let her go.

Clark raced over. "Mrs. Alwine! It's so good to see you! How are you feeling?"

"I'm great. You were right. The extra week of recovery time worked wonders."

He was right? He'd spoken to Mrs. Alwine and never told her?

"That's great."

Mrs. Alwine laughed. "Yeah. It's great. But I know you need someone to cook for your holiday and I'm back."

Althea watched as Jack slid on a stool and Clark chatted happily about how they'd gotten on without her because of Althea.

"That's good. Jack's grades are up then?"

Clark said, "Yes."

He talked to her almost the same way he'd spoken to Althea. Friendly. Inclusive. Mrs. Alwine knew as much about Jack as Althea had. With her here, it was as if Althea had no place. Worse, she wasn't the fifty-year-old woman Althea had pictured her to be. She was probably thirty-five. Young. Happy. Energetic. She probably made cookies. Made supper. Remembered the laundry. And Teagan loved her. So did Jack. So did Clark. Not in the romantic way she'd thought he felt about her. But he clearly loved seeing her, having her back.

"So I can be here tomorrow morning." She tickled Teagan's tummy. "We can bake cookies."

Teagan laughed.

"We made cookies." And didn't she feel like an idiot for pointing it out.

Mrs. Alwine smiled. "What did you make?"

"Snicker doodles and shaped sugar cookies. We painted them."

She tickled Teagan's tummy again. "Then we'll make chocolate chip."

Jack said, "All right!"

Clark smiled.

And Althea suddenly wondered if she hadn't misinterpreted everything.

Was she so desperate for love that she read things into everything Clark said that he didn't really mean?

CHAPTER TWELVE

MRS. ALWINE LEFT with a promise to return in the morning. Althea was on her way to her room, when Clark said, "Hey, why don't we make hot cocoa and sit in front of the tree?"

The kids cheered, so Althea headed for the cupboard with the pans. Jack pulled the cocoa and sugar from the pantry. Clark got the milk. Teagan sat on a tall stool by the center island, her elbow on the marble island top and her chin on her closed fist.

They took the tray of four cups of cocoa into the living room, and Clark turned on the tree lights. Teagan gasped. Jack settled on the cushiony area rug beneath the coffee table. Clark and Althea sat on the sofa.

Clark said, "Do we want to sing?"

Teagan shook her head fiercely. Althea laughed. "We're not trying to bamboozle you into talking out loud. Singing is part of the holidays."

She shook her head again.

Jack rose unexpectedly. "Yeah. You know what? I'm kinda tired, too."

Althea's gaze whipped to Teagan who all but drooped at the coffee table. "Oh." She'd been so wrapped up in herself and Clark that she hadn't noticed. She rose. "Well, let's put Teagan to bed then."

Clark waved her down. "I'll get this. You take a break. You've been busy all day."

When Clark and the kids were gone, she leaned back on the sofa, telling herself to calm down. But she couldn't.

Part of her worried that she didn't fit into this household as well as she'd believed. The other part was worried sick about her dad. In her head, she knew the two things were connected. That if she could talk about her dad with Clark then she would relax, stop noticing stupid things and fit again.

She sucked in a breath, staring at the pretty tree. As Clark had mentioned a time or two, Carol had had excellent taste. Though the tree had no theme, the pristine multicolored balls and bells were uniform in size. The multicolored lights shimmered. Silver tinsel bowed from limb to limb leading to the angel who sat on top, like a guardian.

Clark strolled into the room. "Well, that's done for the night."

Althea nervously picked up her cocoa.

Clark plopped down beside her. "You look tired yourself."

"I am. And I—" She faltered. Though it hadn't seemed difficult to tell him the story of her past, she couldn't seem to find the words to tell him her dad was very much in her present. Every time she opened her mouth, she remembered him angry with Carol, wondering what she'd been thinking, bringing this much trouble to their door, and the words choked back. Logically, Carol hadn't thought she'd die. She hadn't known Teagan's paternity would be called into question. She hadn't thought her affair would become public.

Althea, on the other hand, knew her dad, knew he wanted money.

Clark scooted over, slid his hand across her shoulders.

She jumped, then winced. "Sorry."

He leaned in and kissed her. "Don't be sorry. I just real-

ized how preoccupied I'd been." He smiled. "I hoped I could
make it up to you."

She wanted him to. With every fiber of her being she
wanted him to. She brushed her lips across his lightly.
"What'd you have in mind?"

He returned her kiss. "Oh, a little of this and a little of
that."

She laughed. Her tension ebbed. She also remembered
that she had a plan to handle her father. Maybe she shouldn't
tell Clark until she'd taken care of it?

He slid closer, pushed her down on the sofa cushion and
kissed her again. It felt like coming home. Until the last few
days, being with Clark had always been easy. Then Jack's
grades came back good and that problem was solved. DNA
results showed Teagan was Clark's. Mrs. Alwine returned...
and no one needed her.

She stopped that thought. Clark wouldn't be kissing her
if he didn't need her. The oddness she suddenly felt wasn't
from Clark. Ever since her dad had shown up she'd been
suspicious, antsy, nervous.

Just as she had been when she'd lived with him.

She knew she was going to take care of him, pay for the
car, but she hadn't been able to tell Clark about her dad's
visits—

She suddenly realized she wanted to talk. She needed to
get this out. To share it. That was part of what being a couple was all about.

She stopped kissing him, angled up a bit so that he rose
too.

"I...um..."

He gave her a hand to help her up. "It's all right." He
smiled. "I don't want to force you into something you're
not ready for."

"I might actually be ready. Except—"

He laughed. "I know. Everybody's tired. Jack fell asleep as soon as his head hit the pillow. Teagan didn't even hear her whole story. What'd you and the kids do today?" He shook his head with another laugh. "Whatever it was tomorrow will be better. With Mrs. Alwine here again, you don't have to worry about dinner or laundry or tidying up. And I'll be home all day." He kissed her again. A quick, smacking kiss.

"It's not that. My dad—"

He stopped her by putting his index finger over her lips. "Sweetie. This is our first holiday together. Don't spoil it for yourself by remembering things that will make you sad. Enjoy it."

She blinked, confusion and despair overwhelmed her. She was drowning and he didn't see. That was the real problem. She'd been there for him every step of the way, helping him handle his problem with Jack and Teagan, but now that she needed him, he wasn't hearing her.

Still, she might have been nervous and distracted, but he wasn't a mind reader. Though she'd told him about her dad in the past, she hadn't told him he'd shown up at their front door.

"It's just that he—"

He shook his head. "Althea, he's spoiled every Christmas for you from the time you were a baby. Get it out of your head!"

"He's *here*."

"What?"

"He came here the other day. He wants the money for the car."

"We'll give him the money for the car."

"It's not that easy."

He rose, extending his hand to her. "Come on. Go to bed.

Get some sleep. In the morning, when you're not so tired, you'll see this isn't as terrible as you think it is."

She almost stomped her foot and demanded that he listen to her, but the very fact that she wanted to rant and rave made her wonder if he wasn't right. Maybe she was tired?

In her bedroom, she picked up her cell phone and saw a text from her dad.

Do you have my money yet?

She squeezed her eyes shut. She knew Clark was being supportive, but it wasn't enough. She wanted her dad gone. She didn't want to involve Clark and the kids. This family was finally healing, and if Clark got involved she would bring more trouble to their doorstep.

She barely slept that night, so the next morning she didn't find the relief Clark had assured her she would. Mrs. Alwine had breakfast made—bacon, eggs and toast. Clark stared at his computer screen while he ate his. Teagan grinned happily. Jack chattered about playing another online game with Owen.

When breakfast was done, she excused herself to her room, showered, put on clean jeans and a sweater. She walked through the kitchen, on her way to the den to find the kids, but the kids weren't in the den. She checked the living room with the tree and their bedroom and Clark's office.

Finding no one, she ambled back to the kitchen where Mrs. Alwine was leafing through a cookbook.

"Where is everybody?"

Mrs. Alwine laughed. "Special, private mission."

"Oh."

And they hadn't invited her. They hadn't even told her they were leaving.

Still, she smiled at Mrs. Alwine.

Clark and the kids returned an hour later. They'd had

lunch at the mall, so when Althea suggested they all sit down to eat, they told her to eat without them and raced away.

She sat at the kitchen table alone, while Mrs. Alwine puttered around.

"We're making chocolate chip cookies this afternoon if you'd like to join us."

Althea glanced up. "Sure. That would be fun."

Mrs. Alwine brought her coffee to the table and sat. "I know it always seems odd when people come and go mysteriously. But it is Christmas."

She smiled.

"And the kids must love making cookies with you because they've talked about it nonstop."

Althea nodded.

Mrs. Alwine shook a finger at her. "So don't be so blue."

She laughed and helped with the cookies that afternoon, but everything was different.

She was nervous about her dad, unsure about what was going on with her and Clark and now the kids were behaving oddly around her.

That night after the kids were in bed, eager for Christmas Eve the next day, Althea found Clark and confronted him.

"I get it that I'm not a member of the family. But you've told me things even you admitted you'd never told anyone else. So the only reason I can figure out that you and the kids left without telling me today is that you left because of something to do with me."

He sat back on his chair. Gave her a shuttered look. "It does."

Her heart deflated. Dear God. She was so sure he was about to tell her she was paranoid that when he said their secret *was* about her she nearly collapsed.

"I see."

She turned to go but he caught her hand and yanked her to

him so hard she fell to his lap. "Althea! It's Christmastime. The kids had me take them out to buy you gifts."

Embarrassment overwhelmed her. Oh, God.

He laughed. "They wanted it to be a surprise."

Tears filled her eyes. "I'm so sorry."

"You're tired! You're a single woman who spent an entire month being a mom to two troubled kids. Now that it's over you're decompressing or something."

He placed a smacking kiss on her lips, pushed her off his lap and smacked her bottom. "Go to bed."

She walked back to her room like a zombie. Her fears forgotten. Her suspicions obliterated. Her mind numb.

She'd felt left out when they were actually doing something nice for her.

She walked into her room, closed the door and leaned against it. It was like being fourteen again, suspecting her dad was mad at her, worried that he'd find out something she didn't want him to know.

She flopped to the bed, put her head in her hands. This wasn't about her dad. Clark and the kids weren't wrong to want to surprise her. They were sweet and she didn't know how to deal with sweet. Hell, she didn't know how to deal with normal.

The tears that had gathered in Clark's office spilled over. He thought she was tired. But she wasn't tired; she was ruined. She didn't know how to trust. She did her best work in problems. That's why she was so good, almost normal, when Jack had troubles and Clark was worried.

Now that they were normal, she floundered.

She swiped her hands across her cheeks to brush away the tears and felt their shaking.

She didn't deserve this family. She most certainly wouldn't put wonderful Clark through another bad relationship. Damn it! He'd suffered enough—three long years—because of Carol.

She would not put him through anything else.

Sobbing uncontrollably, she rose from the bed, retrieved her suitcase and began packing. Tomorrow was Christmas Eve so she wouldn't ruin the kids' Christmas. They had Mrs. Alwine. Clark was healed and whole and able to give them their best Christmas ever. But if she stayed and they gave her their gifts, she would crumble. She'd never be able to leave and Clark would be stuck with another woman who only gave him heartache.

With her clothes packed and her laptop strap over her shoulder, she sneaked through the dark downstairs. All the lights off meant Clark had already gone to bed. She breathed a sigh of relief. Not letting herself take one last longing look toward the upstairs or the Christmas tree twinkling in the moonlight pooling in through the big window, she reached for the doorknob.

"I want pigtails."

She froze, then spun around. "Teagan," she whispered. A laugh bubbled up. "I told you when you really wanted something you'd talk."

Teagan displayed two matching hair ties she held. "I want pigtails."

She set her suitcases on the floor, slid her laptop beside them. "Honey," she whispered. "You're supposed to be in bed."

Teagan's response was to shove the two hair ties at her.

She laughed. Rifling through her purse she found a comb. "Okay. We'll do this quickly."

She pulled the comb through Teagan's long dark locks, quickly parted it down the middle of the back of her head and spun the hair ties around two loose ponytails, one by each ear.

She smiled, turning Teagan to face her. "You look adorable."

Teagan grinned. "I know."

She shook her head. "So you're going to talk now?"

She nodded. And Althea felt the door closing on this chapter of her life. With Teagan talking everything that was wrong when she arrived had been fixed.

"Where are you going?"

"I'm just taking a little drive."

Teagan frowned. "I want you to stay."

Pain poured through her. She wanted to stay, too. More than anything she'd ever wanted. But she was broken. Ruined. And this family had just healed. She wouldn't put them through living with her doubts and insecurities.

She stooped in front of Teagan who stood on the third stair up. "I would like to stay, but I can't. I have to go see my sister." That was a bit of a lie, but not really. She'd see Missy before she left town.

Teagan looked down at the stair below her. "But I want you to stay here."

"Sometimes people can't stay. Sometimes people come into our lives when we need them, but they're only here to do a job then they leave."

She peeked up. "Like an angel."

She laughed. She'd hardly call herself an angel. Still, if it made Teagan happy… "Yes. Like an angel. Now go to bed."

Teagan nodded and turned to go up the stairs. But she stopped suddenly and came back down, propelling herself into Althea's arms. "I wub you."

Althea pressed her lips together. "I love you, too."

CHAPTER THIRTEEN

CLARK WOKE UP excited, happier than he'd been in years. It was Christmas Eve and he was in love. In *love*. Real love.

He'd known there was something different, something special about Althea from the day he interviewed her. But he never would have realized that trusting her would lead him to face his fears. And the reward was the freedom to love her.

He sleepily walked into the kitchen. Jack sat at the center island, eating a bowl of cereal and reading a book.

A book.

Dear God. Could that woman have had any more of a positive impact on them? He'd said he didn't deserve her and maybe he didn't. But he would spend the rest of his life loving her.

He glanced longingly down the hall. Her door was closed, which meant she was still sleeping.

"We should do something special for Althea."

Jack looked up. "Like what? We already got her a gift."

"I know, but maybe we should go out to dinner tonight?"

Even as the words came out of his mouth they felt wrong. What was he doing inviting Jack and Teagan out on his first date with Althea? He couldn't leave the kids with a sitter on Christmas Eve, but the day after Christmas he intended to take her out. Someplace special.

Mrs. Alwine burst into the room from the garage entry.

Unwrapping her scarf, she said, "What are you two doing up at six?"

Jack said, "I was hungry."

Clark laughed. "I thought it was later."

"It's still dark out!" She cast a quick glance at Jack's cereal. "I was going to make apple pancakes."

Jack shoved his bowl away. "Make 'em."

Clark sat beside Jack as Teagan walked into the room, rubbing her eyes. "Hey, pumpkin."

Her hair in cockeyed pigtails, which, given their sloppiness, she'd probably done herself, she frowned and walked over to him. He lifted her into his lap. "It's Christmas Eve! Little girls aren't supposed to be grouchy on Christmas Eve. Althea's gonna be mad at you."

"No, she's not."

Clark froze. Jack's head snapped up. Mrs. Alwine faced them with a gasp.

"Teagan! You talked."

Jack high-fived her. "Way to go, Chai Tea."

Teagan snuggled into her dad's shirt. "She doesn't wuv us. She said she does but she doesn't."

The sadness in her voice finally penetrated. "What? Are you talking about Althea?"

She nodded.

"Don't be silly. She adores you."

"She weft."

The joy of hearing Teagan speak was quickly shoved aside by paralyzing fear. "What?" It was early. Way too early for Althea to have gone to the store. Plus, Teagan had just gotten up. How could she say Althea had left?

"Did you have a bad dream?"

She shook her head. Her cockeyed pigtails swung from side to side.

Clark bounced her once on his lap. "Come on, now.

You're talking. You're not going back to nods and frowns. Tell Daddy. Did you have a bad dream?"

"She made my pigtails then told me she had to weave."

Clark froze. Took another look at the pigtails. Especially, the tightness of the brightly colored hair ties. They weren't the handiwork of a three-year-old. They'd gone cockeyed from Teagan sleeping on them.

He spun her around on his lap. "She left last night?"

Teagan nodded.

"Did she have her suitcases?"

She nodded again.

Clark's heart fell to his feet. He plopped Teagan on the stool beside Jack and raced to her room.

Neat as a pin, the bed had been made. The drapes drawn. The closet emptied. He spun to the dresser and saw the note leaning against the mirror.

He grabbed it and ripped it open.

"I'm sorry to leave like this. But with Jack's studies completed and Mrs. Alwine back I realized I could go. My dad wants restitution for the car and thanks to you I can give it to him. But he's a royal pain in the butt and if I stay, he'll always hound us. I'll never forget you guys."

He threw the note on the bed, raised his gaze to the ceiling. He'd felt she was a little nervous the past few days, but he thought that was because everything was happening between them. So he'd given her space, distance, to work out how she was feeling.

"Do you wuv her, Daddy?"

He spun to face Teagan. Mrs. Alwine raced behind her

and put her hands on Teagan's little shoulders. "I'll just take her to the kitchen and let her help me make pancakes."

She turned Teagan to go as Clark stared around the room feeling something akin to despair. She was worried about them. He got that. He could handle her dad. But he sensed she didn't want him to.

Confused, disheartened, he returned to the kitchen.

At the center island Teagan was crying. "I want Alfeea."

He slumped on the stool beside her. "I want Althea, too." His brain scrambled for answers. What had he done? Why had he decided to give her time and distance? He should have pushed her. He should have let her know what she meant to them.

But, no. He'd had to be logical. And now he'd lost her.

Althea walked down the dark, silent Main Street of Newland. Cold air turned her breath to mist as she strode purposefully to the diner. She stopped at the door and squeezed her eyes shut, but popped them open again. This was something she had to do.

Then she could go. Away from Missy. Away from Clark. Away so that people with normal lives didn't have to be hurt.

She pushed open the door and the bell sounded. The sweet scent of cinnamon rolls filled the air. Empty booths and tables sat silently in the semidark dining room. Christmas Eve. People would pour in for fresh cinnamon rolls around nine. Until then, he'd be alone.

"Gimme a minute, early bird," he called from the kitchen. When it came to his customers, he was Mr. Personality. That's how she and Missy had known no one would believe them if they sought help. Who would possibly believe such a great guy, a solid business owner, hurt his wife and daughters?

He walked out of the kitchen wiping his hands on a dish-towel. When he saw her he stopped and smiled. "Well, hey, baby girl. Merry Christmas."

The nickname went through her like a knife. She crushed the check in her pocket. Fear trembled through her, but she remembered that the check in her sweaty hand meant free-dom. She took two steps to the counter.

"So what do you want? Free pancakes? A dozen cinna-mon rolls to impress your boyfriend?" He snorted a laugh. "Ain't nothing comes free in this life. You pay like every-body else."

"I paid more than everybody else."

His face scrunched in contempt. "Excuse me?"

"What are you going to do? Hit me?"

Before he could reply, she slapped the check on the coun-ter. Every cent of money she had. "This is for the car."

His face brightened. "Well. Well. I see you do have some money after all."

She slid the receipt and release onto the counter and handed him a pen. "Sign this."

"What is it?"

"It's a receipt for the car. If you don't sign it, I stop pay-ment on the check."

Without a second's hesitation, he leaned down and signed the receipt.

She scooped it up and shoved it in her purse. "That's it." She sucked in a breath. This *was* it. Get him out of her life now or spend the rest of her life worried, running. "Seri-ously it. That's what I was paid for tutoring Jack. I have no more money."

"Well, now, baby girl. Missy made something of herself and you're the one with the college education. You can prob-ably do twice what she did."

Anger rumbled up in the pit of her belly. Sharp and hot, it filled her blood, raced through her veins. He had every intention of using her!

She looked at her dad. He was older than he had been, but that didn't faze her as much as the fact that he was a man, picking on a girl—his own daughter. He wasn't just scum. For the first time in her life she also saw he was a coward.

"If you ever even try to contact me again, I will call the police."

He slapped the check against his palm. "Yeah. Sure. Fine."

"I'm serious." Part of her wanted to yell. The other part was suspiciously calm. She walked around the counter, stood in front of him, feeling a power she'd never felt before. "When I file for a restraining order, I won't just tell the police you beat us. I'll air every piece of dirty linen this family has."

"Now, baby girl…"

"Don't baby girl me. I'll tell the police how you threw bleach at us when we got out of reach of your fists. I'll tell them that you broke my arm. I'll tell them how you used to burn our clothes, blacken mom's eyes, break her ribs and refuse to take her to the hospital."

He took a pace back.

He was afraid. Not of her but of the truth.

She could have said more. She could have said so much more. But he'd cost her Clark. He'd cost her the kids. Even confident that he'd never come near her again, she couldn't go back to the family she'd come to love. She didn't even know how to be in a normal family, forget about being a wife or mom.

She strode out the diner door.

Once again, she was alone on Christmas Eve.

* * *

Clark paced his office, waiting for an hour or so to pass so he could call Missy. He had absolutely no idea why Althea had felt she could or should leave…except that she was trying to protect him and his family from her father. It was skewed logic at best, but a man who'd spent three years refusing to get a DNA test for his daughter could understand. Sometimes fear of possibilities was so strong that a person couldn't see the obvious.

He walked to the window, saw the snowman and scrubbed his hand across his face. He remembered her determination to beat him in the snowball battle. He could see her butt in the air as she rolled the big snowball to make the middle of her snowman. He could feel her submission when he kissed her cold face.

The wonder of it filled him again.

He could not let her go.

He would not let her go.

The hell with waiting!

He raced out of the room, grabbed his coat. "Mrs. Alwine! I'm leaving for a few hours. Can you watch the kids?"

Althea got in her car and headed out of town. But as the sun began to rise, pale beams hit the silvery tinsel that shivered in the light breeze and it winked at her.

She blew out a relieved laugh. She'd done it. She'd faced her dad. She'd paid her debt like an honest woman and she'd faced her dad.

She wanted so much to tell Clark. She wanted to grab his shoulders and kiss his face and tell him she'd faced her demon just as she'd forced him to face his.

And wouldn't that be embarrassing? Because after she kissed him she'd have to admit that she didn't have the normal life experience to be in a family. She hadn't even had the common sense to realize they'd gone shopping for *her* the day before. Worse, she hadn't had the common sense to take the kids shopping for a gift for their dad.

Her life had been so screwed up there was no hope for her. And she wouldn't tie him to her. After the holidays, he could walk out into the street and realize there was a whole world of women out there. And he'd find someone who wasn't scarred. Someone who knew how to be a mom. Somebody really pretty, who'd make a good hostess.

Her foot eased up on the gas pedal. Sadness trembled through her and she began to cry.

Her life sucked and—damn it—she wasn't spending another Christmas Eve alone.

She swung her car down a street that would take her to her grandmother's old house. She raced into the driveway, parking behind the humongous RV, and shoved the gearshift into Park.

She didn't consider the time. The kitchen lights were on. At least one of them was up. She pounded up the back porch steps and knocked on the door.

When Missy opened it, she fell into her arms.

"Hey. Hey!" Missy soothed. "What's up?"

"I talked to Dad."

"Oh."

"Damn it! I don't care about that."

Missy pushed her out of their embrace. "That's even better. It's about time you shook off his hold." She frowned. "So why are you crying?"

"I left Clark."

"Oh, honey. Why?"

"I fell in love with him and the kids…and the big dog."

"Oh. Oh." She pulled her into the house. Lainie, Claire,

Owen and Wyatt sat at a long black kitchen table. New cupboards had been installed. Granite countertops. Hardwood floors. And the wall that had once separated the kitchen from the rest of the house was gone.

She took a few steps toward the huge living space. Leather sofas sat in front of a stone fireplace currently decorated with five red stockings. Thick area rugs defined conversation spaces with comfortable-looking chairs. A huge Christmas tree sat in front of a wall of windows on the far side of the room. Lights and shiny ornaments twinkled at her.

She swallowed. "Wow."

Missy smiled at Wyatt. "We like it."

Her sister had everything she needed. Everything they'd both always wanted.

Fresh tears threatened to erupt.

Wyatt sprang from his seat. "Why don't I make the French toast while you two go and have a chat?"

"I don't want a chat." She wanted to be loved. She wanted to be able to love. Was that so much to ask?

"Yeah, but maybe you need a chat," Missy said, leading her toward the leather sofas just as someone knocked on the front door. "Now who the hell could that be?"

Althea's first thought was that it was their dad. But instead of fear racing through her or even anger, she merely felt tired. If he wanted her to tell him to take a hike one more time, she'd happily do so.

Her shoulders straightened. "I've got this."

Missy said, "What?" and tried to catch her as she marched through the big room to the front door, but Althea was too fast for her.

She reached the door, yanked it open and said, "What? You didn't understand what I said this morning?"

But it wasn't her dad on the front porch. It was Clark, who simply frowned. "Actually, I didn't."

Her heart about leaped out of her chest. "Clark."

"Teagan talked."

The wonder in his voice made her smile. She'd felt that same wonder the night before for the little girl they both loved. "I know. She asked me to give her pigtails last night." Her face reddened. Last night when she was sneaking out.

He shoved his hands in his jeans pockets. "Why'd you go?"

"I had to face my dad."

He reached inside the door and caught her arm. "Come on. If you want to face your dad, we'll do it now. Together."

"I already talked to him."

"Sheesh, woman. Give me ten minutes to catch up. I wanted to go with you. To help you like you helped me."

"Oh." Her pounding heart slowed. His being here was payback. "Well, thanks for the offer but I handled it."

"Really?"

"Yeah. I just stood up to him." And saying that made her feel strong again. She desperately wanted to share this with Clark, but as a mate...not some guy who thought he owed her. And she already knew she couldn't be his mate. She didn't know how. But she wouldn't embarrass herself by telling him that. She straightened her shoulders. "I'm sure you've got better things to do on a Christmas Eve morning than stand on a cold porch." Tears threatened again. She loved him. *Loved him.* Crazy dog. Adorable kids. Scruffy beard and all. If she didn't soon get away from him she'd throw herself into his arms and beg. And she was done begging. What she really wanted, what she *needed* was somebody who could accept her as she was. She started to close the door. "So, Happy Christmas."

He shoved his foot in the door. "Wait!"

She lifted her chin. "What?"

"I know these past couple of weeks have meant something to you. Don't you want to spend Christmas with me and the kids? Remember, we were making the perfect family Christmas?"

An arrow hit her in the chest. "You have Mrs. Alwine back."

"And I pay her handsomely to make Christmas dinner. I want you with us."

She shook her head. "I can't come back."

"Why not?"

She shifted to close the door again. "I'll be sharing Christmas with my family."

He lodged his foot more securely on the threshold. "I thought we were your family."

Her lips trembled and she couldn't help the words that came out of her mouth. "I thought you were, too."

His voice softened with confusion. "So why won't you come home with me?"

She would not spell it out. It was embarrassing enough that she knew she couldn't be what he needed. She refused to say it.

Refused to beg him to accept her as she was. "Goodbye, Clark."

"Goodbye? You make us love you and then you leave?"

Her gaze sprang to his. "You love me?"

"Well, yeah." He ran his hand along his neck. "I know I've been preoccupied. But I also didn't want to scare you." He winced. "It always seems like I'm pushing you into something you don't want because I'm so needy."

Oh, if he only knew she was so much better with people who were in trouble. It was people who were normal that she couldn't handle. "I'm not what you need. I don't know how to be a mom. I'm not even sure how to be a good girlfriend."

"I don't want you for a girlfriend. I want you for a wife." He stepped closer. "And as for not being what I need?" He laughed. "Who the hell knows what they really need? You're what I want. You make me laugh. You love my kids. You renamed my dog." He smiled. "That took some gumption."

She laughed, but she quickly sobered. "I panicked when you left to buy gifts yesterday. Two days away from Christmas and I didn't think gifts. I thought you were dropping me."

His voice softened. "Why would I drop you?"

Her lips trembled. "No one's ever really wanted me."

"We want you. A lot."

"Well, you should have let me finish. Because no one's ever wanted me I don't know how to behave with people who do."

"Technically, no one's ever wanted me, either."

Her gaze ambled to his.

"You're my first real love." He patted his stomach. "The one who gets me here." He touched his heart. "And here. So I don't know any more about love than you do. We'll learn together."

"You won't care if I forget the laundry?"

"We have Mrs. Alwine for laundry. I want you to love me."

Her trembling lips stilled. Tears fell off her eyelids.

"And you want me to love you?"

She nodded. "Yes."

"Well, I do." He waited a second then said, "And you love me, too?"

She nodded again.

He growled. "Say it."

She raised her head slowly, met his gaze. Staring into his pretty amber eyes she swallowed. He loved her. She loved him. She'd taken a chance with her dad. Maybe she should take the greatest risk of all? "I love you."

He scooped her into his arms and kissed her thoroughly. The way she'd seen handsome men in the movies kiss their leading ladies. Their mouths fused, their tongues danced. Happiness bubbled through her, eradicating her paralyzing fear until she couldn't even remember she'd been afraid.

When he pulled away, she clung to his jacket collar, never wanting to let him go. Someone who knew her past and present wanted to be part of her future.

"If you guys wouldn't mind coming inside, Wyatt's got French toast."

Althea laughed through her tears. "I think we should go home to the kids."

"They'll be fine with Mrs. Alwine for a few hours."

She peeked at him.

"This time they're wrapping gifts."

She frowned, but he squeezed her shoulders. "Give you one or two Christmases and you'll catch on to all this silliness."

"I don't think it's silliness." She smiled. "I think it's magical."

Missy happily led them down the hall. "Why don't you guys come to our house tomorrow for Christmas Day?"

"Why don't you come to our house?" Clark countered. "Mrs. Alwine's baking a ham. My mom brings a turkey."

"Sounds fun." Missy said, "I'll make a cake."

Althea caught her bottom lip between her teeth. "I hate to have Mrs. Alwine work all Christmas Day for us."

"Oh, she doesn't. She just puts the ham in the oven. My mom and I take over after that."

"In that case," Missy said, "I'll also bring a loaf of bread and maybe a salad."

"Hey, salad is my department," Wyatt said as they walked up to the table.

"I can bring cookies," Claire announced, pointing to the cooling cookies on the cooking island.

Althea stood back, watching it all, feeling the love, but most of all basking in a sense of belonging. Of family. She'd finally have the family Christmas she always wanted.

EPILOGUE

THAT SUMMER, CLARK and Althea honeymooned at a hotel Wyatt owned on the Gulf coast of Florida. Lying on a hammock, drinking pink drinks served in tall glasses, garnished with pineapple, Clark couldn't have been happier.

Althea, however, nervously sat up. "Do you think the kids are okay?"

"Spending four days with my parents at Disney World? Sheesh, woman, how much more okay could two kids get?"

She cuddled against him, then sprang up again. "Did we pack Teagan's bear?"

"If I remember correctly Teagan packed an entire bear suitcase. Something she wouldn't have been able to do without Wyatt's private plane."

"It is handy to have a rich guy for a brother-in-law."

Clark feigned offense. "Hey. I don't do so badly in the money department."

She laughed. "No. You don't."

"What? Do I have to buy you a hotel or an airplane to prove it?"

She smiled shyly and looked down. He caught her chin and lifted her face again. "What?"

"It's just all so unreal sometimes."

"What? The money? The fact that you were suddenly a mother?" He waggled his eyebrows. "Or me?"

She smiled. "You. I never ever thought I'd find somebody who would love me."

He laughed, tightened his arm around her and snuggled down in the hammock. "What are you complaining about? I didn't even know what love was."

"But we make it work."

His eyes drooped. "Every day."

She snuggled against him. "Are we really going to nap?"

"Yep."

"Nothing else on your mind?"

"Not while I'm sitting beside a hotel pool with a hundred spectators. But just wait till we get back to the honeymoon suite. Then I'm going to—" He whispered a suggestion in her ear that made her laugh. And he settled into the hammock again. He loved her laugh. Loved making her laugh. She was so warm and open and honest he knew he could make her laugh forever.

And that was the point.

* * * * *

"What about the military? Didn't they do anything for the holidays?"

He paused by the front door. His back went ramrod-straight.

"I always opted to be on duty," he said, his tone clipped.

"You're home now. Time to start over. A chance for new beginnings..." Her voice trailed off. She didn't want him to misconstrue her words—to think she wanted *them* to have a new beginning. "You should try joining in the fun. After all, it's the most joyous time of the year."

Kara forced a smile. She couldn't believe she was trying to talk him into celebrating the exact same holiday in which he'd broken her heart. If he wanted to be an old, cranky Scrooge, why should she care?

Jason didn't say anything as he opened the door and stepped aside, allowing her to enter. In the narrow opening her arm brushed against him, and even through the layers of clothing an electrical current zinged up her arm, warming a spot in her chest.

Staying here wasn't a good idea.

Being alone with her new boss was an even poorer idea.

This whole situation constituted the worst idea...ever.

SNOWBOUND WITH THE SOLDIER

BY
JENNIFER FAYE

First published in Great Britain 2013
by Mills & Boon, an imprint of Harlequin (UK) Limited,
Eton House, 18-24 Paradise Road, Richmond, Surrey TW9 1SR

© Jennifer F. Stroka 2013

ISBN: 978 0 263 90148 1
ebook ISBN: 978 1 472 00538 0

23-1013

Harlequin (UK) policy is to use papers that are natural, renewable and recyclable products and made from wood grown in sustainable forests. The logging and manufacturing processes conform to the legal environmental regulations of the country of origin.

Printed and bound in Spain
by Blackprint CPI, Barcelona

In another life, **Jennifer Faye** was a statistician. She still has a love for numbers, formulas and spread-sheets, but when she was presented with the opportunity to follow her lifelong passion and spend her days writing and pursuing her dream of becoming a Mills & Boon® author, she couldn't pass it up. These days, when she's not writing, Jennifer enjoys reading, fine needlework, quilting, tweeting and cheering on the Pittsburgh Penguins. She lives in Pennsylvania with her amazingly patient husband, two remarkably talented daughters and their two very spoiled fur babies otherwise known as cats—but *shh*…don't tell them they're not human!

Jennifer loves to hear from readers—you can contact her via her website: www.JenniferFaye.com.

This book is dedicated to the real life Sly. A beautiful, sweet black cat who crossed my path and stole my heart. She was my muse for this heart-touching story.

Sly, you passed through our lives far too quickly.
You are missed.

CHAPTER ONE

OLD MAN WINTER huffed and puffed, rattling the doors of the Greene Summit Resort. Kara Jameson turned her back on the dark, blustery night. She didn't relish heading out into the declining weather to navigate her way home after a very long day at work.

She took a moment to admire the massive evergreen standing in the lobby of what had once been one of Pennsylvania's premier ski destinations. The twinkling white lights combined with the sparkling green and red decorations would normally fill her with holiday cheer, but not tonight. Not even the rendition of "Jingle Bells" playing softly in the background could tempt her to hum along.

The resort had been sold. The somber thought weighed heavily on her shoulders. It didn't help that rumors were running rampant that all the management positions were being replaced. Why did it have to happen with Christmas only a few weeks away?

Everything will work out. Everything will work out. She repeated the mantra over and over in her mind, anxious to believe the old adage. But something in her gut said nothing would ever be the same again.

"Kara?"

The deep baritone voice came from behind her. She froze. Her gaze remained locked on a red bell-shaped ornament as her mind processed the sound. Even in the two syllables of her name, she knew that voice, knew the way her name rolled off his tongue as sweet as candy.

Jason Smith.

It couldn't be. He'd sworn he would never come back.

"Kara, won't you even look at me?"

Her gaze shifted to the glass doors that led to the parking lot. Her feet refused to cooperate, remaining cemented to the swirled golden pattern on the hotel carpet. Seven years ago, she'd bolted out those exact doors after Jason had broken their engagement. Back then she'd been unsure and confused by the depth of her emotions. Since then life had given her a crash course in growing up. Running was no longer her style.

She sucked in a deep breath, leveled her shoulders and turned.

Clear blue eyes stared back at her. A slow, easy grin lifted the tired lines around Jason's eyes. She blinked, but he was still there.

This couldn't be happening. The overtime and lack of sleep must be catching up with her.

"Are you okay?" He reached out to her.

She jumped back before he could touch her. Words rushed up her throat, but clogged in her mouth. She pressed her lips together and willed her heart to slow. Her pulse pounded in her ears as her fists clenched at her sides. A breath in. A breath out.

"You're so pale. Sit down." He gestured to one of the overstuffed couches surrounding the stone fireplace. "You look like you've seen a ghost."

She didn't move. This surreal moment struck her as a clip from a movie—a visit from the ghost of Christmas past. Only, this wasn't a Hollywood soundstage and he wasn't an actor.

She studied the man before her, trying to make sense of things. The dark scruff obscuring his boyish features was a new addition, as was the two-inch scar trailing up the right side of his jaw. His hardened appearance was a visual reminder of the military life he'd chosen over her. Her fingers longed to reach out and trace the uneven skin of his jaw, but instead she gripped the strap of her tote even tighter. A bit older and a little scuffed up, but it was most definitely Jason.

Just pretend he's a mere acquaintance from years ago, not the man who threw your love back in your face and walked away without any explanation.

"Jason Smith. I can't believe you're here," she said, trying her best to sound casual.

"Actually, I go by Jason Greene these days...."

The fact he now used his mother's maiden name came as a surprise, but Kara supposed she shouldn't find it too shocking, knowing the stormy relationship between him and his father. The name change had presumably contributed to her inability to track him down and notify him of his father's failing health. A question teetered on her tongue, but she clamped her lips shut. Playing catch-up with Jason was akin to striking a match near fireworks. One wrong move and it'd blow up in her face. Best to stick to safe topics.

His gaze implored her for an answer, but to what? She'd lost track of the strained conversation. "What did you say?"

"How are you?"

He wanted to exchange pleasantries as though they'd parted on good terms? She didn't have time to beat around the bush. She should already be home, getting dinner for her daughter before they went over her homework.

"When you left Pleasant Valley, you swore you'd never

return. So what happened? What finally changed your mind?"

His expression hardened. If he'd been expecting a warm welcome, he'd been sadly mistaken.

He shrugged. "Things change."

Well, most things did, and generally not for the better, but not in Jason's case. He hadn't gained so much as a beer gut or a receding hairline. Even the jagged scar on his face added to his sexiness.

Kara's gaze rose to meet his. At first glance, she thought his intense blue eyes were the same as she remembered, but a closer inspection revealed a hard glint in them. He no longer resembled the warm, lighthearted guy she'd dated for nearly four years. Or had he been that way all along? Had those rose-colored glasses she'd been wearing back then obscured his real character? Had she ever truly known him at all?

Jason hitched his thumbs in his jeans pockets. "I'm sorry about what happened between us. I handled it poorly."

"You certainly did."

"If I could explain, I would, but I can't—"

"Don't." She held up a hand, stalling his too little, too late explanation. "Nothing you say will change what happened."

Her pride refused to let on that his presence affected her, that even after all this time she longed to know what had changed his mind about marrying her. She reconciled herself to the fact that she was better off not knowing—not prying open that door to her past.

Jason shifted his weight from one foot to the other. "I guess it was too much to hope that you'd be willing to put the past behind us."

She lifted her chin, drawing on the strength she'd used

to manage this place in the recent absence of her boss, who also happened to be Jason's father. "I've moved on."

It'd taken time—lots of time—but she'd gotten over him and the way her life had unraveled after he'd dumped her. She refused to let him get under her skin again. Besides, she had enough on her plate already.

After working her way up through the ranks, to now be dismissed from her hard-earned position would be utterly demoralizing. She'd like to think she was needlessly worrying, but the rumors said the new owners wanted their own people running the show—people with more education and experience.

She went to step around Jason, but he snagged hold of her arm. "Wait. I need to apologize."

Even through her coat she could feel his warmth radiating into her body. She yanked at her arm, to no avail.

"Let go," she said with a hard edge. He couldn't just worm his way past her defenses with an empty apology. She refused to let him off the hook that easily. "If you were truly sorry, you'd have said something before now. You wouldn't have ignored me all these years or returned your father's letters unopened."

His hand slipped from her arm. "You know about that?"

She tightened her hold on the strap of the tote bag slung over her shoulder, which held the red scarf she was knitting for Jason's father for Christmas. "Yes. He told me. After you left, he was never quite the same. Not knowing if you were dead or alive seemed to age him overnight."

Jason's body visibly stiffened. "I think you've mixed my father up with someone who cares."

"He's sick, Jason. Real sick. I've done what I can to help him, but he needs you."

"I don't want to discuss him."

She should turn away and walk out the door before the

snow grew any deeper, but her feet wouldn't cooperate. There was one thing she needed to know—one nagging question that demanded an answer.

She licked her dry lips. "If it isn't because of your father, then why have you suddenly returned home?"

"Do you really care?" His gaze never left hers.

"No. Never mind. I shouldn't have asked."

Her pulse quickened. Heat scorched her cheeks. Even though it was a lie, she refused to let him think that she cared anything about what he said or did. He was part of her past...nothing more.

"I have to go." She needed space to make sense of things.

"Kara, I know we can't go back to the way things used to be, but it doesn't have to be this awkward. We were friends for years before we dated."

They had been the best of friends. She'd told him everything about her life, but apparently that openness had been one-sided. She wouldn't make the mistake of trusting him again.

"Does this plea of friendship mean you're planning to stay in Pleasant Valley?"

"Yes."

The blunt response lacked any telling details of what had prompted his unexpected return. Her errant gaze strayed to his bare ring finger. Still single. Still available. Been there, done that. She glanced away.

"Welcome home." She buttoned her black peacoat. "I really do need to go."

"Be careful. The snow's picking up." His gaze moved to the glass doors. "It looks bad out. You should spend the night at the hotel."

She shook her head. "The resort's closed for renovations. You shouldn't even be here. Who's been showing you around?"

They weren't the only ones there late. With the new owner, GSR Inc., arriving on Monday, a number of people were working late even though it was a Friday evening. Everyone had gone above and beyond their duties, hoping to make a good impression on the new owner. Though Jason had been away for years, a number of employees knew him and would have volunteered to give him a last look around the place.

She glanced up at him, waiting for a response. His lips were pursed as though he was about to say something, but had refrained.

"I don't have all night," she stated.

"I don't need an escort."

Kara squared her shoulders. "Since I'm in charge around here, I'm telling you that either you have an escort or you must leave. Now."

This close to the new owner's arrival, she wasn't taking any chances. The last thing she needed was for anyone to get hurt on her watch.

Jason's brows arched. "You like being the boss, don't you?"

"I do whatever needs to be done to keep this place going."

"Good. I hope all my employees are so devoted."

"Your employees…?" Alarm tightened her throat, smothering her next words. Surely she hadn't heard him correctly. Or she'd misunderstood.

"Yes, my employees."

This nightmare couldn't be unfolding right before her eyes. "You…you're GSR?"

"I've gone in with a couple of investors. This place needs to be reorganized. A lot of cutting needs to be done, but I think it's possible to turn the business around with the right management."

A lot of cutting? Right management? The implication of his words shattered her dream of keeping her job. Fragments of her hopes scattered over the freshly laid carpet. Finding an equivalent job would not be easy without a college degree. She inwardly groaned.

She might even have to move. Her thoughts turned to her parents, who had been involved in their only grandchild's life since the day she was born. To tear her daughter away from them now would devastate not only them but her little girl, as well. But Kara wouldn't have a choice. She would have to move wherever she could find reasonable employment.

"Time to start job hunting," she muttered under her breath.

"What?"

"Nothing. I have to go before the snow gets too deep to drive in." She yanked on her gloves. "Good night."

Kara forced herself to take measured steps, training her gaze on the glass door. She hadn't run away when the locals had clucked their tongues and shaken their heads at her youthful mistake. Now she wouldn't give Jason the satisfaction of witnessing how he could still shake her to the core.

Jason Greene clenched his hands. He'd heard enough of her mumbled comment to know she had no intention of working for him. He couldn't leave things like this. Her assistance and knowledge over these next several weeks were essential to the resort's success. He'd risked everything he owned on restoring the Greene Summit. And he couldn't afford to lose it all now.

He started for the door. Large snowflakes fell, adding to the several inches of accumulation on the ground. He'd forgotten how fast the weather could deteriorate in the Laurel Highlands. An overwhelming urge settled in his chest to stop her and convince her to stay over in one of the hotel rooms, where she'd be safe and warm during this stormy night.

His steps grew quicker. Damn, he still cared about her. This was bigger than when they'd grown up together— back when Kara was 100 percent tomboy and he'd protected her from the school bully. The emotions brewing inside him now had an adult edge.

He lingered at the glass doors, staring out into the stormy night. He couldn't tear his gaze from Kara's petite figure as she braved fierce winds while crossing the snowy parking lot. Her appearance had changed, from jeans and snug T-shirts that nestled against her soft curves, to casual business attire. A short haircut replaced her ponytail. Everything combined to give her a mature, polished persona. He certainly wasn't the only one who'd changed.

Was she worried about her trip home? Or was she doing the same as him and reliving the past? He still had time to stop her. He pushed the door open. The bitter wind stung his face as he followed her footsteps. She would demand once more to know the sordid details behind his seven-year absence. His pace slowed. Could he bring himself to explain that dreadful night?

He stopped. No. No way. If he knew the words to make everything right between them, he'd have said them years ago. As the cold cut through his coat and over his exposed skin, he realized he'd played out all the scenarios in his mind thousands of times. Each ended with her looking at him with repulsion. No way could he put either of them through that experience.

Jason rubbed the back of his neck, trying to ease the

stiff muscles. His return to the Summit was going to be just as rough and bumpy as he'd imagined, but he'd get through it. He turned and limped back to the lobby. Only one day on his feet, with the cold seeping into his bones, and already the wound in his thigh throbbed.

He exhaled a weary sigh. The last time he'd worked at the resort, Kara had been his priority. Now, with no significant other in his life, he could sink his dreams into restoring this place without all the emotional entanglements of a relationship and raging teenage hormones. His experience in the military had forced him to grow up. He now realized what was important and why.

He shoved his fingers through his hair, hating the selfish boy he'd once been. This time he'd prove himself worthy of the trust others placed in him. He wouldn't repeat the mistakes of his past.

Muffled footsteps drew his attention. He glanced over his shoulder to find his childhood friend Robert Heinze approaching him. He looked every bit the professional in his navy suit, and definitely fit the part of a distinguished attorney.

"Jason, what are you still doing here?"

"While I was walking the grounds, I came across some maintenance men working on a problem with the towrope for the bunny hill."

"And from the grease stains on your jacket and jeans, I'm assuming you couldn't just let the staff handle it on their own."

Jason shook his head. "I'm not good at standing around watching when I could pitch in and lend a hand."

"You'll have plenty of time to play Mr. Fix-it after tomorrow. By the way, I heard the roads are getting bad. If you don't leave now, you might find yourself riding out the storm right here."

"Before I go, I want to thank you for finalizing this sale with my father. Without you going back and forth between us, I don't think an agreement would have ever been reached."

Robert flashed a small smile. "I think you give me too much credit. You were the mastermind behind this whole venture. I hope it turns out the way you planned."

"It will." He'd returned a couple of days ago, and until the deal had become official, he'd intentionally kept a low profile. "By the way, I just ran into Kara Jameson."

He didn't know why he'd mentioned it. Maybe he just wanted someone to talk some sense into him. After all, before Robert had moved away to be an attorney in downtown Pittsburgh, he'd grown up right here with Kara and Jason.

"Did you tell her you bought this place?"

He nodded.

Robert shrugged on his coat. "How'd it go?"

"The news took her by surprise."

"Seems like an understandable reaction. You've been gone for years." His old friend paused and looked intently at him. "What else is bothering you? Did she quit on the spot?"

"Not exactly."

"Then why do you look like you just chugged a carton of sour milk?"

"Kara lit into me about ignoring my father. He must have fed her some kind of lies to gain her sympathy." Jason didn't bother to hide the loathing he felt.

Robert let out a low whistle. "Boy, you didn't exaggerate about the rift between you two."

If anything, he'd understated the distance between himself and his father. Every muscle in Jason's body grew rigid at the thought of their insurmountable differences. He refused to dwell on something that could never be fixed.

With the help of a couple of investors, he'd at last gained ownership of his heritage—the resort his grandfather had founded. His gaze moved around the lobby, taking in its splendor.

"I've thought of nothing else for the past year but of making this place mine, of restoring the Greene Summit back to its former glory, like when my grandfather was alive. I'll make him proud. No matter what it takes."

Robert patted him on the shoulder. "Then you might want to start by being honest with Kara. I've talked with her and she's bright. When your father's health started to decline, he leaned on her to keep this place running. By now, she must know where each and every skeleton is buried. You're going to need her."

"I know. I'll tell her everything Monday." Well, not everything—just the parts pertaining to the Greene Summit.

Robert's brow furrowed and he began patting his pockets. "I must have left my phone in the office. I'll run back and grab it."

"Okay. I'll see you in the morning."

"Get some sleep. We've got work to do."

Jason turned to the lobby doors and gazed out at the parking lot. He rubbed his thigh, trying to ease the persistent throbbing. He had a business to rebuild and no time to slow down.

The grand reopening in three weeks had to go off without a hitch. All his investors would be on hand to take part in the festivities, and their approval was of the utmost importance, especially if he wanted more capital to undo the years of neglect.

He knew he could never again be the man in Kara's life.

Still, he had to find a way to get her to stay on at the resort. He needed her knowledge to make this a smooth transition.

But when she preferred braving a snowstorm to staying safe here with him, how in the world would they be able to work side by side?

CHAPTER TWO

THE HYPNOTIC SWIRL of flakes made it difficult for Kara to focus on the winding mountain road. The cascade of snow hit the windshield harder and faster with each passing minute. She flicked on the wipers. The built-up ice on the rubber blades made an awful ruckus. *Swish. Thunk. Swish. Thunk.*

The knowledge that Jason was now her boss haunted her. She'd thought that, with the resort sold, any lingering ties to him would be severed. How could she have been so wrong?

A bend in the road loomed ahead. Her foot tapped the brake a little too hard and the car lost traction. Her fingers tightened on the steering wheel as she started to skid.

Stay calm. You know how to drive in this weather.

Thoughts of Jason vanished as she turned into the skid. Like a pinball shot into action, the vehicle slid forward. Trees and the guardrail whizzed by in a blur. In an attempt to straighten the car, she spun the wheel in the other direction. Her throat constricted. At last, she came to a stop in what she hoped was the middle of the road.

That was way too close.

The pent-up air whooshed from her burning lungs. She

rested her forehead against the steering wheel, trying to calm the frantic thumping of her heart. She silently sent up a thankful prayer.

On her way to work that morning, the radio announcer had mentioned the possibility of light snow flurries this evening but never alluded to a foot of snow. And it still continued to fall.

She let off the brake and crept forward, anxious to put as much distance between herself and Jason as possible. Would she ever be able to sweep away the tangled web of attraction, woven tightly with strands of resentment? She sure hoped so, because as long as she lived around here, they were bound to run into each other. After all this time, she'd expected to feel absolutely nothing where he was concerned. So why did she let him get to her?

She exhaled a frustrated groan and glanced down to crank up the heater. When she looked up again, a brief flash caught her attention. Her gaze focused off to the side of the road, where her headlights reflected off a pair of eyes staring back at her. A millisecond later, a deer darted into her path.

A screech of terror tore from Kara's throat as she tramped the brakes, braced for the inevitable collision. Like a skater on a sheet of ice, the car careened over the slick pavement. At the last second, the deer jumped over the hood, just as the front tires dropped off the pavement.

Kara's foothold on the brake slipped, sending the car off the road. She pitched forward, but the seat belt jerked her back, slamming her into the door. With a thud, her head careened into the driver's side window. Pain splintered through her skull. The sound of ripping metal pierced the inky darkness.

At last the car shuddered to a halt. The air bag thumped hard into her chest, sending the breath whooshing from her lungs. She clung to the memory of her daughter's sweet smile.

With newly attached chains on the SUV's tires, Jason drove cautiously down the curvy mountain road. Soon he'd be home, enjoying a piping-hot bowl of leftover stew. His stomach rumbled in anticipation.

He stared out the windshield at the dark, desolate road. When he was a kid, there would have been a string of headlights passing him as anxious skiers flocked to the resort to try out the fresh snow. Tonight, the only evidence of another soul on this road was the faint outline of tire tracks.

Was it possible they belonged to Kara?

The thought of making peace with his childhood sweetheart weighed heavily on his mind. He didn't blame her for still being angry with him. She had every right to be furious over the way he'd walked out on their engagement. He'd probably act the same way if their roles had been reversed. No, he'd have been worse—much worse.

If only there was a way to make her understand that even though he'd handled it poorly, his leaving had been the only answer. But he had no idea how to convey that to her without going into the details of that fateful night, and that was not something he was willing to do. Not even to save the Summit, his birthright.

The wipers were beginning to lose their battle with the thickening snow. He turned on the vehicle's fog lamps, hoping they'd give him a better idea where he was on the road.

The tire tracks he'd been following suddenly veered to the right. His stomach muscles tightened. Trying to get a rescue squad out for an accident during this storm would take hours. He'd best go investigate first. He gently applied pressure to the brakes. The tires fought for traction, sliding a few yards before the SUV stopped. He glanced around, not spotting anyone standing next to the road. Not a good sign. They could be injured or worse.

He grabbed a flashlight from the glove compartment and flicked the switch, sending a light beam out the window. He squinted, trying to see through the thickening snow. At last he spotted the tracks. They led off the road into a gulley. Concern sliced through him. *Please don't let it be Kara.*

He threw the SUV into Park, switched on the flashers and jumped out. Wet snow tossed about by the biting wind stung his face. If Kara was out here, he'd find her.

With his hand shielding his eyes, he marched forward. Piercing pain shot down his thigh as he forced his way through a drift. He gritted his teeth and kept moving. From the edge of the road, he shone the light down at what appeared to be a ten-foot drop. At the bottom was a car with its front end smashed against a tree trunk. Whoever was in it was in need of help.

He'd just started down the embankment when his foot slipped. Hot pain shot through his knee and up his thigh, and his eyes smarted as he choked back a string of curses. Beads of perspiration ran down the sides of his face. But he couldn't stop now. He had a mission to complete.

His fingers curled around a branch and, using his good leg, he regained his balance and sucked in an unsteady breath. He massaged his knee, hoping he hadn't just undone the surgeon's long hours of reconstructive surgery, and weeks of physical therapy. Cautiously Jason flexed the joint. A new wave of agony swept up his body and socked him in the gut. It might hurt like the dickens, but it still worked. That had to be a good sign.

When he reached the two-door coupe, he tapped on a snow-covered window. "I'm here to help. Open up."

The window inched down, letting the buildup of flurries spill inside. Jason flashed his light into the dark interior. A hand immediately shot up, shielding the occupant's eyes from the glare.

"Jason?"

"Kara?" He leaned down, trying to see her better. "Are you all right?"

"I don't know. I think so." Her breathy voice held an eerie squeak. "There was a deer. Then the car skidded off the road. The door's stuck and my phone won't work."

"Okay, slow down. First thing we've got to do is get you out of there."

She started pushing on the door with her palms. He tried pulling on the handle. Without warning, she slammed her shoulder into the door. A grunt followed, but she pulled back, ready to repeat the process.

"Stop!" He used his drill sergeant voice, hoping to gain her attention. "Sit still."

"But I smell gas."

The mention of a gas leak shot a dagger of fear through his chest. Jason surveyed the area with the help of the flashlight, soon spotting the reason the door was stuck. The bottom was jammed against the embankment. The passenger door was pressed against a tree trunk.

"I need out!"

"Wind down your window the whole way."

"It's stuck." Her eyes grew round as her palms pressed against the glass. Her fingertips slipped through the opening and curled over the edge. "Help me."

The frigid wind continued to throw snow through the opening. With these low temperatures, he needed to get her out—fast. He kicked the ground, hoping to find a rock beneath the white blanket of frozen moisture.

At last, armed with a decent-size rock, he used his drill sergeant voice again. "I've got to break the window to get you out. Turn away. And cover your head with your coat."

She did as he instructed, and soon he was assisting her through the opening. When her foot sank down into the deep snow, she lost her balance and pitched to the side. He caught her, hugging her slight form to him. Her hands clutched at his shoulders, pulling him closer. When her head came to rest on his chest, he breathed in the faint scent of strawberries. The feel of her body next to his and the enchanting smell of her all came together, jumbling his senses.

Unable to resist the temptation, he ran his fingers over her golden locks. "It's okay," he murmured. "You're safe now."

Her weight shifted fully against him. Warmth filled his chest. After all those long, lonely nights in different towns and countries, Jason felt as if he'd finally found his way home. He never wanted to let her go.

A gust of wind threw wet snow in his face, bringing him back to his senses. He shouldn't be holding her. It was wrong to enjoy their closeness. He'd sacrificed that liberty years ago. And he was no longer the same man she'd once known.

He held her at arm's length. "You're bleeding."

"I am? I don't feel a thing."

He cupped her face in his hands. A crimson streak trailed from her forehead to her cheek. *Please don't let it be serious.*

"Are you sure? No headache? No double vision?"

"Nothing."

Ever so gently he wiped away the blood with his thumb.

When he found only a minor cut, he breathed a little easier. "Tell me if you start to feel bad."

She nodded.

He pulled his phone from his pocket, punched in the numbers for help and held the device to his ear. After a few seconds, he moved, positioning the phone in front of him. "I can't get a signal. Looks like we're on our own."

She shivered, wrapping her arms around her midsection. "How will I get my car out of there?"

He gave her a quick once-over. Aside from the small cut, he didn't see any other signs of trauma. "The car's not going anywhere tonight. And if you smelled gas, we aren't taking any chances. The tow truck people can deal with it tomorrow."

Her body shook and her teeth chattered. "Now…what… am I going to do?"

He worried about shock settling in. He was certain the accident had been horrific enough, but then to be trapped, even for a brief time, might have been too much for her.

"My SUV's up on the road. We need to get you warm."

He ushered her up the short embankment to his vehicle, which still had the engine running. After she climbed in, he reached behind the seat and pulled out a blanket. "This should warm you up."

He was about to close the door when she said, "Wait. I need my stuff from the car."

She started to climb back out, but he placed a hand on her shoulder, holding her in place. "I'll get your stuff. You wait here and turn up the heater."

"My purse is there…in the backseat…and my cell phone."

Jason closed the door and yanked his gloves from his pocket. He hobbled along, doing his best not to stumble on the uneven ground. The coldness seemed to freeze all but one of his thoughts: *Kara.* He'd missed her much more than he'd been willing to admit to himself. Between her pouty lips and soulful eyes, it was tempting to forget the demons that lurked in his past.

But that couldn't happen. He couldn't let himself go soft in the brain. It wouldn't be fair to her. Soon they'd be off this mountain, he assured himself. Once he gathered her belongings from the car, his only agenda was to deliver her safely to her doorstep and leave.

He limped to the wrecked vehicle and ran the flashlight's beam from trunk to hood. A sour taste rose in the back of his throat. In the military he'd witnessed the tangled metal wrecks and human carnage caused by IEDs, so this accident scene shouldn't evoke a reaction—certainly nothing like the wave of nausea washing over him. But he couldn't escape the fact that Kara could have died here tonight.

He blocked the awful thought from his mind. She was safe, he assured himself. All he had to do now was retrieve her belongings and drive her home.

Long minutes ticked by before Jason reappeared in the glow of the headlights. *Thank goodness he's back.* Soon she'd be home, snug and warm, with her family. Still, something struck her as not quite right. She gazed through the window, giving him a second, more intense inspection. She noticed he moved with a limp. The knowledge that he'd been hurt while rescuing her gave her pause.

When he yanked the back door open, she asked, "Are you all right?"

"I'm fine."

After placing her belongings on the backseat, he closed the door with a loud thud and climbed in beside her. It'd been a long time since they'd been together, but as close as they were physically, they'd never been so far apart in every other way. And it would remain that way. It was for the best.

But that didn't mean she could ignore his physical pain. "You aren't fine. You were limping."

"Don't worry. I'll be fine after I rest my leg for a bit."

The lines etched around his eyes and mouth said the pain was more severe than he'd admitted. Once again he was holding back the truth.

"Can I do anything—for your leg?"

He shook his head. "The, uh, weather—it's getting worse. We better get moving. Are you ready?"

"Definitely. I'm anxious to get home. I don't want my family to worry."

He yanked off his snow-covered hat and tossed it in the backseat. When he unbuttoned his coat, a fluff of pink fur poked out. Kara gaped at him. Nothing about him either in the past or now screamed pink fuzzy anything.

He withdrew the object. "I found this on the floor in back when I was searching for your purse."

"Bubbles." Her daughter must have forgotten the stuffed animal that morning, when Kara had dropped Samantha off at her grandparents' house before school.

"Huh?" Jason's gaze darted from the teddy bear with Baby Girl embroidered on its belly to her. "Bubbles? Really?"

Kara reached for the stuffed animal. "Something wrong with the name?"

"Uh...no." He tossed her the ball of fluff. "Not at all."

"Hey, it's the color of bubble gum—hence the name Bubbles."

"Logical. I guess."

She glanced at him, expecting to find humor easing the tense lines marring his face, but his expression hadn't changed. What had happened to the old Jason, the one with a thousand and one fast comebacks and an easy grin? Sadness burrowed into her chest. She mourned the boy who had always made a point of making her smile, even during the worst teenage crisis.

She hugged Bubbles to her chest. "Thanks for rescuing him."

"The bear is really yours?" Suspicion laced every syllable. "You carry a baby's toy around in your car?"

She stared down at the bear. It had been her daughter's very first stuffed animal. Even though Samantha had accumulated an army of plush toys over the years, she still reached for Bubbles when she was tired or upset.

Kara considered pretending she hadn't heard the question. However, she recalled how Jason had been worse than a hound dog rooting around for a bone when he wanted information. He would continue to hunt and dig until he found exactly what he was after.

Maybe a glib answer would suffice. She did know one thing: she certainly wasn't prepared to blurt out the entire truth about her daughter. So she'd give him the basics, and hopefully, he wouldn't ask any more questions.

"The bear belongs to my daughter."

CHAPTER THREE

SERIOUSLY, COULD THIS night get any worse?

Kara didn't say anything more, hoping he'd get the hint that she didn't want to talk. Her daughter was off-limits to him. She turned her head and stared out at the starless night, which mirrored her dismal mood.

"So you're a mother?"

The astonishment in his voice set her on edge. This was the very last topic she wanted to discuss with him. After all, she didn't owe him any explanations. She didn't owe him a single thing. Her daughter was no secret, but that didn't mean she had to share the circumstances of her birth with him.

"A lot changed after you left."

"Obviously. So who's the lucky man in your life?"

Kara suddenly hated her single status. The thought of lying tiptoed across her mind, but she'd never been any good at it, even as a kid. Best to stick with the truth. "There is no man."

"Thought you'd have guys lined up, waiting to take you out."

"And you'd be wrong."

She smothered a sigh. After he'd dumped her and she'd found out she was pregnant, it was a very long time until she was willing to trust any man. When she finally did dip her toe in the dating pool, finding a man with the right personality, who was ready to take on a young mother, was a challenge. Most of the guys she met simply didn't want the hassle of a ready-made family. And they certainly weren't thrilled about having their social calendars dictated by whether or not Kara could secure a babysitter.

Not that she'd become a nun or anything. She'd dated here and there. The evenings out were nice, but that's all they were—nice. She shielded her daughter from her dating life. She didn't want Samantha getting attached to someone, only to lose him when things didn't work out.

Sensing Jason giving her periodic glances, Kara refused to meet his gaze. Instead, she continued to stare into the night. The thickening snow kept her from spotting the pond where they used to skate as kids. In those days, they'd been practically inseparable. Did Jason ever think about the good old days? Did he even regret his abrupt departure from her life and this community? Was that why he'd finally come home? To make amends?

She sneaked a glance at him. His long fingers clenched the steering wheel, fighting to keep the vehicle on the road. When he turned his head to glance at her, she jerked her gaze away, focusing on the hypnotic swish, swish of the windshield wipers.

A loud crack echoed through the night as a tree limb fell onto the road. "Watch out!"

He cut the wheel to the left. The driver's side tires dropped off the snow-covered pavement. Kara's upper body jerked to the left, where firm muscles pillowed her and held her steady. Jason's body was rock hard. The kid she'd planned to explore the world with was long gone, and in his place was this man she barely recognized. The army life had transformed him into a human tank. And in that moment, she knew he'd protect her.

Thankfully, the vehicle slowed to a stop. With some effort, Jason eased it back on the road. "Sorry about that. You okay?"

Realizing she was still leaning against his arm, she pulled herself upright. "I'm fine."

But was she? Her heart continued to palpitate faster than a jackhammer. The blood pounded in her ears. It was the near miss with the tree limb that had her all riled up. She was certain of it. She settled back in her seat and took a calming breath.

"Hang on tight." Jason released the brake and the vehicle crawled forward. "The weather's getting worse. I can barely make out the road."

The tires crunched over the snow blanketing the pavement. The wind created white sheets that draped over the vehicle. All the while, the wipers worked furiously to clear the windshield for a second or two at a time. How in the world was she going to get home tonight? It'd be dawn before they got down the mountain at this inchworm pace.

"What are we going to do?" She didn't bother to hide the quaver in her voice.

Jason patted her leg. "We'll be okay. Trust me."

He was the very last person she should trust, but in these extreme circumstances, she didn't have much choice. Heat emanated from his lingering touch and radiated outward, sweeping through her limbs. Her gaze zeroed in on his fingers gripping her thigh. She should pull away, at the very least shove his hand aside. Before she could act, he withdrew it himself, to grip the steering wheel.

"Kara, why are you still there—at the resort? Working for my father?"

Not exactly a subject she wanted to broach with him, but at least it kept him from asking about her daughter. "You mean why didn't I leave him like you did?"

"That isn't what I meant." A note of bitterness wove through his tone. "Why haven't you moved on with your life? Gotten away from here? You always dreamed of traveling the world. Why give it all up for an old drunk who ran my grandfather's dream into the ground?"

She straightened. "Don't you dare judge me. Your father and I did our best to keep the resort up and running. Maybe if you'd been here, you could have helped."

"I was busy at the time, getting shot at while defending our country." He turned to her, his eyes glittering. "And recovering from a bomb blast."

Her brain stuttered, trying to imagine the dangers he'd faced. "I had no idea."

"You weren't supposed to. I shouldn't have mentioned it."

"What happened? Are you okay now?"

"I'm fine."

"If you're so fine, why are you here and not still overseas?"

A muscle flexed in his cheek. "They gave me a medical discharge."

She realized abruptly that something awful had happened to him. For all she knew, he might have come close to dying. A shiver washed over her body. Common sense said she should let the subject drop. After all, he was no longer part of her life, and she couldn't afford to let him back in.

But the tense silence set her frazzled nerves on edge. Maybe some light conversation would ease her anxiety about the weather. "Your father must be so relieved to know you're home. That you're safe."

"I haven't seen him. And I don't know if I will."

Shocked at his admission, she paused. It wasn't right that these two men, who had only each other, should be so distant. She fiddled with the blanket's satin binding while staring out at the storm. Time was running out for his father. She felt compelled to try to help them.

"You have to go to him," she insisted. "His liver is failing. I tried to put him on the transplant list, but with his history, he isn't a candidate."

"You can't expect me to act surprised. No one can drink at breakfast, lunch and dinner without paying for it in the end."

"Jason!" She glared at him.

In all the time she'd known him, he'd had a strained relationship with his father. Kara surmised it had started with the death of Jason's mother, but none of that explained why Jason had turned his back on his dad after so many years. She couldn't imagine ever cutting herself off from her parents. They didn't have a perfect relationship, but her folks were always there when she needed them, and vice versa.

Refusing to believe Jason could be so cold, she said, "The next time I stop by the nursing home, I'll let him know you're in town."

"Don't interfere. That man and I took care of everything we had to say to each other years ago. There's nothing left between us."

Jason's rigid tone told her she was pushing her luck, but she couldn't help herself. "But he's changed. He's sober—"

"No more." Jason's hand slashed through the air, as though drawing an imaginary line she shouldn't cross. "I can't argue with you. I need to focus on the road."

She sagged back against the seat with a heavy sigh. He was right. Now wasn't the time to delve into the situation with his father. At best, Jason would be only partially listening to her while he worked to keep them out of a ditch. At least she'd had a chance to make her point about his father's condition. There wasn't much more she could do now. She just hoped Jason would come to his senses and make peace with his dad before it was too late. Regrets were tough to live with. She should know.

She reached for the radio, then paused. "Do you mind if I turn on some music?"

"Go ahead."

At the press of a button, an ad for a local grocery store resonated from the SUV's speakers. Kara turned the dial, searching for her favorite country station. The headline news greeted her. She glanced at the clock on the dash. With it being the top of the hour, news would be on most every station.

"This bulletin is just in from the National Weather Service," the radio announcer said in a somber tone, garnering Kara's full attention. "The arctic express is supposed to dump twenty-four inches of snow in the higher elevations by tomorrow."

"Two feet," she said in horror.

"We'll be okay." Jason reached over and gave her hand a reassuring squeeze. An army of goose bumps marched up her limbs. She assured herself it was just a reaction to the dire forecast and had nothing to do with his touch.

The radio crackled as the announcer's voice continued to ring out. "That isn't even the worst of the storm. Sometime this evening, a blast from the south will raise the temperature, only to have the thermometer quickly sink back below freezing. I know you're thinking this is a good thing, but let me tell you, folks, those pretty little flakes are going to change into an ice shower, and with a wind advisory due to kick in at midnight, it's going to get dicey, resulting in downed trees and power lines...."

After another advertisement, strains of "Let It Snow" began to play. Someone at the radio station had a sick sense of humor. Outside, the flakes were continuing to come down hard and fast. A glance at Jason's squinted eyes and the determined set of his jaw told Kara the conditions were already beyond dicey.

Minutes later, when the vehicle skidded to a stop next to an old elm tree, outside a modest log home, she turned to him. "What are we doing here?"

"The roads are too dangerous. We'll hunker down here until the storm passes."

"Here?" A half-dozen snow-covered trees surrounded them. "In the middle of nowhere?"

"This isn't the boonies. There's heat and shelter. You'll be fine. Trust me."

There he went again with that line about trust. The words grated across her thinly stretched nerves. What in the world had she done for Fate to conspire against her?

"I can't spend the night with you," she protested, even though she knew her daughter would be safe with her parents.

Jason leveled a frown at her, as though he wasn't any more pleased than she was about the situation. "You aren't scared of being alone with me, are you?"

"Don't flatter yourself," she said a little too quickly, refusing to meet his intense stare. "I grew up a long time ago."

Her lips pressed into a firm line as she surveyed the sprawling log structure. Being snowed in with Jason, of all people, would be more stressful than sliding down the slick mountain road. Her hands clenched. She and Jason had too much history, and she hated how he still got under her skin, evoking a physical awareness she hadn't experienced in ages.

"Do you even know who lives here? Or are we about to commit an act of breaking and entering?"

"This is now my home. Don't you remember it? I

brought you here a couple of times to visit my grand-mother."

Her gaze moved past him to the covered porch, with its two wooden rocking chairs. She searched her memory. At last she grasped on to a vague recollection that brought a smile to her lips. "I remember now. She fed us chocolate chip cookies fresh from the oven. I liked her a lot."

"She liked you, too." His lips quirked as though he'd been transported back in time—back to a life that wasn't so complicated. "I inherited this place from my grandpar-ents, along with a trust fund my father couldn't squander."

Glowing light from the dashboard illuminated Jason's face, highlighting the discomfort he felt when mention-ing his dad, as he opened the door, letting the frigid air rush in. "Wait here. I'll leave the heat on while I shovel a path to the porch."

She refused to let him overexert his injured leg again on her behalf. With a twist of the key, she turned off the engine and vaulted out of the SUV. She sidled up next to him as he limped along.

He frowned down at her. "Don't you ever listen?"

"Only when I want to. Now, lean on me and take some pressure off your leg."

He breathed out an exasperated sigh before draping his arm over her shoulder. She started to lean in closer, but then pulled back, keeping a respectable distance while still assisting him. She refused to give in to her body's desire to once again feel his heat, his strength. She had to keep herself in check. This was simply a matter of he'd helped her and now she was returning the favor—that was all.

On the top step, they paused. Her eyes scanned the lengthy porch. Her gaze stopped when she noticed a freshly cut pine tree, all ready to be decked out in colorful orna-ments and tinsel. She remembered as a child accompanying her father and grandfather to the local Christmas-tree farm to cut down their own tree. The fond memory left her smiling.

"I'm so jealous," she said as Jason pulled away to stand on his own. "You have a real Christmas tree. All I ever have time for is the artificial kind. I remember how the live trees would bring such a wonderful scent to the whole house."

"A neighbor asked to cut down a tree on my property, and thanked me by chopping one for me, too. The thing is, I don't do Christmas."

"What do you mean, you don't do Christmas?" Her eyes opened wide. "How do you not do Christmas? It's the best time of the year."

"Not for me." His definite tone left no doubt that he wanted nothing to do with the holiday.

Her thoughts strayed to her daughter and how her eyes lit up when they put up the Christmas tree. Even in the lean years before her promotion to office manager, Kara had managed to collect dollar-store ornaments and strings of lights. With carols playing in the background, they would sing as they hooked the decorations over the branches.

The holiday was a time for family, for togetherness. A time to be grateful for life's many blessings. Not a time to be alone with nothing but your memories for company. The thought of Jason detached from his family and friends during such a festive time filled her with such sorrow.

"I haven't celebrated it since…my mother was alive." His last words were barely audible.

Kara recalled when they were dating how he'd always have a small gift for her, including the silver locket at home in her jewelry box. But he'd always made one excuse after another to avoid the Christmas festivities.

"Surely after all these years you've enjoyed Christmas

carols around a bonfire, driven around to check out the houses all decked out in lights or exchanged presents with various girlfriends?" Kara didn't want to dwell on that last uneasy thought.

He shook his head.

"What about the military? Didn't they do anything for the holidays?"

He paused by the front door. His back went ramrod straight.

"I always opted to be on duty," he said, his tone clipped. "I'll get rid of the tree the first chance I get."

"How could you possibly throw away such a perfect tree? You're home now. Time to start over. A chance for new beginnings..." Her voice trailed off. She didn't want him to misconstrue her words—to think she wanted them to have a new beginning. Not giving him time to ponder her statement, she continued, "You should try joining in the fun. After all, it's the most joyous time of the year."

Kara forced a smile. She couldn't believe she was trying to talk him into celebrating the exact same holiday during which he'd broken her heart. If he wanted to be an old, cranky Scrooge, why should she care?

Jason didn't say anything as he opened the door and stepped aside, allowing her to enter. In the narrow opening, her arm brushed against him, and even through the layers of clothing an electrical current zinged up her arm, warming a spot in her chest.

Staying here wasn't a good idea.

Being alone with her new boss was an even poorer idea.

This whole situation constituted the worst idea ever.

CHAPTER FOUR

ALARM BELLS CLANGED loud and clear in Kara's mind.

There had to be a realistic alternative to staying, but for the life of her, she couldn't come up with anything reasonable. One hesitant step after another led her across the threshold and into the log house. Warmth enveloped her in an instant.

"It's getting really bad out there." Jason slammed the door against the gusting wind before stomping the caked snow from his boots. "Let me get some lights on in here."

He moved past her to a table and switched on a small antique lamp with little blue flowers painted around the base. The soft glow added warmth to her unfamiliar surroundings.

"Thanks." She clasped her shivering hands, rubbing her fingers together.

When her eyes adjusted to the lighting, her curious gaze meandered around the place Jason called home. Worn yet well-kept maple furniture stood prominently in the room, with a braided, blue oval rug covering a large portion of the oak floor. Nothing flashy, but not dingy, either—more like cozy and comfortable.

Jason favored his leg as he made his way to the fireplace and arranged some kindling. He struck a match, and soon a golden glow gave his hunched figure a larger-than-life appearance. What would it be like to curl up with him on that leather couch with a hot mug of tea and a fire crackling in the stone-and-mortar fireplace? To sit there and discuss the day, or make plans for the future?

She gave herself a mental shake. This wasn't a romantic vacation. Nor was she interested in curling up with him now or ever. She'd keep out of his way and wait out the storm. Once the weather broke and the plows cleared the roads, she'd be gone. And it couldn't be soon enough.

She tugged her soggy jacket tighter, trying to ward off the chill that went clear through to her bones. All the while, she continued to examine her surroundings. A wadded up pile of white sheets lay on one of the armchairs, as though Jason was still in the process of making himself at home. Her attention moved to the oak coffee table with a folded newspaper and a tidy stack of what appeared to be sports magazines.

"Something wrong?" he asked.

"You mean other than being snowed in here with you?" She couldn't resist the jab. She didn't want either one of them to get too comfortable in this arrangement and forget about all the problems between them. "Actually, I'm surprised to find this place so clean. I guess I just don't think of men as being neat freaks. Unless, of course, you're living with someone...."

The thought hadn't occurred to her until then, and it annoyed her that it even made a difference to her. Yet the presence of a girlfriend would assure their past remained in the hazy shadows, along with the snarled web of emotions.

"I'm not involved with anyone." The flat statement left no doubt in her mind about the status of his bachelorhood. "I learned to clean up after myself in the military. You've got to be prepared to move out on a moment's notice, and you can't be ready if your gear is in a jumbled heap."

The tension in Kara's stomach eased. Instead of examining her worrisome response to finding out he had no one special in his life, she chose to stick to safer topics.

Glancing up, she said, "I love the cathedral ceiling and how the chimney rises into the rafters."

"Wait until you see this place with the morning sun coming in through the wall of windows on the other side of the room."

Preferring not to dwell on the idea of watching the sunrise with him by her side, she pointed past the fireplace. "What's over there?"

"My grandfather used the area as a study, and I didn't feel a need to change things."

She glanced around, taking in the winding stairs. "Where do those go?"

"To the loft. When I was little my grandparents used it as a bedroom for me. I'd spend hours up there playing. Now the space is crammed full of junk. Maybe this summer I'll get around to throwing it all out."

"Why would you want to do that? There are probably heirlooms up there that you'll one day want to hand down to your children."

His thick brows puckered. Storm clouds raced across his sky-blue eyes. "One man's treasure is another man's junk. And since I'm not having kids, I don't need the stuff."

Not having kids. The knowledge knocked the air from her lungs. He made it sound so final, as though he'd already given the subject considerable thought. She'd never heard him say such things when they'd been dating. In fact, they'd discussed having a boy and a girl. A little Jason and a little Kara.

In that instant, she realized a stranger faced her. *What could have changed him so drastically?* She bit back the question. None of her business, she reminded herself.

Dredging up these old memories stung worse than pouring rubbing alcohol over a festering wound. Her judgment concerning men seemed to be made up of one painful mistake after another.

"I'll get us something warm to drink," he said, ending the conversation. "You can get out of those wet clothes in there." He pointed to a door on the opposite end of the great room.

"I don't have anything to change into. Besides, I need to call my family."

"You need to get warmed up before you come down with pneumonia. Then you can phone home. It's not late, so they shouldn't be too worried yet."

She hoped he was right.

When Jason bent over to untie his boots, he groaned in pain. She grabbed his arm, tugging him upright. He started to pull away, but she tightened her grip, noticing how his muscles rippled beneath her fingertips. In spite of her awareness of his very muscular build, she dragged him over to a wooden chair beneath the picture window.

"Sit," she commanded, in the same tone she used when Samantha was being uncooperative. "You don't need to put any more pressure on your sore leg."

His startled gaze met hers. Then, ignoring her words, he once again attempted to loosen his laces. She swiped his hand away.

"I'll do it," she insisted, kneeling before him.

Her cold fingers ached as she dug her short nails through the chunks of ice, trying to loosen the laces.

"So this take-charge woman you've become, is it part of being a mother?" he asked, startling her with the intimate question.

"I suppose so." The mention of her daughter, combined with his nearness, flustered her. Her fingers refused to cooperate. "I almost have your boots untied. There's just this one knot…"

She bit down on her lip, forcing her attention to remain on the frozen tangle and to ignore how easy it'd be to end up in his capable arms. With one last pull, followed by a solid yank, she loosened the laces. And none too soon. This proximity was short-circuiting her thought processes.

She jumped to her feet and strode over to the fireplace. Why did this log home have to be so small? She supposed *small* wasn't a fair description, as this all-purpose room was quite spacious. But it didn't allow for any privacy, any breathing space away from Jason.

Her gaze shot to the two doorways off to the side, below the loft. Maybe she could wait out the storm in one of those rooms.

"I'll find you something to wear." Jason got to his feet. "Come on."

He led her to the nearest bedroom. Before he even opened the door, she guessed it was his. Definitely not her first choice for accommodations. She couldn't imagine sleeping in his bed, surrounded by his things.

"What's in the other room?"

"Wall-to-wall furniture. My grandmother had the great room loaded with so much stuff you could hardly get around."

So much for that great idea.

She stepped into his room. It wasn't spacious, but roomy enough for a dresser and a double bed. Her gaze lingered on the bright colored scrap quilt covering the mattress. The thought of being here alone with Jason had her lingering at the doorway.

Her mind reeled back to the summer of her sophomore year in college. Jason had told her that he wanted to leave Pleasant Valley, that he was joining the army. In the very next breath, he'd proposed to her. He wanted to elope with her after she earned her journalism degree. The answer had been a no-brainer—a very definite "Yes!" But she hadn't wanted to wait. She'd planned to drop out of college and earn her degree via the internet while following Jason around the world. She'd been so certain she could make it work.

She recalled how they'd made love over and over, celebrating their impending nuptials. At the time, she'd thought her heart would burst from the abundance of love. Never once had they been bold enough to come together in the luxury of a bed. Their special spot had been a remote pasture near a creek at the back of the resort, where the warm rays of the sun had kissed their bodies. The place hadn't been important, only that they were alone to talk, laugh and love each other.

When Jason abruptly left Pleasant Valley—left *her*—seeing the world was no longer an option. As the only child of two loving parents who worked manual labor jobs to get by, Kara realized as soon as she learned she was pregnant that she couldn't burden them with another mouth to feed. The day after she'd finished her junior year of college, her job at the Greene Summit Resort went from part-time to full-time.

Youthful endeavors and girlish dreams were lost to her. With the most sweet, well-behaved baby counting on her, Kara grew up overnight. Her parents were supportive, but the bulk of the responsibility for child care fell to her, whether she'd been up half the night for feedings or exhausted from a strenuous day at work. It was a lot to adjust to, but she would do anything for her daughter—then and now.

The dresser drawer banged closed, jarring her back to the here and now. When Jason handed over a pair of gray sweatpants and a flannel shirt, their fingers briefly touched, causing her heart to skip a beat.

"Thank you." She jerked her hand away.

"The bathroom is just through that door." He pointed over his shoulder. "I'll go get you something warm to drink."

"You should rest your leg," she protested.

"I'm fine. But you won't be if you don't get out of those wet things."

Before she could utter a rebuttal, the door thudded shut. Irritation niggled at her. Did that man always have to have the last word?

She rushed over to the door, only to find it lacked a lock. Nothing like feeling utterly vulnerable. With a sigh, she turned and leaned back against the door. She stood there for countless minutes with his clothes clutched to her pounding chest. She inhaled deeply and Jason's manly scent assailed her senses. She couldn't resist burying her face in the soft flannel. Even though it had obviously been laundered, spicy aftershave clung to the material. He wore the same brand as he had years ago. Okay, so maybe not everything about him had changed. She smothered a groan of desire.

After everything that had happened, why did she still have a weakness for him? But no matter how many memories bombarded her, they couldn't go backward. What was broken between them couldn't be undone. The only thing for them to do now was to take a step forward—in opposite directions.

Determined to stave off her lingering attraction to him, she rushed off to the bathroom. The pulsating water eased her achy muscles and the billowing steam soothed her anxiety. She refused to let the crush of memories overwhelm her. She just had to treat Jason in the same gracious manner she would anyone else who rescued her.

Minutes later, dressed in the warm clothing, she glanced in the oval mirror mounted above the chest of drawers. Kara didn't need to inspect her reflection to know she looked ridiculous, as though she'd just fallen out of a Salvation Army donation bin. She cinched the baggy sweats around her waist so they didn't slip down over her hips, and rolled up the dangling sleeves.

That left dealing with her hair, which was an absolute mess. She attempted to finger-comb the waves, but it didn't help. Surely there had to be a brush or comb around here. She scanned the dresser top, taking in the papers and envelopes haphazardly dropped in the middle. She noticed how there were no photos of people from his past or ones currently in his life. It was as if he was a clean slate just waiting to be written on, but she knew that was far from the truth.

A small, flat box sticking out from beneath the papers snagged her attention. Though she knew it was none of her business, a longing to learn more about this man from her past had her reaching for the box. It creaked open. Suspended from a red-white-and-blue ribbon was a gold five-point star with a laurel wreath surrounding a silver star in the center. Her heart swelled with pride for Jason. Her eyes grew moist as she realized he must have put his life on the line to receive such a great honor.

With her thumb, she lifted the medal and read the engraving on the back: For Gallantry in Action. A tear dripped onto her cheek. Jason was a bona fide hero. Just not *her* hero.

A brief knock at the door drew her attention. "Uh... coming."

She repositioned the medal and snapped the lid closed.

Just as she was about to return the box to its original spot, the door squeaked open.

Heat swirled in her chest before rushing to her cheeks and ears. Nothing like getting caught red-handed, snooping. Still, part of her was glad she'd learned this important detail of Jason's life. Knowing their country had taken time to recognize him for risking his life touched her deeply. Before her stood a rock-solid hero with broad shoulders, hefty biceps and a chest any woman would crave to be held against—except her.

Kara refused to let his gallant acts or obvious good looks change what she knew about him. When a relationship got too serious or hit a snag, he'd rather skip town than talk out their problems. She refused to get involved with someone she couldn't trust.

His blank stare moved from the box in her hand to her eyes. "I have the water heated up. I just need to know if you want tea or coffee."

"Tea." Her mouth grew dry and she struggled to swallow. Giving herself a moment to suck down her embarrassment, she took her time returning the box to the dresser top. At last she turned. "I didn't read about your heroism in the paper."

He leaned against the doorjamb and crossed his arms. His eyes needled her. "Snooping, huh?"

She didn't know if her face could get any hotter without catching fire. Unable to deny his accusation, she went with a different tack. "Such a great honor shouldn't be kept a secret."

"And that justifies you going through my things? Digging up unwanted memories?" The roughness of his voice spoke of a deep emotional attachment to the memories.

"Why were you honored?" she asked, needing to understand what had happened to him during those missing seven years.

"I did what had to be done. End of story."

"Does everything have to be some sort of deep dark secret? Or is it just me that you refuse to be honest with?"

Pain reflected in his eyes, but in a blink, it was gone—hidden behind an impenetrable wall. Regret for snapping at him rolled over Kara. She hadn't meant to make him defensive. She truly cared about what had happened to him.

"I'll get you some tea."

"You don't need to bother." She didn't want to be even more of an imposition. "I can just wait in here, out of the way, until the snowplow digs us out."

"I don't think that's a good idea."

"It's for the best. This way we don't have to get in each other's way. You can go about your business like I'm not even here."

"This room isn't very warm. You'll be a lot more comfortable in front of the fireplace."

"I could just bundle up in a blanket."

Why was he being so difficult when she was trying to make this awkward arrangement as tolerable as possible for both of them? Surely he wasn't any more interested in spending time with her than she was about spending it with him.

"Suit yourself." He shrugged. "But you should know that as soon as I get your tea, I'll be in to get my shower. And with the bathroom being a bit cramped, I tend to strip down in the bedroom."

Heat scorched her cheeks until she thought for sure her hair would go up in smoke. So much for her idea about keeping distance between them.

"I'll be out in a minute," she said. "You wouldn't have a comb handy, would you?"

He pulled one out of his rear pocket and tossed it to her before walking away.

She turned back to the dresser, catching sight of the box containing his medal. She hated that he refused to open up to her. But he wasn't the only one keeping secrets. She had things in her past that she preferred not to discuss—especially not with him. Maybe he was right. Nothing good would come of them opening up to each other.

After doing what she could with her hair, she walked into the living room to find the fireplace crackling with a decent-size blaze. The glow of the burgeoning flames filled the room with dancing shadows.

A movement on one of the chairs drew her attention. A black cat stood and stretched, arching its back. Kara stepped forward. The cat poised at the edge of the chair, ready to scamper away.

"It's okay. I won't hurt you."

The cat sent her a wide-eyed stare, as though trying to make up its mind about her. Finding her not to be an immediate threat, it sat down.

"Well, aren't you a cutie? I'm surprised you'd live here with Mr. Scrooge. You know, he wasn't always so grouchy."

Kara glanced around, making sure they were alone. A clank followed by a thud assured her Jason was still in the kitchen. Now would be a good time to contact her family.

"I'll be back," she told the cat, whose golden eyes followed her every movement.

With her outerwear wet, Kara borrowed Jason's far-too-large boots and a dry blue coat that was hanging on a wooden peg by the door. She rushed out into the driving snow to retrieve her belongings from the SUV. She hoped and prayed her cell phone hadn't been damaged in the accident. Once back on the covered porch, she dropped her stuff on one of the rockers. A quick search of her tote revealed her phone had survived the accident. The lights twinkled across the screen and displayed a weak signal. It'd have to do.

Her parents would be anxious to hear from her. She always called when she was going to be late, and she refused to take advantage of their generosity. Only tonight, there was no way she was going to make it home. She hit the speed dial and pressed the cold plastic to her ear.

Crackle. Crackle. Ring.

By the fourth ring, she began to worry. Surely her parents hadn't done anything foolish, like heading out in this storm to hunt for her. She paced back and forth. *Please let them be safe.*

As though in answer to her prayer, her father's voice came over the line. "Kara? Is that you?"

"It's me, Dad."

Crackle. "…been so worried."

"Dad? I can hardly hear you."

"Kara…" *Crackle.* "…and Samantha are all right. Where are you?"

"I'm at the resort." The answer was close enough to the truth without having to get into the sticky explanation about spending the night with her ex-fiancé. "The roads are impassable. I'll be home tomorrow."

"Okay, be…"

Crackle. Crackle. Silence.

Time to deal with Jason. What in the world would they discuss? Her mind raced as she rushed back inside to warm herself by the fire. There had to be some sort of casual conversation they could make to keep the tense silence at bay.

The weather? A mere glance outside pretty much summed up that depressing subject.

The resort? It was bad enough being snowed in with

the new owner. If firing her was part of his reorganization plan, she didn't want to find out tonight.

The past? The mere thought soured her stomach. That subject was best left alone.

Perhaps in this case silence truly was golden.

Jason reached into the far corner of the cabinet above the stove. Luckily, a neighbor had presented him with a welcome basket containing some tea bags. Not knowing what to do with them, he'd stashed the bags in the back of the cabinet. He never imagined he'd be serving Kara, of all people, some chai tea.

His mind was still reeling from the news that she was now a mother. As he placed the mug of tea on an old tray, an image of her with a baby in her arms filled his mind. Uneasiness settled in his gut. Years ago, when he'd proposed marriage, he'd been too young to think much about kids, other than someday they'd have two. A boy and a girl.

Even though he'd wanted her to move on, he'd never thought he'd be around to see her again. And he'd certainly never imagined she'd end up a single mom. A fiery rage slithered through his veins and burned in the pit of his stomach. The guy who'd abandoned Kara and her little girl better hope Jason never crossed his path.

Jason opened the fridge, removed a jug of milk and banged it down on the counter. What excuse did this man have for walking away from Kara? Sure, he himself had done the same thing, but there hadn't been a baby involved. He'd left in order to protect Kara from what he'd learned about himself. At the time, he'd been in shock, and repulsed by the ugly words his drunken father had spewed at him. Emotionally wounded and in trauma, he'd needed to get away from everyone he knew, including Kara.

The memory of the tears streaking down her cheeks,

dripping onto her new green Christmas dress, still bowled him over with self-loathing. His jaw clenched. He'd totally botched the entire situation. Now he deserved her contempt, and anything else she could throw at him. He was a mature man, a soldier, he could shoulder her wrath. Besides, she couldn't say anything about him that he hadn't thought at some point.

"Do you need any help?" she called out from the other room.

"I'll be right there."

He gathered his thoughts while retrieving a big bag of sugar from the cabinet. With everything balanced on the tray, he headed back to the living room, expecting to find Kara on the couch, snuggled under one of his grandmother's quilts. When he found the cushions empty, he paused.

"Hey, sweetie," Kara's soothing voice called out.

The tray rattled in his hands. Sweetie? Every nerve ending stood on high alert. Had he heard her correctly?

"Come on over here," she crooned.

His heart careened into his ribs with enough velocity to leave a big bruise. Where was she? In the bedroom? A flood of testosterone roared through Jason's eager body, drowning out the pleading strains of his common sense.

"Hey, big boy. You know you want to. I promise I won't bite."

CHAPTER FIVE

JASON SNAPPED HIS gaping mouth closed. His jaw clenched, grinding his back teeth together.

The tray in his hands tilted. The tea sloshed over the rim of the cup, while the sack of sugar slid to the edge. He righted the tray before the contents could spill onto the floor. In haste, he safely deposited the armload on the table.

"Kara?" He cleared the hoarseness from his voice. "Where are you?"

"Over here."

He scanned the couch and the two easy chairs, but saw no sign of her. "Quit playing games."

"I'm down here."

His gaze fell to the floor, and in the corner, behind the easy chair, he spotted the most enticing derriere sticking up in the air.

"Come on, sweetie," she coaxed. "A little closer."

His heart rate shot into the triple digits and showed no signs of slowing down. He reached for the back of the couch to anchor himself. His ears must be playing tricks on him. She despised him...didn't she?

"Please," she crooned. "I promise to be gentle."

"Kara," he said. "What are you doing?"

"There's the sweetest kitty under this chair."

"You're talking to the cat?"

She raised her head to look at him. Amusement danced in her green eyes. "You thought I was talking to you?"

Her lips bowed and a peal of laughter danced through the room, making him all the more uncomfortable.

"It's not funny!" The air grew uncomfortably warm and he yanked at his shirt collar. He shouldn't have built that fire up so much. "Leave the cat alone. She'll come out if she wants to. Your tea's on the table. I'm going to grab a shower."

He headed for the bedroom, needing a cold, cold shower to set him straight. On second thought, he'd be better off to go outside and roll around in the mounting snow. He could just imagine the steam billowing off his body. How was it possible that woman could still drive him crazy, like some hormonal teenager?

With the door firmly closed, he raked his fingers through his hair. He sucked in a ragged breath. The cat. He shook his head in disbelief. Wow, he'd been alone way too long.

Maybe once he got the resort back in operation, he'd consider spending an evening or two with a cute snow bunny. The problem was when he closed his eyes and sought out the ideal woman to spend time with, his mind automatically conjured up Kara's image.

Jason groaned. Boy, he was in deep trouble. If he couldn't keep his feelings for her in check for this one evening, how in the world would they work together?

Kara got to her feet, giving up on her attempts to befriend the cat, for now. Still chilled, she grabbed the red-white-and-blue patriotic quilt from the back of the couch and draped it over her shoulders. She made her way to the scarred oak table, where her now lukewarm tea waited.

A smile pulled at her lips as she thought of Jason preparing her tea.

She pulled out one of the ladder-back chairs and made herself comfortable. The table was strategically placed in the room, giving the occupants somewhere to dine while admiring the landscape, which at this moment was hidden beneath a fluffy white blanket of snow. Coldness radiated through the windowpanes, sending goose bumps cascading down her arms. She clutched the quilt tighter.

Some hot tea would help warm her up. She dug a teaspoon into the five-pound sack of sugar and ladled out three even spoonfuls. All the while, her mind replayed the moment when Jason thought she'd been calling out to him and not the cat. She couldn't help but notice the flame of desire that had burned in his eyes. Knowing he was still interested in her unfurled a ribbon of excitement within her. Long-ignored needs swept over her, making her weak in the knees.

The spoon clanked against the mug a little too hard, jarring her attention back to stirring the tea without making a mess. They weren't meant to be, she reminded herself. She'd learned that unforgettable lesson the hard way. She didn't need a repeat. Someday she'd find the right man. He was out there somewhere.

Still, she was intrigued to know that beneath Jason's grouchy, war-hardened veneer was a kind, caring heart—one capable of opening up his home to a stray cat and an old love. She thought of mentioning her observation to him—but what was she thinking? She needed to stop dwelling on her sexy host. But being stuck with him in this cozy log home, she had no way to avoid him.

What she needed to do was keep herself busy. But doing what? She couldn't remember the last time she'd been faced with having to find something to occupy her time. Usually there weren't enough hours in the day, to help Samantha with her homework, do the laundry, cook dinner...the list went on and on. But here in Jason's home, Kara felt out of sorts.

She had just lifted the warm mug to her lips to savor that first sip of tea, which was always infinitely better than the rest, when Jason entered the room with his hair still damp from the shower. His scowl was firmly in place. In fact, the only time he'd appeared the slightest bit at ease was when he'd thought she was flirting with him. *Not going there,* she reminded herself.

"When did you get a cat?"

"I didn't."

She glanced across the room, finding the aforementioned feline sitting on the coffee table. Kara couldn't help but smile as the sleek feline let out a big yawn, showing off its pink tongue. "Are you going to try to tell me there isn't a black cat sitting across the room, staring at us?"

His forehead creased. "Of course there's a cat. But I didn't get her. She just made herself at home."

"So it's a girl. And let me guess, she was hungry and you started feeding her."

He shrugged a shoulder. "Something like that."

So the curmudgeon wasn't as hard-hearted as he wanted to let on. "What's her name?"

"Sly."

A kitty with a name was a kitty with a permanent home. "Sly? Hmm...what kind of a name is that for a girl cat?"

"For a person with a stuffed bear named Bubbles, I wouldn't be casting any stones."

Kara, feeling childish, stuck her tongue out at him. His blue eyes grew round and his pupils dilated. All the blood swirled in her chest and rushed up her neck. Obviously, that wasn't the right move to make around a man who'd just moments ago thought she was flirting with him. She inwardly groaned, wondering if she'd ever figure out how to act around him.

"Do you think Sly will ever let me pet her?"

"The way to make nice with that cat is through her stomach. If you feed her, you'll be friends for life."

Kara paused at the mention of friends for life. She wouldn't be around after tonight. In fact, she had no idea where she'd be this time next year, after Jason replaced her at the resort. Not that she intended to give him any reason to fire her. When she left she wanted it to be on her terms—with a stable job waiting, to support her and her daughter.

"How about I fix us some food?" she asked, anxious to do something—anything.

"Dinner's already taken care of," he said, getting to his feet while keeping his gaze averted. "You'll have to make do with leftover stew."

If he was anticipating an argument, he wouldn't get one. "Sounds good. Anything I can do to help?"

"No, it only needs to be warmed. Shouldn't be long. Then you can feed Sly. She eats when I eat. Keeps her occupied so she isn't stealing my food."

Kara laughed, trying to imagine such an innocent-looking thief. "Just call if you need me."

Of course he wouldn't *need* her. He'd made that abundantly clear seven years ago.

His plan was working. He'd made it through that conversation like a true host. No errant thoughts or overtly awkward moments. He just had to keep his cool a bit longer.

With the bread buttered and the stew ladled into bowls, Jason returned to the living room. He couldn't help but notice how Kara looked at home. Her hair was in disarray, and her cheeks were rosy, as though they'd just spent a lazy afternoon making love. His gaze drifted downward, catching sight of his plaid shirt with just enough buttons undone that when she leaned toward the cat he caught a glimpse of her lacy white bra. His mouth grew dry.

In some distant part of his brain, Jason knew he shouldn't be staring, but the sight was too delicious to turn away. He never would have imagined that old flannel shirt could look sexy on anyone, but he doubted Kara could look bad in anything.

Every muscle in his body grew rigid and he swallowed hard. This wasn't right. She shouldn't be here. It would be way too easy to slip back into an old, comfortable routine with her. His gaze continued to drink in her beauty, impressing it upon his memory, because that was as much of her as he'd allow himself.

When she cleared her throat and straightened her top, his gaze jerked upward, meeting her jade-green eyes. He resisted the urge to tug on the collar of his T-shirt to let out the steam coming off his heated body.

"Here, take this," he said, his voice gruffer than normal. He held out a bowl of hot stew. "I'll— It'll warm you up."

"Thank you. Smells good." She sat up, tucking her feet beneath her and reaching for the bowl and plate. "Is this homemade bread?" She sniffed it and ripped off a healthy chunk.

He nodded. "Just bought a bread machine."

Sly leaped onto the sturdy coffee table and plopped down in front of him. Her piercing gold eyes seemed to question him about why she didn't have her dinner, too.

"You'll get yours in a sec," he muttered, before leaning over and holding out a spoon for Kara. "Here."

"The stew smells so good. I can't wait to try some."

She lifted a steaming spoonful, her full lips puckered.

He couldn't turn away as she blew on the spoon, then devoured the stew. He waited, wondering what she thought of his culinary skills. When she moaned in approval, his mind spiraled in a totally different direction. His hand tightened at his side. He needed to concentrate on anything other than this infernal effect she was having on him.

He glanced back at her. Her eyes were lit up, and his chest warmed at the sight. He struggled to maintain his outward composure. Then the tip of her tongue slipped out and licked her lips. His mouth grew dry as his mind filled with the most sizzling images. A frustrated groan swelled deep inside him as he continued to stare, mesmerized by her sensuous act. Thankfully he had just enough functioning brain cells to squelch the sound before Kara realized how much power she could still wield over him.

"This is excellent," she said. "Aren't you going to eat?"

An indignant meow sounded, drawing him back to reality. He glanced down at the annoyed feline. "I'll go get yours."

He strode past the glaring cat. Right now, food was the absolute last thought on Jason's mind. The only thing he hungered for was Kara. This was going to be the longest night of his life.

If he intended to stick with his plan, his sole focus had to be on reopening the resort. Playing the friendly, considerate host was only going to get him in trouble. After all, he'd rescued her, sheltered her—heck, he'd even given her clothes to wear and a warm meal. No one could expect him to do more.

He needed to distance himself. He couldn't let his desires run unchecked, because Kara wasn't a casual-fling kind of girl. Of that he was certain. And with his past, marriage and children weren't in the cards for him. Not with Kara, not with anyone.

He had to break this spell she had over him, for her sake as much as his own. Thinking of her as just another old friend wasn't cutting it. Time for a new plan. When he returned to the living room, he'd start by reminding them both that their relationship was a professional one now... should she agree to stay on at the resort.

CHAPTER SIX

WITH THE STRAINED dinner over, Jason turned to Kara. She wasn't paying the least bit of attention to him. Instead, she was crooning over the silly cat, which was lapping up her attention as it would warmed milk.

"Kara, it's time we talked."

She scratched behind the cat's velvety ear. "With us stuck here, now probably isn't the best time to get into something serious."

"Might as well get it out of the way. There's really no time to waste."

She shot him a puzzled glance. He thought she'd have guessed he'd be extending her a job offer. After all, she'd worked her way up in the company and though he would have preferred it if things were different, she was a vital employee.

"Since you're determined to talk," she said, "get it over with."

"I want you to stay on at the resort." Her pencil-thin brows shot upward, but not giving her a chance to turn him down before he finished, he rushed on. "I want you to work for me as my assistant."

Her mouth opened, but only air came out. Why did she look as though he'd just handed her a life sentence? Couldn't she be the least bit happy, or appear interested?

"Say something," he demanded, getting to his feet to put another log on the fire.

"I...I don't know what to say. I thought you'd be replacing me, and I'd be moving on. A new town. A new job. A new life."

Did he detect a hint of regret in her voice? Was she upset because he'd messed up her plans to get out of Pleasant Valley? Was this her chance to escape, and he was standing in her way?

He knew what it was like to want to move away. Sure, when he was a little kid, things had been good at home. Back then he couldn't imagine ever leaving the Greene Summit. But his entire life had changed the day his mother died. His father's drinking had increased. The yelling and fighting quickly escalated. Nothing Jason did was right. His waning ego craved a chance to prove himself as a man. Yet he couldn't leave behind the one woman who loved him—Kara.

Swept up in his need to show the world he wasn't the screwup his father accused him of being, he'd convinced Kara to become his army wife. When she'd suggested dropping out of college and starting their adventure right away, he'd agreed. Even then he knew he wasn't being fair to her, but he'd convinced himself he'd find a way to make it up to her.

Looking back now, he realized how wrong he'd been to attempt to drag her into his messed-up life. After learning Kara had dropped out of college anyway—she'd never finished her degree—he felt awful. Another of her dreams dashed. The guilt on his shoulders doubled. Holding Kara back now wouldn't be fair to her. If moving on was important to her, he wouldn't stand in her way.

But above all, he was a businessman. The success of the resort had to be his priority. He had employees relying on him for a paycheck. And more importantly, he wasn't the only investor in this endeavor. He had people to answer to if he didn't produce a profit.

When he glanced up, the worry in her green eyes ripped at his gut. He needed to come up with a solution that would work for both of them. That would leave Kara with an out.

"Work for me at the Summit until after the New Year. Just until I get a handle on everything," he offered, even though he'd much rather have her and her wealth of knowledge on hand for a lot longer.

She eyed him. "What's in it for me?"

He couldn't resist smiling at her resilience. She would definitely land on her feet, no matter where she ended up. "How about three months' severance?"

"And?"

"And...a glowing recommendation. Do we have a deal?"

"Maybe."

"Maybe?" He jumped to his feet and turned toward his home office. "Fine, you think about it. I have work to do."

"While you're working, what do you expect me to do?"

He paused and faced her. "There's got to be something around here to amuse you. Maybe check the stash in the loft. You should find some of my grandmother's books. Feel free to bring down whatever you want. I don't have any use for that junk."

He strode away, disappointed that she hadn't jumped at the chance to stay on at the resort. Still, the worry over whether she'd accept his offer was a welcome distraction from his continual battle with his blasted attraction to her.

In hindsight, he had to concede that she was right to weigh her options. He certainly would if he were in her shoes. Now he just hoped she came to the conclusion that would benefit them both.

* * *

Kara watched until he disappeared into the shadows. He wanted her to work for him—well, temporarily. The fact he wanted her input for the reopening had her straightening her shoulders as a tiny smile tugged at her lips. The knowledge that he recognized her accomplishments was quite satisfying.

But even with this recognition, was it possible for her to set aside the past and work closely with a man who could melt her insides with one heated glance?

She'd tried so hard to put the past behind her. She couldn't let him tear down all her defenses. The surest means of doing that would be to turn down his offer. No pondering. No wondering. Just a simple "no."

Oh, who was she kidding? She couldn't just walk away—she didn't have another job lined up. How would she make the mortgage payment at the end of the month? Or buy Samantha some desperately needed shoes after her latest growth spurt?

In desperation, Kara considered turning to her parents, but they simply couldn't afford to help her out financially. Her father had been laid off last year from the job he'd held for more than two decades, and had had to take a lesser paying position with the local mall security. No, approaching them for assistance wasn't an option.

Until she found the right position, Kara had no choice but to deal with working with Jason. But for now, he didn't have to know she'd made up her mind. He could sweat it out a little while. If he thought she had alternatives, he might not take her for granted.

Eager to find a distraction, she glanced around. Her bag of knitting supplies was waiting by the front door, but Jason's invitation to explore the books in the loft was too good to pass up. She rushed over to the spiral staircase.

Their steepness forced her to slow down, having already had enough accidents for one night. At the top, she pulled on a chain hanging from a bare lightbulb, which illuminated the area. Stacks of cardboard boxes littered the floor. Surely not all of them contained books.

Like a kid on Christmas morning, she grabbed the first unmarked box and carried it to a vacant spot near the stairs. She dropped to her knees and flipped open the flaps. Inside, she found heaps of old clothes—shirts and pants that definitely had seen better days. What in the world had his grandmother been thinking, to keep this stuff?

Then a thought struck Kara. Maybe she'd stumbled across a way she could repay Jason's generosity for letting her ride out the storm here. She scampered back down the stairs and found a pen on the coffee table. Once back in the loft, she marked the box "Old Clothes. Trash."

Box after box she visually inventoried. There were old newspapers, magazines, threadbare towels and other unnecessary items. All of which she tagged for disposal.

With no more room to stack the sorted boxes, and growing tired, she pulled one last carton from the heap, hoping to at last locate a romance novel. She folded back the flaps and lifted some discolored tissue paper, to find an assortment of handblown glass balls. She grinned, feeling like a child who'd found buried treasure.

These Christmas ornaments had been lovingly wrapped and stowed away with great care. Kara vowed then and there that they would not see the inside of a Dumpster, even if it meant her taking them home.

A piece of red felt stuck between two small boxes. Intrigued, she pulled it out, to discover a stocking with white fur around the edge, with Jason's name stitched in gold thread along the instep. Her index finger traced the stitches. This had been created with love, a love she was certain Jason hadn't felt in a very long time.

He might avoid anything Christmassy, but maybe it was time he got a dose of holiday spirit sprinkled with a dash of childhood nostalgia.

Jason stared at the stack of mail on his desk with zero interest. His thoughts kept straying to the occasional sounds that came from other parts of the house. A loud thunk followed by a thump emanated from the living room. He paused in his attempt to locate where he'd placed his checkbook. Damn. What was that woman up to?

Not hearing anything else, he pulled open the left-hand desk drawer. She'd call if she needed him. He refused to accept that he was hiding from her because of the crazy things she did to his body with a mere look or a casual touch. He had responsibilities. He was a busy man with things he had to get done. He simply didn't have spare time—

Bang! He jumped to his feet. The desk chair rolled back, crashing into the credenza. With long strides, he hurried to the great room, where he blinked, unable to believe his eyes.

"Are you just going to stand there? Or are you going to help me?" Kara glowered at him as she yanked on the trunk of a pine tree that was now wedged in the doorway.

"What are you doing?"

"You told me to find something to do. I'm doing it." She gave another tug and the tree suddenly came loose, sending her stumbling back into his arms.

His heart leaped into his throat. She was soft. But her body was chilled from being outside. A longing to pull her closer and warm her up swamped his senses. This was not good. But it wasn't as if he'd done anything wrong. She couldn't hold it against him because he enjoyed the way her soft curves felt.

All too soon, she was steady on her feet. He jerked his hands away and stuffed them in his back pockets. "I meant for you to find a book to read. Not destroy my house."

She held on to the pine with one hand and turned to him. Her cheeks were rosy from the cold and begged to be warmed with a kiss.... No! Don't go there. He'd just extended her a job offer. He had to start thinking of her as an employee, no matter how much she reminded him of a sexy, tempting snow bunny.

"Since we're stuck here tonight," she said, distracting him from his errant thoughts, "I have nothing else to do...."

"We've discussed this. I don't do Christmas."

"Come on. You'll have fun stringing lights and arranging the ornaments."

His lips pressed into a firm line. "I can't think of anything I'd like less."

"Okay, Scrooge. I'll decorate the tree by myself. If you hate it, you can toss it tomorrow, after I'm gone. Okay?"

He frowned. It would keep her busy and out of his way. Ah, what could it hurt? As she said, after she left he could get rid of it. No harm, no foul.

"Just don't break anything with that bushy shrub." He started for the study.

"It's a tree—a Christmas tree," she called after him. "And where are you going?"

What could she possibly want now? He clenched his hands, his temples pounding. If she hounded him again about decorating that blasted tree, he swore he'd cut it into kindling. "I have work to do."

"Not before you help me move the table. I think the tree would look best in front of the picture window, don't you?"

He groaned. Kara smiled as though she took the utmost pleasure in his misery. With a twinkle in her eyes and a shake of her head, she turned her back on him and set to work. Once they'd moved the table, she needed a little more help. This time he had to hold the six-foot tree upright while she screwed on the base. Then the tree had to be adjusted, to make certain it was straight in the holder.

Jason clenched his jaw until it ached, holding back a string of gripes. He moved the tree this way and that way until she deemed it was in the perfect location. He knew where it would be perfect—in the burn pile. But not wanting to go another round with Kara, he choked down his sarcasm. No wonder he didn't bother with the holidays. They were a big waste of time.

"Are you sure you don't want to stay and help?" she asked, as if it was some great honor. "There's plenty to do."

He shook his head, but the enthusiastic glow on her smiling face made him wonder what he was missing. How could hanging doodads on a dumb tree make Kara glow with happiness? Although even if he didn't understand what the fuss was about, he enjoyed seeing Kara happy, he reluctantly admitted. She should definitely smile more often.

"I'll be in the study if you need me." He inwardly cringed at his choice of words. Kara could do quite well, fending for herself.

He took a few steps, then paused and turned. She'd already started digging through the cardboard boxes, lifting out smaller containers. For some reason, he was having a hard time walking away. But why? This was what he wanted: Kara occupied, so he could go off on his own. Then why did he feel he was about to miss something special?

Back in his study, Jason paused by the window and

noticed how the storm had intensified. The fallen snow was being scooped off the ground by howling gusts of wind, causing a virtual whiteout. With a disgusted sigh, he turned away.

He sank down in his desk chair and forced himself to read over the latest credit card statement. Not much later, the desk lamp flickered. At first he thought there was an electrical short, but when the light flickered again, he noticed that it affected the whole house. If they got the predicted ice on top of those winds, they'd be plunged into darkness. He raked his fingers through his hair and leaned back in the chair. Being alone in the dark with Kara, with nothing to do but snuggle in front of the fire, would be his undoing.

Her sweet voice floated through the house as she sang "Jingle Bells." Happiness rang out with each note. He could just imagine her dancing around the tree, hanging decorations here and there, a goofy look plastered on her adorable face. What he wouldn't do to watch her.

He gave his head a quick shake. He refused to let her singing draw him back to the great room. His gaze scanned the desk. Something was missing tonight, but what? His laptop. He'd left it in the other room, where Kara was pretending to be one of Santa's elves. Jason wasn't going back in there to get anything. No way. Besides, it wasn't the laptop that was bothering him.

Then it dawned on him. Sly was missing. The little black-as-night scamp usually followed him around the house in the evenings. Sometimes he wondered if the cat mistakenly thought she was a dog. He affectionately referred to her as his puppy-cat.

When he worked at the desk, she'd make herself at home on the left corner. She did it so consistently that he'd actually cleared a spot for her. Tonight the spot was empty.

Kara had not only invaded his home and his thoughts, but also had stolen his cat's affections. What was next?

Kara sorted through the open boxes scattered around the living room. Wads of paper flew. Little boxes were tossed aside. They had to be here. She started her search over again, beginning with the first box.

When her fingers at last wrapped around the crystalline icicles, she sighed. They were just what she needed to reflect the colorful lights. One by one, she attached a metal hook to the end of each ornament.

In the background, the sound of crinkling tissue paper filled the air. She glanced over to find Sly batting around a blue satin ball Kara had set aside for the garbage. The cat grabbed the small ball in her mouth and, with a jerk of her head, tossed the ornament into the air before taking off in hot pursuit.

Kara laughed at the cat's antics. If only her daughter was here to witness the shenanigans. On second thought, it was probably a good thing Samantha wasn't here or she'd start pestering Kara about wanting a kitten for Christmas—not that the subject was ever far from her daughter's lips.

Kara had started singing a round of "Deck the Halls" when the little hairs on her neck lifted. She had company. Resisting the urge to turn around, she finished hanging the icicles. She took a couple of steps back and inspected her work. Each light had been positioned with care, and then the garland had been added. And last but not least she'd used an assortment of ornaments, small at the top and large at the bottom. She'd been thrilled to find some with Jason's name on them.

"Well, what do you think?" she asked, admiring her handiwork.

Secretly, she longed for him to ooh and aah over the

trouble she'd gone to. She waited, wringing her hands together as the silence stretched out. At last Jason stepped up next to her, but he remained silent. He hated the tree. She was certain of it. Her heart sank.

She turned to apologize for overstepping, and to offer to take it down, but the wonderment reflected in his blue eyes halted her words. He stood transfixed, seemingly lost in memories. She hoped he'd gone back in time—to happier days, when his mother was alive.

Kara had never known his mother, but on the rare times he mentioned her it was always with devotion and reverence. He made her sound as if she'd walked on water. Kara used to wonder if that was what had happened to their own relationship. Had he matched her up to his mother and found her lacking?

"These ornaments," he said. "Were they in the loft?"

She nodded, but realizing his gaze hadn't moved from the tree, she added, "Yes. Do you remember them? Some have your name on them."

He stepped toward the tree and lifted an ornament of a little blond-haired boy on a rocking horse. His name was scrolled in black paint along the runner.

"I can't believe you found these."

"Surely you don't think your grandmother would have tossed them out?" He obviously hadn't glanced in those boxes to see what the woman had packed away. He was in for a surprise.

"They weren't hers. These," he said, holding the rocking horse ornament, "belonged to my mother."

"You didn't know they were up there?"

"After my mother died…my dad threw out everything. Pictures. Books. Anything that reminded him of her."

Kara's heart ached for Jason. No wonder as a kid he'd never wanted to spend time at that house. It'd been stripped of everything that was important to him. His mother. His past.

"Even the Christmas ornaments?" she asked, trying to keep her voice level to hide her astonishment.

"This was my mother's favorite time of year. She died the week before Christmas."

Her death had happened years before Kara knew Jason. At last she understood his Scrooge-like attitude.

"My grandmother must have known what my father was doing, and salvaged what she could." He turned to Kara. "Thank you for finding them."

She swallowed the lump of emotion clogging her throat. "I'm happy you were able to reconnect with your past." At least part of it. But there was one more thing he needed to do. "Maybe it isn't too late for you and your dad."

"Yes, it is."

Jason's frosty tone warned her not to go any further along this path, but being so ill, the man wasn't capable of tracking down his son and pleading his own case. Jason's father needed her help, and after he had helped her move up through the company, providing her with the means to support her daughter, she wanted to do this for him now. Somehow she had to convince Jason it wasn't too late to rebuild that broken bridge.

"Christmas is a time for love and forgiveness." She placed a hand on his shoulder, feeling his tension. "If not for your father, then do this for yourself. Forgive him for the past. Let it go."

He pulled away from her. "You don't know what you're asking."

"I'm asking for a Christmas miracle."

CHAPTER SEVEN

IN THE STRAINED silence, Jason helped hang a few last ornaments. All the while, he tried to understand why a bunch of colorful ribbon, satin and molded glass should cause a lump to form in his throat. He swallowed hard, trying to push down the sentimental pang in his chest.

Still, his mind tumbled back in time. He clearly recalled being an excited little kid going with both his parents to pick out a Christmas tree. He knew his father would rather be at home watching football, but his mother insisted they search the mountainside for the perfect tree. Through the snow they'd trudge until his mom gave her stamp of approval on a very special pine tree.

Of course, that had been before his dad lived only for his next drink. Before everything went so terribly wrong.

His father, for all his faults, had loved his wife. And he'd played along with the festive plans for the holidays, making Jason's mother very happy. Would playing along with Kara make her just as happy? Maybe in this one instance Jason should follow the old man's lead.

He turned to her. The expectant look on her face immediately had him uttering, "You did a great job with the tree."

Her smile blossomed and her straight white teeth peeked out from behind her lush lips. An urge mounted within him to cave in to his desire to sample her sweetness—once again pull her close and see if her kisses were as good as he remembered.

"You can help me with one last thing." She knelt down next to an open box. "And what are you doing in here, little one?" She straightened, holding Sly in her arms. "Guess you don't have the same aversion to the holiday as some people we know."

Jason rolled his eyes at the cat's silly expression. And Sly's purring was the loudest he'd ever heard. It seemed Kara had totally won over his cat. What was next?

After Kara placed the cat on the quilt on the couch, she turned back to the box and pulled out an elongated container. Something about it rang a bell in his mind, but he couldn't quite pull the fuzzy memory into focus.

"I found this earlier and knew it would be the perfect final touch."

She peeled back the tissue paper and reached inside. With great care, she lifted out a Christmas angel. His Christmas angel. The breath hitched in his throat. Each year, his mother had helped him put the angel on top of the tree.

"Could you help me with this?" Kara asked, holding the delicate object out to him. "I'm too short to reach."

He accepted the angel and gazed down at her painted blue eyes, graceful wings and golden halo. The white material had yellowed over the years, but she was still beautiful. His vision blurred. Damn, dust from these boxes must be irritating his eyes. He turned his back to Kara and swiped an arm across his face.

Then, clearing his throat, he rose up on his toes and placed the angel atop the tree. He took a moment to make sure it was properly positioned, just as his mother would have insisted. Then he stepped back.

"Looks perfect," Kara said.

He nodded, not yet trusting his voice.

"I'm so glad I was able to find it. Childhood mementos can be so precious."

His gaze remained on the angel. A powerful sensation came over him, as though his mother was trying to send him a message. He knew it was impossible. Ghosts weren't real. People couldn't talk to you from the great beyond. Still, there was this feeling that she wanted to get a message to him. But what?

"It's like it's a sign," Kara said, startling him with her choice of words.

He turned to her, noticing how the Christmas lights highlighted her delicate features. Here in this setting, she didn't look like someone he needed to hold at arm's length. Maybe if he let his guard down just this once...

The lights flickered. A surprised gasp crossed Kara's lips. Then they were plunged into darkness, except for the glow of the fireplace.

"Don't worry," he said. "We've got plenty of wood to keep us warm."

"You don't think the power will come back on like it did before?"

"Not with those fierce winds. We'll be lucky to have power by tomorrow."

Even though the strings of lights on the Christmas tree were darkened, the silver garland shimmered in the firelight.

"We'll need more blankets before this night is out," he said, starting for the bedroom. "I'll grab some from the closet. They might be a bit musty, but better smelly than frigid."

Not only was he stuck with an unwanted houseguest, but they'd be a lot closer as they huddled around the fire for warmth. What in the world were you supposed to do while snowed in with your ex? Okay, well, he knew what he wouldn't mind doing....

That couldn't—it wouldn't happen. His teeth ground together. *Stick with the plan,* he reminded himself. *Remain cool and detached.*

With an armful of old blankets, he headed back to the living room. "I found these to keep us warm."

"Do you really think we'll need all of those? It's pretty warm in here already with the fire."

"For now. With the winds whipping around out there, the temperatures will plummet. The house will cool off quickly and you'll appreciate some extra blankets."

He stood rooted to the spot, watching as the light danced across her porcelain-like face. Most women looked better with a touch of makeup, but not Kara. She didn't need any paint to enhance her wide green eyes, her pert little nose or those pouty lips that always drew his attention.

Not wanting to be called out for staring, he turned around to stoke the fire. Thinking it could use another log, he grabbed one from the dwindling stack.

"I better haul in some more wood to hold us over for the night," he said, not relishing the thought.

"You can't go out there. It's too cold and windy. We can make do."

"We don't have enough logs to keep the fire going all night."

"What about your knee? It won't be good having it out in the cold."

"You've certainly got that fussing and worrying bit down pat. Your daughter is very lucky to have you." Jason couldn't be sure, but by the way Kara ducked her head, he'd bet she was blushing. "Don't be embarrassed about it."

"I'm not." She lifted her gaze to meet his. "I'll fetch

the wood. You've already done enough with getting dinner and cleaning up. It's my turn to help out."

Their gazes locked and held. At first there was a challenge in her eyes, as though she was tempting him to look away first, just as they'd done numerous times as kids. But then there was something more, something deeper. His breath lodged in his throat. He should turn away, but couldn't.

He was entranced by her eyes, seeing not only their beauty but also a hint of pain. What had put it there? Was it him? Had he hurt her that deeply all those years ago when he'd taken off for the army?

He ran his hand over his short hair. His thoughts strayed back to his time in the military, with its camaraderie and the way it kept him on the go, not leaving him time to dwell on his past mistakes. Even in basic training, there hadn't been anything they could taunt him with worse than what he'd already heard from his own drunken father.

Jason had worked his butt off, proving himself to the world. As his rank rose, his bruised ego gained strength. He was a soldier, an identity that had filled him with pride. And he'd been a damn good one…until he'd lost control. He'd let his dark side out. And the price had been devastating.

But how did he explain any of it to Kara? How did he open up to her and tell her that he was still groping around, trying to figure out how to keep his unsavory side under wraps?

Anxious for some physical labor, he headed for the door. "I'm the man. I should be the one getting the wood."

"You're the man?" Her fine brows lifted. "Where the heck did that come from?"

He sighed, realizing far too late that he'd said exactly

the wrong thing. "I just meant that you'd want to stay inside next to the fire."

Her lips pursed and her eyes narrowed. Apparently that wasn't the right thing to say, either. Why did it seem as if he suddenly couldn't open his mouth without sticking his boot in it? Military life had been so much easier. He knew what was expected of him—follow orders and don't complain. Being a civilian left him grasping for the right actions, the right words.

"Does the power outage constitute us being thrown back into the dark ages?" She planted her hands on her hips. "Me woman. You man. Let me hear you roar—"

"Hey, that isn't what I meant." He chuckled at the ridiculousness of this conversation. Definitely the wrong move, as Kara's expression grew darker. "I was just trying to be nice. After your car accident, I figured the last thing you'd want to be doing tonight is stumbling around in the snow again."

When the fury in her eyes dimmed, he breathed easier. "I'll be right back."

Sly got up from her spot on the couch. She stretched, before jumping down and running past him on the way to the door, where she stood up on her hind legs and pawed at the knob.

"Oh, no," he said. "You aren't going outside tonight. You'd blow away."

"Here, Sly. Stay with me, sweetie."

Jason's shoulders tensed at the sound of Kara calling the cat by a name she used to call him.

Just let it go. That was then, this is now.

Minutes later, a thump followed by a crash sent Kara scurrying to the door. After shooing the cat away, she reached for the handle, but before she could grasp it, the door swung open.

A gust of frigid air swirled around her, sending goose bumps racing up her arms. Jason stood there with a layer of ice on his hat as well as his coat. Purple tinged his lips while his lashes and brows were caked with snow. But it was the dark scowl on his face that had her worried.

"What's the matter?"

He shook his head, then he handed over his armload of wood, before exiting back into the stormy night with a pronounced limp. She wanted to call after him to stop and rest, but she knew he wouldn't listen. Kara ran to the side of the fireplace and dropped the split wood in a heap. They continued working together until all the wood was piled on the floor. With the door locked, barring Old Man Winter, Jason limped to the chair by the door.

"Here, let me," she said, rushing over to help him with his boots. "You obviously aggravated your knee. And it's my fault. If I hadn't insisted on you retrieving my belongings from my car, you wouldn't have…done whatever it is that you did."

He reached down, grabbing her hands in his. "It's not your fault."

"Of course it is." She yanked free of his hold and continued her fight with the iced-over knot.

"Kara, you aren't listening to me. The limp. It's permanent."

This time she stopped fiddling with his laces and stared up at him. "What are you saying?"

"Remember how I told you I have a medical discharge?" She nodded and he continued, "Well, it's because of this injury to my leg."

A sickening feeling settled in her stomach. "How bad was it?"

"Bad enough."

She needed more than that. The pile of secrets and omissions between them was unbearable. She wouldn't stand for any more. She lifted his wet pant leg up to his knee, revealing an ugly red line snaking down his calf.

The breath locked in her lungs. Her vision blurred. It tore at her heart to think of him bleeding and alone in a foreign country, miles from home. He'd had no family by his side in the hospital to talk to him, to hold his hand. No one should ever be that alone.

Jason lowered his pant leg. "It's an ugly mess farther up. So much for those sexy legs you used to go on about."

She dashed her fingers over her eyes. "Tell me what happened?"

He shook his head, once again blocking her out. "Just write it off to 'shit happens.'"

Sensing he hadn't opened up about it to anyone, Kara pressed on. After seeing the sizable wound, she knew keeping the memory all bottled up inside wouldn't allow him a chance to heal. "I'd like to know, if you'll tell me."

He rubbed his injured knee as though unearthing those memories increased his discomfort. "It wasn't anything spectacular. Just a normal day in the Middle East. Our unit was out on patrol...."

He paused and his gaze grew distant, as though he were seeing the events unfold in front of his eyes. His jaw tensed, as did the corded muscles of his neck. She wanted to reach out to him, but hesitated.

Jason cleared his throat. "My buddy Dorsy was on foot patrol with me. Earlier that day, he'd spotted a Christmas card addressed to me. The return address had a girl's name on it and he jumped to the conclusion that I had a secret girlfriend."

The thought of Jason in another woman's arms left a

sour taste in Kara's mouth. But she had no claim over him. Who he chose to spend his time with shouldn't matter to her.

"Were you and this girl serious?"

He swiped a hand over his face before rolling his shoulders. "No. I didn't even know her. Besides, I don't get involved in serious relationships. Not anymore."

"I noticed," Kara muttered under her breath. His arched brows let her know her slip hadn't gone unnoticed. "Sorry. Please go on."

"The card was from a high school student whose class had sent them to deployed soldiers. But Dorsy wouldn't drop the subject. He kept pushing, wanting to know… It doesn't matter now. The thing is I couldn't take his digs any longer. I told him to shut up, but when he wouldn't, I lost control—I shoved him."

Kara placed her hand over his cold fingers. "Yelling and giving him a push isn't so bad. I'm sure he forgave you."

Jason pulled away. "He never got the chance. He stumbled into the opening of an abandoned building, triggering a booby trap."

"Oh! I'm so sorry." The words were lacking, but they were all she had. "He was lucky he had you as a friend."

Jason shook his head. "No, he wasn't. If I hadn't lost my temper, he'd still be alive. I always end up hurting those closest to me." He paused yet again, as though to pull himself together. "Now, how about you finish untying my boot?"

Kara blinked repeatedly before making short work of unstringing his laces. "Is there anything that can lessen the pain in your knee?"

The tension in his face soothed as they moved on to a new topic of conversation. "Sometimes I use a heating pad, but without power that isn't an option."

She tried to think of a substitute. "Do you have a hot water bottle?"

He broke out into a chuckle. "Do they still make such a thing?"

She shrugged. "Hey, I'm just trying to help."

"I know. And I appreciate it."

The sincerity in his eyes sent a warmth swirling in her chest. When he smiled, her heart tripped over itself. She needed some distance. Some air. Anything to calm the rush of emotions charging through her body.

"I'll be back," he said. "I need to change into something dry."

She nodded and made her way over to the mess of wood on the floor. Work was a welcome distraction, but all too soon she had the logs neatly stacked, and had no idea what to do next. She plopped down on the couch and reached for a magazine. It was a sports issue, but thankfully, not the swimsuit edition. When she lifted it, something fluttered to the floor. A photograph.

It landed upside down. She wondered what image was on the other side. His ex-girlfriend? Did he sit here at night thinking of her? The chance that she'd been letting herself get all tangled up in old emotions while he was secretly pining for another woman left Kara spinning. The old Jason wouldn't have done that, but this new Jason she knew next to nothing about.

Anxious for an answer, she snatched up the photo. Her gaze riveted to the image of two young men with similar blue eyes and brown hair, each holding a colorful snowboard. Their appearances were so strikingly similar that they'd been mistaken numerous times for brothers.

Shaun...

At that moment, the floorboards creaked, announcing Jason's presence. He joined her on the couch. "Ah, I see you've found the picture of Shaun. Do you remember that time?"

Did she remember? She was the one who'd taken the photo.

"I remember." She swallowed hard. "We were sixteen. And life was so much easier back then."

Jason took the photo from her and held it in front of him. "Never thought we'd be sitting here nearly twelve years later, and things would be so screwed up. Back then we were the Three Musketeers. Now you and I hardly speak to one and other. And Shaun's..."

"Dead." The word pierced her chest.

"I know. It's been what? Seven years since he died in a car accident."

"How do you know about it?" She turned to him. "When you left, I thought you cut off all contact with Pleasant Valley. Or was it just me and your father you cut out of your life?"

His brows furrowed together. He reached out to her, but she scooted to the far end of the couch. "It wasn't like you're thinking."

"Then how was it?"

"When I left, I vowed I wouldn't look back. It was easy to get lost in my job, my mission. In the beginning, I'd volunteer for whatever assignment came up—regardless of the risk—but as the years passed, my curiosity about what went on back here grew."

She crossed her arms and glared at him. "So who did you contact?"

"You've heard of the internet, haven't you?"

She released a pent-up breath. "Oh."

"That's where I came across the *Pleasant Valley Journal* and stumbled over the article about Shaun's car accident. Damn shame. He was so young. He had his whole future to look forward to."

She nodded. Unable to find her voice, she thought of the boy who'd always followed Jason around, from childhood through their high school days. He'd always been there for Jason and her. Trusted, funny and dependable. Those were the traits she'd loved about Shaun.

It wasn't until Jason left town that she'd learned Shaun had been harboring feelings for her. With her being madly in love with Jason, she'd never even considered that Shaun's devotion was anything more than a deep, caring friendship. But the night Jason broke her heart at the Christmas dance, Shaun had been the one to drive her home. And again, a couple of months later, he'd been there at one of the lowest points in her life. He'd reached out to her and...

"Kara, are you okay?" Jason asked, moving next to her.

She glanced back at the photo, seeing Shaun's sweet smiling face...so much like her daughter's.

"I'm fine." Her voice was barely more than a whisper.

"It's okay. You aren't alone. I miss how things used to be, too."

The wind howled outside, while Jason's heated gaze warmed her soul. The past and the present collided. His thumb brushed over her cheek and down her neck. Kara's heart thumped madly. Could he feel the blood pulsating through her veins, making her head dizzy with need?

His gaze dropped. His pupils dilated. He was going to kiss her. Her breath caught in her lungs. This was wrong. But it'd be only once. For old times' sake. Drawn to him in the same manner a hummingbird craves sweet nectar, she licked her lips with the tip of her tongue.

His head lowered. She should turn away.

Instead, her eyes drifted closed. His mouth pressed to hers. A moan of long-held desire formed at the base of her throat. This was crazy. Utter madness. And in that moment she wanted nothing more than to be here with him, like this.

She slid her arms over his shoulders. Her fingers stroked his short tufts of hair, enjoying the texture.

His hands moved to her waist, pulling her closer. Her chest bumped against the hardness of his. Her palms slid down his shoulders, savoring the ripple of muscles. No man had a right to feel so good. She attempted to impress every delicious detail, every spine-tingling sensation to memory. She never, ever wanted to forget this moment.

His mouth plundered hers. She welcomed him with an eagerness of her own. Her protective walls fell away, leaving her open and vulnerable to this man who made her body sing with desire.

Her breath came in rapid gasps. Her hands slipped inside the collar of his shirt. His skin was smooth and hot.

"Kara," he murmured, as his lips traced up her jaw. "I want you so much."

She wanted him, too. The years peeled away. Lost in a haze of ecstasy, she couldn't form even the simplest of words. Instead, she sought out his lips and showed him how much she wanted him.

A thundering crack sent her jumping out of his arms. Dazed, she glanced around the room.

"What…what was that?" she asked, her breathing labored.

"It's okay," he said, running a hand over her hair. "Probably a tree limb snapped in the wind. As long as it doesn't come through the roof, we're in good shape."

Satisfied they were still safe in their little bubble, away from the realities waiting for them just outside the door, she turned her hungry gaze back to him. She leaned forward, eager to taste him once more. Thirsting for him like a person lost in the desert thirsts for water, she pressed her lips to his mouth.

Yet his lips did not yield to her.

They were pulled tight, resisting her advances.

Confused, she sat back.

The flames of desire in his eyes had died out.

"This can't happen." His voice was raspy and his chest heaved. "You and me. This thing. It can't happen. Not now. Not ever."

CHAPTER EIGHT

EVERY MUSCLE IN Jason's body tensed, bracing for the fire-storm brewing in Kara's eyes. She yanked herself out of his hold.

"You're right." She ran a shaky hand over her mussed-up hair, failing to smooth the unruly waves. "I don't know what I was thinking. You rejected me once. Why in the world did I think it'd be any different now?"

"It's not you. I never rejected you."

"Really? That's odd. I seem to recall you making me promises of forever, and then just leaving, with no explanation." Pink stained her cheeks as her voice rose almost to a shout. "You didn't even have the decency to tell me what I'd done wrong. You never gave me a chance to fix things."

He smothered a swear word and shot to his feet, ignoring the ache in his leg. With a pronounced limp, he moved to the fireplace. He had to tell her. He had to explain the terrible secret that drove them apart—the one that would keep them apart forever.

"It wasn't you. It was me," he said, turning to meet her glare.

"Sure. Whatever you say." Her eyes said she didn't believe him.

"I already told you how I got my buddy killed. Isn't that enough to convince you that I'm bad news?"

"That was a very unfortunate accident." She settled her hands on her hips. "It has nothing to do with this... with us."

He'd have to go into the whole sordid story to make her see that his hasty departure had been in a moment of shock—of self-defense. And it had absolutely nothing to do with anything she'd said or done.

Refusing to give in to the pain in his leg, he paced to the end of the fireplace mantel, then turned, with a precision drilled into him during his time in the military. He'd never divulged his shameful secret to anyone. At least his father had done one decent thing in his life and kept it to himself. Except for the fateful night when he'd flung the gruesome secret in Jason's face.

His gut churned as the nightmare began to unfold in his mind.

Jason paused. Looked at Kara. Opened his mouth. Then closed it.

With a jerk, he turned away. The pain in his leg was no match for the agony in his chest. He continued pacing. Where did he start? And what did he do when his worst nightmare came true—when Kara looked at him with revulsion? An acidic taste rose in the back of his throat and he swallowed hard.

"Don't do this again. Don't shut me out," she insisted. "Talk to me."

"I can't—"

"Yes, you can. Tell me what awful thing drove you from your home—from me. Or is it that there isn't any secret? Did you just chicken out when things got too serious? Instead of facing me and explaining why you wanted out of the engagement, did you find it easier to bolt?"

Did she really think him such a coward? He considered not telling her, considered holding back out of spite, but that would be childish. After everything, she deserved the truth. No matter how much it cost him.

"It all happened the night I was supposed to meet you at the Christmas dance." His voice grew uneven and he paused to clear his throat.

He searched for the right words. There were none. His palms grew moist. Puzzlement lit her eyes, as though she was trying to guess what he would say next.

"I was on my way out the door when my father stopped me."

Jason inhaled an unsteady breath and blew it out. "We started arguing about his expectations for me around the resort. I'd had enough of him criticizing my job performance, nitpicking my every move. I blurted out that I planned to enlist in the army. He was livid. I'd never seen him so angry. He told me I was an ungrateful, sniveling brat and that I owed it to him to run the place."

Jason glanced up to see the color wash out of Kara's face. Her eyes were large and round, prompting him to keep going.

"I said I was tired of being a slave to a man who lived his life inside a bottle. I didn't stop there. I also told him you and I were getting married and leaving this place. He laughed in my face. His alcohol-laced breath made me want to puke."

Jason forced another breath in, then out. "He said no woman would want to marry me when she found out the truth. I told him there wasn't anything he could say or do to keep me from marrying you."

Boy, had he been wrong.

He swallowed hard, fighting back the wave of fear over Kara's impending repulsion. He wanted more than anything in the world for her to understand, but how do you understand the incomprehensible? How do you reconcile yourself to the fact that the person you thought you'd once known was a stranger?

He just had to say a little more and then it'd be out there. There'd be no more fighting this attraction, because she'd never let him get close to her again. And he wouldn't blame her.

"My father staggered up to me. He stabbed his finger in my chest and stared at me with those bloodred eyes. He told me I was an ungrateful bastard. His words were slurred, but their point came across loud and clear."

Kara's hand flew to her mouth. Her eyes shimmered with pity.

When dreadful seconds of silence fell over the room, she asked, "Why in the world would he say such hateful things to you? No parent wants to see their child leave home, but…"

"But he was drunk, and furious at me for what he saw as betrayal, for leaving him here to deal with a resort that was losing money left and right."

After seven years, the events of that night stood out crystal clear in Jason's mind. His father's words still held the power to stab at his heart, forcing him to blink repeatedly to clear the blur in his eyes.

In his mind, he could still recall his father's last blow—the one that shattered any hope he'd had of having a life with Kara. He wasn't his father's biological son. Under the strained circumstances, that should have given him some comfort—but it didn't.

The truth about his origins was so much worse. He'd run from it for so long that now there was no place left to hide.

He was the spawn of a monster.

The breath hitched in his throat. Kara would never be able to look at him the same if he told her. The thought ripped at his gut.

"Still, you were barely twenty years old," she said, drawing him from his jagged thoughts. "How could he do such a thing? I understand why you left, but why didn't you take me with you? Or at least talk to me so that we could make plans?"

With his head hung low, Jason turned away. "I couldn't."

"Why? What aren't you telling me?"

"You won't understand," he shouted.

Frustration balled up in his gut over his cowardice to spit out the real reason he'd left, the reason he could no longer be with her. He was the son of a rapist—his mother's rapist.

"I never knew you thought so little of me." Pain reflected brightly in Kara's eyes. "I thought...I thought back then that we could tell each other anything."

His vision blurred. His throat started to close. He had to stomp down these tormenting emotions. He was a soldier. He was strong. He could get through this and be honest with her.

He lifted his head. His gaze met hers. He opened his mouth, but nothing came out. The thought of her being repulsed, or worse, being afraid, silenced him.

Besides, what did it matter now? They'd both been reminded that they weren't good for each other. Nothing more needed to be said.

"I have to get some more wood," he muttered, needing to be alone for a moment to collect his thoughts.

"Right now, in the middle of our talk?" Disbelief and frustration laced her voice.

"We're going to need it tonight." He walked to the wood pegs by the door to grab his coat.

"But you just got some—"

"Not enough."

CHAPTER NINE

THE FOLLOWING MORNING, the rumble of a snowplow signaled their freedom. Jason didn't waste any time calling the towing company for Kara's car. Learning there was a considerable wait for service, he ushered her out the door. He needed to get her home. Now. He couldn't let his thoughts become any more muddled.

The ride down the mountain, though still treacherous in some places, was a far cry from the night before. Kara leaned against the door, leaving as much space between them as possible. She stared straight ahead while an ominous silence filled the SUV.

"Turn right here. My dad said they'd be at my house, checking to make sure none of the water pipes froze during the night. I can't wait to see my little girl."

Excitement laced the last sentence. Love for her daughter had filled that part of her heart he'd broken so long ago. If only things had been different—if he'd been different—he'd have a place in her heart, too.

"You can drop me off here," she said, at the foot of the long driveway.

"That's okay. Since someone took the time to plow the drive, the SUV shouldn't have any problems making it to the top of your hill."

The little white house with deep blue shutters held his

full attention. It was so small. Not that his log home was a mansion, but he'd swear her whole house could fit in his great room. How did she live in such tight quarters—with a toddler, no less? She'd constantly be stumbling over discarded toys.

"You own this?" he asked.

She nodded. "It's cozy, but it's home."

He took note of the pride glittering in her eyes over owning this gingerbread house. "It's a real nice-looking place."

"Thanks." She grabbed the door handle. "I'm sorry for imposing last night."

"I'm glad I was there to help."

The door swung open and she grabbed her things before slipping out of the vehicle.

"Wait," he called. "You never answered me about staying on the payroll until after the first of the year."

Her pink lips pursed. Little lines formed between her brows, as though the decision was a real struggle for her. He'd thought his offer had been sweet enough. Could she sense his desperation? Was she holding out for more money? Or did she simply hate the idea of working for him?

"Come on, Kara. Don't make me beg. I've sunk everything I have into the resort. If you're worried about working together, don't be. The past is behind us."

"How can you say that when I still don't know the whole story about why you called off our engagement and skipped town?"

His back teeth pressed together and his jaw ratcheted tight. Why did she have to keep harping about the past? Nothing he could say would make it any better for her; in fact, it would make things so much worse.

He gazed into her eyes and saw steely determination reflected there. She was clinging to this need to know worse than a cat holding on to a catnip mouse.

An exasperated sigh passed his lips. "If I agree to tell you, will you stay on at the resort until we have it up and running?"

"Are you still willing to provide the severance package and reference?"

He didn't want to see her go, but he didn't have any right to stop her. If she could just help him get through the re-opening, he'd be able to take it from there.

"I promise you'll get the severance package and the reference. Now do we have a deal?"

"I'm still waiting." She crossed her arms. "You owe me one more thing…?"

"You surely don't expect me to dig into my past right here in the middle of your driveway." He checked the time. "Besides, the tow truck guy will be waiting for me to guide him to your car."

She bit down on her lower lip as though weighing his words. "But you'll tell me?"

He nodded. The hum of the idling engine and the occasional gust of wintry air were the only sounds as he waited, hoping she'd see reason.

"You have a deal," she said. Before he could breathe a sigh of relief, she added, "But don't think I'll forget about your end of the deal. I expect a candid explanation from you."

"I understand."

"Then I'll see you Monday morning."

As the door thudded shut, he took comfort in the fact that there was no time limit on her request. Kara had always been persistent when it came to something she wanted, but she wouldn't be the first person he'd put off. Eventually she'd get tired of asking, wouldn't she?

A groan grew in the back of his throat. His temples started to pound. He needed a distraction. He glanced down to turn on the radio, then spotted the pink bear on the passenger seat.

With the fluffy thing in hand, he jumped out of the vehicle. "Hey, you forgot this."

Kara turned as he rushed up to her. "Oh, can't forget Bubbles. Samantha would never forgive me."

"We wouldn't want you getting in trouble."

"Mommy. Mommy," cried a child's voice. "Can we put up the Christmas tree?"

A young girl dressed in jeans and a pink winter coat ran toward them, her arms pumping. This was Kara's daughter?

Where was the baby—the toddler—he'd imagined? This little girl was so much older. She looked to be school-age. He glanced from mother to daughter. The child's pert nose, rose-petal lips and dimpled chin resembled her mother's, but there was something else. Something very familiar about her. The eyes. They were the same shade as his. So was her brown hair....

Could she be mine?

The air whooshed from Jason's lungs. The stunning suspicion bounced around in his mind at warp speed, making him light-headed.

Even though he and Kara had taken precautions when they'd made love, he wasn't foolish enough to think that accidents didn't happen.

The girl looked about the right age. His heart hammered his chest with such force his ribs felt bruised. The child had to be his.

He turned a questioning stare at Kara, but she wouldn't look at him. Did she really think she could keep his daughter a secret forever?

The little girl attempted to stop on the icy driveway and ended up sliding. Jason instinctively reached out for her. His arms wrapped around her slight shoulders and steadied her.

She eyed him tentatively with wide blue eyes. "Who are you? And why are you holding Bubbles?"

"This is Mr. Greene," Kara told her. "He helped me during the nasty storm and saved your bear from the snow."

The girl looked at him again, hesitantly at first. Then her hands rested on her little-girl hips, bunching up her padded coat. "You were smiling at Mommy. Do you like her?"

Jason choked back a laugh.

"Samantha Jameson," Kara shrieked. "Apologize."

Samantha—he liked the name. It also didn't miss his attention that the child had Kara's surname.

"Sorry, mister. Can I have my bear now?"

The *mister* part jabbed at him. She had no idea he was her father. Obviously, Kara hadn't showed Samantha any pictures of him.

He crouched down and held out the stuffed animal. "Here you go."

"Do you like Mommy?"

She was certainly a cute kid—and quite persistent. "Your mother's an old friend of mine."

Both females shot him surprised looks. Before Samantha could continue her inquisition, Kara's mother called to her from the doorway. Then, catching sight of him, Mrs. Jameson waved, a much friendlier greeting than he'd been expecting. This trip certainly had been filled with one surprise after another.

Samantha waved goodbye and ran to her waiting grandmother, oblivious to the turmoil going on inside him.

When the front door banged shut, Kara turned to him.

Her narrowed eyes shot daggers at him. "What'd you go and say that for? She didn't need to know anything about you and me having a past. Now she'll be full of all sorts of questions that I don't want to answer."

Certain Samantha was their daughter, a daughter he never knew about until now, anger bubbled up in him.

"You haven't told her about me, have you?"

Kara's brows scrunched together. "Of course not. Why would I?"

"How long were you going to keep this from me?" Betrayal pummeled him. "I'm her father. I should have been told."

"No. You're not."

"Come on, Kara. Don't lie. She's the right age and she has my blue eyes."

Kara's hands balled up at her sides. "She is *not* your daughter."

"Are you sure there's not someone else in your life?" he asked, driven to know if he'd been replaced in his daughter's life. "Someone your little girl calls Daddy?"

"No. There isn't."

Kara glared at him as though warning him to drop this line of questioning. But no amount of denials and icy stares would convince him to let go of this subject. There were simply too many coincidences to come to any other conclusion. Samantha was his little girl.

He wanted to push the topic, but backing Kara into a corner wouldn't get him any closer to his daughter. He needed a different tactic to get Kara to open up to him. And making things even more tense between them wasn't the right course of action. He needed to retreat and regroup. After things cooled down, he'd come at the situation from a different angle.

"Fine. I understand," he lied, watching the tension ease in Kara's shoulders.

What did she have to gain by continuing to deny he was the child's father?

Then it dawned on him what she was doing, protecting their daughter from him. She didn't trust him to stick around. And the fact that he was keeping the past from her was just one more strike against him.

The thought of missing out on his daughter's life overwhelmed him. For one crazy moment, he considered blurting out the awful truth. But how on earth would the revelation that he was the son of a monster—a rapist—going to help his cause? His chest tightened. The truth about his past certainly wouldn't make him a candidate for Father of the Year.

It'd be best for everyone, his newly found daughter included, if he kept his secret to himself. He'd just have to keep Kara distracted until the past was forgotten.

Besides, he wasn't the only one who'd been holding a secret. Anger simmered in his gut over being kept in the dark for so long. If the snowstorm hadn't brought them together, he might never know he was a dad.

Still, Kara thought she was doing the right thing by protecting her daughter—their daughter. The phrase stuck in his brain.

"You should get inside," he said, letting the subject drop for now. "I've got to go."

Saturday evening, after spending the afternoon scouring the internet for job opportunities, Kara sent out her résumé to five companies advertising for an office manager. Hopeful that someone would take an interest in her application, she headed to the Pleasant Valley Care Home.

After signing herself in, she paused and scanned the list of recent visitors, searching for Jason's name. No such luck.

To her utter frustration, her thoughts had dwelled on him since their winter storm odyssey. When he'd first laid eyes on Samantha, she'd noticed how he'd struggled to hide his surprise. And after he'd boldly stated he wasn't planning to have kids, she'd been shocked by his insistence that he was Samantha's father. Thankfully, he'd finally accepted the truth.

Maybe she should have explained her daughter's background, but the circumstances hadn't been right. Standing outside in the freezing cold while Samantha waited inside for her hadn't lent itself to a heart-to-heart talk. Besides, what did it matter? Kara wasn't in a relationship with him. There wasn't even a possibility of it.

After seven long years, he still couldn't face her and explain what had made him break her heart. He didn't trust her then and he sure didn't trust her now. But he did owe her the truth…and she intended to collect.

Kara's footsteps echoed through the empty corridors of the nursing home. No matter how many trips she made here, she could never shake the unease that came over her when she entered the well-kept facility. Maybe it was the idea of her own mortality—that she might one day end up here, too.

Halfway down a brightly lit hallway, in front of room 115, she stopped and gently rapped her knuckles on the open door.

"Come in," Joe's voice rumbled, followed by a coughing spell.

She stepped into the room, finding him propped up in bed with a college football game on the TV. His roommate was lying wrapped in a sheet, with his back to them and the privacy curtain partially drawn.

When Kara's gaze settled on Joe's gaunt features, her heart clenched. His thinning white hair was a stark contrast to his yellow pallor. Some people had good days dotted with occasional bad ones, but it seemed since he'd put the Summit up for sale, his days had all gone downhill.

"And how are you?" she asked, as was her habit. But she truly cared about his answer.

"Awful," he grumbled, hitting Mute on the television. "They won't let me have a cigar while I watch the game."

"You can't smoke. You're on oxygen."

His whiskered face contorted into a frown. "Didn't say I was gonna light it."

"Oh." She didn't know what else to say.

Joe had had to give up a lot of vices when his health collapsed and he'd ended up in this place. He still fussed about wanting a juicy, rare burger with fries, and the cigars, but not the alcohol. Maybe at last he realized how it'd destroyed his life.

"My boy. You've seen him?" A wet cough ensued.

Kara filled his glass with water from a plastic pitcher and handed it to him.

"I did see him. You could have warned me you sold the Summit to him." She wanted to be angry at Joe for keeping such an important fact from her, especially after all she'd done for him over the years. But it was hard to be upset with someone so ill.

He at least had the decency to drop his gaze to his bony hands. "I need you to convince him to come see me. Tell him I'm sorry."

Kara wrung her hands together. Maybe she should back out of being the go-between for these two. After what Jason had told her about what went down between him and his dad, it might be asking too much of Jason to reestablish the father-son relationship.

"I tried," she said, still not sure how to proceed. "He's very stubborn."

Joe made an attempt to reach for something on his nightstand.

"What do you want?" she asked, ready to do whatever she could to help.

"Jason's picture."

She grabbed the framed graduation photo of the boy she'd once loved with all her heart, and handed it to his father. Joe pulled off the back and yanked out a wrinkled envelope.

"Give this to him...." His words faded into a string of coughs. "Make him read it."

Her mouth gaped. How did Joe expect her to do this when Jason wouldn't discuss his father, much less have anything to do with him? But she couldn't turn her back on this man who didn't have anyone else to look out for him. She couldn't give up hope that somehow father and son would be reunited.

Joe reached for her arm and placed the envelope in her hand. His cold fingers squeezed hers. "Find a way. Jason has to know I regret what happened. Please, Kara."

CHAPTER TEN

"LET ME LICK them. Please." Samantha held out her hands for the beaters from the mixer.

"You can have one and I'll have the other." Kara couldn't resist the sweet buttery taste of cookie dough.

They were both licking at the creamy batter when a knock sounded. Sunday afternoons were notorious for impromptu visits from her parents. She continued savoring the sweet treat on her way to the door. She peered through the window, finding Jason.

Jason? What was he doing here? Maybe she'd forgotten something at his place yesterday in her haste to get home.

She yanked the beater down to her side and wiped away any evidence of her childish behavior before opening the door. When she looked into Jason's dreamy blue eyes, her heart started beating in double time. "Hi. What are you doing here?"

"Thought you might want this." He moved to the side, revealing a lush evergreen lying on the sidewalk.

"You got us a tree?"

"You said you always wanted a real tree, so here you go." He peered around her and she turned, finding her daughter lurking behind her.

"Samantha, you remember Mr. Greene, don't you?"

She nodded and moved to stand beside Kara. "Is that for us?"

"Yes, it is. Do you like it?"

Samantha's head bobbed up and down, while a huge grin showed off her pearly whites.

Kara ushered him inside. "You're letting in all the cold."

"I didn't mean to stay. I just wanted to drop this off. Unless, of course, you already put up your tree."

"We didn't," Samantha volunteered. "Mommy didn't have time. Can we have it, Mommy? We've never had a real tree. Ple-e-ease."

Kara eyed her pleading stare. "Fine. Mr. Greene, can I help you carry it into the living room?"

"I've got it," he said.

He picked it up with ease and moved forward, favoring his leg more than usual. Concern swirled in Kara's chest as she quickly ducked into the kitchen to drop off her licked-clean beater. She wanted to ask him about his leg but reminded herself that it wasn't her concern. They each had their own lives to lead, and he didn't need her nagging him about his health.

Kara held the door wide-open while he maneuvered the chubby pine through the doorway. Her living room was small and cozy. She didn't have a clue what they'd do if the tree was too big. Samantha would have a fit. But they'd cross that bridge when they got to it.

"Put it here," Samantha called, pointing to a spot in front of the window. "This is where we always put the *other* one."

Jason glanced at Kara and she nodded in approval. "Just give me a second to slide the chair out of the way."

In a matter of seconds, the tree stood prominently in front of the window, with a few inches of clearance between the tip-top and the ceiling. Kara breathed a sigh of relief. Jason had already anchored it in a red-and-green metal stand, attached to a piece of wood. All she'd have to do was add water and a tree skirt.

Samantha clapped her hands together and beamed. "Mommy, isn't it great? Now you don't have to find time to drag down that dang tree—"

"Samantha! That's enough." Kara's cheeks warmed with embarrassment. Apparently her daughter had overheard her muttering to herself in frustration at the overwhelming prospect of putting all their Christmas decorations up this weekend.

"Sorry." Samantha didn't look the least bit sorry as she grinned at the tree as if she'd never seen one before.

But when her daughter's blue eyes settled on Jason with that same ear-to-ear smile, Kara knew she was in trouble. She didn't need these two to bond. No way.

"We're making cookies," Samantha said. "Wanna decorate 'em with me?"

Jason rocked back on his heels. His hesitant gaze traveled to Kara. Working with him would be tough enough. She didn't need him befriending her daughter. She gave a slight shake of her head, praying he'd get the message.

"Thank you. That sounds great...." His gaze ran to Kara again, as though he was actually interested in spending time with a six-year-old.

Part of Kara wanted to relent and have him stay, to make her daughter happy, but she knew in the end that it'd end up hurting Samantha when he walked out of their lives. He wasn't a forever kind of guy. When the going got rough, Jason got going. *Reliable* definitely wasn't in his vocabulary.

And what was even worse was that he represented the one thing Kara couldn't give her daughter—a father. Up until this point, Samantha hadn't shown any curiosity about her dad, but the day was coming when she'd be full of questions. And Kara couldn't help but wonder if her little girl would blame her for never marrying and giving her a father figure. Still, Jason wasn't an ideal candidate.

Kara steeled herself and gave another shake of her head. Jason was a gentleman and explained that he had a previous engagement, causing her daughter's smile to morph into a frown. Kara couldn't blame her. If she wasn't careful, she, too, would get sucked in by his charms.

He walked to the door, then turned to Samantha. "I almost forgot. I have something else for you. I'll be right back."

Samantha raised her bright eyes to her mother and practically bounced with excitement. "I wonder what it is."

"I don't know." Truly she didn't, but she had to admit she was curious.

When he rushed back up the walk, he was holding a small box. It looked familiar, but Kara couldn't quite place it.

He held it out to Samantha. "This is for you, but on one condition. You have to finish baking with your mother and help with the cleanup before you open it. Can you do that?"

Her head bobbed. "Sure."

"What else do you say?" Kara prompted.

"Oh, yeah. Thank you. Come on, Mommy." Samantha pulled at her wrist. "We have cookies to make."

Jason chuckled. Kara hadn't seen him this relaxed in all the time she'd spent with him at his place. Apparently he related to little girls more easily than he did to big ones.

"Have fun baking." He waved and strolled down the walk, whistling a little ditty.

What in the world had put him in such a good mood?

"Mommy. Mommy. Look at this."

Kara closed the door and turned, to find her daughter

had ripped away the snowman wrapping paper and opened the cardboard box. "You promised to wait to open it, remember?"

Samantha shrugged, peering inside the box. "I know. But I just wanted to peek. Isn't she beautiful?"

She held up the box for Kara to get a good look at the contents. The angel. Jason's Christmas angel.

When Samantha made a motion to reach inside the box, Kara yelled, "Don't! Your hands still have cookie dough on them. Hand me the box." Samantha frowned, but did as instructed. "Now go wash up. We have cookies to finish making before we decorate the tree."

Kara carried the heirloom into the living room. What had Jason been thinking when he'd decided to give away this treasured memento from his childhood? She'd thought for sure, with the memories of his mother the angel invoked, that he'd hold on to it. This just went to prove that she really didn't know him at all.

After another quick glance at the angelic figure, she placed it atop the bookshelf for safekeeping. He might not be ready to appreciate such a fine gift from his past, but she'd hang on to it for him, until his heart was open to the joy of Christmases past and the hope of Christmases future.

Jason Greene, for all of his faults, was hard to resist when he turned on the charm. His visit today had chipped away at the hard edges around her heart. She glanced out the window, but he was long gone.

She still needed to talk to him about so many things. Not only did they have the past to straighten out, but now his father's Christmas wish was weighing on her. She prayed there was some way to broker a bit of peace between the two men. The sands of time were running out for this father-son reunion.

* * *

Jason sat behind a large, solid wood desk—the same desk where his grandfather used to hold him on his knee and tell him that one day this place would be his. That day had finally come. He'd just never imagined he'd be working alongside Kara.

His gaze lifted and met hers. He'd been doing most of the talking for the past hour, explaining his vision for the future of the resort. He'd noticed her raised brows a couple of times when he'd covered how he thought they could cut back on expenses. However, she never interrupted, just continued to take notes.

Now it was time to get to the part where she could really be helpful to him. "While I work on finding the appropriate balance between year-round and seasonal workers, I'd like you to get new quotes from all the available vendors."

"Which one did you have a problem with?"

"It isn't that I have a problem with any of them, but it's a smart business practice to periodically get quotes and make sure no one is gouging us."

She shook her head. "They wouldn't do that. We've been doing business with these companies for years now—"

"And when was the last time you received quotes from the competition?"

"Never, but—"

"Exactly what I thought. My father always did take the easy route. I'm sure that's why this place is in the red."

"I should have been on top of this. Is this really what has the business in trouble?"

He didn't want her blaming herself. "There are many things that contributed to the financial mess, but it's not one single person's fault. We're going to put into place new procedures and policies, so we don't end up in a rut again."

"Which vendors did you want me to work on?"

"All of them. From the liquor to the vegetable supplier and everything in between."

"But surely you don't want to get rid of Pappy Salvatore's."

Jason searched his memory. The name didn't ring a bell. "Who's this Pappy?"

She cast him a look of disbelief. "He's a childhood friend of your father's. He and his sons have been providing us with the freshest vegetables longer than I've been here. They're punctual and their produce is of the finest quality."

Jason paused and stared at her. Throughout this meeting, she'd accepted what he'd said about overhauling the mechanics of the place. Her occasional frown let him know she didn't always agree with his methods, but she'd kept her mouth shut. Why in the world would she pick this one particular vendor to defend? Was it possible there was more going on with the Salvatores than just business? The thought soured his stomach.

"How well do you know this Pappy? Or perhaps you're more familiar with one of his sons?"

She glowered at him. "Don't twist this into something it's not. Yes, I know Pappy. He used to come to the resort once a month to go over the order with me…and your father. He's a sweet man and his whole family is involved with the business."

Still not getting the reason for her to defend their business ties so ferociously, Jason prompted, "And…"

"And he was instrumental in convincing your father to give me the promotion to office manager. He was so impressed with how I'd reworked the various menus, giving each of our food outlets a different ethnic flair."

"Of course he was. He wanted you to swing him more business."

Her eyes narrowed and her chin lifted. "He didn't need to. Your father had already awarded him the resort's full order years ago. He did it because I impressed him with my ideas."

Jason rocked back in his desk chair. He liked this Pappy and he hadn't even met him. He also liked Kara's strong sense of loyalty. He could only wish she'd hold *him* in such high esteem one day. But how he'd manage to get there, he didn't know.

"That still doesn't put the Salvatores above review. Get the quotes. We'll talk later."

Kara's lips pursed together as her pen flew over her notepad. "Is that all?"

"There's one more thing. Could you check on the furniture we ordered for the Igloo Café?"

She nodded, got to her feet and headed for the door.

Not wanting her to go just yet, he said, "I meant to ask you if Samantha liked the tree."

Kara clasped her notepad to her chest. "She did. Depending on what time I get home, we're supposed to finish trimming it."

"There's no need for you to hang around here tonight," he said, deflated by the fact that she hadn't extended him an invitation. "I've got all the files I'll need. Go home and enjoy the evening."

Her green eyes widened. "Are you sure? The reopening isn't far away."

"Positive." He wanted this Christmas to be special for their daughter, whether Kara let him share it with them or not.

She hesitated at the doorway. Was she having second thoughts about inviting him over? Hope rose in his chest. Christmas still wasn't one of his favorite holidays, but for Samantha's sake, he could learn to like just about anything.

"Did you need something else?"

She nodded and pulled an envelope from the back of her notebook. "I need you to read this."

Disappointment hit him hard and fast. He struggled to keep his poker face in place as he held out his hand. "Is it something I need to go over tonight?"

She worried her bottom lip. "Time is of the essence."

"Pass it over and I'll give it top priority."

When he glanced at the envelope and saw the return address, he groaned. Now he knew why she was acting so strange—it was from his father.

"Kara, take this back." It'd be filled with more accusations about how he'd failed as a son. He couldn't—no, he wouldn't let that man inflict any further pain.

"You said you'd read it. You said you'd make it a priority." Her brows scrunched together as her eyes pleaded with him. "You can't pretend he doesn't exist. And you'll regret it if he dies before you have a chance to make peace with him."

Jason didn't want to hear any of this. "I'm the injured party here. My father was the one who pulled away after my mother died. He's the one who turned to a liquor bottle for comfort. He never thought of me or my needs."

"I'm so sorry, Jason. To lose your mother and then for all intents and purposes to lose your father, too, must have been devastating for you. But it's not too late to try and undo some of the damage."

"Why is this so important to you?"

"This will be your father's last Christmas." Her voice cracked with emotion. "If a person can't forgive, they can't know real love. It's a lonely life. Is that what you want for yourself?"

"You think I can't love?"

She shrugged. "Joe wasn't always a bad father. You told me."

Jason's jaw grew rigid. She was a good talker, but he just couldn't put himself out there for his father to throw all his misdeeds back in his face.

Jason held out the letter, but she turned her back and walked out of the room.

With a sigh, he leaned back in his chair as her last comment settled in. It was true. His father hadn't always been a bad man. In fact, Jason could remember a few fishing trips to the state park. They'd hardly caught a thing, but his dad hadn't seemed to mind, as the two of them talked a lot about sports. Jason had just been glad to have his father pay some attention to him.

Then his mother had gotten sick and there were no more fishing trips. It was at his mom's bedside that he first saw his father cry. That was when Jason knew his mother was never going to get better—and that was when he'd really needed a father. But his dad retreated to his study and wouldn't let anyone in. Bottles of Jack Daniel's and Jim Beam had kept him company, putting him into a numbed, drunken stupor.

"Damn." Jason threw the envelope on the desk.

Since the first night he'd run into Kara, she'd been on this blasted campaign to reunite him and his father. And no matter how much Jason wanted to please her, he couldn't do what she asked of him. Too many damaging words had been inflicted. The deep emotional wounds had festered over time, not healed. It was best to leave them alone.

He shook his head, trying to chase away the unwanted memories. His teeth ground together. This was Kara's doing—unearthing his past. She'd wanted him to remember, but it wouldn't work. This was one Christmas miracle even she couldn't pull off, with all her good intentions.

But if she truly thought he couldn't love, she was wrong. As much as he wanted to deny it, she had a permanent spot in his heart. And as for their daughter—he'd fallen for her at first sight.

Now he just had to find a way to show Kara that he wasn't the heartless creep she imagined him to be.

CHAPTER ELEVEN

MEETING AFTER MEETING about streamlining the resort's expenses kept Kara in close proximity to Jason. However, with so many other employees drifting in and out of his office, she didn't have a chance to ask about the past, and get answers to the questions that had plagued her for so many years.

If she didn't know better, she'd swear he'd planned his open-door policy as a way of keeping them from talking privately. But if he thought she'd forget about their agreement, he was most definitely wrong.

So when the phone rang on Saturday, Kara was startled to hear his voice at the other end. He was all-business, asking for her assistance in finding some pertinent paperwork. When she said that she'd have to bring Samantha with her, his tone softened and he said he had an important job for her, too.

Not wanting to give him any excuse to fire her before the holidays, Kara shut down her internet search for jobs, scooped up Samantha from in front of the television and rushed out the door.

With the late afternoon sun playing hide-and-seek behind the trees lining Greene Summit's winding roadway, she drove up to the lodge. Samantha chattered about anything and everything that caught her attention, as was normal during a car ride. Only today her conversation wasn't about school or Santa. Today her only thought was about seeing Jason.

They parked in the vacant front lot, by the main entrance. Massive timbers acted as supports for the alcove roof, while layered logs made up the walls of the lodge, giving it a natural outdoorsy feeling.

"Mommy, hurry," Samantha said, yanking on her hand. "He said I could help him do somethin' impotent."

"Important," Kara corrected, and released her daughter's hand in order to unlock the door.

Inside the newly renovated lobby, a soft pine scent lofted throughout the two-story space, thanks to the giant Christmas tree that soared up toward the skylights, lights twinkling from every branch. A musical rendition of "Have a Holly Jolly Christmas" played in the background. Since they were the only ones in the building, aside from Jason, she couldn't dismiss the fact that he'd taken time to turn on the lights and music to impress Samantha. Her daughter walked all around the tree, admiring the red and green decorations.

"Wow, look, Mommy. Think Mr. Greene did all of this for us?"

Kara smiled. "I think the decorations are for the grand reopening, but I'm sure he'd be happy if you told him how much you like them."

"I will."

As though her thoughts had summoned him, Jason strode over to them. A smile lightened the tired lines on his face. "Hi. So what are my two favorite ladies up to?"

"Waiting for you." Samantha giggled.

"I hope we didn't take too long. I had a nut roll in the oven when you called," Kara said, trying to ignore the way his smile made her heart pound.

Samantha moved to stand directly in front of Jason. "Mr. Greene, I'm ready to work. Look," she said, holding up her stuffed bear. "I brought help."

He chuckled. "Samantha, I wish all my workers were as eager as you and Bubbles."

"What are we gonna do? Is it fun?"

"Slow down," he said. "I called you and your mom here because I have a little work I need your mother to do for me."

Kara stood next to the towering evergreen, observing the way her daughter's eyes lit up as she interacted with Jason. He certainly could turn on the charm. She'd have to be careful or they'd both be vulnerable to his radiant smile and kind words—and that couldn't happen. She knew how much it had cost her when he'd changed his mind about a future with her, and moved on—alone.

Samantha's lower lip stuck out. "I thought you had somethin' impotent for me."

He chuckled, most likely at her daughter's poor grammar, or maybe the way her bottom lip sagged.

"Cheer up," he said, "I have something in mind for you. A real important job. First, would you like to see the changes we've made to the resort?"

Samantha shrugged. Kara knew she should just take care of business and leave, but she was anxious to take a look around. Since Jason took over the Summit, she'd been tucked away in the office, shuffling papers, making phone calls and attending meetings. She'd missed seeing all the renovations. What would a five-minute tour hurt?

"And afterward—" he knelt down by Samantha and whispered loud enough for Kara to overhear "—I was hoping you could help me test the machines in the game room."

"The game room!" Samantha screamed. Her blue eyes sparkled with excitement.

Kara bit back a groan. What was he up to? The last thing either of them should be doing on a Saturday afternoon was hanging out like...like a family. The thought was so foreign to her. It'd always been enough to know she and Samantha were a family unit. Kara didn't like how being around Jason filled her head with thoughts of what was lacking.

She cleared her throat, gaining the others' attention. "As kind as your offer is, we can't stay—"

"Mommy." Samantha's cherubic face scrunched into a stormy frown. "I wanna stay!"

Kara's gaze moved from Samantha to Jason's pleading look. Why was she the only person who thought this was a bad idea? Didn't he have more important things to do than play tour director?

"Please, Mommy? I already have my homework done."

That was true enough. Samantha had been an angel all week. Kara knew it had a lot to do with Santa, but she'd take what she could get, when she could get it. Her daughter had earned the right to have a little fun. Who was she to take it from her?

"Okay. But we can't stay long—"

"Yay!" Samantha cheered.

"Good." Jason smiled, setting Kara's heart aflutter. "Let's go take that tour. I think someone is anxious to begin her work."

"Uh-huh." Samantha beamed a cheery smile at them before grabbing a hand of each adult and pulling them onward.

Kara glanced past her daughter to Jason, who seemed truly relaxed and comfortable holding Samantha's hand. Letting him field the child's million and one questions about the resort, Kara took in all the recent updates.

The hallway's robin's-egg-blue walls were bare, and a faint smell of fresh paint lingered. A lifetime of memories lived and breathed inside this ski lodge. If these walls could talk, they'd spill stories of stolen kisses, tears and shared promises.

Jason pointed out the new restaurants, spa and indoor Olympic-size pool while the past continued to crowd in on Kara. She remembered how things used to be—how things might be again, if only she could make Jason understand the impossible. But her confession wouldn't fix things between them. It'd only scare him off. She doubted even this business could hold him back if he learned exactly what had happened after he'd dumped her. Not that she'd ever have a reason to tell him. He was her boss, nothing more.

The tour concluded with the game room to the left and a bowling alley to the right. A screech of joy ripped from Samantha's lungs. "There's a bowlin' alley, too."

Both of them laughed at her comical enthusiasm as she tried to decide what game she wanted to try first.

"Mister, can I really play them all?"

His smile lit up his face, making his blue eyes twinkle. "First, call me Jason."

"Jason, can we play now? Bubbles wants to bowl. Can we, huh?"

"We have a lot of games to test, so we better get started." He rolled up his shirtsleeves, then found the power switch. Lights flickered and the lanes lit up.

"Mommy, are you gonna play, too?"

"I don't think so. I can't bowl in these boots."

"Not a problem," Jason assured her. "We've got brand spanking new shoes. What size are you?"

Kara took in the expectant look on her daughter's face and then turned to meet Jason's appealing gaze. How could she turn them down? After spending way too many hours being professional, and a responsible adult, she was just as anxious as Samantha to let loose and be included in the fun.

They placed bumpers in the gutters to keep their balls in the lane. Jason and Samantha nearly doubled over in fits of laughter when in her enthusiasm Kara flung the ball too hard and too soon. It bounced over the bumper and into the next lane. Samantha, with the aid of a bumper or two, pulled off a spare, while Jason scored strike after strike.

After he soundly beat Kara, he surprised them with a takeout pepperoni pizza he'd kept warm in the employee kitchen. When he glanced her way, Kara mouthed, *"Thank you."*

He had outdone himself this afternoon. The man certainly was full of surprises. Her daughter was thrilled with the fun, and to be honest, Kara was thrilled, too.

When they finally worked their way over to the game room, Jason produced a pocketful of quarters. He handed Samantha a few. "Here you go. You can test the machines in here while your mother and I talk a little business."

"Aren't you gonna play, too?"

"In a couple of minutes." He ran a gentle, reassuring hand over Samantha's back, making Kara's heart pinch as she thought of all the father-daughter moments her little girl had missed.

Samantha, seeming satisfied to wait, moved to a claw game where the intent was to pick up one of the colorful plush animals with the shiny metallic prongs and place it in the chute. Before she could utter a complaint about being too short, Jason produced a plastic footstool. This was the thoughtful, generous guy Kara had fallen in love with all those years ago. And if she wasn't careful, the past just might repeat itself.

"Step up here," he said, holding out his hand to assist Samantha. "Better?"

"Yeah. Thanks." She surveyed the mound of colorful stuffed animals. "I want that purple monkey."

"Put your quarter in and give it a shot."

Kara swallowed back the emotional lump in her throat. No man had ever taken such an interest in her daughter. Who'd have guessed Jason's Scrooge-like heart could be thawed out by a little girl? Miracles really did happen.

With Samantha occupied, Jason approached Kara. "She's having a lot of fun, isn't she?"

Funny that he'd need her confirmation when the glowing smile and rosy cheeks on her daughter spoke volumes more than Kara could ever vocalize. "Yes, she is. Thank you for this. Since I started working overtime to prepare for the new management, there hasn't been any time to get out and have fun."

"Jason, aren't you going to play, too?" Samantha whined. "I keep droppin' the monkey."

"I'll be right there." He turned back to Kara. "Do you want to help her?"

"She wants you. But first, what file can't you find?"

He paused as though he didn't have a clue what she was referring to, then a light of recognition sparked in his eyes. "The order for the parts for the lift on the double-diamond slope. They were supposed to be here yesterday. Without a functioning lift this grand reopening is going to be a grand disaster."

He wanted an order form? On a Saturday afternoon? There was nothing he could do about the missing order before Monday morning. What had he been thinking when he'd called her? Of course, he hadn't been thinking. She'd never seen anyone work harder than Jason. He expected his employees to give their all, which she didn't mind during the week, but the weekend was for family—something he knew nothing about.

She glanced up to find he'd moved to the claw machine. His hand worked the joystick and his lips pressed into a firm line as he concentrated on grabbing the toy. Her annoyance faded. This was the most enjoyment she and her daughter had had in a long time.

"I'll be right back," Kara called out. Neither seemed interested, as the monkey hung precariously from the metal claw.

She moved swiftly to the business offices, located the purchase order and placed it front and center on Jason's cluttered desk. Her hand hovered as she debated whether to see if the letter from his father was still there. What would it hurt?

It took a little bit of searching, but eventually she located it beneath a mountain of paperwork. Still unopened. She frowned as she placed it conveniently beneath the folder Jason had requested. He would read his father's words, eventually. Hope burned strong and bright in her heart.

Jason's cheeks grew sore from smiling.

He shook his head in disbelief. Samantha hit the left bumper on the vintage pinball machine. How could this pint-size little girl clutching a purple monkey bring him such happiness?

He regretted each and every minute he'd missed of her life, but it would be different from here on out. As soon as he proved to Kara that he could keep the monster side of him at bay, and show her that he wasn't going anywhere ever again, there'd be a lot more moments like this. He'd make sure of it.

Kara strolled back into the game room. Even though she wasn't wearing anything stylish, he thought she looked positively radiant. A pastel pink sweater stretched across her chest, snuggling against her feminine curves. His mouth grew dry. And her low-slung jeans clung to her rounded hips. If he were to envision the perfect snow bunny, it'd definitely be her.

"I can see by the new stuffed animal in Samantha's arms that you two beat the claw machine."

He swallowed. "It took a few quarters but we got it."

"Samantha looks happy. Has she tried every game yet?"

"Almost." As far as he was concerned, she didn't have to leave anytime soon.

"By the way, I found the order form and left it on your desk. But the supplier won't be open until first thing Monday morning."

"Thanks. I'll straighten it out then."

"We should get going," she said. "I'm sure you've got more important things to do."

"Stay just a little longer." He reached for her hand. His thumb stroked her soft skin. "You haven't told me what you think of the remodel."

He honestly didn't care what they discussed. In that moment, he was at peace, and dare he say it, happy. Peace and happiness had eluded him for years, and he'd give almost anything for it to last just a little longer.

"You've done a marvelous job breathing new life into this place," Kara said, letting her hand rest in his. "The color scheme is cheerful and relaxing. It's a very inviting atmosphere. A great escape from the realities of life."

"Really? That's the impression you get?"

"Isn't that the impression you want to give? Don't people come to resorts to escape the pressures of their everyday lives? Aren't they here to have fun, unwind, and for some, to recapture their youth?"

Their gazes met and locked. The guarded walls around

his heart cracked. The glow of Kara's smile filtered through the crevices and warmed him. He couldn't help wondering if she was moved by the host of memories contained within the newly painted walls.

"Do you remember how we used to be?" he asked, his voice husky with reawakened desires.

A flicker of emotion reflected in her eyes. His breathing hitched as he anticipated her next words.

"I remember. How could I ever forget?"

He touched her cheek. His fingers slid down to her neck, where her rapid heartbeat pulsed beneath his fingertips. She wanted him. And he most definitely wanted her. His head lowered.

"Hey, guys," Samantha called out. "I'm outta quarters."

Jason snapped to attention. How in the world could he have let himself become so distracted that he'd forgotten their daughter was just across the room? He still had a lot to learn about being a dad.

Not willing to lose ground with Kara, he laced his fingers with hers. It felt so natural. And he noticed she didn't pull away. The pieces of his life were at last falling into place.

He glanced down at her. "Shall we go see what our daughter wants?"

The smile slipped from Kara's tempting lips and her hand withdrew from his. In that moment, he realized he'd misspoken. The shocked look on her face dug at him. How long did she intend to keep up this little charade, when they both knew the truth?

"Don't look at me like I said the unforgivable. I'm sorry I let that comment slip about her being our daughter." He paused, not exactly comfortable with apologizing. "Actually, I'm not sorry. I know you denied she's mine because you don't trust me, but it's time we were honest with ourselves and her."

"No!" Kara's eyes were round with worry. She glanced over at Samantha. He followed her gaze, finding their daughter preoccupied with another pinball machine. Kara lowered her voice. "I wish I could tell you what you want to hear, but...but I can't. She's not yours."

He stepped back, crossing his arms over his chest. "That can't be. She has my eyes. She's the right age. And I haven't seen any signs of another man in your life."

"He's not in our life." Kara's eyes shimmered. "You don't know how many times I've wished she was yours... but her birthday is in November. You left town in December. It's simply not possible."

"You'd say anything to protect her, but I swear I'll never do anything to hurt her." He whispered the words past the jagged lump in his throat. "Please tell me she's mine."

Kara visibly swallowed. "I can't lie to you. And I won't lie to my daughter. You both deserve better. I swear she's not yours."

The thought of Samantha being another man's daughter hit him square in the gut. He didn't want to believe Kara. But the anguished look on her face drove home the bitter truth.

This wasn't right. This wasn't supposed to happen. They were finally reunited and...and he'd allowed himself to care about them. He'd been so close to having something he'd never thought possible—his own family. Now, he didn't know what to do with the tangled ball of disappointment and longing churning in his gut.

"Guys, you said you'd play with me," Samantha whined, putting an end to this painful exchange.

"One game," Kara said, glancing over at him, and he nodded. "Then we have to go home."

* * *

The next day, Kara's phone rang. Jason's deep voice echoed over the line, making her insides quiver with excitement. For a moment she forgot she had just filled her kitchen sink with hot sudsy water to wash up the lunch dishes.

"Kara, are you there?"

The air whooshed from her lungs. "Yes. Sorry. I was distracted."

"I didn't mean to bother you. I wanted to check to see if it'd be all right if I stopped by your house this evening?"

Her pulse kicked up a notch. After yesterday, she didn't think he'd want anything more to do with her. "Um...sure."

"I found Bubbles this morning and thought Samantha would be lost without him."

He only wanted to return the bear? Disappointment pulsed through Kara. She tried to assure herself that this distance between them was best for all concerned, but it brought her absolutely no comfort.

She twisted a strand of hair around her finger. "I searched everywhere for him last night."

"You should have called me. I would have checked around here for you. As it was, I came across him in the lunch room when I was raiding the snack machine."

"You're working today, too?" she asked, astonished at his dedication and worried that he might be pushing himself too hard.

"We're making a staggering number of changes and I want to oversee everything. I need to make sure the alterations are having the effect we anticipated."

"Do you need help?" She honestly didn't have time to spare, given the scarves she had to finish knitting for Christmas presents, and more cookies to bake for the nursing home. But she felt a certain responsibility to the business that had kept a roof over her head. Plus she didn't like the idea of Jason hiding away in the empty resort, wolfing down some unhealthy lunch from a snack machine.

"I've got it under control." His voice was cold and distant.

"Samantha will be thrilled to have Bubbles back. You'll be her hero. Not that you aren't already, after that wonderful day we had and you winning her the purple monkey."

"It's nothing I wouldn't have done for any of the other employees and their families."

Kara's heart sank. She knew he wouldn't have gone to those lengths for just anyone. He'd obviously been more hurt by the news that Samantha wasn't his daughter than he'd let on. Kara felt absolutely awful. She hadn't intended to upset him. In fact, that was the last thing she'd ever want to do.

"I'll drop Bubbles off at six."

Her heart thump-thumped at the thought of seeing him again.

He'd already hung up by the time she realized he'd be there at dinnertime. Samantha would insist he join them. How would Jason act around her daughter now that he'd accepted the truth? He was a man who had trouble forgiving people, but would he really punish an innocent little girl? Kara would like to think not, but she couldn't dismiss how he refused to make amends with his dying father.

This was her fault. She'd let him into their lives when she knew better. From here on out, she'd have to be more careful when it came to dealing with him. She'd need to keep her emotions at bay—hold him at arm's length.

CHAPTER TWELVE

HE WAS LATE.

Jason lightened his foot on the SUV's accelerator. The last thing he needed was to get pulled over for speeding, and waste more time. His delay couldn't be helped. When the mechanics he was paying double time to work around the clock let him know the double-diamond lift had experienced another significant setback, he'd dropped everything to go investigate.

With the grand reopening only twelve days away, his priority had to be the resort, but tonight was different. He knew how much the bear meant to Samantha, and he couldn't stand for her to be needlessly upset. It wasn't so long ago that he'd been a child himself. He could remember what it was like to want something so badly and to have to wait. Each second seemed like a minute. Each minute dragged on for an hour. Too bad he hadn't found the little guy sooner.

The fact that Samantha wasn't his—that she belonged to another man—still had him spinning in circles. When he allowed himself to think about it, the realization socked him in the chest, making each breath painful. He should just cut his losses and move on. That was exactly what any sane man would do.

But no one had ever claimed Jason was particularly

wise. And he was already in this thing clear up to his neck. The question was, where did he want this thing with Kara to go?

And the trickier question: Could he accept Samantha without any prejudice?

The little girl was a constant reminder of how he'd messed things up with Kara. And evidence of how quickly she'd gotten over him and moved on. His fingers tightened on the steering wheel. The thought of Kara in another man's arms—a man who'd deserted her and their baby—made him furious. Jason was thankful he'd been too shocked the other night to even think of asking for the man's name. At this particular juncture, with disappointment and frustration pumping through his veins, he didn't want to do anything stupid.

His actions had already cost him a buddy's life. Jason didn't want to make things even worse for Kara and her little girl. The man might be a waste of space, but he was Samantha's father and somehow Jason had to learn to respect that fact.

He glanced at the clock. Twenty minutes after six. Being tardy would not help his already tense relationship with Kara. And until he knew what he wanted, he didn't wish to make things worse. He could only hope she hadn't noticed the time.... He shook his head. His luck wasn't that good. With her lack of faith in him, she'd probably think he'd forgotten and wasn't going to show.

When he pulled into her driveway, he noticed how she'd decorated the edges of her roof with those white icicle lights. A glowing snowman stood front and center in the yard. And in the picture window he caught sight of the Christmas tree he'd brought them, now lit up with colored lights.

The tension in his shoulders and neck uncoiled. A smile

pulled at his lips. Maybe the decorations weren't so bad. Kara certainly was filled with holiday spirit. He'd swear she was one part Santa's elf and the other part Christmas angel.

He pushed the SUV door open and eased out before leaning back inside to grab the pink bear from the seat. He glanced down at Bubbles. For a second, he envied the stuffed animal. He wondered what it'd be like to be so loved by that sweet girl.

His knee throbbed from the cold, but he refused to let it slow his pace up the walk. He'd just raised his hand to knock on the bright blue door adorned with a wreath of holly berries when Samantha pulled it open.

She stood there in a red-and-white sweatshirt with criss-crossed candy canes on the front. "Hi." Her gaze lowered to his hand. "Bubbles!"

He held out the stuffed animal to her. She immediately scooped it up into her arms and gave it a great big hug as if they'd been separated for years. He watched in wonder at the little girl's abundance of love. How could her father walk away from her?

Jason choked down a lump of emotion. "I thought you might be missing him."

Samantha held the bear at arm's length. "Shame on you, Bubbles. You shouldn't have stayed at the resort all night by yourself."

"Hi," Kara said, making her presence known. "I thought you'd changed your mind about coming over."

"I'm sorry I'm late." He opened his mouth to say more, but then closed it. He was certain telling her he'd gotten caught up in his work wouldn't warm up her demeanor.

"Step inside and close the door. It's cold out there."

Not exactly an invitation to stay, but she hadn't told

him to leave, either. Deciding to take his chances, he did as she suggested.

Strains of "Have a Holly Jolly Christmas" played in the background. The fact he even recognized the song surprised him, but it helped that the singers repeated it over and over. He didn't foresee a jolly Christmas in his future, and for the first time since he was a kid, it niggled at him.

The scent of apples, cinnamon and various other spices lingered in the air. He inhaled again, remembering how his grandmother's house had often smelled like this when she had pies in the oven.

"Were you baking?" he asked.

"No. It's warmed cider."

So much for making small talk. By the frown on Kara's face, he was wasting his time. "I should go."

"You can't," Samantha interjected. "Mommy made us wait to eat till you got here."

"Samantha, hush." Kara's face filled with color.

She'd made him dinner? The words warmed a spot in his chest that sent heat spreading through his body. It'd been a long time since someone went to any bother for him.

"It's true." Samantha continued as though her mom hadn't spoken a word. "She said you need somethin' 'sides candy to eat."

Jason chuckled. Samantha's spunk was so much like her mother's. He noticed Kara make a hasty retreat into the kitchen. Her embarrassment only made the moment that much more touching.

"Your mother is very wise. You should listen to her."

After he shed his coat and made sure the soles of his boots were dry, Samantha slid her little hand in his. His heart grew three sizes in that moment. Maybe he'd been wrong all those years—maybe someday he could be a good father. But could he be a parent to another man's child?

Could he set aside the jealousy of knowing Kara had replaced him so quickly, so easily?

Samantha gave his hand a tug, dragging him back to the present. "Come on."

The kitchen was small, but warm and inviting. He took a moment to absorb his surroundings, noticing how Kara had painted the room a sunny yellow, giving it a pleasant, uplifting feel. Sunflowers adorned the curtains, baskets lined the tops of the light oak cabinets and a small arrangement of silk sunflowers filled a blue milk pitcher in the center of the table. Kara certainly had a flair for decorating.

"Are you sure this isn't an imposition?" he asked.

"Samantha's right. We have plenty of spaghetti and meatballs. Besides, you do need to eat a real meal if you keep pushing yourself so hard to make this reopening a success." Kara drained the noodles. "Have a seat."

He pulled out a chair at the table and sat down. He looked up as Kara bent over to rummage through a drawer, and he noticed an electric candle burning in the window above the sink. It was like a beacon, calling him home.

"Mommy, Mommy, can I have more cider?" Samantha held out an empty cup, her bottom lip protruding in a look designed to arouse sympathy.

Jason would have caved faster than a house of cards in a category 5 hurricane. So when he heard Kara tell her that she'd had enough for the evening, he was impressed by such fortitude. Before he became a parent, he had much to learn.

"Go wash up," Kara said. "It's time to eat."

"Okay." Samantha scampered away.

Soon they were all seated around the table. The more he smiled and laughed at Samantha's childlike antics, the more Kara loosened up. Jason was captivated by the easy banter and the abundance of smiles. Kara had really made a happy home for her little girl. Samantha chattered on about everything she'd asked Santa for, while he made mental notes of the unfamiliar toys so he could scout around for them. For the first time in forever, he was starting to look forward to Christmas.

But the second thing he noticed that evening struck him most profoundly. They didn't treat him like an outsider. They included him in their talk, as if he was one of them. As if he was family.

After two heaping helpings, Jason pushed aside his wiped-clean plate. Utterly stuffed, he couldn't remember a meal he'd enjoyed so much, even though he'd barely tasted the food. He was too caught up by the company. Time flew by and before he knew it, he'd helped Kara wash up the dinner dishes, while Samantha watched a holiday movie. He didn't want to leave, but he also didn't want to overstay his welcome.

After he said good-night to Samantha, Kara walked him to the door.

"Thanks for staying for dinner," she said. "Samantha really enjoyed your company. Sorry about her going on and on about her Christmas list. She gets a bit wound up."

"I didn't mind at all. It was actually very helpful. Otherwise I wouldn't have a clue what to buy her for Christmas."

Kara slipped outside and closed the door. "Don't feel obligated. Santa will take good care of her."

"I'm sure he will," he said, stepping closer. His gaze zeroed in on Kara's lips, thinking they presented him with an irresistible temptation. "I would just like to do something special for both of you."

His head lowered and he pressed his lips to her warm ones, feeling the slightest tremble in her. Not wanting to push his luck, he pulled away. He caught the softest sigh from Kara. She wasn't as immune to him as she'd like to think.

He cleared his throat. "Thank you for tonight."

She pressed a hand to her lips and glanced up at him. Their gazes held for a moment before her hand lowered. "We're baking cookies on Wednesday after work and making up trays of them to take to the care home. If you aren't busy you could help."

Things weren't running as smoothly at the resort as he'd like, but he'd work day and night if it meant spending another evening in this gingerbread house with these two lovely ladies.

"Count me in."

At last, Wednesday arrived. Jason glanced down at the bag of goodies on his office desk. He'd run out at lunchtime to buy them for tonight's cookie-baking endeavor. The jaunt to the mall had taken him most of the afternoon, but it'd been worth it.

"Here's the report on the latest quotes we have from alternative vendors." Kara set the spreadsheet on his desk and gazed at him. "So what put the cat-who-ate-the-canary look on your face?"

He cleared his throat, trying not to smile, but found it to be a challenge. "I don't know what you mean."

Her brows arched. "Okay, well, these are the latest figures we received. There's only one vendor, Biggest Wholesales, who's beating out Pappy Salvatore's prices."

"Good. I'll have a look." Jason noticed the frown on her face. "You know it's best for the Summit."

"It's not that. It's Biggest Wholesales. I've heard some things about them."

If he was thinking of switching their food services to another supplier, he was smart enough to know he had to be concerned about more than just the bottom line. Sometimes the cheapest wasn't always the best.

"What have you heard about them?"

"That's just it, I can't remember. But it's chewing at the back of my mind. I'm sure it'll come to me eventually."

"Let me know when you recall. And maybe you could do some checking around about them."

She stepped toward the door and pushed it closed before turning back to face him. "Are you still coming over this evening?"

"Wouldn't miss it for the world. I have a date with a cutie to keep—make that two of them." When Kara smiled, he couldn't hold back a grin of his own. "I'll stop by your desk when I finish up here."

"My desk—for what?"

"I thought we could leave together, as long as you don't mind stopping for dinner." He really liked the thought of ending the workday and going home with Kara. It seemed natural, something he could get used to.

"But we can't," she said, a look of horror on her face. "What would people think?"

He shrugged. "Does it matter what they think?"

The fact he'd been able to utter those words and truly mean them stunned him. For so many years he'd stayed away from here, worried about what people would think of him. But now things were changing—he was changing. With Kara and Samantha in his life, he realized he was more than just the genetics that created him—he was a man with wants and needs that surpassed any gossip.

"I care what my coworkers think." Kara tilted up her chin. "They'll start saying we're a couple. I don't want that."

Jason's chest tightened. "You don't want what? Us to be a couple? Or for people to talk about us?"

"I...I don't know. Both I guess." But her gaze didn't meet his. "We still have unresolved issues."

He hadn't forgotten. He just needed a little more time before he tested the ultimate strength of their relationship. And his invitation for Christmas-cookie detail was going to help his cause.

"What are you smiling about?"

"Uh, nothing. Don't worry. I'll be discreet when I leave in about..." he glanced down at the work on his desk "...about a half hour. Do you have a preference for dinner?"

She shook her head. "But that isn't necessary. I can throw something together."

"You'll have your hands full, baking. Dinner is the least I can do."

Just as promised, a half hour later, not caring that he hadn't responded to the last five emails in his in-box, Jason shut down his computer and promised himself that he'd be in early the next morning to deal with them.

On the way to Kara's house, he made a detour to pick up an assortment of sandwiches and side orders from a little mom-and-pop shop. The restaurant been around since he was a kid, and he loved the homemade food.

Armed with food and gifts, he pulled into Kara's driveway, his heart tap-dancing in his chest. Jason didn't know much about making Christmas cookies, so he felt a bit out of his element, but he swallowed hard and climbed out of the SUV. He'd just made it to the sidewalk when the front door swung open and Samantha appeared. With the door left wide-open and a toothy grin on her sweet face, she ran up to him.

"You came! I knew you would," she said excitedly.

"You doubted my word?"

She shook her head, swishing her brown ponytail back

and forth. "Mommy said you might not come. I told her you would."

So Kara still didn't trust him, not even to keep his promise for an evening of Christmas-cookie baking. Seemed tonight he'd have to make certain she knew he intended to stick around. The thought of making it permanent floated into his mind, but he still had his doubts about taking on the role of father.

What would Samantha call him? Jason? Daddy? Did he even want her calling him Daddy? After all, he didn't know much about being a good parent. The throbbing of an ensuing headache had him rubbing his forehead. Now wasn't the time to contemplate "forever."

"Jason, hurry." Samantha grabbed his free hand and started to pull him toward the kitchen. "We have to make the cookies."

"Not so fast," Kara said from the doorway. "We're going to eat first."

"Ah, do we gotta? Jason, are you hungry?"

He might not know much about kids, but only a fool would insinuate himself between mother and daughter—and he wasn't that foolish. "We better listen to your mother. She knows what's best."

He glanced up to catch a look of approval on Kara's face. He schooled his features to hold back a grin, but his chest puffed up just a little. Score one point for him tonight. If only he could keep it up the rest of the evening, he'd definitely be in Kara's good graces, and those kisses would become reality.

Kara ushered them out of the cold and in no time they were working their way through a chicken Parmesan sub, an Italian sub and a meatball sub. Seemed as though he'd found something each of them would eat. He sighed in relief. They were off to a very good start.

With everyone's stomach filled, he pulled out his bag of goodies. He handed a ruffled, white apron to Kara that read: Don't Mess with This Cook, I Carry a Rolling Pin... and I Know How to Use It.

She laughed. "And let that be a warning to both of you."

"Do I get one, too?" Samantha stretched her neck, trying to peer in the bag.

"Hmm...let me see." He took his time, as though unable to find anything.

"You forgot me?" she asked, sounding dejected.

Then he pulled out a smaller pink apron that read: Professional Taste Tester. It also had the picture of a chocolate chip cookie with a big bite taken out of it.

"I love it!" Samantha moved over and threw her arms around his neck. "Thank you."

Jason's heart thumped hard against his chest as he tenderly hugged her back. In that moment, the thought of forever got just a little less scary.

"You're quite welcome."

And last but not least, he dumped the bag on the table and a large assortment of cookie cutters spilled out. "I bought every single kind they had in the store. I can take them back if you don't want them."

The girls oohed and aahed over the various shapes, from Christmas trees to reindeer. He smiled broadly. He thoroughly enjoyed making them happy. Once the new cookie cutters were scrubbed up, they set to work making cookies for trays to deliver to the care home where Jason's father was staying. Jason tried to block out the image of his once strong dad, now sick and needy. Uneasiness laced with guilt churned in his gut. No. He refused to let that man steal this wonderful evening from him—he'd already missed so much....

Kara was in charge of rolling out the already made and

chilled cookie dough, as well as working the oven. That left him and Samantha to do the decorating. Bowls of various colors of icing lined the table. In addition, there were red, green and white sprinkles of varying shapes and sizes. Kara certainly seemed to think of everything.

"What's that?" he asked, gesturing to the cookie Samantha was about to decorate. "A pony?"

She giggled. "Mommy, he doesn't know what a reindeer looks like."

"He doesn't. Well, I guess you'll just have to teach him these things."

"See? These are the antlers." Samantha grew serious and pointed to the cookie. "And if I put this red ball on its nose, then it's Rudolph."

Every time the child smiled it was like warm sunbeams hitting Jason's chest. He couldn't resist a bit more teasing. "I don't know. Still looks like a pony with a bad cold."

The sweet chimes of Samantha's laughter pealed through the kitchen. Even Kara was smiling and shaking her head. He had no idea until that moment how rewarding he found the sound of laughter from these two special ladies. So why was he hesitant to lay the whole truth on the line with Kara? Why couldn't he take the next step necessary to ensure he didn't lose her, now that he'd broken through her stony barrier?

"What's that?" Samantha scrunched up her button nose and pointed at the cookie he was currently smearing icing on.

"It's Santa Claus."

She shook her head. "Santa doesn't wear green."

He glanced down and realized his thoughts had meandered, and he'd accidentally grabbed the bowl of green icing. "Well, my Santa wants to be different."

"But Santa can't be green."

"He can't, huh?" Without thinking about the trouble he'd be in with Kara, he dipped his finger in the green icing and dabbed his fingertip on Samantha's nose.

Her mouth gaped open. Her eyes rounded with surprise. It took only a second for the shock to subside. She dunked her finger in the same bowl and reached out, giving him a matching green nose. They both started to laugh.

"What are you two up to?" Kara turned and he braced himself for a stern lecture. "You're supposed to decorate the cookies, not each other." With a smile tugging at her very kissable lips, she turned to check the oven. It appeared he and Samantha weren't the only ones enjoying this evening.

By eleven o'clock, Samantha was asleep in bed and they had just finished wrapping the cookie trays. Kara walked him to the door. "Thank you for all the help. We couldn't have gotten so much done tonight without you."

"I'm glad I could help. Samantha is a great kid. And her mother isn't so bad, either." Thoughts of kissing her bombarded his mind.

"She isn't, huh?" Kara smiled up at him and that was all the encouragement he needed.

He pulled her to him. With their lips a hair apart, he paused. When she didn't move, he brushed his mouth over hers. She tasted sugary and delectable. It surprised him when she didn't resist his advances. In fact, she sidled up against him, chest to chest, lip to lip. He moaned. This was the sweetest torture he'd ever experienced. He'd been wrong—kissing Kara wasn't enough to appease his mounting desires. In fact, it just made him want her even more.

"Let's go back inside," he murmured.

Kara's hands pressed against his chest. She tilted up her chin. "Are you ready to talk about the past?"

Part of him was willing to say anything just so this

moment wouldn't end. It'd been so many years since he'd made love to her…but tonight wasn't the right time.

If he was to stay here and make love to her, it would be tantamount to declaring that he was ready to spend forever with her, and he just wasn't there yet. Kara and Samantha were a package deal, and until he was ready for all that it entailed, he'd be left with nothing but sweet kisses at the door.

"I should go."

"You know you could stop by tomorrow and we could deliver the cookie trays to the care home—"

"I can't." He just couldn't go, knowing his father was there. Not even for Kara. "I still have a ton of stuff to do before the resort's grand reopening."

Her smile faltered. "I understand."

"But I'd like a rain check. How about Friday I take you and Samantha out to see a holiday movie?"

The smile came back and lit up her eyes. "You have yourself a date."

CHAPTER THIRTEEN

FRIDAY EVENING, KARA loosened her seat belt, allowing her to twist around in the passenger seat of Jason's SUV to check on Samantha. The little girl's head had lolled to the side and her eyes were closed. The hint of a smile still pulled at her lips, while bits of buttered popcorn dotted her chin.

It had been quite an evening, with dinner out followed by an animated Christmas movie. In fact, the whole week had left Kara breathless, from her phone interview for a promising junior management position in Ohio, to letting her guard down with Jason and remembering what a good friend he could be.

She tried telling herself that with things improving with him, she wouldn't lose her job. But she couldn't hang her and her daughter's future on wishful thinking. Not only hadn't he mentioned the possibility of her staying on at the Summit, but they still had so much left unsaid between them.

She'd put off talking to him about what had happened all those years ago, thinking that once he understood he wasn't Samantha's father, he wouldn't be back. But he'd surprised her. He'd been so thoughtful, so attentive. Now that this thing between them no longer seemed so casual, she had to tell him the whole story. Her insides shivered with anxiety.

Although it really worried her that Jason was unwilling to forgive his father. Would he be as unforgiving with her when she explained the circumstances of Samantha's birth? The soda and popcorn she'd had at the theater suddenly didn't sit so well in her stomach.

At her house, Jason carried Samantha inside.

"I've got it from here," Kara said, taking hold of her daughter.

His searching gaze went from her to Samantha and back. "I should get going—"

"No." She wanted to get this talk over with, now that she'd finally worked up the nerve. "Stay, please—unless you have someplace to be."

He shook his head.

"Good. You can wait in the living room while I tuck this little one into bed. I'll be right back."

"But Mommy, I'm awake."

Kara let her stand on her own, but made sure to grab her hand, not wanting her to scamper away. "You're still going to bed. It's way past your bedtime."

"Aw, Mom."

"No 'aw, Mom' with me. Scoot."

Samantha yawned and headed to her room. The lack of protest told Kara her daughter was beyond exhausted. She'd be asleep in no time. Once they got her teeth brushed, her clothes changed and the covers turned down, Samantha begged for a bedtime story. Kara firmly believed reading to children should be a priority, but she had really hoped Samantha would be too tired to notice tonight.

"Read me 'The Night Before Christmas.'" Samantha sent her a pleading look.

"But sweetie, Jason is waiting for me." Kara pulled the pink comforter up and tucked it under her daughter's arms.

"He can read to me."

What? Jason reading to her daughter? No, not tonight. Before they got any closer, Kara had to talk to him—had to set things straight.

"Jason! Jason!"

"Samantha Jean, quit screaming," Kara said in a stern but hushed voice.

In the next moment, she heard hurried footsteps in the hallway.

"Is something wrong?" He peered into the room.

"Will you read me a story?" Samantha held up the Christmas storybook while clutching Bubbles with her other arm. "This is my favorite."

He looked at Kara. At this point, she supposed making a fuss would only cause more problems. She nodded her consent. She took a seat at the foot of the twin bed while he approached Samantha and accepted the book.

"Sit by Mommy," her daughter insisted.

His glance met Kara's and she nodded again. She scooted over and he eased down beside her. His thigh brushed hers. The heat of his body permeated her jeans, warming her through and through.

He opened the book and cleared his throat. Samantha settled back on her pillow as his lyrical voice read each line with intensity. Kara closed her eyes and listened. His voice wrapped around her with its warm tones, like a plush blanket being draped around her shoulders.

The coziness of the situation swept over her. She longed for it to continue forever. *Don't get too comfortable.* She forced her eyes open. Tonight might be the last time they saw Jason. If he couldn't handle the truth behind Samantha's birth, he'd bolt—like last time.

When Jason flipped to the last page, Samantha let out a great big yawn. Kara peered around him and witnessed her daughter's struggle to keep her eyes open.

"The end." He closed the book. "Time to go to sleep."

Kara saw this as the perfect opportunity to put a little distance between them. She slid off the bed and took the book from him.

"Aw, one more, please," Samantha whined, but without her usual enthusiasm.

Another yawn escaped her lips and Jason chuckled. "Maybe another time."

Kara replaced the book in her daughter's abundant collection and turned to find Jason standing in the doorway, waiting for her.

She straightened the covers once more and hoped he didn't notice the slight tremble in her hands. It was time for the "talk." Time to clear the air. Suddenly it no longer seemed like such a good idea. Like her daughter, she enjoyed Jason's company—but she'd already delayed telling him for way too long.

After a kiss and an "I love you," she flicked off the light. She turned and caught the warmth glowing in Jason's eyes. Reading a story to Samantha had gotten to him, too. Kara's fate was sealed, but she had to make sure he understood about this family he was insinuating himself into. This time around she didn't want secrets or omissions to come between them.

She followed him to the living room. When he stopped to turn on the tree lights, she nearly ran into him.

He turned to her and stroked his thumb down her cheek. "Thank you for sharing the evening with me. You have no idea how much it meant to me."

Her mouth went dry and she swallowed hard. "Samantha...she likes you, too. A lot."

His finger traced Kara's jaw. Her heart pounded in a most irregular rhythm. "I like her, too." He stepped closer. "And I really, really like her mother."

Drawn into this enchanting spell, she heard herself utter, "And her mother really, really likes you."

In the soft glow of the Christmas tree, her gaze locked with his. Common sense warred with her body's desires. With her exhausted daughter tucked in bed, her plans for talking began to give way to the crazy sensations Jason evoked in her. Why ruin such an enchanting evening?

His hand slid to the back of her neck as his head lowered. His lips gently brushed hers, but the restrained eagerness was undeniable. She wanted him more than she'd thought possible. And his hungry kisses were so much better than her dreams.

Snuggling closer to him, she trailed her hands behind his neck. Her soft curves pressed to his rock-hard body and a moan escaped her lips.

Suddenly, Jason grabbed hold of her shoulders and held her at arm's length. In a passionate haze, she sent him a baffled look. He wanted her as much as she wanted him, so what was the problem?

His breathing was heavy. "Remember how I owe you an explanation about my leaving?" When she nodded, he continued, "I think you better hear it now...before we go any further."

The seriousness in his voice and the worry in his eyes sent an arrow of alarm piercing her chest. She wanted to talk to him, too, but something told her that if he didn't get this off his chest now, he might never do it.

Jason drew an unsteady breath. He'd been thinking about this talk all week. And he didn't see where he had much choice. Kara deserved to know what kind of man she was getting involved with before they took this relationship to the next level—something he'd come to desire with all of his being.

But first, he had to give Kara the facts—every last horrid one. He knew he was kidding himself. She would despise him once she knew everything, and toss him to the curb. Still, since he'd been spending time with her, he was starting to believe in miracles. He had to at least take the chance, even if it was a long shot.

Kara perched on the edge of the couch and looked at him expectantly. "It's okay. Whatever you have to say, we'll work through it."

He really wished he could believe her. With his shoulders pulled back, he said, "Remember the fight between me and my father?" She nodded and he went on. "There was more to that argument than I told you.... My father was drunk, and livid that I was leaving him to deal with the resort on his own."

She didn't interrupt, even though part of Jason wished that she would. Facing combat and his own mortality had been easier than what he was about to do.

He paced the floor, searching for the exact words. When he found them, he stopped in front of her. "He told me no son of his would abandon him like I was about to do. He yelled that I was not his son...that I never had been and never would be." Jason's voice caught and he swallowed hard. "He said I was the spawn of a monster."

Kara pressed a hand to her chest as her eyes shimmered. "How horrible."

Jason's head hung low. "There's more. He told me no woman would ever accept me as a husband, much less want me for the father of her children."

He forced himself to stand ramrod straight, his shoulders rigid. He drew on the discipline hammered into him over the course of his military career. He would complete his mission.

"My mother was raped...just after my father met her." Jason ignored Kara's horrified gasp and kept going, or he'd never get it all out. "I was the consequence of her rape. My dad is not my biological father. Some unidentified monster brutally attacked my mother and..." His voice cracked and died in his throat.

In an instant Kara was standing in front of him. Her arms wrapped around his shaking body, pulling him close. The self-loathing and pain surfaced. In her embrace, he let himself feel everything he'd kept bottled up for years.

Kara held on to him, whispering words of comfort. He desperately wanted to believe it'd be all right, but it wouldn't be. It couldn't be. There was no way to rip that bastard's DNA from his body.

But now it was all out there. In the open. Kara knew he was damaged goods, inside and out. Jason pulled back and turned away to swipe his flannel shirtsleeve over his cheeks. Now it was time to face the moment he'd been dreading for years, seeing the repulsion in her beautiful eyes.

Suck it up, soldier. Facing her can't be avoided. Get it over with and move on.

He lifted his head, pulled his shoulders back and turned. With him towering above her five-foot frame, his gaze shot over her head.

Look down, soldier. One glance and it'll be done. The damage will be evident.

He forced his eyes down over her rumpled hair—hair he'd only moments ago been running his fingers through. The air became caught in his lungs. His gaze skimmed her forehead, passed her gathered brows and settled on her eyes, which held no hint of repulsion or disgust.

How could that be?

Kara stood there, returning his stare, as though he was the same man she'd always thought him to be.

"Say something," he ordered. He wanted this over. It'd already dragged on for too many years.

"I'm sorry..."

"Sorry? For what?" This wasn't making any sense.

"For your father being so horrible to you. Obviously you were never meant to know any of that. I'm sorry that in a drunken rage he'd say such hateful words."

Jason's gaze bored deeply into hers. He had to be missing something. "Do you understand what I said? My biological father is a rapist. A monster. And I have his blood pumping through my veins."

Empathy glistened in her eyes. "You're nothing like that man. You're the son of a very wonderful and loving woman."

He recalled his mother and her eternal smile. She had always been an upbeat person. His dad used to refer to her as a Mary Poppins wannabe. Always looking for the good in people. And she'd most definitely loved him.

"Can you honestly say you don't see me differently?"

"You had no control over your conception. And your mother loved you. She never held the past against you. So why should I? You're nothing like your biological father."

Jason took a hesitant step toward Kara, watching for any sign of fear in her. She didn't budge. Her steady gaze continued to hold his.

"You really believe I'm a good guy, inside and out?" His breathing stopped as he waited for her ultimate decision.

She stepped up to him. Her gaze never wavered as her hand reached out and caressed his cheek. "Absolutely."

With a smile, he swept her up into his arms and held her tight. With her feet suspended, he swung her round and round. In that instance, he knew what he wanted—what he'd always wanted.

"Jason, there's more we need to talk about."

CHAPTER FOURTEEN

KARA NEEDED TO get this over with as soon as possible. But before she could utter another word, Jason's lips were pressed to hers. She should pull away so they could finish talking, but after what he'd just told her, she didn't have the heart. He needed to know without a doubt that he was still worthy of love.

As the kiss intensified, desire flooded her body and short-circuited her best intentions. For so long now she'd been holding herself back from him, but no longer. She met his kiss with a burning heat of her own. Her arms wrapped around his trim waist, pulling him to her. His body was hard and solid against hers. She could barely believe this was happening, that he was holding her close again.

She'd dreamed of this moment for years, never believing it'd happen. Perhaps her fairy godmother was lurking in the shadows of the Christmas tree, waving her magic wand.

Jason sank down onto the couch, pulling Kara with him. His lips still teased and taunted hers. He tasted buttery, like the big tub of popcorn they'd shared at the theater. She traced his lips with her tongue, savoring the added saltiness.

His kisses trailed up her jaw to her earlobe, where he probed and tickled her, sending waves of shivers down her spine. His fingers played with the hem of her sweater, sneaking underneath to her bare waist. More goose bumps swept over her skin.

He stopped kissing his way down her neck long enough to say in a breathy voice, "We've wasted too many years apart. Marry me?"

"What?"

She yanked herself out of his embrace. He couldn't be serious, could he? Her breathing still rushed, Kara moved to the far end of the couch, trying to gather her composure. She straightened her clothes before running a hand over her hair.

"That's not exactly the reaction I was expecting."

"You're serious?" When he nodded, she continued, "You're not just getting caught up in the moment?"

A broad smile lit up his eyes. "It shouldn't be that big of a shock. After all, this isn't exactly the first time I asked you."

"But there's Samantha to consider."

"I know. But you said the biological father isn't part of her life. We'll just petition him to relinquish his rights." When Kara didn't say anything, Jason squeezed her hand. "Will the man give us problems?"

The backs of her eyes stung and Jason's image blurred. "Not like you're thinking. But there's something important you need to know."

Jason's gut churned as it used to do when he was out on patrol in hostile territory. Right now his internal radar system was telling him to duck for cover.

Until this moment, he didn't understand how much Samantha had come to mean to him in such a short period of time. Only a couple of months ago, if someone had told him he was a father, Jason would have been in total denial. Now, he'd no more be able to deny his connection to

Samantha than he could deny his love for her mother. He was more than ready to step up and accept a role in Samantha's life—in both of their lives.

"We'll deal with it together," he said, with all the confidence in the world. "What's the guy's name?"

He'd had long enough to come to terms with Samantha being another man's child. He didn't like it, but at least now he could think about it without losing his temper.

"You don't understand...."

"I know this is hard, but just tell me his name."

Kara's face paled to a sickly white, and her bottom lip trembled. "Before I do, there's something you have to understand."

The raw emotion in her eyes ripped at his gut. Jason stood on the cusp of losing the future he'd come to dream of—the future he desperately wanted. His arms dropped to his sides and his hands clenched into tight balls. *No, this can't be happening.*

"Don't do this." The hoarse words tore from his throat.

A single tear dropped onto her cheek. She swiped it away.

"I'm sorry, but you need to hear the truth—the whole truth."

He was a man who'd been on the front line of combat, who'd faced the enemy and never considered backing down. But at this moment, he wanted to make a hasty retreat. His eyes searched out the door, yet his feet wouldn't cooperate. Running from the truth wouldn't change it.

"Whatever you have to say, I can deal with it," he said. He had to.

He loved them.

The revelation stole the air from his lungs. He wanted Kara and Samantha more than he'd ever wanted anything in his life, including restoring his family's resort.

He couldn't let this thing between them end before it had barely begun.

Surely whatever she had to say couldn't be nearly as bad as what he'd told her. Kara was just overreacting. If she could forgive and accept him, then he could do the same for her now. After all, wasn't that the foundation of a good relationship—being able to forgive each other?

"When you left—" Kara's voice cracked. She started again. "After you'd ended our engagement with no explanation, I was devastated."

She pressed her lips together and swallowed. "For a couple of months I hid in my room. I cried my eyes out, trying to figure out what I'd done wrong to make you leave. I hoped and prayed you'd change your mind and come back for me." She paused, sucking in an unsteady breath. "I even asked your father for your phone number or address, any way I could get in contact with you."

"I didn't let him know where I was stationed. I even changed my last name, to make it impossible for him."

"Your father sounded so broken up when he told me he hadn't heard from you. I was totally lost and I hurt so badly. My friends rallied around me. They said I needed to forget you and get on with my life. They insisted I go out with them to a party. But they didn't understand. How could they understand what you and I shared?"

Her words were like a sledgehammer, beating at his chest. Jason opened his mouth, searching for an apology. Unable to find words to express the depth of his regret, he closed his mouth. She wouldn't even look at him now. Her hands were clenched in her lap. He wanted to reach out to her, but his nerve faltered.

Kara had never been a partier. She'd much rather be doing outdoor sports than watching her friends get drunk.

Something must have happened at that party. His chest struggled for each breath as he waited.

The silence flowed on. Her pink lips trembled. He'd always been drawn by them. Surprised he'd noticed them now of all times, he continued to stare. The temptation to smother them in a reassuring kiss and erase the rest of this doomed story overrode his apprehension. He stepped forward. Maybe just one kiss could change this perilous course they were on, but logic told him it'd only delay the inevitable. This journey had been preordained years ago.

He pulled his foot back and took a firm stance. "Kara, whatever it is, just say it."

"At the party," she said, giving him a hesitant glance, "I found a dark corner and stayed there. I regretted going, but since I hadn't driven, I had to wait for my ride. Anyway, someone decided I needed to loosen up, so they spiked my drink. When I realized what they'd done, I hesitated. I wasn't thinking clearly, but they convinced me that the drink would take the edge off the pain."

She paused, her eyes not meeting his. One by one, each muscle in his body grew rigid, while a sickening feeling brewed in his gut.

"I was young and stupid. I don't have any other excuse for what happened next. One drink led to another and another. You know I didn't drink, so it didn't take long before I was feeling good—too good." She rubbed her hands together. "Shaun showed up. Someone had called him when they found me wasted. He took care of me...."

Jason's uneasiness ramped up to an excruciating pain, as though he'd been riddled with bullets, left on the side of the road to die a slow, agonizing death. He wanted to be there for Kara, just as she'd been there for him, but this... this was different.

"I was wrong," he said, his voice hoarse. "I don't want to hear this."

He took a step toward the door.

"You have to listen." The eerie, high-pitched tone of her voice put a stop to his retreat. "You can't run away. Not this time."

His teeth ground together. His jaw flexed. The door was in sight, but the determination in Kara's voice told him that she'd follow him this time. He summoned up the courage he'd clung to on the battlefield, and turned.

Kara stood now. Her gaze held his with a fierce determination. "You weren't there to help me—but like always, Shaun filled in. He was your lifelong best friend. We had been the Three Musketeers. I trusted him almost as much as I trusted you."

She dashed away another tear. "He attempted to sober me up. He took me to his car, intent on getting me home."

Jason felt trapped on a runaway train. His life whizzed past him and there was no way to get off. He could only hold on, bracing for the devastating collision with the truth.

"On the way, I started to cry. Shaun pulled off on one of the desolate country roads. It was late and there wasn't any traffic. He tried to comfort me—"

"Stop." Jason's voice thundered in the room. He couldn't bear to hear any more.

The stabbing pain in his chest had him glancing down, searching for blood. He took a moment to gather his shattered illusions.

"Shaun is Samantha's father?" he asked, stumbling to latch on to this fact.

Kara nodded. Silent tears streamed down her cheeks. "Yes, he is."

The brown hair and blue eyes made sense now. Jason

and Shaun had been mistaken all their lives for brothers because of their similar looks.

Shaun. His best friend.

And Kara. Kara! The only woman he'd ever loved.

How was it possible his girl and his best friend had created a baby?

Pain spanned from temple to temple. This couldn't be happening. It had to be some kind of sick, twisted nightmare. Kara and Shaun never would have betrayed him like this.

Jason's breath came in short, rapid puffs.

"This can't be right. Kara, tell me it isn't true. Tell me you're saying this to get even with me for leaving you, and none of it is true."

"I can't."

"But how? Why?" The questions tumbled through his mind. "Did you always have a thing for him?"

"No. It was a mistake. A combination of too much to drink, a deep aching loneliness and hearing that Shaun loved me."

"He loved you?" Would the blows never stop coming?

"He admitted that he loved me, but up until then he hadn't been able to do anything about it, because of you...."

Jason ran a hand over his mouth, trying to remember some sign, some hint he'd missed. "I had no idea. How could I have been so blind?"

"You weren't the only one. I didn't know, either."

Her words didn't comfort him. Inside, he was mortally wounded, worse than when his father had smacked him in the face with the truth about his parentage. Jason had thought nothing could hurt worse than that, but he had been oh so wrong.

His vision grew blurry as he looked at Kara, no longer seeing the woman he loved, but rather the woman who'd betrayed him with his best friend, and stolen away the child he'd so wanted to be his little girl.

"Why?" His voice croaked out. "Why him?"

If it had been anyone else in the world, he'd have been able to deal with it. But not the one guy he'd considered a brother.

He had been wrong.

He couldn't forgive this.

If that made him less of a man, more a coward, so be it.

Shaun being the father of Kara's little girl made Jason's stomach lurch. The thought of his best friend and the woman he'd wanted to marry clinging to each other—Shaun's lips on hers—made the bile rush to the back of his mouth. Jason swallowed hard, pushing down the sickening thought.

When Kara opened her mouth to speak, he held up a hand to stop her. "Don't answer. I don't want to hear it. I can't believe you betrayed me with my best friend."

He couldn't stay here any longer. He was going to be ill.

In a few quick strides, barely noticing his injured knee's protest, he reached the door. His hand paused on the doorknob for just a moment. With a shake of his head to clear away the image of Kara in Shaun's arms, he yanked open the door and rushed into the frigid, dark night.

He'd never been so sick or so alone in his entire life.

CHAPTER FIFTEEN

HER PREDICTION HAD come true.

In this instance, Kara hated being right. But just as soon as Jason heard about her youthful mistake, he'd done exactly what she'd worried he would do...run. Of course, part of it was her fault. She'd waited too long to tell him about Shaun, and she hadn't prepared Jason at all. The whole situation couldn't have been handled any worse if she had tried.

Days had passed since that fateful night and Jason had completely avoided her, both in and out of the office. The devastation of him turning away like this made her anxious to find a new job. She'd let herself get in too deep with him. She'd let herself trust him, rely on him. In that instant, she realized how he'd sneaked past her best defenses.

She'd fallen in love with him.

She wasn't in love with the boy he used to be, the youth of her memories. No, she loved the man who'd saved her from a snowstorm and opened his home to her. The man who'd put her and Samantha's happiness above his own by taking time away from renovating the resort to decorate cookies and read a bedtime story.

What if Kara had told him she loved him? Would he have still walked out the door? Probably. He was unable to accept that she'd had a child with his best friend. The fact that their engagement had been officially dissolved at the time seemed completely immaterial to him.

But none of it mattered now. Whatever she'd thought they were building together was over and done. She had to focus on the new job she'd been offered in Ohio. It was in the next state, not that far from her family...or Jason, not that he'd ever visit them.

"Mommy, Mommy, look." Samantha hurried into the kitchen, holding a folded piece of red construction paper.

"What do you have there?"

"A Christmas card. See?" She held it two inches from Kara's face.

A step back allowed Kara's eyes to adjust and focus on the highly decorated paper. She noticed the green cutout of a Christmas tree and the shape of an angel at the top, reminiscent of the tree topper Jason had given them. Kara's bottom lip started to tremble at the thought of never having him drop by their house with little gifts for Samantha, or just to share a cup of hot cider and discuss his day with her.

"Do you like it?" Samantha asked, jarring Kara back to the present.

"It's lovely. You did a great job. But didn't we have a long talk about you not using the glue without asking?"

"Uh-huh. But it was a surprise."

"I understand, but don't do it again." She didn't have the heart to be more assertive. "You're quite the artist. I like how you used glitter to make the garland on the tree."

Her daughter ducked her head and shrugged. "I wanted it to look just like the tree Jason gave us."

Kara swallowed the lump that formed in her throat at the mention of his name. She had yet to tell Samantha that he wouldn't be coming to visit anymore. She knew it must be done sooner rather than later, but she also knew how attached her daughter was to him. How in the world was Kara supposed to break her heart?

"I have another picture I have to finish." Samantha turned and started out of the room.

"Wait," Kara called. "Don't you want me to put your card on the fridge?"

"Uh-uh. I made it for Jason."

Kara picked up the card and opened it. *"Merry Christmas, Jason. We miss you. XOXOXO Samantha."*

This was the moment she'd been dreading. Kara backed against the counter for support. "But honey, he's really busy with the resort. I don't know if he'll have time to visit again."

Samantha pressed her hands onto her hips. "Then you can give it to him at work."

"I'll try."

"You have to. Promise?"

Unable to deny helping her daughter with this gesture of kindness, Kara said, "I promise."

"Don't forget."

She wouldn't forget the card or Jason. Although she couldn't wait around for something that obviously wasn't meant to be. She'd been down this road before, but this time she knew she had to move on—to do what was best for her and Samantha. No matter how much it hurt.

Jason leaned back in his office chair late Thursday morning. He ran a hand through his hair, not caring if he messed it up. He didn't have any appointments, just a huge stack of mail, files to review and invoices to sign. He'd spent most of the week working on the lift on the double-diamond run. It'd taken three tries to get the right parts for such an old piece of equipment, but at last they'd done it. Things were finally on track for the grand reopening in two more days.

He'd spent months working toward this moment, and now that it was almost here, he should be excited, bursting with happiness. But without Kara and Samantha around to share his accomplishment, he was empty inside. They'd provided him with the driving force to overcome unforeseen problems and the strength to push through the long hours.

He picked up the phone to dial Kara's extension, but then slammed it back down. He had no idea what to say to her. Now that he'd had time to calm down and think everything through, he realized how poorly he'd reacted to her admission. What had he expected? For her to be a saint, and loyal, after the horrible way he'd ended their engagement and left town without even an explanation?

He had only himself to blame for everything that had happened. His heart pounded with unrelenting exasperation. How could he have handled this situation so horribly? Maybe he was more like the man who raised him than he'd ever imagined—unreliable. Jason found it strange how he found himself in such a similar position to the one his dad had been in years ago, both of them loving a woman who had a child by another man.

Jason's head hung low and shame washed over him at the way he'd failed while his father had succeeded. His dad had moved past the fact that Jason's mom was pregnant with another man's child. He'd married her and raised her baby as his own. Jason had to give the man credit; he'd tried to be a good father.

Jason shook his head. He hadn't even stepped up to the plate and welcomed the woman he loved and the daughter of his heart into his life. His hands clenched. Instead, he had lived up to Kara's worst nightmares and walked away from her. Again. She'd predicted that this was how he'd react when things got to be too much for him, and he'd proven her right.

There'd be no going back this time.

He ran his hands over his face. He'd really screwed up. Anger over his knee-jerk reaction balled up in his gut. After she'd forgiven him for leaving her, and accepted him, screwed-up genes and all, he'd overreacted to something she'd done years ago in a moment of confusion and pain.

A deep, guttural groan grew in the back of his throat. He'd ruined everything. His eyes closed as he tried to block it all out. Kara's image refused to fade away. The anguished look in her green eyes ripped at his gut. He clenched his hand and slammed it down on the desktop, making everything shake. The desk calendar fell over, a pen rolled off the edge and the stack of paperwork requiring his attention teetered over, spilling onto the floor.

With a frustrated sigh, he rose to his feet, surveying the mess of files and correspondence. He placed everything in a haphazard stack on his desk. Maybe some work would take his mind off the chaos he'd made of everyone's lives.

With a sigh, he sank down on his chair and tackled the very first item on the intimidating heap of paperwork. More than an hour later, he came across a plain white envelope. Jason looked at it and frowned when he found it still sealed. It was customary for his assistant to open everything and date stamp the correspondence. It wasn't like her to miss things.

He slipped a finger beneath the flap and yanked, ripping open the envelope. He pulled out a folded piece of red construction paper. When he saw the crude cutout of a Christmas tree, he was quite puzzled. He flipped it open and smiled at the scribbled, green crayon message, with Samantha's name printed across the bottom. He blinked repeatedly as he stared at the prettiest card he'd ever received.

Was it possible Kara didn't hate him? His hands began to shake as his hopes started to mount. Was this her attempt at a peace offering? Or had Samantha merely insisted she deliver the card? Either way, he was deeply touched by the gesture.

He set it on the desk and sucked in a deep, calming breath. He couldn't go off half-cocked—that was what had led him to this mess.

He glanced down. An old weathered envelope caught his attention. It was the letter from the man who'd hurt him so deeply—the same man who had taught him to fish and how to play ball. Jason stared at the envelope, remembering his promise to Kara to read it.

Maybe there really was such a thing as a Christmas miracle. Or maybe he needed to make a Christmas miracle of his own. He needed to prove to Kara that he had changed into a man she could trust with her heart, through the good and the bad. Words wouldn't be enough. He needed to do more. Perhaps this letter was the perfect place to start.

He ripped open the envelope, bracing himself for a string of hateful words. But when he read: *"Son, I'm sorry..."* his gaze blurred. He blinked repeatedly and kept reading the heartfelt note. His father hadn't meant what he'd said in his drunken rage. Jason checked the date, finding it'd been written almost seven years ago, while he was still in basic training. He'd wasted all these years being stubborn, thinking his dad hated him. But he'd been wrong.

Jason's throat grew thick with emotion. Kara had been right all along. This was the season for hope and forgiveness.

A plan started to take shape in his mind. He'd show her

that he could embrace the spirit of the season. He knew what must be done—the most important mission of his life. Operation: Win Kara Back.

And he didn't have a moment to lose. He'd already wasted seven years. He could be a reliable, steadfast man for Kara and a father to the little girl who'd already claimed a permanent spot in his heart. He wouldn't repeat his or his father's mistakes. He'd make sure both Kara and Samantha knew how much he loved them.

Jason shoved back from his desk. With long strides he headed for the office where Kara's desk stood. When he found her chair vacant, he spun around, scanning the shelving units, file cabinets and other desks. No Kara.

What if she'd quit? His chest tightened.

"Mr. Greene, do you need something?" asked Sherry, a redhead wearing a festive reindeer sweater.

"First, it's Jason, remember?"

She smiled, then nodded.

"Do you know where Kara is?" He'd track her down to the ends of the earth if that was what it took. He couldn't lose this chance to set things right. Something told him it would be the last chance he got.

"Oh, well…"

"Spit it out," he said, lacking any patience.

"I took a message for her when she stepped out to get some coffee. When I gave her the note, she grabbed her things, said she didn't know when she'd be back and ran out the door."

Had something happened to Samantha? Jason's heart lodged in his throat. But surely Kara would have said something. Then he realized, with the way he'd left things between them, he'd be lucky if she ever spoke to him again. And he couldn't blame her after the ass he'd made of himself.

"Do you remember the message?" he asked, praying for a little help here.

Sherry nodded. "It was the Pleasant Valley Care Home."

Regret sucker-punched him. His breath hitched. Kara's prediction had come true. Something had happened to his father and Jason had been too stubborn to go to him, to hear him out. Now it was too late to give his dad some peace of mind. Or was it? Was his guilty conscience jumping to conclusions?

"What did the message say?" he asked, poised to rush out the door.

"For her to come to the home—that Joe needed her."

Jason still had a chance to make things right.

He bolted toward the parking lot, hoping he wouldn't be too late to put his father's mind at ease. Jason might not have liked the drunk he had become, but the man he used to be, when Jason's mother was alive—he owed that man a bit of peace.

And Kara shouldn't be shouldering this all by herself. She might not want him there, but he owed it to her to at least make the attempt.

Jason clung to the hope that he wouldn't be too late as he tramped the accelerator on the way to the sprawling facility. He took the first available parking spot and ran to the door.

Out of breath, he said to a small group of women behind the counter, "I'm here to see my father."

One with bleach-blond hair and blue eye shadow directed him to sign in, gave him directions to the room and buzzed him through the double doors. Though the process took only a couple of minutes, each second dragged on forever.

The muscles in his shoulders and neck grew rigid as Jason strode down the wide corridor, checking each room number, his hands balled up at his sides. At last he reached room 115. He fully expected to see a flurry of nurses shouting out lifesaving orders, but instead the lilt of laughter echoed through the doorway. Kara was laughing?

He stood there in the hallway, breathing a sigh of relief. Little by little, his body began to relax. His father had to be okay or she wouldn't be laughing.

Suddenly he was caught up in a wave of second thoughts. Neither Kara nor his father knew he was standing just outside in the hallway. He could easily slip away and nobody would be the wiser. He'd be back…soon. Once he gave this reunion some thought and planned out what to say. Somehow "Hey, Dad, how's it going?" didn't quite work in this case.

His gaze swung back to the double doors leading toward the parking lot. It'd be so much easier, and he had so much work to do at the resort.

He'd stepped back when he heard someone say, "Mr. Greene, I see you found your father's room. You can go ahead in."

A pretty, young nurse with a brown ponytail was headed down the hall, carrying a white blanket. He vaguely remembered seeing her at the reception desk.

"Thanks."

More footsteps sounded and then Kara stood before him, her face lit up with a smile. In fact, he'd say she was glowing.

"I knew you'd eventually find your way here. In your own time."

His instinct was to deny he was here for any other reason than to check on her, but he couldn't. The time had come to be truthful about the feelings he'd been running from for too long. As crazy as it sounded, if there was a chance to see the man who'd called him son, Jason wanted to take it.

"They said at the office there was an emergency." He glanced into the room, but could only see the end of a bed and a couple of empty chairs.

"Everything is okay. Your father got worked up when a doctor he didn't know tried to examine him. His doc went out of town for the holidays and the newest associate drew the short straw, pulling holiday duty."

"You were able to sort it all out?"

She smiled and nodded.

Kara shouldn't be here, dealing with his father and the doctors. She had enough on her hands being a single mother. It was time he started shouldering the responsibilities where his father was concerned.

"Kara," a gruff voice called out, followed by a string of coughs.

"I'll be right there." She moved closer to Jason and lowered her voice. "Prepare yourself. He's a mere ghost of the man you left seven years ago."

Jason nodded, still not exactly sure what to expect. He couldn't imagine Joe as anything but six foot four, with shoulders like a linebacker and a stogie hanging out the side of his mouth.

"One more thing," she said. "If you came here to settle up on an old score—don't. He can't take the strain. He isn't strong enough."

Jason nodded once more.

"I mean it." Her tone left no uncertainty about her seriousness.

"I get it."

First, he'd deal with his dad, and then he'd talk to Kara. He started for the door, letting her follow him inside. His steps were slow but steady.

When at last he saw his father's face, he stopped. A word of greeting caught in his throat. He blinked, unable to imagine someone could physically change so drastically from a vibrant man to barely more than a skeleton with yellowing skin.

Jason choked down his alarm. The pitiful sight doused any lingering resentment inside him. There was nothing he could say to hurt this man any worse than he'd hurt himself. His father had suffered enough.

"Son, you came." A round of hacking coughs overtook him.

For a moment, Jason stood frozen, bombarded by his dad's appearance, from the oxygen tube aiding his breathing to the sunken eyes and the bony hand covering his mouth as he struggled through the fit of coughing. It was the distressed look on his father's face that finally kicked him into action. Jason stepped alongside the bed and filled a glass with water.

"Yes, Dad, I'm home."

After handing over the glass, Jason peered over his shoulder to make eye contact with Kara, but she was gone. Their talk would have to wait a little longer.

"I...I was worried." Joe paused to catch his breath. "Thought maybe I'd never lay eyes on you again."

"I'm here." He placed a reassuring hand on his father's bony shoulder. Jason schooled his features, hoping to keep his pity and shock under wraps. "Whatever you need, all you have to do is ask."

"You'd do that...now...after everything?" He coughed again.

"Yes."

The one syllable said enough. Jason didn't want to rehash the bad times, knowing they'd wasted too much time looking over their shoulders instead of appreciating the here and now. Besides, the letter had already told him everything he'd ever need to know. Too bad it'd taken him all these years to read it.

"Hey, Dad, remember those days when we'd head out with our fishing poles in hand to catch dinner?"

The corners of his father's thin lips lifted. "You remember back then?"

"I remember, Dad."

"We never did catch much."

"But it was fun trying."

"That it was." This time it was his father who reached out to him, squeezing his forearm with cool hands. "I was worried you'd forget those times." Another coughing fit overtook him and Jason offered him more water. When his breathing calmed, Joe continued, "I'm sorry it all went so wrong. I couldn't handle your mother's death, and I let you down."

Knowing this was no longer about him, but about giving his father everlasting peace, Jason added, "But before that you were the best dad. I wouldn't have made it to quarterback in high school if it hadn't been for you teaching me to play ball at an early age."

A twinkle came to his father's sunken eyes just before his eyelids began to droop. Obviously, the emotional reunion and the coughing had zapped his energy.

"It's okay, Dad. You rest now."

"Son, tell Kara I still want my Christmas present."

"I will." Jason hoped she knew what his father was talking about, because he certainly didn't. "I'll be back tomorrow to check on you."

"Promise?" Joe murmured. His eyes were completely closed now.

"I promise. You don't have to worry anymore. I'll be here when you need me."

And he knew without a doubt that he wasn't going anywhere—no matter what fate threw at him. He would be here for the loved ones in his life. Now he just had to convince Kara to trust in him.

CHAPTER SIXTEEN

FRIDAY EVENING KARA's heart hammered harder and faster the closer she got to Jason's log home. She could hardly believe he'd once again called and summoned her to drop everything, grab Samantha and come running.

This time he'd requested the vendor quotes. Of course, she couldn't blame him. She was supposed to have dropped the report on his desk on her way out the door, but a printer snafu and a phone call from her impatient daughter had left her thoughts scattered. Kara had walked right out the door with the printed report in hand.

But she also had some important information for him. After checking around with other restaurants, she knew what she didn't like about Bigger Wholesales—they undercut their competition with inferior produce, and a lot of money was lost due to waste.

As she made a left-hand turn onto Jason's road, she wondered if tonight might be a good time to let him know that she'd done a phone interview with the company in Ohio. Her background check had come back clean and now the only thing standing between her and an office manager position with benefits was for her to accept. She should be excited, or at least relieved, but she couldn't work up any enthusiasm for leaving her family, home or—most of all—Jason. It'd taken years to be reunited and now, in a blink, they were over.

A groan from behind had Kara glancing in the rearview mirror at her daughter, who was squirming in her seat belt. "Sweetie, what are you doing?"

"I dropped Bubbles." Guttural grunts sounded. "Got him."

"Maybe you should leave him in the car so you don't lose him while we're at Jason's. We won't be long."

"Bubbles stays with me."

Not in the mood for an argument, Kara let the subject drop. Jason's driveway loomed in the distance. A nervous energy made her stomach quiver at the thought of seeing him outside the office, where they didn't have to maintain a professional facade.

She glanced at the clock. Seven on the dot. They were right on time. She turned into the drive and was floored to find the entire house decked out in multicolored, twinkling Christmas lights. Her mouth gaped open.

"Mommy, look at all those lights."

"They're beautiful."

Tears threatened as she wondered if Jason's Scrooge-like view on life had at last changed. She quickly tamped down her emotions. It wasn't as if he'd done this for her. He must be planning to invite the investors to his house for a party or some such thing. He probably hated each and every one of the lights adorning his yard.

She glanced down at the gift she'd wrapped for him, wondering if perhaps she'd chosen the right thing to give him. Would he take offense? Still, she just couldn't run out and buy him any of the traditional gifts, such as a tie, flannel pajamas or a cheese tray. Those things didn't say "Jason" to her. But seeing the house all decked out with holiday fare reaffirmed her choice of gifts.

Her insides trembled as she pulled the car to a stop next to the porch. Before she had a chance to decide her next move, Santa stepped out onto the porch.

Santa?

"Mommy. Mommy, look."

When Santa moved in front of her headlights, and stared back at her through wire-rimmed glasses, Kara gaped again. Why in the world was the man she'd commonly thought of as Scrooge all dressed up like the jolliest man at the North Pole?

She swallowed hard, trying to comprehend what was going on here.

"Mommy, doesn't Jason look neat?" Samantha opened the door and scooted out of the backseat.

Too late to back out now.

He walked down the steps in his black boots and out the walk to greet them. Kara immediately noticed his lean waist had grown into a very plump tummy, with a thick black belt and a gold buckle holding everything in place.

"Ho-ho-ho." His deep voice rumbled.

"You make a good Santa," Samantha said, patting his rounded belly.

"And have you been naughty or nice?" he asked, in a Santa-like voice. "Ho-ho-ho."

Kara couldn't help but laugh. What in the world had gotten into him?

When she regained her composure, she asked, "Um… are we early?"

"You're right on time. You and Samantha are my only guests."

Her eyes opened wide. "You planned all this for us? What about the vendor report?"

"We'll go over it Monday at the office. Afraid that was just a ruse to get you here." He smiled sheepishly. "I know how much you enjoy the holidays and I thought you might appreciate the decorations. Do you like them?"

Samantha ran off to check out the various Christmassy figurines lining the porch, leaving the two adults with a little bit of privacy.

Kara gazed up into Jason's blue eyes and her world tilted off center. Giving a little tug on his cottony beard, she said, "I like Santa best of all."

"I'm so sorry, Kara. I was such a jerk the other night—"

"We've both done things we aren't proud of. I should have been totally straight with you from the beginning about what occurred after you left town."

His steady gaze held hers. "I wanted to show you just how much you both mean to me."

She bestowed upon him her biggest and brightest smile. "Well, Santa, you've outdone yourself. Especially today with your father. Thank you for making the effort."

"No, thank *you*. You finally talked some sense into me. It was way past time that my father and I patched things up. We'll never be candidates for a Norman Rockwell painting, but we've made peace with each other, and you won't have to worry about him so much anymore. I'll be there for him."

"I'm glad." She squeezed his arm.

"Let's go inside," he said, climbing the steps and opening the door for them.

When Kara stepped inside, Sly ran up to her with a loud meow, followed by a boisterous purr as she rubbed against her ankles. Kara bent down and ran her hand over the feline's satiny fur.

"Hey, sweetie. I missed you, too."

As though understanding Kara's words, Sly paused, lifted her golden eyes and meowed in agreement.

"Wow. A kitty." Samantha ran over and dropped to her knees.

Sly scampered away to a safe distance before turning and taking in the little girl with a cautious stare.

"Come here, Sly," Jason called to the cat.

Sly paused. Big, curious eyes checked them out before she sauntered over. In one fluid motion, Jason scooped up the cat in one arm and started to pet her.

"This is my friend Samantha," he said close to the cat's inky-black ear. "She's really nice." He leaned toward the little girl. "Go ahead and pet her head."

Kara smiled as Santa did his best to make her daughter feel at home. Her eyes glistened as she took in this tender moment. What in the world did all this mean? She didn't want to jump to conclusions. She was certain Jason would eventually explain.

In the background, she spotted the Christmas tree exactly as she'd left it. She couldn't stop smiling. Jason had let the joy of the holiday back into his heart. A happy tear splashed on her cheek. She swiped it away with the back of her hand.

Samantha ran over to the tree and sat on the floor next to it. The sleek feline followed, eventually rubbing against her arm.

"Look, Sly, at all the presents. There's three with my name on them." Samantha glanced over her shoulder at Jason. "Can I open them now?"

"Sure. If it's okay with your mom."

Kara nodded. As Samantha ripped into her gifts, Jason draped an arm over Kara's shoulders. "I hope I did okay. I've never bought toys for a little girl before. In fact, I've never bought toys before, period."

After Samantha unwrapped a pink plush cat, a jewelry

and makeup kit, and an electronic game, Kara said, "Samantha, don't we have a gift for Jason?"

Her daughter rushed over, removed a wrapped package from Kara's oversize purse and handed it to him. "It's your turn."

"What's this?" he asked, giving it a little shake.

Samantha shrugged.

"Just a little something," Kara stated.

He tore off the wrapping paper in much the same frenzied fashion as her daughter. "The angel." His brow crinkled. "But I gave this to Samantha."

Kara pressed a finger to his lips, stopping his protest. "This is a very precious gift, and Samantha and I enjoyed having her atop our tree. But it was time she came home where she belongs—with you." *The same place I want to be,* she almost added, but held her tongue. A heavy sadness settled in her heart as she blinked back the moisture gathering in her eyes.

Jason disappeared into the kitchen and returned with three champagne glasses. "Here's some sparkling cider. I thought it would fit the occasion." He handed each of them a glass and then held his high. "Here's to the two most wonderful ladies." He paused, clearing his throat. "May your futures be everything you want them to be."

Kara clinked her glass with his and forced a smile on her face. "And to a successful reopening."

She glanced up at him and saw the puzzled look in his eyes. He must have picked up something in her expression. Deep inside, she didn't want to move away. Living in a city meant there'd be no yard to plant spring flowers, and Samantha would have to go to an after-school day-care center while she worked, instead of staying with her doting grandparents. City life would be very different from what she'd imagined for her and Samantha.

And most of all, Jason wouldn't be around to drop by on a moment's notice. Oh, how she'd miss him, and the chance of them being more than just old friends. Sometimes life could be unfair.

Still, she couldn't discuss her reservations about the move. She had to maintain a positive front not only for Samantha but for herself. Kara stiffened her spine and swallowed down her misery. She'd wait until the day after Christmas to break the news of the move to her daughter. She didn't want to ruin the holiday.

CHAPTER SEVENTEEN

JASON TOOK KARA by the elbow and led her to the other side of the living room, giving them a little privacy.

"Will you give me another chance?" he asked, staring deep into her eyes.

"A chance for what?"

"For us. For you and me and Samantha to be together."

She continued to stare at him. Her eyes grew shiny but her lips didn't move.

"Kara." He placed a finger beneath her chin and lifted her head so their gazes met. "Talk to me. You want that, too, don't you?"

She blinked repeatedly while worrying her lower lip, as though internally waging a deep debate. Was it really so hard for her to decide? Was he about to lose her for good?

Jason searched her darkened eyes, detecting the swirl of confusion and utter frustration in them. "Please, say something."

"Why now?" Lines of stress creased her beautiful face. Her eyes pleaded with him to be honest. "If only you'd said something sooner, maybe we could have figured out something. But I've found a new job…in Ohio."

Her words sent his heart plummeting. He'd thought this through before she and Samantha had arrived. He knew there'd be hurdles to cross. Now wasn't the time to give up. If it meant he had to meet her halfway, or more than halfway, he'd do it.

"Come outside with me," he said, taking her arm.

"Outside?" She pulled back. "But why?"

"I need a few minutes to talk to you. Alone." He glanced over his shoulder at Samantha. "Don't worry, she'll be fine sitting next to the tree, with Sly by her side and her toys to occupy her."

"All right. Just for a couple of minutes."

He grabbed her coat from the back of the couch and draped it over her shoulders. After letting Samantha know where they'd be, Jason ushered Kara out the door into the chilly night.

A few inches of snow layered the ground and dusted the trees. With the lights he'd painstakingly strung over the porch rails and small trees and shrubs, it did look magical, if you were into that sort of thing. It wasn't something he'd normally have done; he considered it a labor of love. But as he stood here, looking out over the yard and watching colored lights twinkle on the snow, he had to admit it wasn't so bad.

"I still can't believe you put up all these decorations." Kara moved to his side.

When he turned his gaze back to the woman he loved—the woman he didn't want to let go for a second time—his insides twisted with anxiety. He'd never been so nervous about anything in his life, not even making his way through boot camp or being sent into enemy territory.

"I saw the worried expression on your face when I made the toast," he said. "Is there a problem with your new job?"

She shook her head. "No. Not at all. In fact, they're anxious for me to get settled into my new position."

Not what he wanted to hear, but nothing he couldn't handle. "So you're going ahead with the move?"

"Of course. Why wouldn't I? This is an amazing opportunity."

"I'm sure it is." Jason swallowed back his disappointment.

"You know, it's beautiful here," she said, leaning her hands on the rail. "You're so lucky to have this little piece of nature."

He turned to her and she stared up at him. The gentle breeze carried with it the scent of strawberries from her golden hair. The nippy air also brought out the pink hue in her smooth cheeks. And the red of her lips intensified, drawing his full attention to them. They looked so perfect for kissing.

"*Beautiful* doesn't even begin to describe it," he murmured, never moving his gaze from her.

"The yard looks amazing with all the lights. Did you do all this for us?"

He nodded. "If it's what makes you happy, then it's what makes me happy."

"And that Santa suit… You really outdid yourself." Her gaze slid over him, and he grew self-conscious when she eyed the puffy pillow widening his midsection.

"I need to apologize for being such a jerk the other night. Seven years ago, I dumped you. You were free to do whatever you wanted with your life. And I've accepted that. I'm sorry I overreacted. Most of all, I'm sorry I put you in that position all those years ago."

Her fingers reached out and touched his cheek. "We may have not made the best decisions back then, but despite them something miraculous happened. I gave birth to the most wonderful little girl." Kara turned to the living room window and he followed suit, glancing in at Samantha. "I've never for one instance regretted her."

"Nor do I," he admitted, surprised by his own heartfelt

sincerity. "She may not have my DNA, which is probably a blessing in itself—"

Kara elbowed him. "We had this conversation already, remember? You were created from your mother's love and Joe's best intentions. A child would be fortunate to have you as their father."

Her confidence in him warmed his insides. How could he have ever doubted her and her ability to handle his secret?

"Do you really mean that?"

"Of course I do."

"Santa almost forgot. He has one more gift to hand out." He reached beneath his costume and fished out a small box wrapped in red foil and tied up tight with a bow. He held it out to her. "Here. Open it."

Her eyes grew round. Her searching gaze moved from him to the tiny present.

"Go ahead," he coaxed. "It won't bite. I promise."

Her fingers trembled as she pulled on the ribbon, but they were no match for the quivering in his stomach. The most important mission of his life had finally reached the critical juncture. He had to succeed with this part of his plan. Otherwise his heart would end up a fallen victim on the front line.

Kara deftly made her way past the wrapping to the black velvet box. As though she was afraid to stop, she quickly lifted the lid.

Her lips formed an O.

Unspoken questions filled her eyes. She stood there staring at him like a deer caught in headlights, not knowing which way to go. She didn't throw the box at him and stomp away. Nor did she squeal with delight and throw herself in his arms. He'd take her reserve as a positive sign.

He still had time to convince her that they could make this thing between them work. He *had* to convince her.

"Don't say anything," he said, pressing a finger to those delectable lips. "Just listen. We can make this work."

She shook her head, her eyes shimmering. He fortified his determination with the knowledge that she hadn't heard his proposal yet. Once she did, she'd realize the possibilities for them.

"First, I love you," he said, gazing straight into her eyes. "I've always loved you. I am so sorry for destroying our dreams all those years ago. I wasn't mature enough back then to have faith in you and me—in us—to handle the news about my biological father."

Jason reached out and took her free hand in his. He rubbed his thumb over her cold fingers. He had to speed this up so he could get her back inside, next to the fire.

"I know how important this new job is to you. I can't expect you to change your plans and drop everything to live here in the country with me."

"What are you saying?"

"I'll move with you. You, me and Samantha will be a family."

"You'll move." Disbelief rang in her voice. "But you can't! You've only just come back. Your father needs you. And you're about to reopen the resort."

He'd done some serious thinking about this and he knew what he had to do. "I'll have my father transferred to wherever we are, and I'll sell the resort."

"Sell the resort?" Her brows arched. "You can't!" she repeated. "You just restored it."

He swallowed the jagged lump in his throat. "The Summit is important to me, but not as important as you and Samantha. I can be with the two of you and lose the resort and still be happy. But having the resort without the two most important people in my life would be a hollow victory."

Kara pressed a hand to her chest. "You really mean that, don't you?"

He nodded. "I'll do whatever it takes for us to be a family. I love you more than ever. And Samantha. She may not be my biological daughter, but she's the daughter of my heart."

"Oh, Jason. I love you, too. But I can't let you do this."

He took both Kara's hands in his. "Yes, you can. I was the one who walked out on our plans seven years ago. It's only fair that I fit into the life you've created for yourself, no matter where it is."

"The thing is, I don't want to move. I want to stay right here with you, my family and friends." She stepped into his open arms, resting her head beneath his chin. "Do you really think we can make it work?"

"I do. I've changed. I've grown up. With honesty between us, we can face anything."

She looked up at him, their breath intermingling. He couldn't resist his desire to taste her sweetness. His head dipped low. His lips met hers. She was compliant and eager beneath him. A moan rose in the back of his throat. He'd never, ever grow tired of kissing her.

As much as he hated to pull back from her, they needed to finish this conversation. They still had one more thing to discuss.

"It's starting to snow," he said, remembering the last time they'd been here and it had snowed—the miraculous night when she'd made him feel love again.

She turned, leaning back against his chest as they both watched fat snowflakes drifting down. "Do you think we'll get stuck here?"

He pulled her close. "One can only hope. By the way,

my dad said to tell you he's waiting for his Christmas present. Mind explaining?"

She laughed. The sound was the most delightful he'd ever heard. "Your father won't let me forget. I promised to knit him a red scarf so he can wear it outside. He misses the snow. He wants to feel it on his face once more."

"Is the scarf done?"

She nodded.

"Looks like if this snow keeps up we'll have a Christmas wish to fulfill."

"It'll be a Christmas of miracles."

Now was the perfect moment for the last thing he had to ask her. He dropped to his knee. "Kara Jameson, I've loved you since we were kids, and you mean more to me with each passing day. Please tell me that you'll be my best friend, my lover and my wife." He took the ring from the box and held it out to her. "Say you'll be Mrs. Jason Greene."

Tears dripped onto her pink cheeks. "Yes. Yes! *Yes!*"

His heart felt as if it would burst with joy. He slipped the ring onto her finger, stood up and pulled her into his arms, then swooped in and planted a gentle kiss on her lips. Her arms slipped up around his neck. He'd never felt this deeply for someone in his life.

"I saw Mommy kissing Santa Claus...." They turned to find Samantha grinning at them, happiness twinkling in her eyes. "Does this mean I get the present I really want for Christmas?"

Kara's eyes met her daughter's. Unable to contain her joy, she smiled back. "What present is that?"

"I want Jason to live with us. He can be my daddy."

Jason smiled, and Kara draped her arm around his waist and leaned into him. "I think that can be arranged," she said.

He knelt on one knee again and held out his arms. Samantha rushed into them. "I'd be honored to be your father."

Over her head, Jason's gaze met Kara's. "I can't think of anything I'd love more than to be part of this wonderful family."

* * * * *

A sneaky peek at next month...

Cherish™

ROMANCE TO MELT THE HEART EVERY TIME

My wish list for next month's titles...

In stores from 18th October 2013:

❑ Marry Me under the Mistletoe – Rebecca Winters

& Proposal at the Lazy S Ranch – Patricia Thayer

❑ A Little Bit of Holiday Magic – Melissa McClone

& Stranded with the Tycoon – Sophie Pembroke

In stores from 1st November 2013:

❑ Marrying Dr Maverick – Karen Rose Smith

& A Maverick under the Mistletoe – Brenda Harlen

❑ A Cadence Creek Christmas – Donna Alward

& How to Marry a Princess – Christine Rimmer

Available at WHSmith, Tesco, Asda, Eason, Amazon and Apple

Just can't wait?

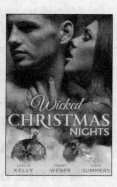

Book Club

Join the Mills & Boon Book Club

Want to read more **Cherish™** books?
We're offering you **2 more** absolutely **FREE!**

We'll also treat you to these fabulous extras:

- **Exclusive offers and much more!**

- **FREE home delivery**

- **FREE books and gifts with our special rewards scheme**

Get your free books now!

visit www.millsandboon.co.uk/bookclub
or call Customer Relations on 020 8288 2888

Wrap up warm this winter with Sarah Morgan…

Sleigh Bells in the Snow

Kayla Green loves business and hates Christmas.

So when Jackson O'Neil invites her to Snow Crystal Resort to discuss their business proposal… the last thing she's expecting is to stay for Christmas dinner. As the snowflakes continue to fall, will the woman who doesn't believe in the magic of Christmas finally fall under its spell…?

4th October

www.millsandboon.co.uk/sarahmorgan

013/MB435

Come home this Christmas to Fiona Harper

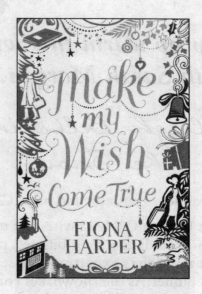

Make my Wish Come True

FIONA HARPER

From the author of *Kiss Me Under the Mistletoe* comes a Christmas tale of family and fun. Two sisters are ready to swap their Christmases—the busy super-mum, Juliet, getting the chance to escape it all on an exotic Christmas getaway, whilst her glamorous work-obsessed sister, Gemma, is plunged headfirst into the family Christmas she always thought she'd hate.

www.millsandboon.co.uk

1113/MB442

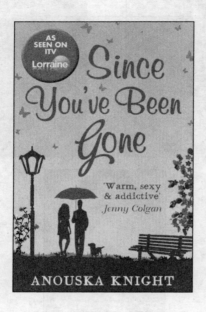

The World of Mills & Boon®

There's a Mills & Boon® series that's perfect for you. We publish ten series and, with new titles every month, you never have to wait long for your favourite to come along.

Blaze.
Scorching hot, sexy reads
4 new stories every month

By Request
Relive the romance with the best of the best
9 new stories every month

Cherish™
Romance to melt the heart every time
12 new stories every month

Desire™
Passionate and dramatic love stories
8 new stories every month

Visit us Online